T0271500

The Dance of Shadows

The Dance of Shadows

Rogba Payne

First published in Great Britain in 2024 by Gollancz
an imprint of The Orion Publishing Group Ltd
Carmelite House, 50 Victoria Embankment
London EC4Y 0DZ

An Hachette UK Company

1 3 5 7 9 10 8 6 4 2

A CIP catalogue record for this book is
available from the British Library.

ISBN (HB) 978 1 399 61261 6
ISBN (ETPB) 978 1 399 61262 3
ISBN (eBook) 978 1 399 61264 7
ISBN (Audio) 978 1 399 61265 4

Typeset at The Spartan Press Ltd,
Lymington, Hants

Printed in Great Britain by Clays Ltd,
Elcograf S.p.A.

www.gollancz.co.uk

In the old days we lived amongst you, in plain sight. You knew the names we told you and some of you knew the names we never told. We cared for you, protected you and taught you. The woe of love.

Prologue

The Alaafin had always thought it would rain on the day he died. Instead, the sun stood at its full height above him with no opposition from the clouds. The heat made his dark skin glisten with sweat. Sunny days usually made him smile, but this was not a day for smiles. Before the day was done, he'd be dead.

'Don't die before you are dead,' Oya said, placing a hand on his chest. 'Be strong, my love.'

She peered up at him and smiled. To smile like that when she knew what was coming was an act of uncommon strength. He tried to smile back but it was in vain. He didn't have it in him. Not a true smile. Only she could do that.

She had skin like smooth earth, with a full head of braids that trailed down her back like thick black snakes. Her boubou of nine colours had loose-fitting sleeves and a bodice tight to her form.

Her love was like honey spooling in a bowl. Sweet and slow; thick and full. A gift he could never truly be worthy of. The Alaafin would have given anything to sing to Oya in the way she deserved, to praise her, to exalt her, and worship her. Now he feared all he would have for her would be screams.

No, I won't scream, I won't let her hear me scream. I have to be strong for her. He straightened.

Their house was no fortress. He'd built it himself with his hands, perseverance, mudbrick, and palm leaves. There was nowhere to hide, nothing to protect them.

They could run, but even if they did, they could not outrun *him*.

There had been a time when he could vault a nation with a stride, part the waters, call the wind to carry him and be sure it would obey. A time before all this; when men still called his name. A time when, if he dipped his toe in the ocean, the world heard the splash. That time was long gone.

It was a cruel way to die, awaiting slaughter like a goat on festival day. The whistle of the wind was like laughter in his ears.

Oya touched the small of his back. 'He is close. I can feel him.'

The cord in his neck pulsed. The Alaafin could feel him, too.

He drew in breath. 'I am going to get my double-axe.'

Oya's hand glided slowly from his back to his shoulder. Her touch still made his skin tingle. 'There is no sense in that, my love. Just hold me – for now.'

He bit down on his tongue and pulled her close, burying her head in his chest. Her nails dug deep into his back as he locked his fingers in her hair. For that small, eternal moment he felt whole; blessed and stout-hearted. But it was only a moment.

A disgusted squall from above drew their attention. A vulture, alone and unafraid, loomed overhead. Its wings stretched wide, as though expecting applause.

Oya glanced up at the bird, her gaze cold as the night sea. The vulture glared back. Daring them, almost. A normal vulture would not goad the living, but this was no normal vulture.

The Alaafin arched his back and stared up at the sky, then he called lightning by its name. A bolt from the heavens struck the bird directly. A shriek rang out as it fell dead to the ground.

If the Accuser wanted to kill them, they would not go quietly.

2

'I am going to get my double-axe.'

This time, Oya did not disagree. He could almost feel her fury flare as her countenance changed.

'I am with you, my husband.'

At last, he smiled. They would die as they had lived, and that was enough.

They gathered their weapons and adorned themselves with every charm they owned. *Damudamu*, to confound their enemy's senses; *isora*, to blunt every enemy blade; and *aferi*, to become invisible to the naked eye.

Oya washed her two-edged *ida* sword with pepper and poison to paralyse at a touch, then wore a necklace with the single black cowrie that warned her of danger. The Alaafin sharpened his double-axe and put on the amulet of Jarishma, which made his skin impenetrable. Their faces were painted with the blood of enemies long dead. Finally, the Alaafin donned his war helmet. Hard iron, wrought in the shape of a snarling dog. It made a sharp sound as he snapped it shut.

They stood as one. Ready to die.

The Alaafin let out a sharp breath. 'Let him come.'

A ripple in the air announced the arrival of their executioner. He was dressed all in white with bleached, near-translucent skin, and pointy teeth like knives. He moved like he had all the time in the world, every step bereft of urgency. Like a man who owned the earth.

The Alaafin narrowed his eyes. *The Accuser.*

A boy appeared next, also dressed in immaculate white. The boy watched the Accuser with all the eager calm of an apprentice watching his master's work. His smile was that of a hunting dog staring at cornered prey.

When he spoke, the Accuser's voice was like water wrenched through an empty husk. A voice that came in an unsteady drip-drop, with high and low notes falling with no rhythm. 'The Alaafin and the Mother of Nine. I know you sensed that I was coming, yet you have not tried to run. Tell me, have you decided to serve the Son?'

The Alaafin parted his lips but Oya spoke first, her voice taut with rage. 'Bind the Son to hell! Dara the Skyfather remains Lord of All.'

The Alaafin smiled again.

The Accuser's stare was pitiless. 'So, it is death. Will you die quietly?'

The Alaafin's eyes narrowed to dark slits. Old strength reared up inside him. 'It will be loud.'

The skies grumbled overhead. It *was* going to rain after all. He etched the crossroads sign of Dara the Skyfather across his sternum and raised a hand, calling forth his shadow. Sheets of effervescent black mist oozed from his skin as his shadow rose in a column of black froth. A sharp and sudden storm wind whipped black fumes into a spiralling updraft. Power flooded him, roaring through his bones and body, calling him to act. He hefted his double-axe in his right hand and stretched out his left. A night-black curved blade coalesced from dust in his outstretched grip. Clouds ambushed the sun, telling all things living to find shelter.

Brimming with the power of his shadow, the Alaafin raised his double-axe high and screamed his own name: '*Xango!*'

The Accuser's expression was almost one of delight, a quirk in his lips the only response to the Alaafin's show of power. They were amusing to him. He chuckled and raised his own hands to the sky. The Alaafin jerked back.

To the eye, nothing had changed – but to the Alaafin, it was a declaration. He could sense the foreboding press of the

Accuser's incredible power. It was as though the air itself was being strangled.

The Alaafin cursed. '*Shege.*'

A thin, grey-white sword materialised in the Accuser's hand and he started to chant.

'And the Son shall cast them down, erase their names, their seed in the land.'

Oya's arms quivered as her sword-grip went slack. Tears trailed down her cheeks, smearing the war paint. *This is not how it should end.*

She glanced at him and when their eyes met, she smiled, for the very last time. 'I love you ... Xango.'

I

A Pigeon Among Swans

RUMI

In this life, it is important to know the truth about yourself. It helps to resist the lies. A dead man told Rumi that.

Rumi knew at least three things about himself. He knew he was Odu down to his bones. Born under a bloodwood tree, with dark rosewood skin and dreadlocks that grew to his waist. He knew he had to keep his pride; it was his weapon and armour in an adversarial world. He knew the smell of Kuba people made him sick.

That afternoon, Rumi was sick.

The triumphal arch above bore the words '*The Golden Room*'. As he stepped forward, the floral stench of Kuba perfume jumped down his throat.

He cursed under his breath. '*Shege.*'

It was the scent of prosperity. Orchid, with hints of bergamot, honey and salt. Doubtless a delight to the local Kuba parvenu, but it made Rumi feel like a jungle wolf that had strayed too close to the village and caught the scent of a hunter.

Always keep a Kuba at least a spear's length away. That was his philosophy, but today, he was deep in Kuba territory with scant protection for his nose.

A short Kuba man stood beside the door. Shaped like a

cookpot, with a thick, obstinate jaw and the Golden Room's crest on his dark blue kaftan.

The doorman looked at Rumi the way a gatekeeper looks at a stray, sickly dog.

'Who you be?' the doorman called out.

Pidgin. He had spoken pidgin to Rumi. When a stranger speaks pidgin to you, it means they think you are a beggar, a village boy or both. Rumi *was* a village boy and he *was* no stranger to begging when the money purse was light, but he could speak the damn Common Tongue.

He forced a smile and replied in clean Common. 'I'm here to audition … sir. I'm a musician.'

The doorman snorted. 'Do you have a reference?'

The moment of truth.

Rumi produced a small note and handed it over. 'From Tinu the Panther.'

The doorman read it slowly. Or at least, it seemed slow. Time always moved slowly in the big moments. Like the moment before the guilotine falls.

'Your name?' the doorman finally asked.

'Irumide Voltaine.'

The doorman blinked, eyed Rumi up and down, then nudged the door open. 'Take a seat in the waiting room. I'll call you when your turn comes.'

Supressing a smile, Rumi brushed through the door. As soon as he was inside, he let out a silent breath, sagging against the wall. A chance. That was all he wanted. A chance to make some *real* money. The kind of money that allows you to plan your life. To leave leftovers on your plate.

He straightened as he looked around. The anteroom was opulence incarnate. A huge window dominated the far wall, bathing the room in sunlight. The curtains and carpet were a shimmering honey-gold, and there was a large, gold-plated table at the centre with four candelabras. By the near wall, marble busts of musicians past stared down at him with stern, disapproving faces.

It was like being in another country. The Palmaine had brought a piece of their nation to Basmine; everything down to the candlewax looked imported.

Rumi was dazzled. Who wouldn't be? Yet, like an over-sugared butter cake, there was something a little sickening about it all.

The place was swarming with Kubas, dressed in colourful cashmere kaftans and soft-sole leather sandals.

Rumi had his best kaftan on, but beside them, he looked like a wretch who'd had an especially torrid year and been robbed on the trip down. A pigeon among swans.

His height – a gift from the father he'd never known – made him an easy target for their reproachful glares. His skin seemed to itch just from being in the room.

He glanced up and noticed a strange ceiling mural. It was a painting of pretty, pale angels having a naked frolic in the clouds. The angel at the centre of the painting was the prettiest of the lot, seated on a throne of clouds with a vulture perched on his shoulder. *Why ruin such a beautiful scene with a vulture?*

Instinctively, Rumi tugged the edges of his leopard-skin scarf to make sure it covered the tattoos on his neck. The last thing he wanted was for some prick to start screaming 'denier' if they saw his tattoos.

In places like the Golden Room, where wealth was a virtue and poverty a vice, Rumi was the devil and his *Darani* tattoos made him worse than the devil to some. Anyone with sense knew there was no place for the old gods in this shiny new world.

A soft sound behind him sent a tremor up his spine. Rumi glanced over his shoulder. A man was fingerpicking an oud;

tuning it. Finally, he relaxed. It was the first thing in the Golden Room to make him smile. Each touch of string was a subtle, delicate test. A search for the taut places.

The old Odu saying went, '*A man's hands tell his story*'.

If Rumi's hands told his story, they would say he had been whipped, that he had climbed trees and fallen from them. That he had scratched flesh when that was all he could do to protect himself. That he had burned his fingertips reading books by candlelight and that he had never caressed a woman the way Belize did in all his mother's secret books. Today was about his hands, nothing else. Not the Kuba, the Palmaine or anyone else.

He scanned the room for Odu people. The Kuba and Odu looked much alike, but Kuba were typically darker in complexion and thinner at the nose. To be truly sure of a person's tribe, you had to look them square in the face. Rumi wasn't in the habit of staring at Kuba, so instead he looked for other signs – well-worn kaftans or sandals dusty from walking.

One man seemed to fit the description. He stood near the marble busts with an easy slouch, in sandals not quite as new as the others.

Rumi made his approach. '*Hashiyeshi*,' he called out in greeting.

The man raised his chin, but his expressionless gaze did not change.

Rumi tried the Common Tongue. 'Hello?'

'Oh, hello,' the man said, his lips curling into a vague approximation of a smile as he stepped close.

The man's accent made music of the Common Tongue. Soft and fluent. It was native to the man.

The man probably lived in the Citadel. He probably ate three courses at dinner. Soup for starters and the like. When Rumi shook his hand, it was like silk rubbing on charcoal. His hair was slick-wet with pomade, parted just left of centre.

The man *was* Odu; the dark brown eyes and wide bridge of the nose screamed Odu. But he was a different *type* of Odu. Tidy as a Palmaine schoolteacher at morning bell.

Tales of the Odu way of life were written all over Rumi, but this man was a blank canvas. Rumi's arms were stiff with lean muscle from a life of lifting, swinging and pulling. The labour in this man's arms likely came from writing bank notes and pointing at servants. He had the straight-backed gait of a man from a good home, and a ten-string harp worth more than Rumi earned in six months.

Rumi's fake smile melted away. He had hoped to find something familiar but had found a man who embellished his otherness.

The light in the man's eyes dimmed as he studied Rumi in return. The man was comfortable in this room. A comfort that must have taken years to cultivate. Fighting to belong, making people forget he was Odu. Getting that hair so soft. The scowl on his face plainly stated he did not, under any circumstances, want to be lumped in with an Odu like Rumi.

So Rumi gave a tight-lipped smile, nodded with understanding, and walked away.

He found an inoffensive spot near the audition-room door where he would be left alone to eavesdrop.

As the minutes slid into hours, the soft tick-tock of the pendulum clock above the door made a slow mockery of his patience. There was no first-come-first-served in the Golden Room. Palmaine first, Kubas next, Saharene just ahead of Odu. Even the soup-to-start Odu had to wait his turn.

By the time the doorman started to call the Odu, fifty-six players had auditioned and only two had been taken. Rumi had fallen into a sort of trance when the doorman finally called his name.

'Irumide Voltaine!'

He gave a start and rose to his feet. Curious eyes settled on him. His name was plainly not an Odu one, nor could it be said to belong to any other familiar tribe. His mother had refused to adopt a familial last name. They were – she explained – not part of Odu culture. She had taken to calling herself Voltaine instead and Rumi had followed her lead.

As he nudged the audition-room door open, he whispered a prayer. 'Dara, father of all, go with me.'

Three people sat before a long glass table on a dais. They glanced down on him like gods at the gates of paradise, appraising his misdeeds. If they really were gods, the looks on their faces said they were ready to send him straight down to hell.

The man at the centre was a young Palmaine with the twin tell-tale combination of raven-black hair and watery blue eyes. It was Zahim Alharan, the proprietor of the Golden Room. His sharp cheekbones and eagle-like nose indicated he was of the oldest, purest Palmaine vintage, with the subtle poise and upturned chin of a person who has never worried about a meal or a warm bed.

The woman seated to the left was Saharene, with skin like desert sand and big hazel eyes. She wore a dark, loose-fitting boubou and a band on her forehead that kept her dark hair pulled back. As her eyes swept through Rumi, she had the look of someone who had been presented with a mule when she was expecting a thoroughbred.

Seated on the other side, the last of the three, was a stout Kuba man with sea-green eyes; thin, greying-black hair; and a heavy, gold-linked chain. He looked like every villain in every storybook.

Tough crowd.

The three of them inspected him for a long moment before anyone spoke.

'Irumide Voltaine, is it?' the Kuba man finally asked.

Rumi bowed. 'My friends call me Rumi.'

'Welcome, Irumide. My name is Kunde; I'm one of the music directors here. How old are you?'

'Seventeen.'

'And where are you from?'

'The brightest village in Basmine, it's called Alara. It's—'

'A village?' Kunde said, raising an eyebrow.

Rumi wet his lips. 'Yes.'

'And what tribe are you from?'

'I am Odu.'

Kunde seemed amused. 'Yes, you look Odu, but your name is *unusual.*'

'I suppose it is.'

Kunde waited for a moment, expecting more of an explanation, but Rumi had nothing for him.

Kunde cleared his throat. 'You speak well.'

Rumi's smile momentarily slipped. He could almost hear the unspoken words 'for an Odu'.

'Thank you,' he said, summoning all his nerve to smile.

'And where have you played before?'

'At the Orchid House.'

Kunde stroked his chin. 'Orchid House … Orchid House … Ah, I remember! It's a fighting club.'

Rumi winced. 'That's the one.'

'You look like a fighter yourself.'

Rumi bit down on his tongue. His smile was tiny now. 'No, I'm no fighter.'

'Good … and why did you leave the Orchid House?'

Rumi's mind flashed to the Orchid House. To Tigrayin, Nataré, the floor wet with blood.

'I want to challenge myself.'

The Kuba man chortled. 'You've certainly come to the right place.'

The Saharene woman interjected. 'Ghastly business, wasn't it? At the Orchid House?'

Rumi's heart thumped his ribs. 'Excuse me?'

'The proprietor at the Orchid House. He was killed, wasn't he? Beaten to death?'

Rumi lowered his chin. 'Yes … ghastly business. Gambling debts.'

There was a moment of silence that seemed to stretch for an eternity.

'What will you be playing?' Kunde eventually asked.

Rumi let out a silent breath and raised his drums. Zahim threw back his head and laughed.

The last vestiges of Rumi's smile vanished. He could feel his stomach slowly sink.

'You came to the Golden Room with … *drums*?' Kunde said.

'Kasinabe drums.'

The Saharene woman made a disgusted noise. 'I warned the doorman, no timewasters.'

Rumi's cheeks melted on his face. *Stupid. Stupid.*

Of course they didn't like drums. He should have borrowed a flute or an oud. His mother had a pretty little kora they would have loved. His chance was slipping away.

Zahim raised his hand to quieten the room. 'Let's hear him.'

'*Drums*, Zahim?' the woman said.

'He got this far with drums, so let's hear him.'

Dara bless that man.

Kunde smirked. 'You have a fondness for crude things, Zahim.'

'A king loves a jester,' the woman said.

'You wound me, the both of you. Courtesy demands we let him play, as we have let others.'

It was subtle, but Zahim was still Palmaine and the other two still natives. He had the binding authority in the room and there was no part of Palmaine hypocrisy that was taken more seriously than courtesy.

The woman frowned. 'Fine. Let's hear it.'

Rumi nodded, giving them no time to change their minds. With no cue, he started to play.

He let his hands speak for him, and they said many things as he lost himself in the music. He felt them fall under his spell. When he finished his piece, the Saharene woman was stony-faced and Zahim's eyes were wet with tears.

'Give us a moment,' said the Saharene woman.

Rumi stepped outside and pressed his ear shamelessly to the door.

Their debate, though spirited, was conducted in whispers and through the door only the ghost of words could be heard. Rumi's heart thumped so hard it hurt his ears.

After a brief deliberation, he was called back in for Kunde to deliver the verdict.

'You have something. You have … *something* … but we don't think drums fit with the players we have here at the Golden Room.'

Everything after the word 'but' hit Rumi like a punch to the gut. It was still horribly bitter, despite being braced for and expected. He bowed and turned to leave.

I should have never come here. I let these butter-eaters have their fun with me. They will laugh when I leave.

He gritted his teeth and found both hands bunched into fists. *I did everything right.*

He glanced at the marble bust at the side of the door. Must have been worth a full year's pay. Twice that. For a moment he was sure he was going to smash it to tiny pieces. But then a thought occurred to him.

He glanced over his shoulder. 'I can play other instruments.'

The Saharene woman lifted an eyebrow. 'What instruments?'

Rumi rushed to speak. 'The flute, the oud, the kora and I can play the harp and—'

She raised a hand, cutting him off. 'Steward!'

The doorman shuffled into the room and bowed. 'Yes, Mistress?'

'Bring me my oud.'

A few moments later, the doorman returned with a beautiful long-neck oud.

Rumi took the oud and traced his forefinger over the wood-work. He had only played the oud a handful of times; he was a drummer.

'Play for me,' the woman said.

A moment of uncertainty washed over him. His mother's words drifted through his ear. *When the music plays, it is better to dance than to stand still.*

So, he played. He wasn't perfect – there were missteps – but he played with an accumulated contempt that made the oud come alive. It was like a weapon. He tugged its strings like a crossbow. He told them about themselves with it, he exposed their lies with it. He shouted his name with it.

Zahim smiled when Rumi was done. 'Come back in three weeks. Bring an oud.'

'And get a haircut,' Kunde added.

Rumi ran a hand through his dreadlocks. *A haircut.* That stung a bit.

Zahim cleared his throat and handed him a folded letter. 'Welcome to the Golden Room.'

Rumi bit his tongue and bowed, his heart pounding as he left the room.

Outside, he doubled over, taking in deep, heavy breaths. *Godsblood. I did it. I actually did it.*

For a moment he allowed himself to dream. A market child, playing at the Golden Room for twenty cowrie shells a week. He stared up at the night sky with a proud smile, almost to say, 'I told you so'.

A bird stared back. Its beady, grey-black eyes locked tight on Rumi. He blinked and squinted.

What on earth is a vulture doing in the middle of the Citadel?

2

A Proper Wagon

RUMI

The vulture sized Rumi up from its perch atop an arched street lantern.

Rumi stared back, reaching slowly for a loose cobblestone.

'What the hell are you looking at?' he whispered.

The bird leaned forward, as though to say, 'What are you going to do about it?'

He let the stone fly. It flew true and struck the long stem of the lantern, making it chime.

The bird only cocked its head, unimpressed; gave Rumi a long, appraising look, then hissed and flew up into the air. *Stupid bird.*

Left alone, Rumi was struck by the jarring quiet of the Citadel streets. In Alara, the village would have been alive with the bustle of bleating goats, skittering chickens, and trouble-minded children. The Citadel was clean as a baby's leg, with no sounds of life. The streets looked more like the work of a master painter than that of men with bricks and mortar. Criss-crossing avenues with endless buildings competing for height and prettiness. Lovely, arable lawns covered with flowers instead of crops. Fountains gushing water clear as glass – clean water, just to decorate the place? *How indulgent.*

After a few minutes of walking, a huge, glistening building

appeared in the distance, dominating the night sky. The sight of it almost made Rumi's eyes jump from their sockets.

The House of Palman.

Rumour was that the House of Palman was the most beautiful thing in Basmine. Rumi had never taken that too seriously. Now the rumour slapped him in the face, plainly true. The building rose above the Citadel skyline like a majestic sword. Atop the tower was an ornamental four-point star, which coruscated in the moonlight with all the brilliance of a real one. It was a Palmaine symbol, and a threat. A building that asked the natives, 'How could you ever defeat a people strong enough to build this for their god?'

As he stared at the building, Rumi understood why so many natives chose to follow the foreign god, Palman. There was no overlooking it now: there was beauty in the Palmaine empire. The beauty of being connected to power. In less than twenty years, the Palmaine had shown all the natives the true meaning of domination.

As stunning as the Citadel was, Rumi did not let its beauty eat him whole – he had been forewarned. The Citadel was like every friend your mother warned you against in school; the sort that baits you with the promise of sweets and leaves you on your own when the storekeeper comes kicking. Rumi was still a trespasser here. Too poor to be targeted by any self-respecting cut-purse, but this hour brought out the sorts of men who wouldn't sleep well until they were piss-drunk and had cracked at least one skull open.

Worse still, there were no caravans around. Citadel people rode their own horses, not caravans.

He felt a slight prick on his arm and slapped a mosquito dead. If there was even one caravan on the Citadel streets, he would find it.

★

It was full dark by the time he spotted a stocky Saharene man beside a high-wheeled caravan. Some called the people of the Saharene tribe 'sandskins', for they were once desert dwellers. They took to calling the other tribes 'mudskins' in return. Both were taboo now, but all the old enmity was still there.

Rumi approached with respectful caution.

'Good evening,' he said with a bow. 'I'm headed south. To Alara.'

The wheelman looked him up and down. 'Not going that far Sout' this late.'

'I'll pay three shells.'

The wheelman's eyes brightened. 'Ten shells. '

Rumi frowned. 'I paid two shells to get here.'

'Then you came in a ramshackle. This is a proper wagon,' he said, patting the caravan with satisfied pride, 'and I'm not desperate for a fare. Keep walking. Maybe you'll find another ramshackle to take you back before the mosquitoes drink you dry.'

Rumi gritted his teeth. The chances of finding another caravan were slim and it would be even more expensive to find board for the night. If he tried to sleep rough, he ran the risk of being caught by the consular guard without a permit. The wheelman had him.

He counted ten cowrie shells from his purse. Each one like a needle pricking his palm. Three weeks of hard work and being miserly, all gone.

He parted the caravan curtain to climb in but the wheelman stretched his arm across, barring his way.

'You ride in front with me.'

Rumi gave him a disgusted look. 'I paid your fare.'

20

'I won't have *you* riding behind me like my employer. Take it or leave it.'

Rumi glared at him long and hard, then climbed on.

They rode through the Citadel gates onto the mainland road.

A marvellous road by any measure. When the four kingdoms were conquered by Palmaine and mushed together to form Basmine, the mainland road was the first thing they built. It was like the spine of Basmine, connecting all its constituent parts. If the Citadel was the head of Basmine, Alara was probably the bum-bum, both in nature and location.

In the moonlight, Basmine looked so ... *vast*. The great Palmaine experiment. Four nations made one. The foremost of the Palmaine colonies and jewel of the Darosan continent. The land where the first man trod.

From the faraway lights and the distant imprints of buildings and nature, the country teased Rumi for knowing so little.

The little Rumi did know about Basmine, he had learned out of necessity. Things that, in one way or another, had become elemental to his survival. As a child he had learned never to eat plantain at an execution; it was unseemly. Today he had learned not to loiter around the Citadel gates if you don't enjoy getting thumped by the consular guard. He could add this new knowledge to his bone-deep familiarity with the south of Basmine where he lived. From its red soil, mudbrick houses, open gutters, and the way people fought the squalor with mindful indifference. Aside from that, he knew very few facts about Basmine.

He had never seen the peninsulas in the east, the fishing villages and the boundless Brown Sea. He had never seen the ruins of old Kasabia where the Palmaine had slaughtered the entire Kasinabe tribe and left nothing but black sand. He had never crossed the Neck and explored the Nyme forest, where animals mingled with the spirits and the waterfalls harboured every forgotten creature. He had never seen the God-Eye mountains in the North, where men made myth through reckless adventure, or the land beyond the God-Eye mountains where the giant people of the Ethiope rode giraffes and drank hot cocoa all day long. One day he hoped to see it all.

Eventually the wheelman spoke.

'Have you heard the joke about the three men in a beer parlour?' he asked.

Rumi pretended not to hear the question, but he was dealing with a man who didn't take hints.

The wheelman nudged his shoulder. 'It's a funny one.'

Rumi set his jaw.

'An Odu man, a Kuba man and a Saharene man walk into an ale parlour,' the wheelman started. 'In the middle of their meal, a fly comes in through the window—'

'I've heard it,' Rumi snapped. He hadn't, but it was predictable. The dimwitted Odu savage was a tiresome trope.

The wheelman frowned. 'What's the punchline then?'

Rumi frowned. 'The Odu man eats the fly.'

The wheelman's lips curled into a slow smile. 'You *have* heard it.'

Rumi considered paying the wheelman another cowrie for a promise to shut his mouth.

The jokes kept coming.

Rumi was halfway to telling him off when a deep voice cut through the night wind.

'Stop in the name of the King!'

Three men stood ahead, dressed in dark tailcoats fastened at the breast by a gleaming four-point star. Rumi narrowed his eyes. *The consular guard.*

The wheelman hauled on the reins, bringing the caravan to a dead stop.

The tallest consular stepped forward – a Kuba man who walked with a peacock's pride. Only a Kuba would wear that uniform with such shameless delight. Theirs was the only tribe to fight under the Palmaine flag against their own countrymen. The lower ranks of the consular guard were filled with Kuba.

A hand slipped out from the man's sleeve as he reached for the clasp on his tailcoat. Rumi drew in a breath as the coat fell open. A weapon gleamed. Shining metal, longer than an arm, two barrels with thick, rounded nostrils at the end.

Rumi had heard one fire, once. Like a god's sneeze. He pulled his leopard-skin scarf up.

The consular – satisfied that the gun had had the desired effect – fixed the wheelman with a stare. 'Where are you going?'

The wheelman fiddled with the reins. 'To Alara, sir.'

'Anyone in the back?'

'No, sir.'

'Search it,' the consular commanded, and the other two officers moved like wolves to a carcass.

The consular's gaze fell on Rumi. The reek of gin was strong on his breath.

'What were *you* up to in the Citadel?'

'I play music, sir.'

The consular sniffed, glancing at the caravan. 'Do they pay you well to play music?'

Rumi's heart slapped against the walls of his chest like a crazed cat in a cage. He held out a cowrie. 'A token, for your service, sir. Long live the King.'

The consular snatched the cowrie with a grunt. 'Long live the King.' Then, 'Be careful,' he said, turning to the wheelman. 'Stick to the mainland road.'

The wheelman bowed. 'Long live the King.'

Thunder fire the King, Rumi thought. The officers waved them on and Rumi let out a long breath of relief.

They rode on for a few more miles before the wheelman drew rein again.

This time it wasn't the consular guard. A man and woman, frail as soil-starved trees, were gesturing for them to stop.

It was plain they were Odu, but not just any Odu. The woman's face was painted with intricate white patterns and her boubou, though tattered, was the dark green of forest leaves.

Rumi's eyes widened. She was a Darani priestess. Her companion, who carried her purse, was an acolyte.

They stared at Rumi with sunken, bulbous eyes as the caravan drew close.

The acolyte held a cowrie up. 'End of the mainland. Please, sir.'

Rumi nodded to the wheelman. 'You can let them on.'

The wheelman's nostrils flared. Rather than slowing down, he sped up, kicking dry soil at them.

'You're going that way anyway,' Rumi said. 'It costs you nothing.'

'Dirty lickheads. I'm not having them on my wagon.'

Rumi glanced back. *The consular guard* ... if they caught them. He looked at the woman. Frail, plainly penniless. The perfect plaything for some idle consular.

'It's not your concern,' Rumi whispered to himself.

The priestess stared at him. Her eyes seemed not to blink.

He drew in a long breath. 'I'll pay you a shell for them.'

The wheelman fidgeted with the reins briefly. 'Two.'

Rumi glared at the wheelman as anger rose within. He closed his eyes and reached into his pocket. 'Fine.'

24

He dropped two shells in the wheelman's hand and the caravan came to a stop.

They both ran over.

The priestess pressed a cowrie into Rumi's hand as she climbed in. 'Thank you,' she said.

'Keep it,' he said, not looking at her.

She did not release his hand.

'It belongs to you ... *kukoyi*,' she said.

Rumi jerked his head towards her. For a moment, her eyes seemed to press down on him. She held his hand and he could almost swear heat welled up from the cowrie.

He relented, accepting the cowrie, and her grip slackened. She smiled for a moment, then dipped into the caravan.

Rumi stared at the cowrie. It was glossy black, smooth as river stone. Likely worthless at any market.

Kukoyi, she had called him. He'd heard the word before. It meant something along the lines of 'he who dodges death' in Odu. Children like Rumi, who were cut from their mother's wombs in childbirth, were sometimes called *kukoyi*. But how did she know he was born that way?

In the background, the wheelman was babbling again. 'Witch doctors on the mainland road. What next? This country is halfway to ruined.'

Rumi set his jaw. *This man blathers for the sheer thrill of it.*

The wheelman lowered his voice. 'The last governor-general had it right. You have to be tough with people. The more power they give the natives, the worse things get.'

Rumi stirred. 'You say the word "natives" like we're a bad thing.'

'We natives have never been able to build anything on our own. We need the Palmaine. They are a civilising influence.'

Rumi gritted his teeth. 'Just because the Palmaine scrubbed

history from our land does not mean we never had civilisation. We had our own great rulers. King Olu the Special. The Nsala of Maroko.'

The wheelman snorted. 'Do me a shegin' favour. If the old kings were still here, we'd probably be fighting over which tribe has the biggest cocks. I'm a proud Basminian. Palman is my god. Long live the King.'

'We could have figured things out on our own. Our time would have come, as it has come for other nations.'

'We would still be deniers, praying to the trees,' the wheelman said.

Rumi's mouth tightened. That one he would not ignore. Slowly, he pulled his leopard-skin scarf down, letting the edge of his tattoos show. The marked impression of leaves and trees on his neck peeked over the yellow-black scarf.

'I *still* pray to the trees.'

The wheelman's eyes widened to the size of eggs. 'You ... you're *Darani*?'

'That's right.'

The wheelman scowled. 'If you still follow the old gods then you know nothing of the past. The slaving. The killing. The barbarism. Your ancestors probably captured and sold my ancestors to the Palmaine for a bottle of gin; it wasn't some honourable time.'

'Has there ever been an honourable time in the history of humanity? You seem to have forgiven the Palmaine, so why not your brothers? We might be from different tribes but we are all Darosan, after all.'

'Forgiveness?' He spat at the ground. 'Well, I'm not surprised to hear that from you. The Odu turned selling Kuba into sport.'

Rumi stiffened, picking his words carefully. 'The Odu say that when you run from your father's sins, you goad his demons

26

to a new chase. The Odu have sinned in this land. But do *not* compare us to the Palmaine. There are slavers on every continent, but only one continent teaches its children that a slave is less than a man and should never be free. Only one continent enslaves babies and uses men to bait bears. If the Odu turned selling Kuba into sport, then it was the Palmaine that made it a religion.'

The wheelman snorted. 'What can a denier know about religion?'

'Your ancestors were Darani too. Do you believe they all went to hell when they died?'

His response was instantaneous. 'Yes.'

Rumi could have left it there. *Should* have left it there. He did not.

'Then you, my friend, are a tree without roots. Bereft of your soul, falling with the breeze. A cheaply bought coward.'

'Tread carefully, *Zarot*.'

The last word hit Rumi like a stone in the back. Though all natives wore that word, it always had a special violence when used against the Odu. *Zarot*. A word that once meant twenty cowries. The price of an Odu slave. The cheapest type of slave.

Rumi's knuckles cracked as he clenched his fists. 'What did you just call me?'

The wheelman steadied himself, weighing the heft of his words.

'I called you what you are ... a slack-lip ... dark-eye ... cowrie-pinching *Zarot*.'

There it was: an end to the chatter at last. After an hour of silent riding, the acolyte called out. 'Let us out.'

Rumi raised an eyebrow. They were still a good half hour from the end of the mainland road.

The wheelman drew rein for them to disembark.

Before leaving, the priestess put a palm on Rumi's shoulder. 'Be careful,' she said.

Rumi grabbed her wrist. 'Do I know you?'

She smiled, making no effort to leave his grip. 'No, you don't.'

A vulture hissed in the sky and her head jerked upwards.

'Get to the Eredo,' the priestess said, ripping her wrist free. 'The tide is rising.'

Rumi watched them leave, shaking his head. They did not look like lickheads. Rumi knew the signs. Milk-white drool, glassy eyes, and a jagged edge to the voice. The priestess bore no signs, yet she had babbled like an addict. *What the hell is an Eredo?* He ran his thumb over the strange black cowrie as the caravan pulled away.

A few miles down the road, they passed a massive iroko tree. To the Darani, the iroko tree was sacred; to everyone else it was good for boat-building and furniture. His mother's words flashed through his mind: *Where the iroko still stands, the Odu will be near.*

'Stop the caravan,' Rumi said.

The wheelman pulled back on the reins and glanced at Rumi. 'What now?'

Rumi's eyes narrowed to slits. 'You may not know this, but there was a time during the rebellion when "Zarot" was the last thing Odu people heard before they were hanged from trees.'

'Listen—'

Rumi seized him by the collar. The wheelman tried to punch him, but Rumi slapped the punch aside and struck with controlled blunt force.

'Zarot! Denier bastard! Fu—'

Rumi backhanded him. It was the sort of heavy-handed slap that left your ears ringing.

28

The wheelman snarled. Rumi grabbed him by his hair and jerked his head back, staring into his eyes.

'We are in the South now. Oduland. Shege any man that calls me a Zarot on Oduland. The Southern soil is full of the corpses of my ancestors and I will not suffer such an insult while they watch. Ride back to the Citadel and remember that in the South some Zarots still bite.'

3

And Now Your Service Begins

SABACHI

Sabachi's only eye snapped open to the moon's full glare. He fitted a small, cast-iron ball into his empty eye socket as he regained full consciousness.

His Master barely moved from beyond the writhing fire. The forest was silent, but for the low whistle of the wind and the cracking of blackened wood in the heart of the flame. Sabachi leaned over to sit cross-legged beside the fire and stared up at the moon, waiting for his Master to speak.

The Priest of Vultures wore an immaculate flowing white kaftan of the purest fabric, stitched by the cleanest hands. His skin was the translucent white of coconut innards and his teeth were like little knives peeking over lips. The fire danced in his coal-black eyes. A beautiful man, a good Master. A holy man. The last hope for mankind. His Master's body was solid as stone, yet when he walked it was with dancerly suppleness.

'What did you see?' his Master said at last.

'A boy,' Sabachi said. 'Near where we found her.' He pointed at the Darani priestess, who they had tied to a tree branch above the fire. 'The same one your bird saw. Just a boy, but he could be...'

The Priest of Vultures gave a hard look. 'The Son of Despair?'

Sabachi nodded. 'His shadow burns.'

'You are sure of what you saw?'

'Absolutely, Master.'

His Master glanced up towards the priestess. 'And the Son shall cast them down, erase their names, their seed in the land.'

The sweat dripped from her forehead directly into the fire.

His Master spoke softly. 'Is that why you gave him the cowrie?'

The woman did not stir. She was no ordinary priestess. Tough as old leather boots. Like in the old days.

They had been slowly torturing her for almost three hours before setting her skin to simmer. She hadn't said a word, not even given the slightest hint she would turn for them. Sabachi had seen people run mad with the telling of secrets after just a few seconds above the fire; he had seen an old soldier give up his wife, child, and cousin. The priestess's lips had hardly moved.

Sabachi launched a stone at her. It struck true, forming an instant gash on her cheek. She took the blow in complete silence.

The Priest of Vultures pinched the bridge of his nose and closed his eyes. 'Bring her consort out,' he called.

A cold wave washed over Sabachi as a tall, manacled figure crept from the shadows. Skin dark as coal, cut from muscle hard as stone with legs tree-trunk thick and arms three times bigger than a veteran blacksmith's. He towered over everything. A brute by any measure, but all this was nothing when set beside the man's most unsettling feature. *The eyes.* They were white as eggs, with no iris or pupil. Sabachi's stomach fell. His Master had summoned an *Obair*. Creatures wrought of skin and shadow. Nightmares made real.

The Obair tugged against a chain and the priestess's acolyte was dragged into the light. The acolyte shivered despite being close to the fire. A man in pitiful condition. It was like someone

31

had taken a corpse, given it a loaf of bread, and told it to live again.

'Stay … strong.' The skinny man coughed. His eyes were fixed on the priestess above the fire. 'You were always the strong one.'

Tears glistened in the priestess's eyes for only a moment before she pulled a mask of grim determination over her face.

The Priest of Vultures' response was pitiless.

'*Break his legs.*'

The Obair's obedience was instant. He set the acolyte down and held out one of his legs, then, with a derisive grunt, stamped down on the man's shin, bending the leg until it snapped like a matchstick. The loud crack of bone and the spatter of blood made Sabachi wince. The acolyte howled in pain, his leg dangling like a banana peel in the Obair's hand.

The Priest of Vultures glanced up at the priestess. 'You can still talk before we break the other one.'

She closed her eyes and set her jaw. The Priest of Vultures let out an exasperated breath and nodded to the Obair.

The sound of the second leg cracking was louder and bloodier than the first. A horrific thing. Worse to hear than even to see.

'Speak now and spare his life!' the Priest of Vultures snarled. 'Why did you give him the cowrie?'

The priestess raised her chin. 'Furae Oloola, my love.'

For a moment, the acolyte stopped screaming, forcing two words through his pain. 'Furae … Oloola.'

The Priest of Vultures narrowed his eyes. 'So be it.'

The Obair threw the man into the fire.

Even for someone as seasoned to blood and death as Sabachi, the screams were unbearable. As the fire peeled flesh from bone, the acolyte's screams filled the night. A shrill, high-pitched thing. The scream a rat makes when the poison is working, the sound of death in his throat. Sabachi covered his ears until the silence returned.

The Priest of Vultures stared up at the woman, his face almost completely inexpressive. 'I will ask once more. Why did you give it to him?'

The priestess twisted her head to stare at the Priest of Vultures, her eyes glistening with tears.

'The Dancing Lion will break all our chains.'

The Priest of Vultures spoke with a note of sadness. 'I will find him, and your suffering will have been in vain.'

He stared at the fire and, as though at his command, it whimpered to death. In the blackened ash and charred remains of the flame was a thick metal collar with a long silver leash.

The Priest of Vultures raised his hands to the sky and a screech shot out from the night. Birds came into view, blotting out the light of the moon. Vultures. Hundreds of them, flying in legion.

They descended on the priestess. Pinkish innards dropped like fruit from a tree as they began to peck at her, ripping the flesh from her bones in a carnival of blood and guts.

The Priest of Vultures steepled his fingers as he watched the birds finish the bloody work. 'And now your service begins.'

Without warning, a sharp, childlike cry shot through the night.

Sabachi glanced over his shoulder. The sound came again. *No, not a child. A cat.*

As always, the Priest of Vultures had sensed her before she even arrived. 'What are you doing here?' he called over his shoulder, without looking back.

A woman stepped into the moonlight. Her flesh was dem-erara brown, hair the colour of syrup bouncing around her face like curly vines. Two black cats with bright yellow eyes nuzzled her knees, purring softly. If Sabachi's mother had seen her dress, she would have covered his eyes – the unguarded areas of her honey flesh drew them like bees. Sabachi drank it all in with his stare; he had killed his mother a long time ago. The woman's eyes enraptured him the longest. Glowing balls of crystal yellow and green with vertical pupils at the centre. Pupils like daggers. *A cat's eyes.*

She smiled at the Priest of Vultures. 'Aren't you happy to see me?'

The Priest of Vultures' eyes narrowed to slits. 'What do you want?'

Her chin drooped at that for a moment. 'I came to amuse myself and watch your pathetic *crusade*. The great Priest of Vultures, reduced to hunting children. What a fall.'

A vulture flew down, hissing, and perched itself on his shoulder. Both the bird and the man looked down on her with malice. 'The fools fight to fell the oak tree. The wise pluck the acorns from the soil.'

The woman glared at him for a moment, then smiled as though he had told a joke. 'When you are done catching grasshoppers, you will be too old and weak to join us in the real hunting ground, chasing the big game.'

'And the Son of Despair shall cast down the holy temple and—'

'Declare himself Lord of All. So shall the tribulation of gods begin,' she snapped, cutting him off. 'I know the scripture. I have not forgotten what we fight against.'

The Priest of Vultures spoke in a low voice. 'He may be the Son of Despair.'

She laughed. 'Don't be a fool. Open your eyes, see beyond the ghosts in your mind. We all have. There is no Son of Despair.'

34

The vulture perched on his Master's shoulder hissed at the woman and a hint of fear passed through her eyes.

She remastered herself and flashed a dark, malicious smile. 'Such conspicuous creatures,' she said regarding the vulture. 'You have never been a subtle man, have you?'

His Master said nothing, staring his dismissal down at her. A committee of vultures had come to rest on the surrounding trees, all with their eyes fixed on her. Sabachi's stomach turned sideways; he was unsure of what was about to happen. A long, tense silence had its way.

The woman let the moment pass and lowered her chin. 'Fine. Enjoy your grasshopper hunt.'

With that, she turned and left without a backwards glance.

Sabachi watched her leave, drinking in her body as she walked away. Then he felt his Master's backhanded slap.

4

Walking with the Panther

RUMI

Only stubborn pride kept him walking, but Rumi had stubbornness and pride aplenty.

His bruised knuckles ached, but he was no stranger to pain. He was reminded of something Tinu the Panther had said once. *You can't be a weakling and an Odu in this country, boy. Choose one.*

Every Odu boy in Rumi's situation who had any genuine interest in living, learned that it was a matter of extreme importance to find a skill, craft or talent to escape the strangle of poverty. In the Orchid House, some had believed that fighting would be Rumi's gift. Tinu the Panther had trained him to be a brutal brawler. But Rumi's heart had always been with music. Now it really could be his way. *Would be.* In the Golden Room, of all places. The finest music house in all of Basmine.

He pulled the old leopard-skin scarf up over his nose. After all these years, it still smelled like Tinu, somehow. He wished he could share this moment with him, but the man was long dead. He tried not to think of Tinu often, but every now and then he found comfort in the memory. *Grief shapeshifts.* Sometimes, you need to remember the pain.

★

The village was fast asleep when he arrived. A cautious, watchful sleep. Cookfires had been doused, lanterns quenched, and the people of Alara had retired to their mudbrick houses. Still, you could almost feel the lingering tension. It was always that way. Undead habits from a time when slavers raided at night.

He came at last to a sturdy bungalow with terracotta pots littered about the doorway and nudged the door open to find his mother, Adunola – or Yami, as he called her – wide awake in her wooden chair. His older brother Morire sat cross-legged on the floor in front of her. Yami's dark eyes studied him as he entered.

It was one of those rare things – a good night.

Morire drummed the floor as Rumi walked forward. At the centre of his being, Morire was a happy man. Growing up, Rumi had done a lot of punching to make the other children leave his big brother alone.

He knew the things that bothered Morire: a crinkle in his routine, a new colour on the house furniture, a chair rearranged. Morire was a man of routine. Drumming was a way to take back control; set the new tempo.

Morire was the taller of the brothers, with a grip like iron and thickly muscled arms, but he was a gentle soul of wordless eloquence. It was the balance of their brotherhood; Rumi had to be fierce, so Morire could be gentle.

Either side of Morire sat two great dogs: Kaat and Ndebe. Lionhounds that were as much Adunola's children as Morire and Rumi. Stories abounded of men and women bonded to beast in the old age, and Adunola acted as though she shared that same psychic connection with her dogs.

Kaat was an old, world-weary bitch with rich black fur, who took long, languid strides as though she owned the ground she walked on. If Kaat had been a human and not a dog, she would have been an aristocrat with an upturned nose, and a straight neck; absolutely convinced she was better than you. Her round, yellow eyes always gave the impression she had figured you out and found you completely uninteresting.

Ndebe was the younger of the two; a handsome mahogany beast with thick hind legs and sharp teeth.

The lionhounds watched Rumi as he nestled in between them.

Yami sucked in breath the way she only did when she was telling a story.

'Story, story,' his mother began.

'Story,' Rumi replied. Morire groaned his approval.

'In the forest, there is a giant tree called the Iroko, it is feared by all men and shunned by even the other trees,' she began. 'In the Iroko lives the spirit of an old man who roams the Nyme at night with a small torch and a staff older than the world, searching for lost travellers or lonely hunters.'

'Or runaway little boys,' Rumi added.

'Oh, yes, even little boys tired of home,' she said. 'Anyone who—'

'Sees his face, dies,' Rumi interrupted. 'We've heard this one before, Yami.'

She raised an eyebrow. 'I see we have a troublemaker.'

Rumi raised both hands, feigning innocence. 'Me?'

Yami frowned. 'I'll tell you what, you *crook*, if I tell you a story you haven't heard before then you're going to massage my feet for two weeks.'

Rumi laughed. 'I'll break kola nut to that.'

She presented a kola nut in her palm. 'Agreed.'

Rumi often wondered where she kept the kola nuts, the way she made them appear almost from thin air. They broke the kola nut and raised a piece each to the sky in agreement.

'You've always been a clever boy, but don't ever think you're too clever. The journey does not end because you think you have arrived.'

'I didn't come for proverbs, Yami, I came for new stories!' Rumi said, biting down on the kola nut.

She smiled, taking a sharp bite of her own piece. 'Very well.'

Rumi leaned forward.

She sucked in a deep breath. 'There was once a monkey caught in a stream against the tide. Try as he might, the monkey could not escape. Drowning with no hope. Death was at the monkey's throat when suddenly, like a rescue from the gods, he saw a fallen tree outstretched across the river – the perfect escape.'

She glanced at Rumi. He sat with his arms folded, suppressing a smile.

'And, so, the monkey climbed, and he rested, for he had tasted certain death. And when he had rested, he saw a friend struggling against the tide, just as he had. He knew then that he had been saved for a reason. He had been saved to save others, to be a hero. He searched for help and found a brave fisherman with a net pledging his support. Together they rushed to the river and saved the monkey's friend. The fisherman, a kind man, promised to take the monkey's friend to safety. Later, in the village square, the monkey boasted, "I saved a fish from drowning today".'

The smile on Rumi's face widened, but he withheld the laughter. His mother regarded him with mock seriousness, then she smiled a smile that said, *I've got you, you little rat.* Rumi's resistance broke and he barked with laughter.

'Two weeks!' she said. 'Massages with ori oil!'

Morire slapped the floor with glee and the room was full of joy.

Rumi raised his hands in surrender. 'You win. I have never heard that one before.'

His mother gave half a smile. 'I keep more stories than I tell. Believe me.'

Rumi glanced up. 'Like the stories about the godhunters? The ones who wander in the night killing our gods?'

Yami's eyes narrowed to serious slits. She formed the sign of the crossroads with her forefingers and closed her eyes. It was a sign to ward away evil. 'We do not speak of such things in this house.'

She spoke each word with a tense effort, her calm voice flecked with a soft tremor of anger.

Rumi raised his chin. 'I am not a little boy anymore, Yami. I don't wet my pants from scary stories.'

'I *said* we do not speak of such things in this house.' The last of her patience had slipped away and her feather-paper voice was suddenly hard and sharp as flint.

Rumi's smile faded as he saw her darkening eyes. 'Yes, Yami.'

She stared at him for a long, tense moment before she relaxed and her face was soft as cotton again. 'Hungry?' she asked.

It was the closest Yami ever came to an apology.

Rumi stiffened, stepped forward and then pulled her into an embrace. 'No, thank you, Yami.'

He waited for her to ask more questions, but none came. He raised an eyebrow. 'Aren't you going to ask me about the Golden Room, Yami?'

'No.'

'Why not?'

'You are my son. You are Darani. You were not born to fail; Dara carved your wood before you could breathe, and you give me more pride than anything I have done in this life. Whether they said yes or no, you have already won.'

40

Rumi could not suppress the smile. 'They told me to come back in three weeks... with an oud.'

Her blossoming smile withered to dust. 'You'd better not take an oud back there.'

'Yami—'

'Don't "Yami" me! The drums are a part of you that you cannot abandon. Play their instruments, you play their music. Our music has more power than that, more meaning.'

'I can't go back to the Orchid House, *ever*. You know that, Yami. It's been almost two years of me hustling from village to village. This is a big opportunity.'

'Dara will provide other opportunities. It is Dara that creates opportunities, not them.'

'Yami...' Rumi said. 'How much does the market still owe in consular taxes?'

She narrowed her eyes.

'How much, Yami?'

She lowered her head. 'Five hundred and thirty cowries.'

'How much of that do we have?'

She pursed her lips in silence.

Rumi put a palm on her shoulder. 'The Golden Room pays a maintenance of twenty cowries a week... with performance bonuses. Twenty cowries a week, Yami! This is how we get the consul off our back, once and for all, and protect the market.'

'It is not your responsibility, son. I will handle it.'

'Yami, I am not a child anymore. Let me help you.'

She let out a deep sigh.

'Rumi, please... please, listen to me. You are worth more to me than all the cowries in the Palmaine empire. Do not go back there with an oud.'

Rumi gritted his teeth. 'All right, Yami,' he lied.

He thumbed the acceptance letter in his pocket, enjoying

the reassuring feel of it on his forefinger. He was going to the Golden Room with or without her blessing. It was their last hope. His last hope.

His mother inclined her head. 'What happened to your kaftan? The hustle?'

Rumi glanced down at his sleeve. A thin line of blood ran down to the cuff.

'A nosebleed,' he said.

She narrowed her eyes and called his full name. 'Irumide.'

Rumi straightened. Whenever she used his full name like that, he knew playtime was over.

She lifted her chin and spoke softly. 'Lie to me again and you will regret it.'

Rumi did not doubt it. His mother *was* a market woman. 'I'm sorry, Yami,' he said

'And what else?'

'I'm sorry for that, Yami. I won't—'

'Sounds to me like another lie waiting on your tongue.'

The words died in his throat.

'I thought you were done with fighting?' she said.

'I am. It was ... The wheelman on the way back called me a Zarot.'

She frowned. In the lantern light her skin was like a glowing black rock, marbled by the siege of the sea, and her eyes were dark brown like his – but without the hint of red. Eyes that seemed to darken when her mood was foul.

She ran a finger over one of the five parallel scars on her forearm.

'Is that the Way of the Darani? To be quick to anger?'

He frowned. 'No, Yami.'

'If you end up bleeding every time you are provoked, you won't live very long and I won't forgive you for not living long.'

42

Rumi narrowed his eyes. 'Are *you* lecturing me on anger now, Yami? *You*? The Market Mama?'

She looked up at him. 'Anger can be useful, but only if you know how to keep it. Like the leopard keeps its speed. You know it's there, but you use it wisely. Next time, ask yourself, am I really angry?'

'Of course I was. He called me a Zarot!'

She shook her head in sober disapproval. 'Anger is what you showed but it isn't what you felt. Shame, pain, sadness. These were the feelings. You only expressed them through anger. I always believed I taught you better than that. If you understood your feelings better, you would know there is no good sense in being angry at a native who is chased by the same terrors as you. If he was a Palmaine man, you would have known restraint, because of course you know getting angry at a Palmaine man could get you killed.'

'What are you—' He bit his tongue.

Her dark eyes were patient as the executioner, waiting for him to respond. Daring him to. He knew enough to know when it was time to change the subject.

He let out a long breath. 'Tell me again how you got your scars, Yami.'

A truce.

She thumbed her scars slowly. 'All I'm saying, Rumi, is put love first.'

Rumi nodded his understanding and pointed to her scars.

And so began a new tale about how she had earned each scar on some impossible task. She told of how she had lived a year selling plantain in the spirit lands and had to prove she could bleed to be allowed passage back to the mortal realm. She told other unlikely stories.

Before long, all the tension was gone and they made their way to their shared bedroom, sated by the spiel.

Rumi lit a stick of incense to ward away mosquitoes, then climbed into his bamboo bed. 'I saw the Citadel, Yami.'

Her face was expressionless.

He pressed on. 'It was ... beautiful.'

Still, she said nothing. In the dim light, her faced seemed not to move.

'They say Palmaine itself is ten times more beautiful than the Citadel, with streets paved with gold. How can they build that? Why couldn't *we* build that? We have iron and gemstones and corn in no short number, but we never *built* anything like that.'

She traced a thumb down the side of her face. 'If you give one nation a table of food and another a table of empty plates, one nation will argue about splitting the food and the other will argue about finding food. Only one nation will be better for it. That is why we say, "beware of the man whose homeland has no trees". Our time will come, Rumi. We need only the story to bind us.'

Rumi smiled. *Simple as that.*

At the corner of his eye, something moved. A bird in flight he thought. He jerked his head round. In a flash, his mother was there turning out the window lantern. Not a bird in sight. *Sleep playing tricks on me.*

'Goodnight, Yami,' he said, lying down to sleep.

She lingered over the window, staring out into the night. 'Goodnight, my son.'

5

The Market Mama

RUMI

The hiss of simmering oil pulled Rumi from sleep. One whiff and he was on his feet – Yami's cooking was not to be missed. Outside, Yami, Morire and the dogs were semi-circled around a cookfire. Dollops of beancake batter were taking form in a large pan of oil.

A dozen golden-brown beancakes were already set out to dry in a large bowl beside the pan. Hand-made, pan-fried gateways to paradise. Rumi dipped his finger in, smiling. 'Good morning, Yami.'

She didn't look at him. 'Have you said your prayers?'

Rumi froze. 'No.'

'You know the rules in this house. Even for Golden Room boys.'

Rumi groaned, walking back inside. With his prayer mat, divination tray and a small bucket of water in tow, he ambled into the bush, towards the bloodwood tree.

The bloodwood seemed to slouch. Rumi laid his prayer mat down and pulled water to his face in cupped hands.

His mother had hammered it into his head half a hundred times. *A child who washes their hands can eat with the elders.* Prayer was to be treated like a dinner with esteemed guests. He scrubbed all the dirt from his face and hands and set the divination tray with a kola nut and a cowrie. Dark red sap oozed from a slash in the tree. He touched the sap, marked a red line on his forehead, then dropped to his knees.

He spoke in Odu, calling names Yami had instilled in him from the day his neck was tattooed. The great ancestors: Walade the Widowmaker, King Olu the Special, Nasir Neverkneel. The Agbara of Oduland: Xango, Shuni, Aja, Kamanu, Ilesha, Gu, and Dara the Skyfather – the first and greatest.

He spoke aloud, as though to a room full of guests. He prayed for wisdom, for strength and for his family. He gave thanks to Dara for the Golden Room and a future of good living. Then he closed his eyes, breathing deep, listening for the ancestors. Perhaps they would finally have something to say.

A soft *thunk* broke his concentration. He glanced over his shoulder. A coconut had fallen behind him. The tree was too young to be dropping full-grown coconuts.

'Renike!'

Renike glided down the tree until her naked feet dangled from a low branch.

She smiled sheepishly. 'I didn't mean to disturb your prayer.'

Renike was the closest thing Rumi had to a sister, though they shared no blood or family. She was at that age where her arms and legs had run ahead of her development, leaving the rest of her body to catch up. Her yellow dress had been stained to near brown from climbing.

'You didn't disturb me,' Rumi said, rolling his prayer mat up.

She gave him a curious look. 'What's that?' she asked, pointing to the priestess's cowrie.

Rumi prodded her neck. 'It's magic.'

Her eyes widened for a moment before she scowled. 'No such thing.'

Rumi raised an eyebrow. 'Then what do you call Yami's beancakes?'

She sniffed the air, catching the scent and a smile spread across her cheeks. 'I'll race you.'

Before Rumi could answer, she bolted.

Rumi grabbed his divination tray and chased after her. Renike was quick for her age, but Rumi had a reputation to uphold. He caught up to her in five strides and used his superior reach to touch the parapet first.

'I almost had you,' she said, gasping for air.

'The old dog never dies,' Rumi said, smiling.

They joined Yami and Morire at the table to eat.

There was reverent silence. For a long, priceless moment everything was perfect. Then a talking drum sounded. Rumi dropped a beancake and rose to his feet.

Yami narrowed her eyes, gesturing for Rumi to sit back down. 'Relax.'

The silhouette of a tall, dark figure appeared from the other side of the house. Rumi's heart sank.

'Baba!' Renike yelled.

A tower of a man stepped forward. He had hair that dropped in greying locks over each shoulder and a face cut from hard lines and sharp sinew. He bent a little to avoid a tree branch and smiled a father's smile.

Rumi let out a relieved breath. 'Lutayo,' he breathed, clutching his chest. It was Renike's father.

'Am I too late for beancakes?' Lutayo asked.

'Far too late,' Rumi said, rubbing his belly. 'Beancakes don't last long in this house.'

Lutayo cursed. 'Shege.'

Renike shook her head disapprovingly. 'Mind your language, Baba.'

'Sorry, Ren, sometimes I need bad language to talk about bad things,' he said.

Adunola met his gaze. 'Why did the talking drum sound?'

One look into his eyes told Rumi all he needed to know: something was wrong.

'Trouble,' Lutayo confirmed.

Rumi's hand tightened on the priestess's cowrie in his pocket.

Lutayo was to the village farmers what Adunola was to the market women. Their leader and champion. They were right and left fist of the village. When Lutayo came to meet Yami, it meant a fight was coming.

Yami went still for a moment, her eyes narrowed to slits. 'Rumi, go answer the door.'

Almost on cue, someone knocked.

Rumi rushed into the house and pulled the door open. A figure filled the doorway. A market woman like his mother, but older and wider with an awkward gait. She was bare-chested and held a long, metal-tipped spear. Around her waist was a rope of thin gold. His face flushed as he averted his gaze from her breasts.

'Never seen breasts before?' she said with a grin. 'Don't be so shy, you were on your mother's milk till you were almost five.'

'Good morning, Mama Ayeesha,' he greeted.

She slapped his cheeks and waddled past him. 'Good morning, Rumi.'

His mother stepped into the house. 'Why did they sound the drum?'

Ayeesha raised her chin. 'Four consular guard headed this way.'

'Shege,' Lutayo said with a grim scowl. 'Where are the others?'

'They aren't coming.'

'Just us then.'

Adunola's nod was slow and solemn, like the guilty accused

accepting a death sentence. She moved to the centre of the house and dragged aside the thick lambswool rug to reveal four straight planks of floorboard. Rumi narrowed his eyes and leaned in close. Yami stamped down on the two centremost planks, snapping them in half in an explosion of dust and splinter.

A small smile spread across Adunola's lips as she pulled at a trapdoor by its inset iron ring and climbed down into the gloom.

'Godsblood,' Rumi breathed. *A secret room.*

She returned with a weapon in her hands.

'What is that?' Rumi asked, as his mother straightened up.

She lifted it above her head. A broad charcoal-black axe-head, topped with a long spike.

'A halberd,' she said.

The light bounced off the black haft like oil. It was as though the weapon was formed from solid, congealed smoke.

Adunola ran her fingers along the axeblade. Rumi stared down into the room and saw a book, marked with Yami's sinuous scroll. He narrowed his eyes.

'What are you doing, Yami?'

She ignored him as she unfastened the buttons of her shirt, exposing the long, curved scar below her navel where she had been cut open for Rumi to be born.

There was a firmness to her now, a quiet strength. She looked twenty years younger. Rumi wasn't looking at Yami anymore, he was looking at the Market Mama.

'Quick, get down there with your brother and Renike,' she said, pointing at the trapdoor.

Rumi stared down into the secret room. 'Yami—'

'Now,' she hissed.

Rumi's jaw tightened.

His heart pounded as he helped Renike and Morire down.

Just before he took a step inside, he saluted with the easy devotion of a soldier affirming his captain's command. 'Come back to me, Yami.'

She gave him a brief, bothered look, then nodded. 'I will.'

She shut the trapdoor and Rumi let out a sharp breath. The last time he had seen that look on her face was almost ten years ago when she'd left to stop the village headcount. That time, there were half a hundred women with her.

A headcount always came before a tax. When the Palmaine came to account for Alara, they met Yami with fifty market women who were wielding spears, machetes and bare breasts. That was where the Market Mama was born: in the Market Mama Riots. For three years they resisted. Then their little rebellion came to the attention of Governor-General Zaminu. Things got bloody after that. Sixteen women were killed and the market women were ordered to pay years' worth of back taxes.

The floorboards creaked and Rumi heard the faint press of bootsteps. The consular were inside the house.

Yami's voice was cool as the river wind. 'Shall we take this outside, officers?'

Rumi didn't catch a response, but the footsteps trudged outside. He pressed his ear to the trap door, listening for more. It had gone quiet.

His jaw tightened as he sank back against the wall. Minutes passed that felt like hours. Every moment was an exercise in agony. *Come back to me, Yami.* Renike squeezed his hand. It was too dark to see her face clearly but the limp desperation of her grip told him she was terrified. Morire sat perfectly still, his breathing slow and rhythmic.

'It'll be all right,' Rumi whispered. 'They will be all right.'

'Are you sure?' she asked.

He was about to answer when the sudden clap of a gunshot made him jump. Renike let out a sharp scream and Morire made a hissing sound. The unbidden question pummelled his mind. *Who did they just shoot?*

Rumi lurched towards the trap door but Renike tugged at him.

'She said we should stay put,' Renike urged, gripping his hand.

Another gunshot sounded.

'Shege that,' Rumi snarled.

He put his shoulder to the trap door and shoved with all his strength. It shuddered at the first barge but didn't give way. Rumi gritted his teeth and tried again.

He couldn't lose Yami. Not now. Not after losing Tinu. The darkness from that loss had wrestled him until he was completely bereft of energy and desire, with thoughts like knives in his skull.

That darkness was still there, waiting like a dog chained to a wall.

Not again.

With a contemptuous hiss, he smashed into the trapdoor and broke off one of the hinges. Without hesitating, he slid the door aside and climbed out.

'You stay with Morire,' he said to Renike.

He didn't get a response before he darted into the next room, snatching a knife off the table as he sped through the door.

Chaos reigned outside as he followed the trail of violence. Broken horsecarts and cookpots askew preceded the market gates. He sped through to a scene of complete and utter bedlam.

A woman screamed ahead. 'My leg!'

It was Mama Ayeesha. A consular guard stood with his gunstock above her knee. The consular's face was eagerly grim.

Like a moneylender's on repayment day. He raised the gun high and brought it down in a wet crack. Ayeesha let out a feral scream.

Rumi moved without thinking. He caught the consular flush, fist to temple, quick and hard. It was the sort of punch that Tinu called 'the wonderbang'. A hit that couldn't get any sweeter if it was dipped in a pint of honey.

The consular went down with a grunt. *When you know a man is stronger than you, don't give him a chance to prove it.* Tinu's words. Rumi brought his fists down with malice until the consular went slack in his grip.

With the business finished, Rumi straightened, wiping his bloody knuckles down on his kaftan. His breathing came in short, sharp gasps.

Ayeesha stared up at him with a look of horror. He realised he was snarling. He had done it again – let himself go.

He backed away from her and tripped over a potato sack.

He glanced back. Not a potato sack. Too thick, too awkward.

He drew back the ragged swathe of cloth and his whole body stiffened.

'Shege,' he whispered.

It was Lutayo, Renike's father. Jaw set strong, lips firmed tight. A large, wet wound dominated his chest. A man would have had to shoot from less than arm's length to create a hole that large.

Rumi's first instinct should have been to jerk back, to cover his mouth in horror. Instead he was frozen, transfixed by Lutayo's wide, accusing eyes.

Mama Ayeesha let out a shuddering breath. 'They shot him for no reason.'

She winced as he ran his hand along her shin, searching for a break. Finding what was little more than a crack he helped her to her feet and she settled against a horse cart.

'Where is Yami?' Rumi asked.

Ayeesha pointed past his shoulder to where a small crowd was gathered.

Rumi moved at speed, shoving through the throng of people.

Adunola stood alone against two consular guards. She stared past them at the oncoming Palmaine captain who was riding at a gallop. The captain drew rein with an exasperated huff and dismounted right in front of her.

She held the halberd slightly to the side. An easy, unaggressive stance.

'Officer, what is the meaning of this?' Adunola asked.

The captain looked Adunola up and down. 'We are here to collect your unpaid taxes.'

'The governor-general agreed to give us time to repay. I have a letter that says—'

'The governor-general is dead,' the captain said cutting her off, 'all his letter decrees are suspended until a new governor-general is announced by the royal conclave.'

The news didn't seem to surprise Adunola.

She raised an eyebrow. 'Is that why your men have brought violence here?'

The captain frowned and shifted his gun slightly so the nose was pointed down. 'I have the understanding that your men struck first.'

'That is not true,' Adunola said, almost gently. She pointed at a stout Kuba officer who wore a gold nose ring. 'He shot a man with no provocation.'

The officer stepped forward with all the coiled rage of a hunting hound. 'Five hundred and thirty cowries in taxes is provocation enough.'

Adunola didn't move an inch but the first signs of anger flashed in her eyes. 'I speak of lives lost and you speak of... taxes.'

She spat the word out as though it was an abomination to say aloud.

The crowd stirred and even the consular officer took a step back.

The captain shot the Kuba officer a levelling look and all that arrogance disappeared. 'It is unfortunate that things came to violence. Rest assured, any officers responsible for excessive force will be duly punished.'

The crowd yelled its fury but Adunola raised a hand, bringing silence. 'We will bury our dead and you will give us a year. Only then will you have your taxes in full.'

The captain snorted. 'We did not come to give; we came to collect.'

Adunola lifted her chin and silently moved her hand into a two-handed grip of the halberd. 'Well, there isn't much to collect right now,' she said, not breaking her stare. Her eyes were a dire threat.

Rumi broke from the crowd to stand beside his mother. Others felt the moment too. The circle seemed to inch closer around the consular. Chattering gave way to silence. Suddenly there were ten men behind Adunola and another ten either side of the consular guard.

The one with the gold nose ring raised his weapon and narrowed his eyes.

Rumi rolled his shoulders in reply and curled his grip around the knife in his pocket. *If it is to end in blood, let it flood to the ankle.*

The captain wet his lips, then placed a gentle hand on his subordinate's shoulder. 'There is no need for more violence.'

Adunola was impossibly still. 'I quite agree.'

The Kuba consular slowly lowered his weapon, glowering at her.

The captain leaned forward. 'Six months. We will return in six months and I can promise you, there will be more of us.'

The Kuba with the nose ring gave Adunola one last look and started to hum a song. At the first note, Rumi's nostrils flared.

It was 'The Boat on the Brown Sea'. An ugly song with a bloody history. It was a celebration of Odu death, though the Kuba often claimed it was about Kuba pride.

> *We danced around their sinking boat*
> *For crocodiles a putrid meal*
> *We clapped to see the drowning throats*
> *Of those who only know to steal*

Rumi's blood rose as the man hummed the tune, but Adunola put a firm, imploring hand on his shoulder. *Don't.*

Adunola watched the consular as they turned away.

'We are just going to let them leave?' Rumi snarled.

'Irumide,' his mother hissed.

Rumi jerked his head back towards her. 'They killed Renike's father.'

'Irumide,' she said again, her voice cold and pitiless.

He bit down on his words.

'We will report it to the consular office,' she said.

'They'll just move the killer to some other post! There'll be no justice!' His words came out with angry flecks of spit.

Yami narrowed her eyes. 'And what kind of justice are you looking for?'

'Yami—'

'It is not our place to mete out justice,' she said with inhuman calm. 'We will report them to the consular office, and we will treat Lutayo's death with the decorum it deserves. What did I tell you about your anger?'

Rumi frowned. 'Keep it. Like the leopard keeps its speed.'

She nodded approvingly. 'So, you keep it. Is that clear, son?'

Rumi's brows drooped in a low, angry V. 'Yes, Ma.'

Yami leaned close and spoke in a low voice. 'You left your brother and Renike?'

Rumi gritted his teeth. 'I heard gunshots – something could have happened to you.'

'And what if you got caught up in it? Who would be there for your brother if something happened to both of us? Think, Rumi, think.'

'I am thinking!' he snapped. His sharp movement caused the knife and priestess's cowrie to fall from his pocket.

Adunola squinted. 'Where did you get that?'

'It's the knife from—'

'Not the knife ... that ...' she said, plucking the priestess's cowrie from the ground.

Rumi raised an eyebrow. 'A priestess gave it to me, on the mainland road.'

She glanced at Mama Ayeesha, who was staring at the cowrie as though she had seen the spirit of her ancestor.

'The tide is rising, Sister,' Mama Ayeesha whispered.

6

The Princess and the Lizard

ALANGBA

Alangba raised his double-edged *ida* sword. The men behind him saw the signal and stopped in their tracks.

They had made it, after two days of hard trekking. Trekking without a drop of wine, ale or gin – the very worst kind of trekking.

A frosty wind tickled his skin and open-mouthed breaths produced small visible clouds of mist. This was Palmaine, *the Coldlands*. He had heard of strange things in these lands. Cold, white rain that fell from the skies like cotton. *Snow* they called it. A part of him would have liked to see it; the other part wanted to put his back to Palmaine forever.

His Commander, the First Ranger, had only allowed him to take four rangers with him. A band small enough to be dismissed if they failed. Had Alangba been First Ranger, he would have brought at least twenty, but you work with the soil in your village. Though they were only four, there were no better rangers to have in all the world.

Two of the best stood beside him. Maka Naki and No Music. Maka, was a fair, thickly muscled man. Handsome as heaven with charm to do more damage with a smile than most could with a sword. Maka's older brother and uncle had been coal miners under Governor-General Zaminu. They'd each lost a hand when the mine failed to meet Zaminu's quotas. One look at Maka's face told the entire story – he came to spill blood by the bucket tonight.

The other man, No Music, was dark as old mud. All sinew and lean muscle. Like a man made from rope. Tough and durable. To Alangba's mind, No Music was the most dangerous man alive. His name, No Music, was the product of someone with a crude imagination, given on account of the fact that No Music was deaf as the dead. The story was, No Music lost his hearing from refusing to plug his ears in his days as a cannoneer. Said he wanted to 'hear the voice of death'. The classic, uncomplicated kind of psychopath. The very sort that every team of killers needs. The one who could keep the fighting up when everyone else was sick of it. When it came to killing, No Music had all the eager calm of an apprentice wheelman at his first chance to take the reins.

The only trouble with No Music was that the bastard made the rest of the team uneasy. It's all right having a cold killer on your side, but a silent, unsmiling one, who looks halfway dead and only ever seems alive when killing? That makes people nervous.

The other two were Phelix and Tanto. Both young but what they lacked in experience they made up for with enthusiasm.

Tonight's was an impossible task, but theirs was an impossible assembly – if any five rangers could do it, it was them.

Alangba stared up at the building. Knowing Governor-General Zaminu was somewhere inside made his heartbeat quicken. A man so flippant with torture that even the Palmaine king had to pull him back. Alangba gritted his teeth. *You escaped Basmine, but you will not escape me.*

The building, now only a few metres ahead, possessed the asymmetrical patterns and façade of archaic Palmaine design. A building sure to rouse the poisoned nostalgia of conquerors past. Marble outer walls, four storeys topped with a Palmaine flag slapping against the evening wind. The image of the flag – a four-point star on a field of red – made sense if you saw the red as blood.

A party was going on inside. They seemed to be playing Odu music, but it was twisted somehow. That was what they did in Palmaine, made natives of the continent play a parody of their music to which they could dance. And dance poorly, too.

He put four fingers in the air. His men moved soundlessly through the shadows to stand beside him, awaiting instructions.

Alangba let out a slow breath and gave his instructions in swift hand signals.

'There will be natives inside. Some will try to stop us. Do not harm them if you can help it,' Alangba said.

There was no response from anyone.

He formed a triangle with his hands and they moved into position. They were good men, *his* men, but duty came before death.

He pulled his robes up over his shoulders and folded them into a burlap sack. They were replaced by a wing-collared, chalk-white Palmaine shirt, a black waistcoat, and close-fitting trousers. The small cobalt collar and leash he always kept on his person fit perfectly in the waistcoat pocket. The scabbard that held his sword trailed on the inside of his trouser leg. Last of all, he fixed a monocle. It was an unnecessary addition, but he loved the look.

He adopted the hunchbacked slouch of a man accustomed to servitude and approached the front door. It was guarded by two men in maroon uniforms bearing the sigil of the Palmaine king.

Both men were over six feet tall and wide enough at the shoulders to struggle through a door.

At their sides, Alangba spotted shiny repeating rifles.

He nodded to each of them politely.

'Guests only,' one of the guards said. 'Servants' entrance is that way.'

Alangba's breath caught in his throat.

'Let him through, he's late already,' said the second guard.

The soft clink-clink of glass flutes and the rumble of drunken laughter seemed to tease Alangba from inside.

'Go on then, quick, hurry in,' the guard said, holding the door open for him.

Alangba bowed. 'Thank you.'

There was barely a hint of suspicion on their faces. *Unlucky.*

The door opened into a ballroom. Tables were covered with food enough to satisfy a village. An almighty chandelier loomed over the proceedings as though to crown the affair. There were women everywhere. Near-naked Odu women in the main. There were men, too – Palmaine men in varying degrees of undress, and Darosan men dressed like Alangba, carrying trays of food or drink and wearing forced smiles.

His task – the most important one – was to infiltrate the upper room where Governor-General Zaminu entertained his most esteemed guests.

Two armed guards stood either side of the door to the upper room. From the way they stood, it was plain they knew the business of killing.

Alangba made a step towards the door and a heavy hand touched his shoulder. Without hesitating, he whirled and pressed his pocket-knife into the figure's armpit, then twisted it. It was done quickly. He guided the man to the ground, made him look more like a drunk than a corpse.

His eyes darted to the door again. *Wait for the signal.*

The music faltered at the sound of shattered glass. The rangers were moving. *Too early.* They were supposed to draw attention *away* from the door.

Confusion and panic took over the room. Alangba stayed focused, closing in on the stairs. The guards raised their rifles, unsure of who to fire at. The signal wouldn't come; he had to do this alone, without the benefit of distraction from a kitchen fire.

Alangba's sword was in his hand mere seconds before one of the guard's aimed his rifle. He swung once, severing the man's hand before he could squeeze the trigger. A bullet whistled past his ear from behind. Someone screamed. Alangba seized hold of the second guard and threw him over the balustrade into the melee below.

Leaning over, he saw Maka with his bloodstained sword held high. Another ranger, Phelix, stood beside two dead guards. One of his own, Tanto, was sprawled out on the floor, his head a bloody mess.

Then there was No Music, cutting guards up like a gardener trimming the hedges. A fat smile on his blood-spattered face. The guards wilted as No Music whipped up a carnival of chaos. Some turned and fled as they watched him work his blood business. The guards here were not warriors. They were well-trained and looked the part but they had no stomach for the work. Domesticated wolves who knew nothing of the hunt.

Maka saw it too. 'They are not built for this,' he cried out.

There was a loud shout of agreement from his compatriots.

Alangba turned back to the door and kicked it open, then rushed through.

As the door slammed shut behind him, something strange happened. The corridor fell quiet as a crypt. It was as though he had stepped into a different dimension and all the noise from the ballroom just behind did not exist. The only sound Alangba could hear was his own staggered breath. The temperature seemed to drop and suddenly it truly felt like the Coldlands. He steadied himself as a chill curled up his spine.

He had the sudden desire to be somewhere else; anywhere else. There was something unnatural in the air. Every instinct in his body told him that something was wrong. But duty came before death. He pressed on.

At the end of the corridor, he came to an open door that led down a flight of stairs.

He glanced down the stairs, barely illuminated by the flickering light below. He sucked in a breath and muttered a prayer. 'Dara, Father of All, go with me.'

Every step was an act of faith and bravery, and his heart thumped harder the closer he got to the dim light. At last, he came to the end of the stairs and stepped into a room. It was a large chamber, supported by four alabaster columns. At the corners of the room loomed the shadows of large objects just out of view.

Just ahead, four men stood around a small table illuminated by a candlelight chandelier. Alangba moved noiselessy into the shadows. He was no novice when it came to sneaking about.

Zaminu still wore the uniform of a governor-general, down to the helmet and socks. Even without the uniform, he would have been instantly recognisable. Alangba had seen that face impressed upon grey-white limestone. Standing proud beside the dock of Basmine with a sword in one hand and the Palman holy book in the other. It takes a certain kind of man to commission his own statue and Zaminu was one such man.

Beside Zaminu was a Palman priest holding an incense-burning thurible.

Alangba could not recognise the other two men but reasoned that they were important. They wore the uniform of high-ranking Palmaine officers.

Zaminu cleared his throat. 'Gentlemen, you may have heard rumour of our discoveries in Basmine. Secrets of lost occult power. Sorcery and *magic*, the likes of which you could never imagine. Perhaps you have dismissed these reports as utter nonsense or foolish superstition. Tonight, I bring you a demonstration.'

The other men smiled with the scavenging anticipation of hyenas. Zaminu gave an approving nod, then gestured to the table where four golden goblets surrounded a large silver plate. He raised a goblet and drained it in a single gulp. 'Drink,' he ordered, and the other men obeyed.

Alangba's stomach turned sideways.

The priest stepped forward to polish the small plate that lay at the centre of the table. *No.* Alangba narrowed his eyes, noticing the markings on the plate. Not a plate at all; a Darani divination tray. The appearance of it in a room like this should have been the height of oddity. Yet, what struck Alangba was the way the Palman priest was treating the divination tray. Not as an object of blasphemy, but one of veneration. Every part of Palman scripture demanded that the priest smash the divination tray to pieces, yet here he was polishing it in the old Darani way.

Zaminu raised his hands to the sky in supplication and closed his eyes. The candles whimpered all at once. A small, hissing sound sprang out from nowhere as a wisp of dark, viscous smoke curled from Zaminu's hands.

Alangba's inadvertent gasp drew their attention. They turned on him with looks of animal hate.

The priest gave a disapproving frown. 'Is he one of yours?'

'No,' Zaminu hissed, his eyes lidded with disgust.

Alangba narrowed his eyes. Around the divination tray was a calabash, a candle, and a golden coin. *This is a ritual.*

The priest muttered something under his breath and Alangba noticed a bloody stripe on Zaminu's forearm.

Without thinking, Alangba reached for the Odeshi collar in his waistcoat. It was an object that had the look of a dog leash but it carried the power of the gods that gave the dog life. The one tool he had to dominate magic. Just as he moved to spring, the priest stepped forward and swung the thurible like a flail weapon. It struck Alangba flush in the face in an explosion of ash, incense, and scalding oil.

Alangba snarled, partially blinded as he staggered back. Something moved at the corner of his vision; smooth and silky as a snake. *No Music.*

By the time Alangba found his feet, No Music had skewered a man and was already turning to kill another. The priest dropped his thurible and ran. Zaminu tried to do the same but Alangba swept his leg and he went down in a tangle. Without hesitation, Alangba snapped the Odeshi collar around Zaminu's neck.

He squinted through the searing pain spreading across his face as he wrestled Zaminu to the ground, putting a knee on the small of his back to pin him down while he tied his hands.

'Governor-General Zaminu, I arrest you in the name of the indigenous people of the nation now known as Basmine.'

'Unhand me,' Zaminu hissed. 'Mudskin bastard.'

No Music stared down at the two corpses he'd made, frowned, and then turned to go after the priest.

Alangba blinked as the burn in his eyes receded. In front of him was a large box with wooden hasps and staples. He forced it open with his ida sword and the smell made his head jerk back. Two rotting black corpses squashed together like snail meat. He slammed the box shut and kicked Zaminu in the chest so hard he coughed blood. He sniffed at the empty goblets and caught the thick, unmistakeable pang of blood. *What were these men doing?*

The answer was obvious – though he did not want to admit it to himself. Juju of the most dangerous kind – human sacrifice and blood ritual. They had broken Dara's sixth commandment. How the Palmaine had come to discover such things was a mystery it hurt to consider.

He glanced down at Zaminu, who was trying to force the Odeshi collar from his neck. Alangba was not entirely certain how the collar worked, so he kicked Zaminu again for good measure.

Elsewhere in the room was a framed map of the world with the continent of Darosa marked blue to indicate Palmaine territories. There were suggestions for names in crude handwriting all across it. His jaw tightened as he saw the word 'Basmine' scrawled over a large blotch of blue.

A rattle of chains came from the darkest corner of the room.

He crouched forward until he saw a large, sheet-covered box. His heartbeat quickened as he placed his hand on the sheet and drew it back. It was a cage.

Inside was a full-grown, barrel-chested lion. The light illuminated its yellow-gold coat as it stalked around the cage, barely bending its thick forelegs with each calculated stride. The muscles beneath its fur bristled and bulged as it stalked forward. Their eyes met and the lion froze. Alangba felt the stillness too. Like cold water in the face. He could almost hear the lion's heartbeat, thrumming in perfect sync to his own. Its eyes widened as it walked to the very front of the cage. Close enough for Alangba to feel its hot breath on his face.

It was an act of violence against nature to cage such a majestic creature. Stripping it bare of everything that made it what it was; as cruel as cutting a bird's wings.

He pulled his sword free of its scabbard and walked to the small gate at the cage's front.

'What are you doing?' Zaminu shouted.

Alangba was wrapped in his own silence. He could feel the lion calling out to him, clear as a bell at his ear. He reached a hand into the cage and the lion bowed for him to touch the centre of its head. He felt something. Something that came from the lion, as tangible and perspicuous as a stone in his hand. *Rage.*

With an overhand slash of his sword, he severed the latch of the cage gate. The lion let out a low growl. It glided towards the gate, each step a marriage between peace and violence.

Somehow, Alangba was sure the lion would not harm him. It was part of him and he of it. He sheathed his sword and ran his hand through the lion's mane.

Zaminu gave a disbelieving laugh behind him.

The lion opened its giant mouth and let out a booming roar, stunning Zaminu into silence.

Alangba seized Zaminu by the collar around his neck. 'What dirty work were you doing here?'

Zaminu's face was almost expressionless. 'Men like you don't ask questions of men like me.'

Alangba flashed Zaminu's face with a backhanded slap. 'You haven't even begun to answer questions; so much pain lies ahead.'

Zaminu yawned dismissively. 'You're not the first man to threaten me.'

Alangba grabbed him by the Odeshi collar and dragged him into the ballroom. Dead bodies littered the floor. Most had fled in the madness but the captives left had been arranged into two clusters at the corner of the room. One cluster of Palmaine, the other a cluster of everyone else.

The room fell into a ghostly silence as Alangba reached the foot of the stairs.

No Music stood perfectly still, staring at the lion as though trying to figure out whether he would have to kill it. Maka's hand was at his sword, staring at Alangba for an instruction.

'It won't hurt you,' Alangba said.

Maka raised a questioning brow. 'I've always thought you were mad, Alangba, but what new madness is this?'

Alangba turned to the lion and raised a hand. The lion crouched to lay flat on the ground, settling its head in between its outstretched forelegs.

Maka's eyes widened. 'A ... a bond.'

Alangba nodded. 'I can feel it, sharp and clear.'

'Godsblood,' Phelix said.

Alangba raised a hand and the lion rose to its feet again.

'Does it have a name?' Maka asked.

Alangba wiped the back of his hand across his forehead. 'His name is Ijere.'

Maka laughed and another ranger smiled. *Rage.*

Alangba threw Zaminu to the ground. 'I want two collars on him.'

Maka turned his gaze to Zaminu, confused. 'Why? He has not been given the Bloods, he can't—'

'I said, I want two collars on him.'

Maka nodded and obeyed, placing his own thick cobalt collar around Zaminu's neck.

Alangba stalked past the corpse of one of his own men. It was Tanto – the youngest of them. Pink pieces of brain leaked from his bullet-battered skull.

He drew in breath. 'Cover him up.'

To himself, Alangba whispered a prayer. '*May the salt of the ocean wash you clean and may its waves take you home.*'

He glanced at No Music and gestured a message with his hands – *did you find the priest?*

No Music shook his head and frowned.

Alangba seized a bottle of wine from an abandoned table and drank deep. Rich, buttery, full-blooded red with a charcoal undertone.

He turned to Phelix. 'Search the rooms and take every single bottle of this wine.'

The ranger smiled and nodded.

'What happened to the signal, Maka?'

Maka smiled sheepishly. 'Someone forgot to bring the matches. We had to improvise.'

No Music gave a sly shrug, his face completely blank.

Alangba shook his head, then took another generous swig of wine. 'Have you told them?' he asked, gesturing to the captives.

'We were waiting for you,' Maka said.

There were not many of them. About forty in all.

He cleared his throat. 'They call us the Chainbreakers. We are here to arrest this man,' he said, pointing at Zaminu. 'He is a criminal like so many others. You can tell your friends and family that the Chainbreakers came tonight and we will not stop coming until every person responsible for crimes on our soil is brought to justice and the people of the continent of Darosa roam free.'

Alangba took another swig.

'We have a ship not far from here, which will be leaving for Basmine tomorrow. To my brothers and sisters who are captives in this land, I offer passage back to the motherland.'

The Palmaine faces were everything between horrified and indignant. A song came to Alangba's mind. *I wonder if you'd still be fine, if you knew what your heroes did to mine.*

Abruptly a woman's voice echoed across the ballroom.

'You are thieves and murderers! You have no right to arrest anyone.'

Alangba smiled. *Murderers and thieves. These people have no sense of irony.*

He glanced in the direction the voice had come from. To his surprise she wasn't Palmaine. She stared back at him with eyes that said 'I want you to die'.

Alangba scrubbed his forehead in consternation. She wasn't dressed like the other native Darosan women; she wore a flowing lilac dress with a high-necked collar and cloth tied in perfect bows at the sleeves. On her finger was a gold ring with an emerald stone the size of a fingernail, and her hair was brushed in the places her own hands could not reach. She looked almost Odu, but he could not tell for sure.

'What tribe are you from?' Alangba asked.

'I am a citizen of Palmaine,' the woman said.

Maka flashed a grin. 'You were brought here under a bill of sale.'

Alangba studied the woman. At the top of her collar, embossed in her brown skin, was the faintest trail of black ink. *Tattoos.*

He pulled her collar down to reveal a neck marked from chin to near chest in the Darani way. Not just any tattoos either – the clear imprint of a tree with a martial eagle on it. Alangba's eyes doubled in size.

He dropped to his knees and bowed his head. 'Princess.'

Maka gasped, staring at the royal markings. They all knelt, wearing the faces of men who had seen a ghost. Even No Music seemed mildly surprised.

'We will take you home, *Omoba*. It has been... many years,' Alangba said.

The woman's face did not change. 'This is my home.'

Alangba's mouth tightened at the corners. 'I am duty-bound to see you home, Princess.'

She glared at Alangba. 'I will not go quietly.'

Alangba frowned. 'I would expect nothing less from a Kasinabe princess.'

Her eyes darkened. 'The first chance I get, I will put a knife in your back.'

Alangba nodded to Maka, who moved to restrain her, muffling her shouts of protest. Turning away from her, Alangba spoke with a voice that carried to every corner of the ballroom.

'Who else wishes to return to Basmine?'

Alangba did not expect many. Most would be afraid – it was always that way. For some it was better to live in familiar chains than to die in search of an unknown freedom.

The first voice startled Alangba.

'I do,' said a woman, rising to her feet.

Maka eyed her suspiciously. She held the hand of a young child barely eight years old whose skin was the dull yellow of a ripe banana. A child born of a Palmaine man and a Darosan woman.

'What's your name?'

She threw something at Alangba. He caught it. He smiled as he opened his grip to find a kola nut.

'Aiyana,' she said. 'This is my son.' Alangba nodded decisively. 'Let them come.' Two others joined them. By the time they had loaded to leave, there were five native newcomers, one full-grown lion, and Princess Falina, the last Omoba of the Kasinabe tribe.

7

Oké-Dar

RUMI

In the days after Lutayo was killed, Rumi found sleep hard to come by. Every time he closed his eyes, he saw Lutayo's dead face staring at him as though in accusation.

Renike fell to pieces when she saw her father's body. For hours she sat with her knees bunched up, shaking with silent, bitter sobs. Morning came and they went to break the news to Renike's mother. It was a strange thing. Renike had cried up until the very point they reached her mother's door. The moment Adunola knocked, Renike pulled silence from some otherworldly place.

The burial, which followed quickly, was a solemn affair. The sadness was there, but there was also something more feral and raw beneath the tears. Rage. Thick as a cloud. Pungent as the fish market.

Renike's mother snapped the moment Lutayo was lowered into the ground. She lost all poise and let out a long, shrill scream. Renike held her up with strength beyond her arms and legs. Completely quiet.

Those days after the burial were ruled by silence. Renike, once a jolt of ceaseless motion, became a child of stillness. Nothing – not even eating – came easy.

71

It took nearly a week for Rumi to find some focus for the Golden Room, and by then he only had a few days left to get an oud and haircut. For both, Rumi knew precisely where to go. Mama Ayeesha lived in the nearby Oké-Dar township. She was Yami's dearest friend and essential for two main reasons. For one, she was a veteran smuggler who kept all sorts of things at home. For another, she was an artist with a razor and had given Morire several haircuts before.

His plan was simple: wait until Yami left for the market, slip out to see Mama Ayeesha in the late afternoon and return when Yami was fast asleep.

Rumi waited till Yami left for the market and made his way into the village proper.

The sun was showing off and it was hot enough to scald a lizard. In that heat, walking to Oké-Dar was unthinkable. He had hoped to avoid paying for a caravan on account of being one ill turn of luck from cowrielessness, but now he had no choice.

He needed an out-of-village caravan to avoid anyone tipping his mother off – so he headed for the village gates.

He strode past the local school as he neared the edge of the village.

Schoolchildren whistled and jeered from the windows as he walked past. He had fond memories of his time there. It was a place, in Yami's words, where Odu children would not be 'torn asunder by the gaps in Palmaine bookshelves'.

Rumi wanted to tell them to enjoy their time there. Most of them would have to leave Alara after school to clean or cook in the Citadel, just to be liberated from the captivity of next-to-nothing wages. Some would search, as he had once searched, for the root of their wretched condition. The lucky ones would find Kuba or parents or ill luck to blame. The rest would find that they despised the mirror, or worse, despised Alara.

Just short of the village gate, he noticed a squatly unfamiliar wheelman with a two-wheeler.

'I'm headed to Oké-Dar,' he said, meeting the wheelman's eye.

The wheelman nodded.

Rumi held out a cowrie and the wheelman raised his left hand to accept it.

Rumi raised an eyebrow at the slight. It was considered rude to accept anything with your left hand. He cleared his throat, staring at the wheelman's left hand.

The wheelman frowned and raised his right arm, which ended in a blunt stump. 'Excuse my left. Coal mines,' the wheelman said.

Rumi winced and dropped the cowrie in the man's left hand. 'I'm sorry, didn't notice.'

The wheelman nodded dismissively.

When he ruled Basmine, Governor-General Zaminu had sent the consular to take a hand for every worker who failed to meet their quota. Seeing a maimed miner up close sent a serpentine shiver through Rumi's stomach.

They rode down sand-soaked village roads until they came to a corridor of sun-beaten huts.

'This will do,' Rumi said, raising a hand.

The wheelman drew rein and pulled off to the side.

Almost as soon as he'd dismounted, a putrid smell slapped Rumi in the face. He jerked his head back and pulled his leopard-skin scarf up over his nose.

The wicked stench comprised at least three layers: vomit, *agbo* and scat.

The quietness was there too; Oké-Dar was eerily quiet. It always made Rumi feel like he was being watched. Crickets bleated, but they were a part of the watchful silence.

'Looking for a taste?' a voice asked.

73

Rumi jerked back, startled.

A seedy-looking man, wearing an oversized *dashiki*, tipped his wide-brimmed hat. He was heavily perfumed, but not nearly enough to mask the smell of burned leather and agbo. *A lickhead.*

Rumi had seen agbo's work up close. What it did to people when they got hooked on it. He had watched agbo leave Tinu the Panther with trembling hands and eyes like dark caves. It had battered the man's wits till he died in a fire after an unholy binge. When agbo had its way with a man, it became difficult to tell his age. The addict could have been anywhere between twenty and fifty. His smile was crooked, with only the faintest hint of sincerity, and his voice was dry and hoarse. If stones could speak, they would sound like lickheads.

'Mama Ayeesha,' Rumi said, dismissing the man's question.

At the mention of the name, the man's smile faded completely, revealing an effortless scowl. 'I'll leave you be then.'

Mama Ayeesha ran a beer parlour of the very worst sort. The kind of dirty and damp place where even a baby might carry a knife. Rumi had seen a baby in there once but didn't dare look twice at it.

He nudged open the swinging door and stepped inside.

The parlour carried the metallic scent of blood and sweat, with lights too dim to make out more than the faint impression of a person from any distance beyond an arm's length. Rumi headed straight for the kitchen.

Rumi greeted Mama Ayeesha by touching his toe in obeisance, the correct way to greet a woman of her age.

'Good to see you, Rumi,' she said.

'And you, Mama Ayeesha.'

She gave him a solemn look. 'I still can't believe what

happened in the market. I swear on my mother's name, those consular will pay in blood one day.'

'They will,' Rumi said, in a tone that was more a vow than a reply.

Mama Ayeesha inclined her head. 'Shall we talk inside?'

Rumi nodded.

She walked with the aid of a cane now, shuffling towards the door at the rear of the kitchen. An iron door with thick bars of metal across it.

Mama Ayeesha breathed hard at the effort to unlock it, then pulled it open. As he stepped inside, Rumi caught the faint whiff of agbo but spoke nothing of it. All the signs said Mama Ayeesha was a dealer but Rumi did not want to know that truth.

Locking the door behind them, she touched her heart and pointed to the ceiling – a gesture of welcome and trust.

As they settled into the front room, she gave Rumi an appraising look. 'How may I help you today?'

Rumi sucked in a deep breath and let it out in a slow gush. 'I got into the Golden Room.'

She stared at him for a moment, plainly stupefied, then her eyes widened and she thumped the ceiling with her walking cane. 'That's my boy! This calls for Saharene wine!'

Rumi raised a hand. 'No, there's no need to—'

'Nonsense! What curses would await me in the Higher World if I didn't open wine for moments like this?' she said, moving towards a table.

'I suppose a glass wouldn't be—'

'It's not every day they let an Odu boy play Kasinabe drums at the Golden Room.'

Rumi's heart punched his chest. 'About that ... They want me to bring an oud. That's part of why I'm here.'

She froze, discarding her smile.

'An oud?'

'Yes.'

She sighed. 'I suppose it's an opportunity.'

'A big one.'

She gave an insouciant shrug. 'I suppose.'

Rumi cleared his throat. 'I need to cut my hair, too.' His voice came out small and stumbling, like a barefoot baby on a wet floor.

Mama Ayeesha's head jerked back. 'What?'

Rumi avoided her gaze. 'I need to cut my hair.'

'What does your mother think?'

'I am eighteen years old, Mama.'

'Seventeen.'

'I'll be eighteen before the rainy season is done. I'm basically there.'

'Seventeen...' Ayeesha thumbed her chin. 'Has your mother told you about the Eredo yet?'

Rumi blinked. *The Eredo.* It was the same thing the priestess had spoken about. *Get to the Eredo as quick as you can,* she had said.

'What is the Eredo?'

She seemed surprised by his question. 'It is a place where you can get away from all this. They train younglings like you.'

'Train to do what?'

'To fight.'

'I gave up the fighting, Mama.'

'No, this is different. Not like Tinu used to teach you. This is...' She glanced over her shoulder. '...Fighting with juju.'

Rumi threw his head back and laughed. After he had given the laugh his best, he realised that Ayeesha hadn't joined in.

His face hardened. 'Oh... You're serious?'

76

'Serious as sleeping sickness.'

'Fighting ... with juju.'

'That's what I said.'

Rumi's eyebrows shot upwards as he thumbed his chin. No one in Alara was a stranger to juju stories, but to believe in them and speak of them as fact was something else. All the suspected juju women in the market – like everyone else – fled when the consular came calling. Yet there was something certain in the way Ayeesha said it. *Maybe she is an addict.*

Rumi tapped his foot slowly. 'Like a fighting club?'

'Much more than that.'

'How much can I make there?' Rumi asked.

She shook her head. 'There are more important things than money.'

Rumi snorted. 'Maybe you can afford that high-mindedness. My family, half the families in Alara, live off the markets. They killed Lutayo over taxes. If we don't pay them back, more men, women and children will die.'

'Your mother can handle the consular, believe me.'

Rumi frowned. 'You don't understand, Mama Ayeesha. You don't have a family.'

Mama Ayeesha's jaw stiffened and Rumi knew his words had caused her pain.

'I'm sorry, Mama, I didn't mean—'

She slammed a kola nut down on the table. 'If I cut this hair, then you're going to have to do something for me.'

'Name your price.'

'You are going to ask your mother about the Eredo. Tell her *I said* it's about time.'

Rumi locked eyes with her. To reject an offer of kola nut was a grave insult. To some it was as good as telling a person they were less than dirt. Even so, it seemed a fair price.

He took up the kola nut. 'Agreed.'

She gave him a long, studying look, then led him into a room with a chair and a collection of small razors. Pinned to the wall was a painting of an old Kasinabe king riding a massive Shinala warhorse. The king was resplendent in a helmet fashioned in the image of a snarling dog. In one hand he held a bloody double-axe and in the other a black, curved blade. Beside him rode a woman with thick braids wearing a multicoloured riding boubou and a necklace, from which hung a black cowrie identical to the one the priestess had given him.

'Who are they supposed to be?' Rumi said, staring at the painting.

'I'm not entirely sure,' she said. 'My guess is that is the third Alaafin of Oduland and his queen, Oya the Mother of Nine.'

Rumi narrowed his eyes. 'I have one of those,' he said pulling his scarf down to bare the priestess's cowrie.

Mama Ayeesha squinted. 'Be very careful with that cowrie. You mustn't show it to just anyone.'

Rumi raised an eyebrow. 'Yami won't tell me what it is exactly.'

Ayeesha rolled her eyes. 'It is a kukoyi talisman – names you a friend of the old gods. There cannot be many of these left in all the world. It will protect you from death and be your light in the darkness.'

Rumi tucked the cowrie protectively behind his scarf and turned his gaze to the next painting. A coal-black Kasinabe man with a white beard stood holding a massive cutlass, staring down at a vanquished foe. Even in the painting, the red eyes were terrifying.

'Who is that?' Rumi asked.

'That is Madioha Alaye. Son of Ikwere the Brave. A great warrior. They called him the Raging Flame.'

The Raging Flame.

'Where did you get these?'

Mama Ayeesha winked. 'Somewhere far from here.'

Rumi snorted. Mama Ayeesha kept secrets like turacos kept fruit; only revealing them when she meant to use them. Pressing her would not work.

Rumi stared into the eyes of the Kasinabe man in the painting. *Fierce.* The Kasinabe were nothing if not fierce. Perhaps the four kingdoms would never have fallen to the Palmaine if the natives had rallied behind the Kasinabe tribe. Instead, the Kuba swore an oath to the Palmaine, the Saharene surrendered. Now all the Kasinabe were dead. Hunted into extinction by the Palmaine.

Rumi recalled a joke he had heard in the Orchid House once – 'How do you stop a native rebellion? Ask to speak to their leader.'

Mama Ayeesha patted the chair in front of him. Rumi's heart sank as she lopped off the first lock of hair. It had not been cut since he was a small child.

When she finally held up a mirror, Rumi had to confess he looked neat. He had stepped in looking like a cattle-rearer and was set to leave looking like Belize.

'Thank you,' he said, trying not to be obvious about admiring himself in the mirror.

Mama Ayeesha looked disgusted with herself. 'And now we drink.'

And drink they did, until their vision grew blurry from the balmy flood of wine. Mama Ayeesha gave Rumi a wineskin to take to Yami.

When the drinking was done, Rumi made his petition. 'I need an oud, Mama. Something I can afford.'

She rubbed her chin. 'Follow me.'

79

Rumi obliged and they made their way to the front room, where she revealed a yellow-brown long-neck oud with copper-wire strings.

'It's yours,' she said.

Rumi ran a hand over it, brushing the strings lightly. It was finely made, with a polished, pear-shaped bowl and goatskin finish around the belly. His stomach fluttered as he asked the big question. 'How much do you want for it?'

Mama Ayeesha stared up at the ceiling as though making some difficult calculation, then lowered her eyes. 'I said it's yours, Rumi. No charge. I owe Adunola much more than you could ever pay me.'

Rumi gave a start, then stared up at her. 'Really?'

She nodded. 'Really.'

A thrum of emotion stirred in his stomach. 'Thank you.'

She gave a wave as though dismissing the thanks. 'Speak nothing of it. Just remember your promise to me. Ask your mother about the Eredo. And tell her the tide is rising.'

Rumi stuffed the oud into his burlap sack. 'I will.'

A knock sounded at the door and Ayeesha glanced over her shoulder. 'It's getting late.'

Rumi nodded, taking his cue. 'I'll be on my way then. Back door?'

She nodded. 'Back door.'

Outside, the wind whipped against Rumi's newly shaven head, inducting him into a life without locks.

He rounded a corner and spread out in front of him was a nightmare.

The seedy-looking lickhead from earlier was spread-eagled on the ground, eyes closed in either death or slumber. Marshalled in a perfect circle around him were eight huge vultures. A ninth vulture was perched on the man's chest, faint crimson lines trailing from the places its talons touched.

Sobriety returned immediately.

The lead vulture's hooked beak jerked open to make a raspy, hissing sound.

Rumi snatched the sling from his pocket. The first stone struck the lead vulture square in the beak, knocking it down. The second struck its companion on an outstretched wing. As he reached in his pocket for a third, the birds took flight. The flock leader hissed bird curses at him as they flew away.

Rumi drew his sling as far back as he could. He didn't like to kill innocent creatures but he was good and tired of being followed. All the same, he made himself miss, knowing the errant missile would serve his purpose. The birds got the message and beat their wings as fast as they could manage.

For the rest of the long, lonely walk home, Rumi kept his hand wrapped tightly the sling, trying not to think about the lickhead in Oké-Dar.

Quiet as a cat amongst sleeping dogs he crept into his house.

Something moved in the dying lantern light. He froze and moved the oud behind his back. He hadn't expected to find his mother still awake – a surprising wrinkle in his plans. She was reading from a thick book. The one she kept in her secret room.

'What are you reading?' he asked.

'Wouldn't you like to know?' she said, smiling.

Only then did she glance up at him. Her face fell to pieces at the sight of his freshly shaven scalp.

She slammed the book closed. 'You ... cut your hair?'

Rumi avoided her eyes. 'Yes.'

'For the Golden Room?'

'No. For myself.'

The light in her eyes seemed to darken. 'All right, Rumi.'

Under her expressionless stare, he felt like a coconut being cracked open. It was as though all the air had been sucked from the room.

In a bid to ease the tension, he presented the wineskin. 'Mama Ayeesha said to give you this.'

She glanced at it then held it up towards the lantern. 'Saharene firewine ... will you drink it with me soon?'

Rumi's eyes brightened. It was an offering of peace, on the brink of war. 'I will.'

She nodded.

'Mama Ayeesha said to ask you about a place called the Eredo. The priestess mentioned it, too.'

Her stare hardened. 'Ayeesha always had a big mouth.'

Rumi raised an eyebrow. 'She said to say the tide is rising.'

'Never mind what Ayeesha said,' she snapped, pulling out a kola nut. 'When you are ready to bear it, I will tell you about the Eredo. Not today.'

She broke the kola nut in two and offered him a half.

'What could possibly be too much for *me* to bear?'

Her gaze finally softened. 'When I told you that the Blackfae didn't really give me a cowrie for each tooth you lost, you didn't talk to anyone for a week.'

Rumi grinned and took half of the kola nut. 'And here you are keeping secrets from me again.'

She gave him a thoughtful look. 'We all have our secrets.'

His chin sagged. Was she talking about the Golden Room? *Probably.* It didn't matter – by the time she woke up, he would be gone.

'Do I smell ... strange to you, Yami?'

She leaned in and wrinkled her nose. 'Not to me, why?'

'I seem to be attracting birds.'

Her head snapped towards him like a lion towards a rustle in the bushes. 'What sort of birds?'

'Vultures.'

Her eyes bulged. For a moment, her age revealed itself. He had seen her edgy, or angry or impatient, but seldom worried. Never afraid.

She stumbled up from her iroko chair and started for the door.

'Where are you going?' Rumi said.

'To pray,' she said.

'Right now?'

'Yes.'

'Can I come with you?'

'No. Absolutely not.'

8

Snake Eyes

ADUNOLA

Adunola placed the divination tray in front of the bloodwood tree. She closed her eyes and sat in silence until she forgot everything. She let her mind wander and heard the sounds of the world start to fill her ears. She neglected to name the sounds, just let them play like music, letting her thoughts come and go as they pleased. An hour passed, or perhaps it was two.

She opened her eyes and a young boy was sitting in front of her. His eyes were obsidian rocks with no trace of white, and he wore a cap that was red on one side and white on the other. He held a dice cup, which he rumbled enough for her to hear the rattle of two dancing dice.

Adunola lowered her eyes. 'Not you again.'

'I thought you would be pleased to see me,' the boy said, smiling.

'Of all the Agbara they could send, I get the Trickster.'

'Oh, but I am so much more than a trickster. Watch this!'

He threw out his hand and sent the two dice flying. The dice exchanged somersaults in the air and landed on the grass presenting two single pips. *Snake eyes.* Before Adunola could blink, he snatched the dice up and threw again. Snake eyes once more.

'I could throw a hundred perfect snake eyes in a row.'

'A cheap trickster,' Adunola said.

'You think I load the dice? You try it!'

Adunola snatched up the dice and threw them in the air.
Snake eyes.

The boy smiled. 'Perhaps I do load the dice.'

'Enough games, Ilesha. What message do you have for me?'
Adunola asked.

His face stiffened.

'Ilesha ... *yes* ... It has been a while since anyone has called
me that.'

Adunola made a weak effort to conceal her smile. 'An old
name.'

'You are a treasure, Adunola. Your skill with names is ... well,
it is divine. Thank you.'

Adunola bowed low before the boy, palms outstretched in
front of her to touch the ground and her knees tight together.

'You have been kind to me and my sons, in your own *troublesome* way,' she said, pressing her forehead to the grass.

'That is why you are here, isn't it? Your sons; it's always about
your sons. You never just want to check in on us, never a "good
afternoon, Ilesha, I hope you are keeping well, I hope the Priest
of Vultures hasn't killed you". *No!* Just once it would be nice
if you came to ask—'

'My son said he saw vultures,' Adunola said, interrupting him.

Ilesha went silent. He rose to his feet and suddenly he wasn't
a little boy at all. He was a man – a warrior – tall as a tree with
legs as thick as festival yams. His smile was gone.

'My daughter,' Ilesha said, putting an arm on her shoulder.
'Do not be afraid.'

'Whatever silly game you are trying to drag him into, stop
it. I won't allow it,' Adunola said.

'You won't *allow* it? *Allow*?'

Ilesha's black eyes were like coals set alight; streaks of flame billowed from the corners of his eyelids.

Adunola's heart beat faster.

'He is … my son, he's just a boy. He has no part in this quarrel of yours.'

'*Quarrel*? Your tongue is a pup let loose tonight,' Ilesha said. 'A loose pup in the jungle. It would be a sad thing if I were to tire of your company, Adunola. A sad thing indeed.'

She swallowed. 'Why is my son seeing vultures, Ilesha?'

'How would I know? This *quarrel* has the Priest of Vultures hunting us down like dogs. For Dara's sake, Adunola! How would I know why the Accuser wants your son? I know he doesn't want to invite him to a bloody bazaar! If the Priest of Vultures wants him, it is for nothing good.'

'Won't you protect us? Protect him? *You* control the gateway to the other side; there must be something you can do.'

'We are trying, Adunola. You think it doesn't hurt to see our people treated like mules? We are so much weaker now – the people don't believe in us anymore, they don't call our names. The Priest of Vultures and the rest of the godhunters pick us off like moths around a lantern.'

'Pull yourselves together and fight back! Where is Xango?'

'I wish it were that simple, my daughter. Xango is dead. You are a good child, a faithful one. Trust in Dara, He will not forsake you.'

'Dara … Dara … *Dara* … Will we die waiting for Dara to return? It is his son, after all, that—'

'End it there, Adunola, and I will pretend that I heard nothing,' Ilesha said, through clenched teeth.

Adunola bit down on her lip. 'Ilesha, please.'

He rubbed his chin. 'What about the Eredo?'

She shook her head. 'He's not ready. Not yet.'

'Adunola—'

'He's not ready, Ilesha!' she snapped.

He let out a long sigh. 'Does your son follow the Darani way?'

'Yes.'

'Then he rests under the shadow of the Skyfather. I will give you something, it is the best I can do to protect him. You have my word.'

Adunola pulled out a kola nut from her sleeve. A lonely tear trailed down from her cheek to her chin.

'Seal it with a promise,' she said, breaking the kola nut with trembling hands.

Ilesha took a piece and broke it. For a moment, pain flashed in his tar-black eyes.

Just as suddenly, he broke out into a wide smile. He raised a hand in the air and a swirling pocket of pure blackness coalesced in the air. A gateway to the other side. He took one step in and looked back. 'Keep him in the Darani way, and keep him away from yellow trees.'

When Adunola looked down, the broken kola nut was in her hand. Half of it had turned a putrid black. The other half was blood-red.

9

The Golden Room

RUMI

Rumi drew in breath, waiting for his moment.

The sun had not shaken off the darkness yet and cockerels were still a ways from crowing. The problem was, his mother slept far too lightly.

He was running away.

The Golden Room was calling.

He began his escape. Every step was made on tiptoes.

He reached the door and glanced back towards the bedroom. There she was. Looking directly at him, her eyes red with tears.

'Wear the cowrie *always*, and stay safe, my son,' she said.

Rumi's heart sank like lead in loamy soil. 'I will.'

With that, he pulled his leopard-skin scarf up and rushed out of the door before she could stop him.

There were eight people in the caravan, but it was built to carry five. A leather oud case hung from Rumi's shoulder. He had brought his drums along too, for Yami's sake. The two straps formed a cross about his chest, slightly wrinkling his smooth grey kaftan.

After about a half hour of riding, a new passenger joined the caravan and was perched in the too-small space beside Rumi. The newcomer took one look at Rumi and his eyes widened.

'Rumi!'

Rumi glanced at the man, only faintly recognising him.

'It's me, from the Orchid House.'

Rumi frowned. 'Of course. "Me" from the Orchid House.'

The stranger smiled. 'We worked the tables together once. Remember? What was the name of that girl you were into again?'

Rumi stiffened, pretending not to hear.

'Come on, you know the one,' he said, prodding Rumi's rib with an elbow. 'The two-tribe one?'

Rumi glared at his rib where the man's elbow had touched him, then he looked up at the man. His glare was both a challenge and a warning. The man's smile vanished as he regarded Rumi with a calculating stare. After that, he was finally quiet.

The damage had already been done. Rumi's mind was full of Nataré again.

Most regarded Odu and Kuba as being like water and oil, irreconcilable even in marriage. Two-tribe children were a rare thing, and the only two-tribe person Rumi had ever really known was Nataré.

Working in the Orchid House, Tigrayin – the Orchid House proprietor – had a chorus of insults for Nataré's tribe-traitor mother and was never slow to remind her she was only half a Kuba. Rumi soon learned that beneath those insults was an unspoken obsession.

Tigrayin had watched Nataré like the raven watches the cookfire. His desperate leer was clear as glass whenever she entered a room. Nataré seldom spoke, and when she did it was never more than a few words.

With time, Tigrayin grew to despise Nataré for her indifference. His insults gradually gained more edge. One day he openly slapped her bottom. It was a show of power to the workers at the Orchid House, an effort to cut her down to size.

Nataré was never cut down. She only ever acknowledged the man with a cold, dead stare. A stare more punishing than words could ever be.

Rumi still wished he had been wiser to Tigrayin's plan, but he was still a fool then.

The night before Nataré disappeared, he was in the Orchid House late, working his hands to wrinkled prunes in the restrooms. It was something he did; he always made sure that the native restrooms were cleaner than the Palmaine ones. That was his own small rebellion.

He wasn't supposed to be there that night. All the lanterns were off, save for the one in Tigrayin's office. The dancing flicker of lantern light from inside the office jutted out into the hallway. Rumi's only thought had been to get gone before Tigrayin caught him. He put all his stealth and silence into creeping past Tigrayin's office but caught the faintest image of a negotiation taking place inside. Tigrayin with three impossibly tall, men, who had white markings on their faces and tattoos from neck to navel.

It was an unusual thing for a Kuba man to consort with witch doctors, but Rumi had been so naive then, so oblivious to the wickedness in the world. It took him weeks after Nataré disappeared to piece things together. By the time he mustered the intel and courage to confront Tigrayin, the man had only a sheepish, almost playful smile in response. The smile of a man who had just sold you a sack of beans that was half-full of stones. That smile was the final violence to Rumi's childishness. He snapped. Let himself go. He put every lesson Tinu had invested in him into his first blow and after that, there was no going back. He beat night and day out of Tigrayin. He squeezed the life from the man.

Though Tigrayin was widely despised, it took all of Adunola's cunning and connections to cover up his killing. Gambling debts was the story they peddled but foul play was widely suspected. It meant the end for Rumi in all the nearby beer parlours and fighting clubs.

He found his mind often returning to Nataré, the memory of her never quite slipping away. The two-tribe girl, sold to witch doctors for the silent abomination of rejecting a wealthy Kuba man.

He got to the Golden Room and was met by a heavy-set, sandy-brown Saharene man when he knocked on the door.

'Good morning,' Rumi said.

The man inspected Rumi from head to toe. 'Who are you?'

'My name is Rumi Voltaine. I'm here to play.'

'I think you are mistaken, young man,' the man said, shaking his head.

'I'm a musician,' Rumi clarified.

The man shook his head. 'We aren't open until much later and it's six cowries to get in.'

Rumi pulled the letter out from his pocket and handed it to him.

'I see,' the man said, nodding as he read. 'I apologise for the misunderstanding, it's just… I mean no offence, but…'

A famously ominous preface for something offensive. Here it comes.

'… but you look like one of those Odu street merchants.'

Rumi glanced down at his kaftan. The remark hurt more than he expected.

The man gave a small smile. 'Well, you're welcome to the Golden Room. My name is Zarouk.'

A Saharene man with a Palmaine name. Fitting for a place like the Golden Room. His accent, however, was strongly Saharene. When he spoke it sounded like rushing water filling a cup. *Sh-* and *ph-* sounds filled all the spaces between the words.

'You must be a fantastic player, and so *young*,' Zarouk said, leading him into the building.

Rumi didn't have a response, so he just smiled.

The Golden Room was beautiful, in the true, original sense of the word. The high ceilings hoisted multi-tiered candle chandeliers and the walls held the busts of great entertainers of early Basmine.

Zarouk showed him every room but one: a low, arched door with high stone steps was the only one Zarouk did not open. The small stone sculpture at the entrance made Rumi's breath quicken. It was the stone impression of a vulture. An eagle, a dove, even an owl would make sense, but who would honour such a vile bird with a sculpture?

'What's in that room?' Rumi asked.

As though to answer, the door creaked open. A tall Palmaine man dressed in the red robes of a Palman priest appeared. He had dark, bloodshot eyes, with two gold chains of rank at his neck and a four-point star on his chest. Blood dripped down from a wound on his forearm.

He gave a start when he noticed Rumi. 'What are *you* doing here?'

Rumi's shoulders fell. The irony of a foreigner asking a native that question seemed completely lost on the man.

Zarouk bowed as if the floor had pulled him close. 'He is a new ... player here, your eminence.'

The priest ran a quick hand through the plume of cotton he had for hair. 'A player, is it?'

Rumi fiddled with his leopard-skin scarf and kept his eyes fixed firmly on the floor. Anything to escape the priest's searching stare. A sudden and slight heat hummed from the cowrie at his neck, but this was not a moment to shift his scarf.

After a moment of uncomfortable silence, the priest gave a nod of dismissal and walked away.

'Who was that?' Rumi asked.

Zarouk straightened. 'That's the Bishop of Basmine and it would be wise to remember it. He's a high priest in the House of Palman.'

Rumi nodded. 'And what's in that room?'

Zarouk shrugged. 'I don't know. It is for the priests alone. The Golden Room is funded by the House of Palman.'

Rumi drummed his thigh, considering the room. 'Are there any bloodwood trees nearby?'

Zarouk scowled. 'Why are you asking that?'

Rumi gave him a plain, knowing look.

'You can't do that here. It's ... not allowed. We are godly people,' Zarouk said.

Rumi raised an eyebrow. 'And only the Palmaine god is godly?'

Zarouk's lip quivered. 'If you're a denier, I don't want to know. Just don't bring any of that mess inside.'

Rumi set his jaw. 'Understood.'

Zarouk nodded. 'There's a bloodwood tree somewhere behind the stable.'

'Thank you.'

Zarouk scratched his chin. 'You'll be looking for a place to stay?'

'I will.'

'Well, rooms round here are expensive, but if you don't think a cowrie too precious, I can find a place here for you.'

A place to stay at a cowrie a night was better than anything Rumi could hope for. A coffin-sized room in the Citadel would cost thrice as much.

He lowered his brow, hiding his eagerness. 'I would appreciate that.'

At the edge of the morning, the woman from his first audition walked in. She moved with authority, giving orders with almost breathless automation. To describe her in a word: *efficient*.

Her orderly stare finally fell on Rumi. 'Come with me,' she said.

He trailed after her and ended up in a room where books littered the only table.

'Welcome to the Golden Room,' she said, nudging a chair forward. 'My name is Olae. Please sit.'

Rumi settled into the chair.

'I see you brought your drums,' she said.

'I did.'

She frowned. 'I am happy to have you here, but you must understand an Odu has never mounted the stage before. You will be the first and that means you have an obligation to be exceptional,' she said, startling him with her directness. 'Anything less and neither you nor any other Odu will mount the stage again, and you will be nothing more than a cautionary tale.'

'I understand.'

'If you understood, you would not have brought your drums. Zahim wants you to play tonight, but I have told him you will not play for anyone but me until I have three months with you.'

She picked a book up from her table and threw it at him. 'Now, play me something.'

Rumi caught the book mid-flight and opened it to the first page. His eyes swept over the notes, written in beautiful cursive.

He shuddered as he pretended to study the notes. Slowly Olae's face morphed into a picture of utter disappointment.

The scribblings in the book were meaningless to Rumi. He thumbed the page pointlessly, his lip quivering at its instructions. He had nowhere to go. So he grabbed the oud and started to play. He played until the oud was damp with sweat. Until Olae could do nothing but nod her head in submission to the music. She raised her hand for him to stop.

'You have talent, we can all see that, but you're impulsive, emotional. That can be good, but not without control. And you must learn to read these,' she said, pointing at the books. 'Three months might not be enough, but I will do my best.'

Rumi cleared his throat. 'How much will I be paid? For the three months.'

She blinked, her eyes softening for a moment. 'Twenty cowries a week.'

Rumi nodded. *That works.*

10

On My Count

RUMI

For the first two weeks, Olae burned Rumi down to the ashes of his being. He plucked the oud until his fingers were swollen.

Zarouk found a place behind the stables for Rumi to sleep, but days spent in a slouched playing posture gave him shooting back pains that made sleep almost impossible. He only ever ate the one free meal available to workers at the Golden Room, and with that regime had managed to save twenty-five cowries in two weeks. If he managed to keep that up, he would have enough to pay half the market taxes within five months. All they had to do was hold out long enough and gather the rest.

In his third week at the Golden Room, Olae got on him about his timing.

'I don't want you to pull too fast or drag this note. It needs to be right in the middle of the beat,' she said. 'On my count.'

She raised a finger in the air, which called for poise. Rumi waited, still as a lizard in the shade. She dropped her finger and he plucked.

'Too fast,' Olae spat. 'You are rushing.'

She raised her finger again, then she dropped it. Rumi plucked.

'Far too late,' she said.

It went on like that for what felt an eternity. She was impossible to please.

'I'm not dragging!' Rumi snapped after she had stopped him for what felt like the hundredth time.

'Mind your tone, Rumi, or you can go back to whatever village you came from.'

Rumi bit his tongue hard.

'How do I find the beat?' he said. He hated the desperation he heard in his voice, but he *was* desperate.

'You cannot find it; you have to feel it. It should be seamless. I should not be able to tell if my finger dropped or your note made me drop it.' She reached out for the oud. 'On your count, let me show you.'

Rumi surrendered the oud and watched her position it in her arms. He raised a finger, but she was not looking at his hand, she was staring directly into his eyes. He dropped his finger and she plucked before it had fully dropped. It was a perfect strike, an arrow through the seeds of an apple. Rumi raised his finger again and dropped it. *Bang!* right on the throat of it.

She handed him back the oud. 'That is what I want,' she said. Her face was expressionless, not a hint of hubris.

Rumi positioned the oud and waited, his eyes fixed on hers, her finger in the periphery of his vision. They flickered a half-second before her finger moved. Rumi plucked the oud like a bowstring, her finger bending as the note finished.

'That's what I want!' she said.

He saw what she meant – the eyes gave the signal and the fingers obeyed. It was a subtle thing, imperceptible to ears not accustomed to the fabric of music, but to Olae, it must have been like a sheet of cold wind. She raised her finger again.

Bang! *Take that.*

She ushered a smile away before it formed.

They went on for hours, until the stroke and drop were like horse and rider. The week went on in that way. She taught him things; mended him in places he did not know he was broken. Her ways were harsh, and she spoke in a stabbing staccato, but she always made him better. Always. She taught him how to build layers in his music, how one instrument could be two if you knew how to use it.

One day he played through the 'Great White Ram':

> *Better the pestle than the yam*
> *Better to die than meet the Great White Ram*
> *Better asleep than awake*
> *Lest you see of men what the Ram doth make*
> *Better foolish than be wise*
> *Lest you glimpse his fury with your eyes*
> *Better silence than speak his name*
> *Lest gentle candle challenge Raging Flame*

It was an old, simple song. A thousand times performed in Alara. Rumi added flourishes of sound in the pockets he found empty and built layers where there once were none.

Olae exhaled like she had been waiting for a decade to breathe out.

'You are joining the others today,' she said.

II

Exposed

RUMI

'I thought you said I needed three months?' Rumi said.

'I can't hide you any longer. We have been chosen to host the Governor's Ball in three months.'

His eyes widened. 'Will there be a performance bonus?'

Olae raised an eyebrow as though that was not the question she'd expected. 'Forty cowries and another five hundred cowries for the best player on the night.'

Rumi gasped. *Five hundred and forty cowries. Enough to pay all our tax at once.*

One great performance and the consular would never bother them again.

'Zahim has it in his head that an Odu player would make it a ball not to be forgotten,' Olae said, 'and besides, our new governor-general will be revealed at the event.'

'Do you think I'm ready?'

'Just don't make me look stupid,' she said as she led him to the other players.

As they approached the door, the swell of anticipation rose with the noise of rehearsing musicians. When Rumi stepped into the room, all went silent. Their eyes fell on him like flies on fresh scat.

Always stand up straight and keep your shoulders behind your ears.
Tinu's words.

Olae moved to stand alongside the chubby Kuba man. Kunde
was his name, the one from Rumi's audition.

'Rumi will be joining us today,' Kunde said.

He turned to Rumi, giving him a moment to say something
or to greet the others. Nothing but silence felt appropriate, so
that was what he gave them.

Frowning, Kunde gestured to a tall, handsome Kuba man
with a Selistre harp in hand. 'Shotuga, give Rumi a demonstration of what we expect here.'

The man nodded and started to play. The tune was immediately recognisable.

'The Kasinabe Marriage Cup,' muttered Rumi.

It was a notoriously complex song, best left avoided by
all but the most talented players. Shotuga had that talent. He
had a relaxed bearing, but produced absolutely spotless work.
Smooth, crisp, no drag in his timing. He had *it* – make no
mistake.

Rumi traced his tongue over his top lip as he listened, anticipation chewing at him.

Kunde clicked his fingers and Shotuga doubled his pace.
Rumi straightened.

Olae stepped close. 'What does he have that you don't?'

Rumi narrowed his eyes. 'A silk kaftan,' he whispered.

Olae snorted softly. 'Control. He has control.'

It was enough. Rumi was good and tired of this show. They
thought they knew music here. *All right, I'll show you control.*

He clutched his oud tight and as Kunde clicked his fingers
twice, Rumi pounced like a cat from a cage. The oud melted
into the medley of sound.

It was a daring jump, but he matched Shotuga's pace with no run-up. His teeth were gritted as his fingers moved like hummingbird wings going stride for stride with Shotuga. More than half the crowd turned to him, bemused.

He was reminded, as he played, of Tinu beating Kuba challenger after Kuba challenger, every bout fought with a smidge of hatred and a good deal of showmanship.

Kunde clicked his fingers three times to double the pace again. Rumi obliged, doubling his speed as easily as one would turn an egg over in a bath of oil. The Kuba man plucked the Selistre like life and death depended on it. The soft intake of collective breath was the only sound beneath the battle between oud and Selistre.

They continued the verse at frightening speed. Rumi locked eyes with the man, not missing a note. Shotuga tried to take it up a notch and mis-stepped. There was a small, suspended window of pure silence. Rumi blinked. *Victory is mine.* Still he was hungry, still he wanted to show them something. He turned his oud upside down and drummed against the bowl.

The furious pace of the chorus left his wrists and he pummelled the bowl with brilliant fury. The room was a tomb, arrested by a ghostly silence from the other musicians as he played. He played until he had nothing left and then he spanked the bowl in conclusion.

Rumi could feel Shotuga's hot glare on his neck. When he met his stare, the fury in the man's eyes was thick as smoke. Kunde gave Shotuga a disapproving look as though to say, *you let him beat you.*

Rumi did not smile. Sometimes making it look effortless hurt them more than basking in the moment. He brushed down his palms and put his oud back in its case.

★

'You definitely made a statement,' Olae said when they were alone. 'They will hate you for what you did today, and I won't protect you. If they play dirty, I will not intervene. Do not think I will make a favourite of you.'

Rumi shrugged. 'I can handle myself. I'm better than all of them.'

'Is that what you're here for? To prove you're better than them?'

'I'm here for my family and for Alara. But if I can annoy some butter-eaters along the way, all the better.'

Olae raised an eyebrow. 'You have a hard head, but a soft mind. You may have made formidable enemies today when you could have made allies.'

'Formidable is good. The quality of one's enemies writes a story. A man with no enemies has no character,' Rumi said.

'Words won't save you on that stage, Rumi, only music,' Olae said.

'Then I will be safe. When I was hungry and alone with no friends, I had music. When the world was dark all around, I had music. I'm fine with just music.'

But she was right, he *had* made enemies. He had seen it in the way the Kuba with the Selistre looked at him. They would not make his time easy.

His next day in practice with them, they left him no seat to work from. He pretended it was what he'd expected and sat cross-legged in front so they could all watch him. He drank their hatred in.

Kunde never made a show of treating him differently but made his disdain felt in subtle ways. He ignored questions, always wore a bemused smile when Rumi spoke and would explain everything a second time in pidgin while looking straight at Rumi. The only way Rumi could hit back was with his music and with that, he hit like a thunderbolt.

If he was going to take the prize at the Governor's Ball, he needed to get much, much better. He would only win if his superiority was overwhelming.

His practice became relentless. He accepted that he had to make sacrifices. Zarouk was kind, and turned a blind eye to the nights when Rumi was too tired to make it to the stables and fell asleep behind the kitchen stove. For the first month, he was a complete servant to his craft.

The other players had a quiet fear of him. He cultivated that fear like a seedling plant. He played up even the smallest differences between them so they thought him unpredictable. He would walk into the room silently and attend to his instruments alone as though he had no voice. If they knew the games he played in his head, just to make them uncomfortable around him, they would boil him in soup. What sealed it was his ability, which they could neither imitate nor understand.

He could make music with nearly anything. He had enchanted them the first time his lips touched a Florinian flute; the Old Nazari trumpet was like a sword in his hand the way he would cut the room into a bloody silence. His finger on the oud inspired awe, but best of all, he beat the hell out of his drums, even though he knew he could never play them on stage. With the music within and the hard lessons Olae had taught him, he built a quiet, solemn, respect for himself. Sometimes when he played the drums, he could feel their hatred on the back of his neck. He could sense the silent hope that he would miss a beat or make a misstep, and most of all he felt the hot, biting jealousy of his gift.

No one wanted Rumi to fail more than Shotuga, the Kuba with the Selistre. He was poised, relentless, fast, and always on tempo.

He was a man of style, too. Palmaine-style shirts with native fabric, silk tunics, leather shoes, all complemented with a self-assured smile and a small hoop earring.

He never called Rumi by his name, not once. Instead, he would call him 'the Odu drummer', 'the Odu', or once he had called him 'the cockroach-brown boy over there'. *Cockroach brown.* The man had a gift for insults.

Shotuga took to sitting just at the corner of Rumi's vision, so that even when Rumi wasn't looking at him directly, he could feel him. Sometimes he whispered things to throw Rumi off. 'The Olae experiment,' he would say. 'This grey kaftan again? That's three times this week.' When Rumi looked at him, his face would turn expressionless as though he hadn't said anything at all.

On an off day with only a few weeks to the Governor's Ball, someone crept up on Rumi while he was rehearsing alone in the stable. He had been doing what Olae called 'learning by rote instead of by note' and was taken by surprise when a voice sounded behind him.

'You don't read notes,' Shotuga said, in a way that was both an accusation and a proclamation.

Rumi was caught completely off guard. Shotuga nodded to himself and darted off before Rumi could say a word in his defence. It wasn't long before Rumi had to pay for that mistake.

The next day, Kunde stood before the gathered players with a new horde of books. 'We will be playing the Eighth Symphonic Verse,' he announced as he passed the new songbooks around.

Rumi frowned – they meant to humiliate him. With new songs, he would have to read the music and that always made him slow. He turned through the pages to find the song and his heart sank. It was a fastrunner.

'Ready?' Kunde asked as the players took their cues.

Shotuga leaned close and whispered. 'You had a good run.'

'One ... Two ...'

The playing began. Rumi was predictably slow – but not hopeless. He picked up the notes more slowly than usual, but Olae's work on him ran deeper than he realised. His music was not sparkling but it was not quite the mess that Shotuga and Kunde had obviously expected.

'Faster,' Kunde hissed.

Rumi grimaced. At double time, he was exposed. He fell behind badly. The other players looked at him with surprise. He was losing his invincibility right before their eyes. He tried his best to catch up but it was no use – at that pace, with a song he hadn't practiced before, it was a hopeless effort. For the first time since he had arrived, he stopped playing.

Kunde, satisfied with the result, brought the song to a merciful end. He didn't need to say anything, everyone could see it.

Shotuga leaned close and whispered. 'Another Odu boob bringing a spear to a gun battle.'

Spear to a gun battle. It was a cutting remark, far too cutting. Rumi had learned to ignore their jibes, but this was a stride too far. He jerked his head round so sharply that his scarf fell. Shotuga's eyes widened at the sight of his tattoos, but Rumi was too angry to care.

The class fell silent as Rumi stepped close.

Shotuga – to his credit – did not flinch, instead he smiled like a smug serpent at a caged dog. Rumi clenched his fists with every intent to punch the grin from his face but then he caught the look in Kunde's eyes; delight. This was it, their excuse. A denier striking his fellow players would be thrown out of the

Citadel with a vigorous kicking on his way out. He noticed the other faces; it was what they all wanted. To remove the Odu stain from their pretty little world. He wouldn't give them that, not when there was so much to lose. The anger leaked out of him like wine from a pierced wineskin. This was the price of playing on their terrain.

Rumi remastered himself and spoke aloud. 'My mother said something once: music is a language – to master it, you must have something to say.'

Shotuga smirked. 'My mother said something once too: the sense of a half-shell whore is no sense at all.'

The other players laughed.

Rumi bit down on his tongue, almost losing composure. 'Do not speak of my mother again.'

Shotuga turned to Kunde. 'This beast is taking someone else's space. He will never be one of us,' he said.

His anger flared. 'Why would I want to be anything like you? I make real music. It is in my blood and bones. Music was with me when I couldn't find two cowries to rub together. I played just to stop myself from thinking about food. You know nothing about music, about the biting present of it, things that cannot be learned in notes.'

Perhaps it was something in his voice, but those words seemed to affect the room. Attention turned to Shotuga, awaiting his response.

Shotuga gave an almost fatherly frown. 'This isn't the Orchid House. They will laugh you off that stage.'

For some reason, that made Rumi relax. He shrugged. 'Maybe they will...'

Pulling his scarf carefully back up, Rumi swallowed his rage and used the only weapon he could; a wide, triumphant smile.

'Lesson over,' Kunde snorted.

That night, still burning with anger from the day's rehearsal, he practiced till the moon was tired. He played the drums, then the oud, turn after turn. It was all he could do to submerge his self-loathing for the time being.

There is an Odu saying: it is in the darkness that you see what is invisible to the eye. That night, when he had played to blisters, it came to Rumi all at once, fully formed and whole, a thing invisible to the eye. A new way to play.

The next morning, Rumi was summoned into Olae's lesson room. She sat with a tabletop decorated with dog-eared manuscripts.

'Is it true?' she asked, not looking up at him.

Rumi blinked. 'Is what true?'

She drew in breath, her face a solemn, expressionless sea. 'Are you a denier?'

Rumi scrubbed his forehead and stared at the ceiling. Then his eyelids slowly fell. 'Do I deny that Palman is the one true god, above all other gods? Yes. Is that a crime? Will I be thrown out for honouring my ancestors?'

Olae spoke softly. 'You have to leave.'

'I didn't—'

'You have to leave.'

Rumi stamped his foot. 'I have done nothing wrong!'

'Don't be naive, Rumi! You knew your rope was thin here.'

He sighed. 'So that's it? I'm done?'

'Yes.'

Rumi looked at her for a long moment before he spoke.

'Would you at least like to hear it?' he asked.

'I've heard it before.'

'This is different.'

She blinked, focusing her gaze on him. 'All right, go on.'

Rumi pulled the oud from his bag and tested the string. It was perfect. He started with gentle strokes. The sound had an arrogant politeness; a king following his own rules. Rumi nodded his head as he played. Olae surrendered to the spell and began a nod of her own, lips pursed tight.

There was freedom in the sound, liberty to do as you please. Rumi would not have been surprised if Olae had jumped to her feet. He let the chorus climb out of his fingers as he cornered the first verse. He balanced the oud carefully as he pulled his drums closer. As he closed out the chorus with the oud, he finger-beat the drums with his other hand, both instruments at once. The marriage was beautiful.

Olae's face was disgusted awe. She was shaken by the audacity, but a helpless, happy captive. She motioned with her hands to and fro at the interplay of the medley. Rumi dived deeper into the music. He started to run away, music never written, a stream of inspired consciousness. He closed his eyes and kept the balance, sweat leaking down over his eyelashes. He finished the verse then spanked the drum with a violent thump.

Olae's palm was pressed to her chin, fingers curled around her teeth. It was a pose with no poise, something alien to Olae's face. Several moments of silence passed as he wiped his sweaty forehead, waiting for her response.

'Shege,' she said at last. 'That was ... Shege.'

Rumi's breath was heavy. He dropped to his knees and clasped his hands. 'Please. Please. I am begging. Just let me play one more time, at the Governor's Ball.'

Olae bit down on her lip and said nothing.

Rumi gulped down saliva and hung his head, forcing back tears. 'Please.'

She furrowed her brow and locked eyes with him. 'There is one way.'

'Anything.'

She lowered her chin. 'You will renounce the Darani way.'

It was like a blow to the gut. 'I can't do that.'

Olae raised an eyebrow. 'Yes, you can. This is the cost of success. Perform as you just did at the Governor's Ball and it won't matter what god you pray to, but you have to give me something to stop an outright expulsion.'

Rumi bit down on his lip. He could almost hear his mother's voice in his ear. There was no doubt what she would tell him to do. Even so, Olae was right. Nothing comes without sacrifices. He met Olae's calm, expectant stare. 'All right, I'll do it.'

12

The Governor's Ball

RUMI

Rumi was given a two-week suspension – set to end on the day of the Governor's Ball. It meant he'd be allowed to play. When he returned to Alara, Yami's reception was cold as the grave. From the day he arrived, she barely said two words to him.

On the morning of the Governor's Ball, Rumi sat waiting for a letter confirming his suspension was lifted.

A knock sounded on the door and Rumi moved in a blur.

A Kuba man stood outside. He wore a dark blue kaftan with a four-point star stitched into the pocket.

He reached into his pocket and retrieved an envelope. 'Are you ...' He paused, reading the name.

'Irumide Voltaine,' Rumi finished. 'Yes, that's me.'

The man gave a satisfied nod, reached into his satchel, and produced a flat bronze box.

Rumi stared at it then back at the messenger. 'What is it?'

The messenger shrugged and turned to leave. 'No idea.'

Rumi cracked the box open. Inside was a black kaftan, embroidered with silver stones along the seam. He lifted it out of the box, examining the cut and the stones.

He stared in awe for a moment before folding it back into the box. Only then did he notice the letter tucked into the corner of the package.

He unfolded it and leaned forward to read.

Irumide,
This is to confirm that your suspension has officially been
lifted. You are cordially invited to play at the Governor's Ball
tonight. Enclosed is a kaftan for the event. I hope the tailoring
fits — I had to estimate your measurements.
    Players for the event are entitled to bring five guests but you
will only be allowed three — seated in the kitchen behind the
stage. It was the best I could get for you.
    If you play as well as I know you can, all will be well.
Olae.

P.S. Do not think you're a favourite, I just won't have you
embarrassing me on that stage.

Rumi laughed aloud as he stepped back into the house.

Yami glanced up at him. 'What's so funny?'

Rumi frowned. 'My suspension has been lifted. I'm invited
to play at the Governor's Ball tonight.'

Adunola bit down on her lip and said nothing.

Rumi straightened. 'I know you are upset with me for leaving, Yami.' He touched her hand. 'But I did it for you, for us.'

'Don't you dare say that,' she snapped.

'But I did.'

'Yes, I was part of it, but there was another part, and you
must acknowledge that, son. You wanted to shine; you wanted
their recognition.'

'I did not—'

'You did, Rumi, and I learned to understand that while you
were away. You deserve it. You deserve to shine; you deserve
people's recognition. Even if it isn't on the drums, they *should*

be applauding you. You came through more than any of them could imagine.'

Rumi let out a long, stretched-out sigh. If she knew he had renounced the Darani Way to make this happen, she would be unable to bear it.

'Will you come to watch me play? As my guest?'

She gave a reluctant smile. 'It would be my honour, son.'

★　★　★

'Are you going to look in the mirror all night or are we going to the Governor's Ball?' his mother yelled from outside the room.

'Just the mirror,' Rumi yelled back.

He heard her laugh through the door. 'What a terror I raised,' she said.

The kaftan Olae had given him made him look the part. When he stepped out of the room his mother's face lit up.

She wore a single-piece blue dress and a smile filled with pride and anticipation. Morire was sharp and neat with a smooth black kaftan and matching sandals. Renike wore a silver dress Yami had picked but ruined the effect by pairing it with leather farmer's boots.

Raucous barking drew them outside to find Kaat and Ndebe snarling at the air.

'To me,' Adunola said.

The lionhounds reluctantly came to her side.

'What's got into you two?' Rumi said, running his hand through Ndebe's fur.

Adunola crouched low and ran a hand along Kaat's belly. 'Kaat is expecting.'

She straightened and backtracked into the house. A moment later she re-emerged with a burlap sack. Satisfied with whatever it was she had collected, she brushed down her dress and ushered the lionhounds inside to await her return.

They chartered a caravan for the night and made for the Golden Room.

Rumi led Morire and Yami through the sparse throng of people outside to the door. They would have been refused entry were it not for Zarouk ushering them inside. On the worst of days, the Golden Room was shockingly clean, but today it was as though every inch of floor had been scrubbed, waxed and buffed to a spotless sheen. Rumi was sure that if he licked the walls, his tongue would remain unsullied. Every lamp seemed to shine brighter; every yard of cloth shimmered in vibrant gold. Never before had he seen such a marvellous jubilation of beauty.

Olae greeted his family with a smile. Rumi had seen her smile all of three times in the months since meeting her, and here she was sharing smiles like they were plantain about to spoil.

'You are welcome to the Golden Room,' Olae said, leading his mother by the hand. 'I will show you to your seats.'

Their seats were in the kitchens with the cooks and servants. An irritating slight no doubt, but at least they had a good view of the proceedings.

The fire of competition bristled in Rumi's belly as he made his way to the player's pit at the side of the stage.

He did not give anyone even a sliver of eye contact. Not a smile, not a frown, not a glare. He kept his eyes fixed on his instruments; polishing them like weapons before a battle with all intent to use them in that self-same way.

The blast of a trumpet ripped through the air.

Rumi glanced up from his position in the pit and his mouth fell open at sight of the governor arriving. This was the great reveal. The entire room rose to its feet, eager to catch a first glimpse of the new governor-general. There was a collective gasp as the man stepped inside. He wore an immaculate officer's uniform, with a ceremonial sword at his hip and a white helmet with the symbol of a four-point star. He was a native, a Kuba man. Unimpressive physically, but he had an air about him. That insufferable, born-to-rule bearing.

Whispers began amongst the crowd. How would Basmine take a native governor-general, and a *Kuba* one at that? The Kuba would be quick to say that Basmine was free and paint it as a triumph for the natives. *How can a leader be for the natives when it was not the natives who gave him power?*

Rumi made to turn back to the stage but could feel a hot, baleful glare at the back of his neck. He glanced over his shoulder. A lean Palmaine man with bushy white hair and bloodshot eyes was staring at him. The bishop of Basmine.

Something about the man made Rumi's stomach turn. A flash of heat from the priestess's cowrie touched his neck. A smile formed on the priest's lips as he raised four fingers in the air. It was a Palman signal, a tribute to the four-point star. *Palman reigns.*

Rumi looked away as the priest moved to his seat on the dais beside the governor-general.

The ball began in earnest. A stout Kuba man on the kora was the first to play. He played with immaculate beauty. Neat, polished, and clean. Rumi understood the beauty in that sort of music, in a way; the man had 'control', as Olae would have put it.

Next came a Kuba woman on the flute. Her melody was exuberant but lacked some of the previous player's polish.

Three more performers quickly passed, all with different styles, every one of them elite in some undeniable way. Rumi slowly started to feel as though he did not belong. The music these people played had a quality to it; it was spotless. His was different.

He drummed his thigh as he watched, reassuring himself.

Shotuga walked directly in front of him and trod on his foot as he moved towards the stage. Rumi watched with pursed lips as Shotuga mounted the stage and dropped in an elegant bow. The audience flared in almost immediate applause. He ran a testing finger across his Selistre and nodded to himself with a self-satisfied smile.

From the first note, Rumi knew what song he was playing. Every native of a certain age knew the song. His heart sank.

The opening chords of 'The Boat on the Brown Sea' filled the air. The vein at Rumi's temple throbbed. His stomach churned as the crowd reacted. There was singing, dancing, and smiling in every corner. No smile was brighter than Shotuga's. With one note Shotuga made Rumi an alien in the room, an opponent to something that they all wanted to enjoy.

It was the best Rumi had ever heard Shotuga play, and the audience felt it. He had practiced hard. Each strum was like a perfect whip lashing Rumi's flesh. He had never endured something so beautiful and terrible all at once.

He brought the song to a slow, perfect close and the entire audience save for the governor rose as one to applaud. Rumi looked behind the stage to the kitchen. Four others had not risen to applaud: Renike, Morire, Yami and Olae. He smiled. It gave him the breadcrumb he needed to nourish himself. A small morsel of support. Their defiance was catching.

Before Zahim could announce Rumi, while the room still rang with applause for Shotuga, he mounted the stage, fingers twitching. Shotuga wore a wide, telling grin as Rumi walked past him, but there was no space for Shotuga in his mind. He was locked in. He set his drums and his oud down and started playing with no cue. No introduction.

He exploded onto the oud in a way that sometimes irritated Olae. Something bubbled inside that he could not completely control.

Crisp, hallowing notes filled the air and the whispers in the room turned to silence. Rumi plucked each string with concentrated fury, creating beautiful spikes in volume that gave the melody character. He let himself enjoy the sound of the strum as he entered the song 'Fabric of the King's Cloth'. He surrendered himself to the music, plucking the strings and nodding his head instinctively as the melody filled the room.

This was the music that would follow the chariots of fire, the music to announce the return of gods, the music that arrogant men heard at the feet of a mirror. It had a contemptuous majesty to it and Rumi gave it everything, investing such measured malice into the music that it arrested the ears and eyes. Wide eyes and open mouths littered the crowd. The silence covered the room and Rumi dominated it. The audience were his hostages and he would do with them as he pleased. They nodded their heads as he did. One woman near the front thrust her hands through the air like she was trying to conduct an orchestra behind him, her eyes enchanted.

Rumi built on the layers of sound – one, then two, then three. He'd never gone beyond three, but he built four layers, then five. Sounds built on top of one another like bricks. Rumi stole a glance at Olae; she held her hand over her mouth, her eyes the size of small plates. When they were all under his command, Rumi took one hand from his oud, lowering the layers back to three, then pounded the drums with his left hand.

He started softly, then built until he had three layers on each instrument. He heard gasps. His tongue lolled from his mouth. He knew he looked like a mad man but did not care.

He searched for Shotuga with his eyes. He wanted to be sure Shotuga was watching as he ruined his night, maybe ruined his life. Rumi could not find him. He searched above and below, nothing. No matter. *Let the applause tell him.*

Rumi's palms were sweaty and his new black kaftan stuck tight to his body, but he did not relent. It rose on his insides, something ominous about the mesh between drums and oud, a dynastic marriage. He finished the 'Fabric of the King's Cloth' and kept going, transforming the music into something else, something the natives knew, something that would make his mother smile. 'Furae Oloola', the song of tomorrow. Rumi could not stop himself from smiling. They could not touch him at that moment; those who hated him were already spellbound captives. Even in hoping he would falter they must have wondered how long he could keep it up.

He fingerbeat the drum with the unblinking pursuit of greatness and plucked the oud's strings like an archer, sinking arrows into every member of the crowd. Then, as suddenly as he started, voices stirred, singing.

> *Furae Oloola! Arise the ever-setting sun!*
> *They will never defeat the victory, our father won!*

He glanced around as natives seemed to appear from the unseen places; cracks and crevices of the room bubbled with sound. Natives serving food and drink, natives wiping tables, natives manning doors. They sang as proudly as Rumi beat the drums. There were barely two dozen natives in the room, but the voices boomed like an army. A retaliation.

A thousand lies won't stop our truth
Age-old weapons won't stop our youth
The fires of war won't stop our rain
The Dancing Lion will break every chain.

One verse was enough. Rumi released the music, with a hard, conclusive thump of his drum.

There was an interval of silence. Shock, despair, disbelief lived in that silence. Then there was a thunderclap of applause led by the governor himself, who was on his feet. Zahim, proprietor of the Golden Room, rushed onstage.

'What should I call you?' he said, whispering under the volume of the applause.

'What?' Rumi said.

'What should I call you? They will want a story.'

'Adunola's Son,' he said.

Zahim raised an eyebrow, then looked to the crowd with a perfect smile.

'Honourable ladies and gentlemen, His Excellency the Governor, we give you, "Adunola's Son",' he said, raising Rumi's hand. The applause detonated into another wave. The priestess's cowrie flashed hot on Rumi's neck.

The other musicians could not contain themselves as Rumi climbed back into the pit. Pats on his back, words of congratulations from people who had barely ever spoken to him. The gates to their acceptance were broken now.

Olae greeted him with an embrace in full view of the others. His mother appeared and gathered him in her arms.

'My heart is full of you, son.'

Rumi beamed with light. He had touched the mountain-top.

After that, the other musicians played with the energy of

a vanquished foe: serviceable, but in the knowledge that the battle was lost.

Near the end of the night, just before the governor departed, Rumi received a message from the House Steward.

'The governor has invited you to his residence this evening,' the Steward said. 'He has arranged a special carriage to take you and your family. Your winnings from tonight have already been placed safely inside. When you step outside, the wheelman will come to greet you.'

The surreal quality of the night seemed to wave finger-thick threads of euphoria around him. *Winnings.*

With the playing done, he rushed to his mother in the kitchen. She clapped her hands over her mouth when he told her. 'Five hundred and forty cowries?' she whispered.

He gurgled a low, delighted laugh. 'Yes, Yami.'

Tears welled up in her eyes. 'My son ... oh, my son.'

'They have invited us to the governor's residence too.'

She frowned. 'Why can't he wait until tomorrow or some other time? It's late. He should respect your time.'

Rumi gave her a soft imploring look and a light sparkle touched her eyes.

'I suppose it isn't often one gets an invitation from the governor-general.'

Rumi smiled.

They stepped outside and were greeted by a uniformed wheelman who directed them to a stunning carriage. It was painted in royal blue, pulled by dark coated horses tacked up in leather harnesses, complete with crests.

The wheelman bowed as he held the carriage door open. It was bigger than their bedroom inside, with cushioned chairs, a carpeted floor and a glass tray that carried a decanter with four cut glasses.

'People cook in here?' Adunola asked, pointing to a pretty cast-iron stove near the centre of the carriage.

The wheelman's lips curled upwards in a smirk. 'That's a foot-warmer.'

Adunola shrugged and rolled her eyes, leaning back into a cluster of pillows.

It was a glimpse into the unexamined world that had no place for the plainly poor. Rumi glanced at his mother and brother. Could they ever find a place in a world of carriage foot-warmers? Would they ever want to?

At the centre of the carriage was a large purse with five hundred and forty cowries in it. Rumi stared down at the purse for a long moment. It was as though a firm, eternal pinch on his nose had been released and he was finally able to suck in clean air. *No more market debt.*

Rumi hiccupped and his eyes welled with tears. He felt something he had once thought impossible: Joy.

13

The Black Crocodile

ALANGBA

The sails of the *Black Crocodile* bulged with captured wind, giving the ship a smooth, steady speed. Sweat trickled down Alangba's beard. His vision was blurry at the corners where his eyes were touched with salty sweat and dirty blood.

He raised his staff. 'Is that the best you can do?'

The three men charged at him again, all at once and coming from different angles. Alangba whirled with his staff. His boot sang through Phelix's chin, sending him to the deck. At the same time, his elbow struck another man in the nose. He brought his staff down in a hammer blow, but he had the wind knocked from him before connection. The third man thrust his staff into Alangba's stomach with such vim that he doubled over. He wanted to gasp for air, but he could not let them see that. He shut his mouth tight, sucking air desperately through his nose.

Wiping blood from his mouth, Alangba rose to his feet, regarding the three men with a satisfied smile. 'You are getting better.'

Phelix sneered. 'You still managed to make us look like fools! Three against one is no honourable fight!'

Alangba picked his staff up from the ground. 'I have been fighting for twenty years. You, barely thirty days. You have fought honourably today. I can count on one hand the times I have been struck like that.'

Phelix's lips curled into a reluctant smile.

Maka slapped the back of Phelix's head. 'Don't get all big-headed about it, now. If those were spears instead of sticks you would have been dead half a hundred times already.'

'Death comes but once,' Alangba said with a smile.

Alangba looked over the three men. It was true, they were in far worse shape than he was. Cuts, bruises and swollen parts decorated their bodies like spots on a leopard. He had beaten them near senseless with the staff in trying to teach them.

They would learn in all the broken places, as he had learned. They were hard young men and that was more than half of it. Phelix had the eyes of a man who would rip your throat out to win a game of cards if he needed to. Good iron; the right blacksmith could mould any good iron.

A woman rushed to Phelix's side with water and cloth. Phelix's hard frown gave way to a smile.

They were out in the open water now, Palmaine far beyond sight. The people were in better spirits. There was singing and dancing and, if he wasn't mistaken, the beginnings of romance onboard. Everyone on the ship bristled with anticipation – everyone except Princess Falina.

A week past, Alangba had caught her out on the deck staring longingly into the ocean. Since then, he'd had Maka follow her everywhere but the chamber pot.

He spotted the princess on the deck and approached. She traced her fingers over the wooden taffrail that marked the border between ship and sea. Her eyes were faraway in thought.

'I greet you, Omoba,' Alangba said, kneeling.

She regarded him with a cold, inexpressive stare as he rose to his feet.

He took a gold Palmaine coin from his pocket and threw it into the sea. 'An offering, to the mother of the sea,' Alangba said.

Her jaw was set tight.

Alangba leaned in. 'Your homeland will not betray you again, Omoba. I swear it on my blood.'

'Your breath stinks,' she spat.

Alangba flinched, discreetly holding a hand over his mouth to check his breath. If looks could kill, her stare was a murderer. *She hates Basmine. Why am I forcing her there?*

He'd had no choice in the matter, not with all his men there. No, as soon as he'd known who she was, the die was cast. No matter how many pretty dresses they'd given her, she was still a Palmaine captive.

'I can teach you,' he said. 'About the Darani Way.'

She snorted. 'So I can throw coins into the sea and burn innocent goats?'

Alangba suppressed a frown. 'Are you a follower of Palman, then?'

'Yes, I am … it is a civilised religion.'

Alangba nodded. 'The Darani Way is not a religion; it is a way of life and there is nothing civilised about the spiritual realm. We do not force men to follow the Way, nor do we deny the truth in the gods of other nations. Only a fool believes he is the only one that knows the truth. It is the Way to exist in harmony with all things. We do not convert people as the Palman do.' He plucked out another coin. 'But sacrifice is part of *our* way of life.'

He dropped the coin into the sea.

'Third Ranger, you are summoned by the First,' came a voice.

Alangba glanced back. A lean woman, a ranger, stood with arms raised aloft in salute.

'Excuse me, Omoba,' Alangba said, kneeling to the princess once more.

Descending to the lower deck, he approached the First Ranger's door and knocked twice.

'Come in,' came a low voice.

Alangba walked into the cabin where Governor-General Zaminu sat bound by two Odeshi on his neck. The First Ranger, Okafor Blaise, was a lean man, bald as an egg with broad shoulders and a neck often likened to a giraffe. He was commander-in-chief of all the rangers and carried his rank with unbelievable poise. The essence of the Chainbreakers, through to the bone.

'This... *man* you brought says all sorts of things,' the First Ranger said.

Zaminu craned his neck towards the First Ranger. 'Speak the word and I'll make you the Governor-General of Basmine. I can do that.'

'You think I would ever rule on your authority?'

'Who cares on what authority you rule? You are an ambitious man. A good leader, too.'

'Save your breath for your trial, Zaminu. You will win no traitor here. I stand on the Rock of Kasinabe; there is no greater rock on which to stand.'

'I could write the order tonight; seal it with my hand and no one will refuse you. You will—'

'Enough!' Okafor snapped.

'Think about it,' Zaminu whispered.

'We cannot let this man near any of the rangers. We don't know who will taste his poison,' Okafor said.

'The rangers stand,' Alangba said.

'Yes, but no need to test their loyalty. Sometimes it is better not to tell a hungry man their neighbour has yam tubers.'

'You have wonderful parables in Basmine,' Zaminu said.

Okafor ignored him. 'I need you and Maka to watch him.'

Alangba wanted to sigh aloud, but he nodded instead. The First Ranger stepped close.

'Are you sober?'

'Yes, Captain.'

Okafor smiled and put a hand at the nape of Alangba's neck.

'That animal you brought. I hear he eats the food of ten men every day.'

Alangba's expression did not change, but he nodded. 'His name is Ijere.'

The First Ranger raised an eyebrow. 'I understand you are ... *bonded* to the thing.'

'Yes, Captain.'

'And were you sober when you—'

'Yes, Captain.'

The First Ranger's face soured as though he had hoped for another answer. 'Very well then,' he said. 'You are a good man, Alangba, and the best ranger I have. I will always remember that.'

'Thank you, Captain.'

He patted Alangba on the back. 'How is the Omoba faring?'

'Well, she's started eating.'

'That's a start, I suppose. Poor girl saw horrible things in Kasabia. Who can blame her for not trusting us?'

'Should she trust us?'

Alangba immediately wished he had not spoken, words that escaped like monkeys from a cage. Okafor eyed him carefully; his eyes seemed to warn Alangba.

'Yes. She *should*.'

Alangba nodded.

'Take him to the hold,' Okafor said, gesturing to Zaminu.

Alangba saluted. 'Yes, Captain.'

Alangba shoved Zaminu to the floor and dragged him out of the First Ranger's cabin.

'You should be First Ranger, you know,' Zaminu said.

Alangba retained an impassive stare.

Zaminu smiled. 'There are things I could teach you ... the secrets of the shadow.'

Alangba's mouth dropped open before he could think to close it.

Zaminu smiled. 'I knew that would wake you up.'

Alangba gritted his teeth.

'What's your end goal?' Zaminu asked. 'You think the Palmaine are any more your enemy than the Saharene, or the Kuba? You mean to tell me that a Palmaine man has never been good to you? I built the mainland road. Me. It is more than your loveless gods ever did for you. We have given you so much more than we have taken. Get rid of us and you people will spend the rest of your lives fighting each other. Nothing *we* do is personal; we are men of conquest. Conquest is the order of the world.'

That made Alangba smile. 'You think this is personal for me?' He crouched low. 'When this ship first berthed in Basmine, it was to collect five thousand cowries in exchange for Palmaine cotton. The captain knew that five thousand cowries would take time to count and load and would be vulnerable to pilfering over the sea journey. At that time, a native man of age was worth twenty-five cowries at the Palmaine slave markets. So the captain – savvy businessman that he was – asked for two hundred men as payment instead of cowries. Easier to count and move, less pilferable.' Alangba leaned in close to Zaminu. 'Every man who crews this ship was once an item of cargo on it; a unit of currency. If I tell them you are just "men of conquest", they might cut out my tongue.'

Zaminu frowned. 'I do not deny our insensitivities, but our goal is noble. Just imagine it for a moment. A world with every nation united under one flag; one god.'

'And the Palmaine mean to rule that world?'

'That is the way of the world. The strongest often rule.'

Alangba snorted. 'That is not the Way. Nor is it strength. Cutting men's hands off? Stealing from our land? You are a nation that makes heroes of your cowards. That stands over children with a gun and tells them to call you master.'

A plume of colour flared in Zaminu's eyes. 'You lack the moral authority to condemn me. I know your kind well. A barbarous people. I know a village up by the God-Eye where they used to kill twins upon birth. They said they were a sign of evil and so they burned them. How many babies died before I turned that village to the light of Palman? Hundreds, perhaps. Babies and mothers call me saviour.'

'It's an archaic, deplorable practice. Long condemned, south of the God-Eye.'

'An ancient *Darani* tradition.'

'Every nation has dark chapters in its story but every nation deserves its chance to evolve, to learn from its mistakes,' Alangba snapped. 'You are not the hand of god.'

Zaminu smiled. 'We are the glove through which His hand is felt. We do what needs doing for the good of the world. That is our burden. We are not so unalike, Third Ranger. We both believe in the necessity of change.'

'I do not believe in domination and forced change. I do not believe in power without tolerance. Your corruption is deeper and more dangerous than any nation because you believe your way is the only way. Your god is the only god. You cannot travel with many nations when the road is so narrow.'

Zaminu sighed as though forced to reprimand an errant child. 'Let me make this easy for you. You are strong, a born leader – we need men like you in Basmine. If I were you, I would name my price before they come to set me free.'

Alangba laughed as he pulled the hold door open. 'Who are *they* and how do they plan on setting you free?'

Zaminu shrugged. 'You don't just take a man like me from his home. They will come and they will overrun you. Name your price now. I'll still pay it. You could be—'

Alangba threw him into a room and slammed the door shut, doubling the lock. *A dangerous man.*

In the hold, he could feel Ijere's quiet rage. At this distance he could find Ijere with his eyes closed, the bond was so strong. He walked towards the lion's door.

The intervening years had not scrubbed his mind of the memories from the hold. The smell of the dead and dying, the buzz of flies on naked flesh. Every door had seen its fair share of horror. He reached Ijere's door and opened it. Ijere lay there, plainly waiting for Alangba to appear.

Alangba rubbed a hand through his mane. 'We will be home soon.'

Ijere's countenance did not change, but he heard a low growl at the back of his throat. *Irritation.*

'Soon, Ijere. Soon.'

14

Blood

RUMI

As the carriage glided over the Citadel roads, Rumi's mind was alive. *The governor himself.* Riding in a carriage had a way of making you forget every problem beyond its doors.

He patted the purse at the centre of the carriage. It shook with the reassuring weight of over five hundred cowries. He rested his hand on it. It was real. He had done it.

The raspy, stretched-out hiss of unwelcome company sounded overhead. Rumi pulled the carriage curtain aside and peered upwards.

A wake of vultures circled the caravan. He shot Yami a quick, questioning look. She peered through the curtain and narrowed her eyes.

'Where are we?' she said.

Rumi looked to the road around them. The interlocking stone of the mainland road was gone, leaving only hard red soil. Only one set of hoof beats pattered the ground. The trees either side of the carriage were yellow and thick.

'What route is this?' Rumi called to the driver.

Silence.

'What route is this?!'

Adunola's eyes bulged. 'Yellow trees.'

The wheelman kicked the horses into a full gallop. Morire roared. They were moving at illegal speed.

Rumi leaned out of the carriage and the wind buffeted his eyes. He reached out and snatched a piece of the wheelman's collar. Gathering the fabric, he pulled with all his strength. The carriage veered left, then right, as the wheelman fought against Rumi's grip.

One of the horses buckled against something in the uneven mud. The carriage started to rock violently.

'Rumi, look out!' Adunola cried.

Rumi glanced up. A man clad in all-white stood at a distance. White hair, white kaftan, thin, near-translucent bleached skin.

He was flanked by two other men, too far behind for Rumi to make out. A twisted yellow tree loomed over them before a massive fire.

The carriage careered towards the men with no hope of coming to a halt. All three stared at the carriage, their breaths as patient as a shepherd at night.

The one with the white hair was beautiful in a terrible way; scary and perfect, his brilliant white teeth like knives against his pink lips. The man nodded as though accepting a challenge and waved his hand.

As his hand moved, Rumi heard the groan of breaking wood overhead, and a large yellow tree came crashing down on the carriage. The world went black.

★ ★ ★

Rumi heard his mother's murmured prayer. His eyes stuttered open. The priestess's cowrie on his neck was burning hot and he could feel the wetness of blood soaking his thigh.

He tried to move, but something was pinning his kaftan down. That was when Rumi saw him.

One side of Morire's face was serene and thoughtful as it always was. The other side was a bloody mask of shredded flesh.

Rumi howled. He had never seen so much blood. His hands grew numb as he pulled them to cover his eyes.

Yami's arm was bent in a way it was not designed to bend, and the exposed bone showing through her skin was a brilliant white in claret-brown flesh. Stifling his sobs, Rumi managed to pull her from the carriage. Renike crawled out from the wreckage seemingly unharmed.

He heard Morire's ragged breathing but they were separated by a thick part of the tree.

'Morire!' he shouted.

There was no answer. He shifted to the other side but it was even harder to look inside. Morire was trapped.

He emptied his lungs with a raw scream. The sound echoed through the forest.

Rumi stepped back out of the carriage and sank to his knees. He heard a ragged cough and glanced over his shoulder. *The wheelman.*

He snatched the wheelman at the collar and lifted him until his legs dangled above the ground.

'Who sent you?'

A smile spread across the wheelman's face, exposing his bloodstained teeth. 'The New Covenant has been sealed. Palman reigns.'

'What?'

He moved his trembling hands to hold up four fingers. 'Palman re—'

Rumi pressed his palm to the wheelman's windpipe and squeezed.

'I will only ask you one more time. Who sent you?'

The wheelman coughed, spraying red mucus. 'I am already dead.'

Pink froth formed on his lips and his eyes bulged. Rumi dropped the wheelman to the floor and staggered back. He watched, open-mouthed, as the wheelman shook convulsively then went completely still.

'Irumide!' his mother screamed.

Her voice was like a slap.

The strange men in the distance were slowly making their way towards the carriage. He could make out the two others now: one was Odu with a glimmering, cast-iron ball lodged in his left eye socket. The other was a giant with manacles around his wrists and a long chain dragging along the floor. His eyes were completely white. Rumi gaped. It was something he had always dismissed as superstition in Yami's stories. A godhunter's slave; an *Obair.*

'Blood of Dara above,' he whispered. Each beat of his heart was like a truncheon against his chest. A trickle of warm mois-ture trailed into his sandals. He tried not to let the terror show on his face, but the fear had mastered him. *Godhunters.*

He shut his eyes with the hope that it would all lose its focus and turn into a dream about climbing a mountain or finding a chest of gold. When he opened his eyes, nothing had changed. The men walked towards them at a funereal march.

His mother tugged the ripped hem of his kaftan.

He crouched low. 'They are *godhunters,*' he whispered.

Adunola glanced at the sky then at the men, her face calm. 'Yes, they are.' She whispered a prayer and looked up to Rumi. 'Help me to my feet.'

Rumi raised an eyebrow. 'You're bleeding, Yami … We have to hide.'

'The time for hiding is over,' she said, planting her arm to stand. 'You have always been the one to complete my story. Dara told me I would have two children. The child who would never speak my name, and the child who would dream in colour, dream in a nightmare … and it all came true. You are my *kukoyi* child; even from my womb you came out with the scrapes of death, but you still came, for me. My story is almost over. But yours begins tonight.'

Her eyes were bright with resolution, her jaw firm with sincerity of purpose.

'Help me to my feet.'

Rumi obeyed, putting his arm under her good shoulder and pulling her up. Her courage seemed to radiate and he stole from it, firming his own shoulders.

'What do we do?' Rumi asked.

'You take Renike and run,' Yami said, coolly.

Rumi looked up at the men approaching. 'What?'

She ripped the cowrie necklace from his chest and stuffed it in his pocket. 'Listen to me, Rumi, please. I need you to run, now.'

Rumi's heart pounded at the bottom of his throat. 'I can't leave you.'

She looked up at him with that same ominous look he had only seen twice before. 'I'll be back.'

With that, she shoved him back and stepped out from the shadow of the wreckage.

Renike looked up at him. This whole time, she hadn't shed a single tear. Not muttered even a word of fear. 'What do we do?'

Rumi closed his eyes and sucked in a deep breath. 'Run.'

They took off, sprinting as they had in so many races before through the muddy path. Rumi glanced over his shoulder once and saw Yami draw a circle in the mud around herself – a cold wind flew through him and it seemed as though something changed in the air. He hesitated.

The man with the translucent bleached skin was tall and thin, with hair that fell to his hips. His eyes were deeply unsettling. It was as if a master artist had painted the face of a man, but let a demon paint the eyes. There was a perfection to the man that was almost inhuman. He had the air of command amongst the three.

Something else was strange about him, but Rumi couldn't quite place his finger on it. He studied the man until his breath caught when it hit him. The dancing light of the fire cast no shadow behind the man.

'The only thing here is death. Is that what you desire?' the man in white said.

His voice was like bad music. It had melody, but the melody was broken and corrupt. Adunola ignored the question, as she rose to her feet. She raised her arm and licked blood from her wound then spoke in deep Odu. The kind even Rumi struggled to understand.

There was silence and staring for a moment, then a groan of thunder. Lightning parted the clouds and water bucketed down. The fire shrivelled to death under the battering rain.

Rumi squinted, staring into the dead flame. Something moved and his heart attempted to escape through his mouth. In the doused fire and spreading smoke, instead of charred wood, was a god.

Kamanu, the great white ram of the Celestial Palanquin, the Agbara of thunder and lightning. Rumi knew it was Kamanu, for his flesh was black as coal. His teeth were like pearls against his black lips, his wrapper like the sky and stars. In his left hand was a monstrous cutlass that shone like furnace fire.

When Rumi looked at him he saw a face like that of a man; white-bearded and strong-jawed, but when he blinked, he saw the face of a ram with a white muzzle. He blinked again and the face of the man returned. The rain touched Kamanu's flesh. His eyes flashed open, and they were red and terrible.

'It begins,' Kamanu said.

His voice was deeper than the grave.

Renike had kept on running but Rumi stood watching, paralysed by fear and wonder.

Adunola stiffened, her face harder than any stone. She lifted her chin to the sky and called Dara by seven names. The iron-eyed godhunter hissed as she approached, pulling a long, grey-white sword from his scabbard.

His mother's eyes turned black as tar and when she spoke a cold wind flew through the forest. A black shroud of smoke seemed to leak from her pores.

She stepped forward. 'You will not kill our gods today.'

'Root and branch shall break and burn!' cried the traitorous Odu with the iron eye.

The Obair stood well over two metres tall. Its white-washed eyes made it impossible to tell where its stare settled. Its chain made a screeching sound as it dragged through the sun-hardened soil.

'I am with you, my daughter,' Kamanu said.

His voice boomed inside Rumi's head. Adunola nodded and stretched her hand out to the sky.

'Old magic ...' the shadowless man said, smiling. 'What a providential convenience.'

But this wasn't magic. Magic was sleight of hand, long sleeves, and theatricality. This was juju.

A whirring sound rang out in the air. Something flew into Adunola's outstretched hand.

Rumi's eyes widened. Clean as a whistle, gleaming black steel and a haft that seemed to be formed of trapped smoke teeming with effervescent silver-black mist. The halberd from Yami's secret crypt.

The shadowless man frowned. 'Are you the Son of Despair?'

She set her feet. 'Perhaps to you.'

He nodded to the Obair. 'Prove yourself to me.'

Rumi shifted forward but came up against something hard as stone. Thick and immovable as a wall but invisible to the eye. He looked down at the ground and saw a thick line scratched through the mud. He followed the line until he realised what it was – *a circle*. He punched lightly at the air and nearly broke his wrist. His knuckles hit something solid as stone that he could not see. *Impossible.*

Smoke streamed from Adunola's eyes as she spoke with icy cool. 'When I was a child, my father told me about godhunters, killing our gods in the night … seeking out shadowwielders, putting them in chains.' Her eyes settled on the Obair. 'One way or another, this will be your last day in chains, brother.'

The Obair grunted and drew a huge black sword from its side.

'You think you'll make a story out of him?' said the iron-eyed man.

Adunola pulled the halberd down and flattened the mud around with her feet. 'One way or another, I will make a story.'

The Obair moved like a flying snake, its speed unbelievable as it lunged towards Adunola. It seemed to glide rather than run, flying as arrows do, death delivered in a dance. Rumi winced as the Obair swung its sword. He never imagined something so big could move so fast.

A sound like a broken bell filled the air as weapons clashed. Adunola sent the sword sideways with her halberd. The Obair staggered back and smiled.

Rumi struggled against the force that held him back, gritting his teeth as he pushed against the unseen wall. It was pointless.

THE DANCE OF SHADOWS

The Obair swung for Adunola again, its sword flying in a circle of death. She pulled her halberd once more, blocking the blow. Adunola staggered back. Her arm was a bloody mess, but she moved as though youthfully spry. The black mist around her seemed to give her strength and speed to match the Obair. She moved in whirls of flowing black.

The Obair swung its sword, splitting puffs of shadow smoke to get to her. She moved like an acrobat, dancing around its overhand swings. She was faster than the Obair, but it was far more powerful. A stallion against a steam engine. Every swing was a promise to kill.

'Do something!' Rumi screamed at Kamanu, pounding the invisible wall.

Kamanu only watched. The shadowless man watched too. Neither of them made a move to intervene. The only one who seemed intent on intervention was the iron-eyed Odu but even he seemed to await instruction from the shadowless man.

Adunola dodged again, pirouetting on one foot in time to thrust the haft of the halberd into the Obair's chin. It was immaculate form. The Obair barely flinched and swung for her head. She struck first with a single-step riposte and the halberd spike bit into the Obair's shoulder. Rivulets of blood streamed down, but it did not let up.

Rumi's throat was bone-dry.

The Obair threw its bulk behind a deadly slash that bit down into flesh on his mother's leg. Dark blood flared from the gash. Rumi groaned as though he was the one to take the wound. He pushed with every fibre of his being to move the wall and glared at Kamanu, who looked back at him with empty eyes. Adunola fell to one knee.

The Obair raised its sword high to strike a killing blow.

'No!' Rumi shouted.

He heard the thud of footfalls ahead. Then he heard another sound, a shout. A familiar shout. It was the roar of a man who was absolutely fed up. *Morire.*

Morire sped into view with a large log of wood in hand, and smashed the Obair on the neck, staggering him. The Obair kept its footing, backhanding Morire to the ground. Morire hit hard, blood drooling from his mouth.

The Obair grunted, lifting its sword again. Something moved behind it. Two shadows. The Obair felt it too. Its upraised sword seemed to hesitate for a heartbeat.

The shadows pounced, snarling; all claws and tearing flesh. Kaat and Ndebe wrestled the Obair to the ground and tore him to bloody strips. How they had traced them from Alara to here, Rumi could not know.

Adunola regained her footing as the lionhounds did their vicious work. Morire rose to his feet too; he swung his club with reckless verve.

Rumi gritted his teeth and pushed. He felt a shifting as he pulsed with strain. Kamanu's eyes widened, staring at Rumi, ignoring the battle.

Rumi gave the force a desperate, powerful heave and felt a sudden coolness. Like cold morning rain. The wall had fallen. He darted into the fight.

The Obair fought back. It threw Kaat aside with one hand and split Ndebe in half from tail to tooth with a rising slash. The dog howled as the blade tore him apart.

Ndebe. Ndebe, the stubborn one who snarled just to scare people even when he meant no harm. Split in two like a tuber of yam.

Rumi tried to attack from the Obair's blind side but the creature caught him with a spinning backfist that sent him spiralling to the ground. Blood filled his mouth as he licked at a tooth that had come loose. The Obair moved for Morire next, but something made it stop completely still. It glanced down at its navel as the spike of the halberd burst from its stomach in a spray of blood. The Obair dropped to its knees, peering over his shoulder at Yami, who stood close.

'Take this message to the ancestors,' she said. Then she whispered something in the Obair's ear.

Pupils bloomed in the Obair's eyes, and for a moment, there was a look of relief. Then it slumped forward, revealing the deep wound in its back.

The shadowless man grimaced, staring down at the lifeless Obair with a look more irritated than aggrieved.

'*Igima Kusibe*,' he murmured.

The Obair's corpse writhed and withered like a fish lathered with salt. A cloud of blackness moved to dominate the night sky: an almighty flock of vultures. They flew down and formed a wake around the Obair, tearing flesh away with ravenous lust. Rumi jerked back from the scene in disgust.

The shadowless man turned to Yami. 'A long time since I have seen a shadowwielder in action.'

'Same here,' she said, her tattered dress stained claret.

'You know who I am, I presume?'

Adunola scowled. 'The Priest of Vultures ... the Accuser.'

The shadowless man smiled and bent over in a mocking bow. 'You are skilled with the shadow ...'

The wake of vultures continued to feast on the writhing Obair's corpse.

'... Join the light. You need not wear chains if you confess your sins and choose to serve. Sabachi wears no chains.' He gestured to the Odu with the iron eye.

'You think you are the light?' Yami said, laughing. 'I'd sooner slit my own throat than serve you. Much sooner.'

She looked over the remains of the Obair in manacles, pecked unrecognisable by ravenous vultures, then she shifted her glare to the iron-eyed man. 'He died more honourably than you will, *Sabachi.*'

The Priest of Vultures stepped forward, his dark eyes purpling at the edges. 'You are ... a taint, a smear. To serve is a great mercy ... but if you will not come into the light, then I will cleanse the earth of your stain.'

Kamanu stepped towards them. The Priest of Vultures clenched his fist, the action seeming to make Kamanu double over in pain.

Adunola lifted her halberd slowly, locking eyes with the Priest of Vultures.

His eyes narrowed. 'Enough games.' He stretched out a hand and a thin, grey-white sword coalesced in his hand. Adunola stepped forward.

'You will not harm—'

'Enough!'

The Priest of Vultures slashed violently. Adunola went down, clutching her stomach.

Rumi howled in a way that no human being should.

Morire moved to stand, but the iron-eyed godhunter moved in a blur, pinning Morire's arm behind his back and doubling him over.

'Morire!'

Only then did the Priest of Vultures turn his attention to Rumi. He fixed his eyes on him and started to chant. 'And the Son shall cast them down, erase their names, their seed in the land.'

Rumi had promised himself a thousand times that if anyone ever did harm to his family he would kill them. That he would do all the violence needed to protect them. But as he watched the Priest of Vultures chanting, walking towards him while his family was dying, he was held back by something more powerful, more restrictive than the force that formed a wall in front of him.

Fear.

The presence of the Priest of Vultures pressed down, crumpling Rumi's confidence. *Fight. Fight.* He balled his hands up into fists and willed himself to step forward, but the fear had mastered him entirely. He froze.

The Priest of Vultures smiled. 'The lamb thinks to challenge the wolf.'

'Leave us alone,' Rumi whispered. 'Please.'

The Priest of Vultures' smile widened, revealing every single one of his brilliant white teeth. He darted forward with blurring speed and grabbed Rumi's neck, lifting him from the ground. The firm press of his palm threatened to squash Rumi's throat stone.

Rumi tried to speak but could only manage short gasps. Cords in his neck bulged as the Priest of Vultures put a blockade on the blood flowing through his body.

The Priest of Vultures stared into his eyes. 'A fugitive from death. I would have expected more fight out of you. You are no Son of Despair. Whatever you thought you were, know that it is a lie. Whatever you thought you would become, know that it is a lie. You are nothing … always remember you are nothing. You could not defend your mother, you could not defend your brother, and you cannot defend yourself because you are a coward. Under the eye of the Son, there is no shelter for the sinner. Remember today how the hand of the one true god took everything you loved, remember—'

His voice pulled away as a cold wind flew through the forest. Rumi stole a hard breath as the deathly grip slackened. The light seemed to leave the Priest of Vultures' eyes as he glanced over his shoulder towards the dead fire. The one with the iron eye looked towards the dead fire too, his face a mask of bitter disappointment. A soft hiss filled the air like a kettle almost at boil.

'*Impossible*,' the Priest of Vultures hissed, staring at the dead flame.

Adunola straightened, still holding her stomach. 'Some call him the Skyfather, some call him the Dumaré-Adandan. I call him Dara, the Dancing Lion. He still lives.' She locked her eyes on the Priest of Vultures and her voice was like the harmattan wind, cold and cutting. 'You forget yourself… *Tahinta*.'

The Priest of Vultures stared at her in disbelief, mouth agape.

'Oh, you thought I did not know that name,' she said. 'Now I do.'

Kamanu lifted his chin, lizards crawling around him.

'Now!' Adunola shouted.

As one, Adunola and Kamanu stretched their hands out and the mist covering her formed a swirling pocket of black in the air.

Rumi's eyes doubled wide. *A gateway to the other side – just like in her stories.*

The iron-eyed godhunter reached for Yami but Morire hurtled into him. The force toppled them both into the blackness and they were swallowed whole.

Rumi jerked back, free of the Priest of Vulture's grip, choking as he finally breathed deep.

The Priest of Vultures' eyes widened. He reached for Rumi, but his feet were sucked into the swirling oblivion. As the hole swallowed a leg, he drew his sword. Rumi raised a hand to protect himself, but the grey-white sword shot out at him so fast he barely saw it move.

A dull flash of pain pulsed through him as the gateway sucked the Priest of Vultures in to his waist.

Rumi blinked, lurching forward with the release of breath. The Priest of Vultures had missed. He saw sharp teeth pressed in a smile. Then he felt the incredible pain. He looked down and saw the grey-white sword lodged in his stomach. He coughed up bloody spittle as he dropped to a knee, eyes wide with shock. The Priest of Vultures hadn't missed at all. He had gutted Rumi, so fast he hadn't seen it.

'Pray that you die before I return to find you, for when I do, my birds will pick your corpse clean.'

He snatched the sword free from Rumi's stomach, making him double over as ropes of intestine spilled out. With that final act, the black hole swallowed the last of the Priest of Vultures and dissipated like smoke in strong wind.

Rumi clutched his stomach, as though trying to push the blood and guts back in. The pain was complete and yet distant somehow. He stretched towards his mother. The Priest of Vultures' words echoed in his mind. *Always remember you are nothing. Your pride is built on nothing.*

'Yami,' he said, blood fountaining from his belly. 'I ... I ...'

His vision blackened and he faded into the abyss.

15

A Heavy Cost

ADUNOLA

Rumi did not stir. His eyes closed as though closed forever. Adunola gripped him by the shoulders.

'No.'

Her voice was hoarse, like a woman starved of water. Blood dripped from the gaping wound at her own stomach. Only her firm grip on the shadow kept her alive.

'Rumi!'

There was no response.

'Morire?'

Silence.

Kamanu touched Rumi's neck. 'He'll be dead before sunrise. Your other son was dragged into the Originate.'

Adunola was no surgeon, but she knew a killing wound when she saw one. She moved to stripe her arm but Kamanu grabbed her wrist.

'You can't do anything. You can't go after him. The gateway we made could have taken him anywhere in the Originate.'

She covered her eyes and fell back. 'I know. Godsblood, I know.' Her eyes fell on Rumi and she touched his forehead. 'His story is not over.'

'It would appear that it is, my daughter.'

Her attention was drawn to the hissing sound of the cowrie necklace around his neck. Her eyebrows lifted.

'We can save him,' she said.

'We cannot.'

'Yes, we can!' Adunola cried, her voice trembling. She traced her fingers over the charred skin on Rumi's neck and shuddered at the roughness of his blood-broken flesh beneath her fingers. Her next words were uttered with cold, resigned calm. 'Call the old gravedigger.'

Kamanu stared at her in amazement. 'Whatever the Accuser wants from your son, let him have it. Bury him and put as much distance between yourself and the grave as possible. I can still heal you. I haven't seen one with your skill with the shadow in generations. To steal his name and open a gateway to the Originate, all while fighting an Obair one-handed? Incredible.'

'Agbara, you do not understand.' Adunola pulled up the halberd. 'Call the old gravedigger. *Now*.'

She drew herself up and put the edge of the halberd at Kamanu's throat stone. Steely eyed, straight-backed.

Kamanu's red eyes flickered like a lantern short of oil. 'You are serious? You believe in *him*?'

'With all of my being. He is the best of me. He has Gu's heart. Loving and unrelenting. Has a way of inspiring people. A true kukoyi child. His story is far greater than mine.'

'He is a youngling. Rash. Impulsive, a captive of his passion. Afraid,' Kamanu snapped.

Adunola glanced down at her dying son and knew, with no doubt, exactly what she had to do.

'Whatever it takes,' said Adunola. 'He will live. He *must* live.'

Kamanu spat at the ground. 'Even if I agree … we have no conduit.'

Adunola reached into her pocket and produced Ilesha's kola nut. Red on one side and white on the other. 'There's your conduit.'

Kamanu squinted as he held the kola nut up to the light. 'Who gave you this?'

'Ilesha himself.'

Kamanu narrowed his eyes. 'You know that such a thing would be ... costly. The gravedigger only accepts one currency.'

'Whatever it takes.'

Kamanu closed his eyes and held out a dark kola nut of his own. 'Very well.'

The kola nut's bitter juice filled Adunola's mouth as she sank her teeth into the husk.

The sky flickered with light and the roar of thunder shattered the quiet. Kamanu stretched out his hand and stray branches and logs of wood congregated at his feet. In a moment of brightness, a smile flashed across Kamanu's face.

The moment passed and the smile was gone. Lightning came down and struck Kamanu, turning his eyes white as chalk.

'He's coming.'

Kamanu clutched her hand and traced over Rumi's markings, making new inscriptions with the tip of his forefinger.

Tears rolled down Adunola's cheeks. 'Will I go to hell?'

'Why would you think that?'

She glanced at the remains of the enslaved shadowwielder, the Obair. 'I killed a brother. An enslaved brother.'

Kamanu frowned. 'Long enslaved. I'd wager that one had worn chains for over a hundred years. You gave him freedom.'

'I suppose I will know soon enough.'

A deep sonorous voice sounded behind them. 'Why, Kamanu, why would you summon me down here?'

Adunola glanced over her shoulder. A man approached

wearing a wide-brimmed top hat, a black tailcoat, dark lens glasses and cotton plugs in his round nostrils. His face was painted the bony white of a skull and he held a fat cigar in between his teeth. One of his teeth shone a brilliant gold. Slung across his left shoulder was a long, pristine shovel. Where he walked, grass died.

Kamanu straightened, holding up the kola nut. 'We have an offer for you, gravedigger. One you will find irresistible.'

The old gravedigger sank his shovel deep into the ground and drew hard on his cigar. 'I'm listening.'

16

Home Sweet Home

ALANGBA

Alangba inhaled deeply, taking in the pungent smell of the Basmine dockside. It was good to be back. Three years at sea and on foreign land had aged him. He glanced up at the statue of Zaminu and smiled. The men and women going about their business could not know his joy.

Okafor, the First Ranger, bartered with the customs officers to find a fitting price for them to look the other way.

Alangba turned back to the ship as people climbed down. 'Our journey now is at an end. But for any of you who have no place to call home, we have a place for you.'

He spotted Princess Falina climbing down with Maka and offered his assistance.

'Omoba, I greet you,' he said, kneeling.

She frowned. 'It's far too hot. I'll break out into a sweat soon.'

Alangba smiled. 'The sun is greeting you.'

Okafor appeared, gripping Alangba's shoulder. 'I want you and Maka keeping an eye on our ... package over there,' he said, nodding to the crate which contained Zaminu, sedated and bound with a black sack over his head. 'Take the princess with you. I will ride a few minutes behind.'

Alangba made a circle with his thumb and forefinger and Okafor responded in kind.

He walked over to Maka and nodded to the crate. Maka's eyes flashed understanding and they moved to the back of a large wheelwagon.

Three rangers rode with Alangba. Maka, Phelix and No Music, who seemed eerily happy to be back in Basmine. Alangba motioned Phelix to stay close. Men like Maka Naki and No Music couldn't help but radiate lethality but Phelix was a more plain-looking man.

Though Phelix looked ordinary, he was no scrub. He kept a quarterstaff on his person and he was mean as a snake with it. One would need to knock Phelix down dead to stop him from getting up.

Maka crept into the crate to keep Zaminu company and opened the small, grated window at the front so Alangba could see inside. Okafor gave the signal and Alangba gave his horse a soft kick. The wagon began to move.

They had been riding about an hour when Zaminu rose from his sedation. 'I knew you'd want to stay close to me,' came the voice from inside the wagon.

The sharp slap of a palm hitting skin followed. Maka's work. When it came to giving a good slap, Maka had everlasting experience.

'You just never shut up, do you?' Maka said.

'Where's the fun in that?' Zaminu coughed. 'I'm excited to be back. I haven't had this much fun since I was in the coal mines. I understand some of your family members were there too.'

Alangba glanced over his shoulder at that. 'Maka—'

'Don't worry, I won't let him get to me.'

'A bit late for that, wouldn't you say?' said Zaminu. 'How many people did you kill to get me here? Ten? Twenty? Men

149

just doing their jobs. Seems to me I got to you a long time ago, Zarot.'

Alangba kept his hands firm on the reins.

Maka's voice was cool as the night breeze. 'They say when the Palmaine man is about to leave a garden for good, he wrecks it. That's what you're trying to do – wreck the garden, because there's no joy left for you. Every breath you have left will be harder and more helpless than the one before. Save your energy, Zaminu. I won't be your figure of fun. Every time I hear your chains rattle, I am reminded that my joy is just beginning.'

Alangba could not see Zaminu's reaction, but Maka's words had shut him up.

They came across a small settlement after an hour or so of riding. Alangba glanced to his right. Crude buildings with iron roofs and bare walls loomed over them.

'Maka,' Alangba said, softly.

Maka pressed his face to the grated window. 'Third Ranger?'

'How long has this settlement been here?' Alangba asked, staring up.

'Hard to say. I've never seen it before.'

Alangba's forehead wrinkled as he studied the settlement. 'Why would anyone settle way out here? There's better ground up by the Agede peninsula. Can't be anything to farm or fish out here.'

Maka stared at the buildings then narrowed his eyes. 'I'll get the flatbow.'

Alangba nodded.

At that moment there was an almighty roar from the wagon behind. *Ijere.* Alangba's head whipped back and almost immediately pain seared his face. He reached up to his cheek and felt blood.

Arrows. Had he not looked back to Ijere, he would be dead.

'Away, move away from the buildings!' he said, drawing the reins to veer left.

Maka emerged from the crate with his flatbow at the ready.

'There are two, maybe three archers on the right.' Blood trickled down Alangba's beard as he spoke. 'They are good. They won't miss many.'

'What do we do?'

'We keep moving. If we stop, they'll pick us off like fireflies. If you see anything, take the shot. Don't think, just shoot.'

Maka whirled with his flatbow drawn and scrambled to the top of the wheelwagon.

'We keep moving!' Alangba shouted.

Alangba heard air parting – another arrow had been loosed at them.

'Keep moving!'

He heard another arrow loosed in counter strike. *Slfft* came the sound as an arrow notched in Zaminu's box. Three arrows had come their way in quick succession. It was a targeted attack.

'Keep moving!'

The sound came again. *Slffft.*

'Got one!' Maka shouted.

'Now get another one!'

Maka let another arrow fly, then another. Eventually the enemy arrow fire slowed to a halt and they were out of sight of the buildings.

Maka came up beside him.

'What did they want?' Maka said.

'Who knows?' Alangba said, frowning. 'Bandits, perhaps, looking to catch out some lonely wagons.'

Even as he said it, he had already dismissed the idea. Bandits were often organised, but the traffic this way was too sparse to chance a living on passing stragglers.

Nothing else needed to be said. There was a traitor amongst them.

Zaminu laughed. 'I told you they were coming to get me.'

17

The Originate

RUMI

Rumi blinked. The rain came down in a riot. Thunder announced itself with a guttural groan.

Cold, hard hands gripped Rumi's wrist. A stream of power shot through him. Awesome, wondrous power, bubbling through his veins like water filling a cup. The loud crack of bones and the hiss of sealing flesh thrummed in his ears. The pain leaked out of him. Kamanu, with his deep, unmistakeable voice, chanted in languages long dead.

Sensation returned to his limbs. Like warmth after the desperate cold. Dead things inside sprang to life.

'Get up.'

The words hit him sub-vocally, crashing against the insides of his skull. Rumi attempted to wriggle his toes and succeeded. Then something licked his elbow. *Kaat*. He opened his eyes.

A man stared down at him. 'He's alive.'

Rumi blinked and rubbed his eyes clear. He knew that man's face. It was a face from old books and forgotten paintings. A face born on the ships that left Basmine with men and women in manacles. *The new Agbara of death. The gravedigger.*

'Saturday,' he whispered.

A gold-toothed smile etched slowly across Saturday's face.

He drew hard against his cigar and exhaled, sending a large puff of black smoke into the air around Rumi. Half the cigar shrivelled to dead ash, sprinkling the ground in front of him.

'Most people only live to see me once,' he said coolly. 'What a lucky one you are.'

He turned to Kamanu. 'I've done my part, Kamanu. I'm no good with what comes next.'

He threw what was left of the cigar to the floor and doffed his top hat. 'Pleasure doing business with you. I hope to see you again. For your sake, I hope it's not too soon.'

He stamped out the remains of his cigar and disappeared into the shadows.

Kamanu stood a few metres ahead. His wide back blocked most of Rumi's view of what seemed to be an unlit pyre. Kaat scratched at the pyre, trying to climb it. The cutlass in Kamanu's hand was shiny with fresh blood. Rumi stood.

Yami's body lay still on the rough pyre.

He ran to her; brushed his hand along her wound, ripping swathes from his kaftan to bind her stomach. Her eyes had no signs of life. He pressed his palm firm against her bloodied chest, praying for the faint beat of a heart or the slow intake of breath. There was nothing.

'There is nothing to be done,' said Kamanu. 'She is dead.'

Rumi pressed frantically. 'Yami! Fight for me! Stay with me. Godsblood! Come back to me.'

Kamanu stared down at him. 'She is gone.'

'I am taking her home. We do not need you. Stitches is all … Mama Ayeesha will stitch her up good before breakfast.'

'Gone!'

Kamanu's word pounded in his head like pestle pummelling mortar. *Gone.*

THE DANCE OF SHADOWS

'What did you do to her? You killed her!'

Kamanu locked eyes with him and suddenly Rumi felt very, very stupid. The Agbara's presence pressed down on him, dominating all of his thoughts.

'Listen to me. You are not a child anymore. A child can hide in his mother's shadow, but a man must face the glare of the sun. She gave the most precious thing one can give, that we might bring you back and make you whole again.'

Tears streamed down Rumi's face. 'Her life?'

He knew the answer before Kamanu spoke.

'Her soul.'

Kaat gave a low, mournful growl.

Rumi clutched her tight. 'You should have left me alone! Why couldn't you help her instead?'

'Believe you me, I would much rather she was breathing now than a youngling like you. She could have become an Agbara; she could have done so much more. But she chose you. You have gained a great ancestor.'

Rumi buried his face in his hands. 'Why did this happen? What did *he* want with us? With me?'

Kamanu unclenched his fist, revealing Rumi's necklace with the priestess's cowrie. 'I think he suspected you were something that you are not.'

'Something like what?'

Kamanu narrowed his eyes. 'Their scripture speaks of the Son of Despair. The one who will bring down their temple and commit the abomination of declaring himself Lord of All.'

'Why would they think that was me?'

Kamanu snorted. 'I don't know.'

'How do you know it isn't me?'

'Because there is no Son of Despair. It is a lie. A false scripture.'

Rumi glanced at the cowrie; it looked as small as a fingernail in the Agbara's massive palm. His family destroyed, over a case of mistaken identity.

'What happened to my brother?'

'He is in the Originate, far beyond our reach.'

'How do I find him?'

Kamanu shook his head with irritation. 'The Originate is a place with no beginning or end, no time or space. You've a better chance of finding a raindrop in the ocean. It is a Higher World – where spirits reign. The spirit realm.'

'I have to—'

'Listen to me! Our time is long spent. The Accuser *will* return, and he *will* search for you. I need you to focus on what I am saying.'

Rumi's hands trembled and his lips were bone-dry.

'Focus!' Kamanu said again.

The skies echoed his mood, two claps of thunder following one another like twins from the womb. He gripped Rumi by the arm.

'Promise me that you will not make a fool of your mother! Prove her right!'

A jolt of lightning danced on a cloud at his voice.

Rumi nodded as tears filled his eyes. 'I … I promise.'

'Don't be a child about it. I need to hear it true. Swear it on your blood.'

'I swear it on my blood!'

Kamanu nodded and eased his grip.

Rumi's stomach churned. It was too much.

'Where did she keep it?' Kamanu asked.

Rumi blinked. 'Keep what?'

'The book.'

Rumi narrowed his eyes. The book. There could only be one book. *The one from her secret room.*

'I don't know,' Rumi said.

'Find it,' Kamanu said softly. 'It is called the *Sakosaye*. It contains the knowledge of the Agbara, passed down to our priests. You are not a priest like she was. You must not read it without divine instruction. The Agbara have many things yet to say to you, but you cannot hear them now. Everything has a season; even the knowledge of things has its time.'

Kamanu's words only made the nightmare more real. Rumi clutched his head, digging his fingernails into his scalp, praying to wake up.

Kamanu held out the priestess's cowrie.

'You are of the old blood, Rumi, born to be a shadow-wielder. You know the Accuser's true name now; never speak it to anyone unless you mean to use it.'

'What do you mean, "use it"?'

'My goodness, did your mother teach you nothing at all?'

Rumi frowned.

Kamanu turned away. 'When you find the book, you have my instruction to read my story.'

'You are leaving me?'

Kamanu glanced over his shoulder. 'You need me to hold your hand?'

Rumi narrowed his eyes and scowled.

Kamanu's face was expressionless. 'You have questions; I understand. I can't give you the answers you need. I am no scholar or priest. I am a warrior. My answers are of the blade. Find a safe place where you can shelter from the Accuser and his servants. If you need my blade, you know my true name. When you call it, I will answer.'

'I don't know your—'

The applause of thunder cut Rumi off. Kamanu let out a shout that seemed an announcement to the world.

'Arise, Rumi, for your story begins anew!'

A bolt of lightning tumbled from the sky and set Kamanu's body alight. A blinding flash of light followed and when Rumi looked where Kamanu had been standing, there was nothing.

'Kamanu!'

Nothing.

Snakes of lightning raced across the sky, turning the darkness into intermittent light.

Rumi lifted his mother from the pyre and cradled her. Her chest shifted and he jerked upright, pressing his ear to her bloody chest. Waiting for a second confirmatory breath. It never came.

With Yami cradled in his arms, he threw himself to sleep with all his strength. He wanted it to last forever. He dreamed of Yami and Morire and plantain, and when he woke he lived the nightmare all over again.

Why had this happened? Why couldn't he have done something? Why did he freeze when confronted by the Priest of Vultures? The darkness came, unbidden, whispering the answer: *Because you are nothing, Rumi. Spineless.*

He curled into a ball, his hands wrapped tight around his knees. He could feel death crawling up from his toes, pulling him down. He welcomed it, waiting for it to drag him away, give him a reprieve. But he lived.

Somehow, after a long time in the mud, he found the strength to climb to his feet.

He scratched at the earth with limp, shaking hands until he had a large mound of upturned mud. Kaat joined in the effort, clawing away at the ground. It was long, gruelling work. By the time they were done, Rumi's hands were clammy with soil and blood. He stepped back from the resting place and said a prayer. Though Kamanu had built a pyre, Rumi would not set her body to flame. He buried them, in the old way, Yami and Ndebe together – where flowers might grow again.

18

Whistle in the Wind

NATARÉ

Going after a witch doctor when they knew you were coming was a thing to be done only after serious contemplation. As Nataré crept past the skinny iroko tree with her blade in hand, she finally began to seriously contemplate her future. *I might die tonight.*

Her heart thumped, pleading for them to turn back. She repeated her mantra to herself. *You are the knife edge.*

'Are you sure he came this way?' Tito whispered behind her.

She nodded and stalked forward, her back tight to the tree.

Tito would take any reason to head back now. They had gone deep into the forest. Deeper than they had any right or reason to go.

'You can go back,' she said.

'We're meant to stay together,' Tito said.

She glanced over her shoulder and fixed her eyes on him. 'I won't tell anyone if you leave me.'

Tito's shoulder's sagged as he swallowed. 'I won't.'

She shrugged. 'Then stay close and stay quiet.'

The sounds of crawling lizards and crooning songbirds did little to distract them from the watchful silence beneath. Nataré heard every crunch of grass underfoot. Every step forward was a dare, a wager in a deathly dance.

A bush-shrike flew past her ear and her heart lurched.

'Shege!' Tito shrieked, jumping forward.

Nataré glared at him. If the witch doctor was within a mile of them, he had certainly heard that.

'Sorry,' Tito whispered.

Nataré kissed her teeth and stared ahead into the scattered corridor of trees.

Each moment seemed to stretch out as they pressed forward, one careful step after another. They came to a clearing in the forest, a sudden decline in the density of trees. Nataré froze, her eyes jerking left and right in surveillance. *They are close.*

Tito tapped her shoulder. 'I don't like this. I think we should—'

Something whistled past her cheek and struck Tito in the neck. Instinctively, Nataré ducked. The whistle of wind passed overhead. She whirled as Tito slumped to the ground. She did not need to check to know he was dead. His neck was pierced with a red-feathered dart.

Nataré rolled, expecting another dart. The whizzing sound came from the opposite direction. She gritted her teeth. *Two witch doctors.*

She glanced up towards the sky and let out a heavy breath. *You are the knife edge.* She charged in the direction of the thickest tree, blade held low, straining her eyes to spot him in the darkness. A shift in the clouds allowed a small spray of light. Just enough to spot the silhouette. A big witch doctor with a blowpipe. She doubled her speed.

Startled by the suddenness of her charge, the witch doctor fumbled, trying to fix a dart for his blowpipe.

Her lips tightened. *The one good thing about having ill luck. You learn not to hesitate when good luck comes your way.*

She jutted out to the right, expecting a dart from behind, then immediately moved further right.

'Die,' she shouted, raising her blade high.

The witch doctor squeezed the blowpipe. She ducked and, mercifully, the dart flew overhead. He fumbled for the dagger at his hip, but it was all too slow.

Her blade punctured his stomach and pinned him to the tree. She pressed her mouth to his ear. 'You killed six rangers today. *Six.*'

The witch doctor opened his mouth, spattering blood. 'Seven,' he spat.

Nataré ducked. The dart from behind struck the witch doctor in the forehead.

She turned in the direction of her second assailant. She could not make him out among the trees. She took cover behind a wide tree, breathing hard.

She called out into the darkness. 'Before I reach you, my guess is you blow two darts my way. Three at the very most. So, if you miss three times, you are dead.'

A dart blew past the tree. The witch doctor knew exactly where she was.

'I won't miss again,' came a hell-deep voice.

She narrowed her eyes and let out a heavy breath.

She charged in the direction of the voice, not completely sure where the witch doctor was.

She snaked right and left, waiting for a dart to fly. Pain exploded in her right arm and she glanced down, feeling the wet trail of blood dripping from her elbow. She was hit. A black-feathered dart protruded from her forearm. Red feathers were instant death, but black? What were black feathers?

She snarled, moving forward as her arm went numb. The dark figure of a man appeared in the near distance. The blowpipe was fixed like a flute in his lips as he aimed to shoot. She moved the moment his cheeks expanded; a sharp step left. Another flare of pain shot through her shoulder. *Hit again.*

The blood in her veins slowed. Pain marched up her arm and shoulder like a colony of ants. Her blade clattered to the ground as she lost her footing. She fell back and stared up at the sky, death certain.

The deep voice came again. 'Don't worry, I'm not supposed to kill you.'

He stepped fully into view, standing over her like death. She gritted her teeth and tried to stand, but her muscles had surrendered to the dart's poison.

'My Master has a task for you,' said the witch doctor.

The world faded to black.

★ ★ ★

Nataré woke to the smell of boiling meat. The pain in her forearm and shoulder had disappeared without a trace.

An open cookpot sat atop a small fire, producing an audible hiss and a great uprush of steam. A man stood with his back to her, stirring the cookpot with a long wooden spoon.

'Do you know who I am?' said the man without looking back.

She raised an eyebrow. 'How in Dara's name would I know who you are?'

The man glanced over his shoulder and she caught the twinkle of moonlight in his obsidian-black eyes. He stopped stirring and turned around. He was tattooed from neck to waist and on his bare chest was the imprint of two large eyes. He moved with slow, sinewy ease.

Nataré stifled a gasp as she met his eyes. 'Jarishma,' she muttered.

He smiled and tilted his head. 'In the flesh; though I must say, these days I prefer to be called the jungle mage. Skip the exposition.'

She set her jaw. Any other day she would dismiss the man as an impostor, but something in his slow, sinewy bearing and easy command of witch doctors gave her pause.

'What do you want with me?' she asked.

He narrowed his eyes. 'I need you to help me find someone.'

'What makes you think I would be any help with that?'

'I've seen the way you hunt witch doctors. You are ... relentless.'

'I'll hunt witch doctors until the forest is clean of them. You know their work,' she said, glaring at the pot.

Jarishma followed her gaze. He raised an eyebrow, then laughed.

'Oh no, that isn't ... That's just goat meat,' he said, and chuckled. 'I do not get involved with any of that sort of *work*.'

Nataré dusted down her riding trousers. 'My companion. What became of him?'

The man looked perplexed. 'Death, I presume. I told them to bring you, I don't know anything about a companion.'

Six sentries lost to witch doctors. Nataré bit down on her lip. 'So that's it, then? You want me to help you?'

'Yes.'

'What if I say no?'

He smiled. 'I don't think you want to do that. Besides, you know the young man I am trying to find. Quite well I believe.'

Nataré raised an eyebrow. 'Who?'

'His name is Rumi Voltaine.'

Nataré's heart lurched. The man smirked, noting the effect the name had on her.

'What do you want with him?'

'That is for me to know. Don't worry, you can take him back to the Eredo when I am done with him.'

Nataré narrowed her eyes. The man *was* Jarishma. If he knew about the Eredo, he had to be.

'If you are who you say you are, why are you working with witch doctors?' she asked.

Jarishma frowned, scratching at his neck. 'When you have fought the battles I have fought, you learn that no weapon is beneath you.'

Nataré considered the man. Always ask for something in return, her mother used to tell her.

'If I am to help you, then I must ask something in return.'

'Go on.'

'Tell me where their lair is. The witch doctors, the jazzmen. Tell me where their lair is and I will find Rumi for you.'

With his wooden spoon, he drew from the goat meat broth and drank deep, tilting his head back.

'We have a deal.'

19

Billisi and the Son

RUMI

Rumi woke to the clatter of horse hooves. He thought it was the chariot of death coming to take him home. It wasn't. It was an Odu man and woman on a mule.

Kaat was at Rumi's side and he had soiled himself again, but the rain had stopped. The man looked at the tree-struck carriage and gasped as Rumi shifted on the ground.

The woman screamed. 'He's moving!'

The man dismounted and approached with all the deliberate caution of a houndsman approaching a rabid.

'Are you all right?' the man asked.

Rumi stared blankly at him. *Does it look like I'm all right?*

'Can you walk?' the man asked instead.

Rumi groaned as he moved his legs to test his will to stand. His knees were weak, but not from pain. He nodded.

The man took a step closer, then froze. Rumi followed his eyes to the bloody black halberd and the freshly dug graves.

The man stepped back. 'What happened?'

Rumi juggled the truth in his head. This was no time for the truth.

'Our carriage crashed.'

'Why were you riding here, way out in the Nyme?' He

climbed back onto the mule. 'Let's go. Could be a flytrap. There's robbers in this bush,' he said to his companion.

'It's no trap, I promise. Please,' Rumi begged.

The woman looked to the man. 'Tope, he's afraid. Look at him.'

'Young Odu boys are capable of anything these days; don't be fooled. That doesn't belong to him,' he said, pointing at the bloodstained carriage.

The man turned the mule away and kicked it into a trot. Rumi screamed a feral, desperate scream, but the man did not turn back. He was abandoned. He kept screaming. Screaming until his voice broke and his throat ran dry.

He woke before the sun and lay still on the jungle floor, dirty and hungry. With every small move he made, he felt pain.

The sun stirred in the east, colouring the sky and spreading light. Rumi sat up with his decision made. The halberd still lay by the unmarked grave. That would be too cumbersome, too painful. He did not want to suffer, he wanted something swift. A song sounded in his head. The last song in *Belize's Dialogues*.

> *I want to run in the forest without trees,*
> *I want to taste the honey without bees,*
> *I want to sleep, to sleep without dreaming,*
> *I want to live, to live without breathing.*

Rumi sang softly as his vision grew blurry from tears. *Why did this happen?*

He turned away from the halberd and searched the wreckage. He found his drums and oud fastened in their case beneath crystalline white specks of shattered bone. He tossed the case aside.

He needed something small and sharp. Amongst the torn fragments of his kaftan he finally found something that would serve. Broken cut-glasses and a miraculously intact decanter. He opened the decanter and threw back the liquor in one long gulp, then he moved towards a broken cut-glass. His toe thudded against something thick on the carriage floor.

He pulled back ragged cloth to find his mother's burlap sack. He opened it. The book from her secret room was there, her writing scrawled against the front. Why had she brought it along? She must have known, even then, that all was not well with the night.

He opened the book. On its first page was an index with the names of dozens of Agbara. He ran his finger down the index till he found the page marked for the *Book of Kamanu*. Then he started to read.

In the old days we lived among you in plain sight. You knew the names that we told you and some of you knew the names that we didn't tell you. We cared for you, protected you, taught you and loved you. Centuries passed and soon your adoration turned to jealousy and hate. You thought yourselves wise and thought us foolish for loving you and not destroying you. So many of you turned from us, plotted our demise, abandoned our teachings. Even so, Dara commanded us to love you and to protect you. You were just children, He said; we must protect you, He would say. Some grew tired of Dara's patience and thought we should destroy your kind for your sinful, hateful nature. But Dara was stronger than us all, and the strength of His axe would separate flesh from bone as easily as you might un-purse your lips to speak. There was peace so long as Dara lived, for none of us would chance His arm; no one would risk His fury.

Now Dara was not born alone. He had a sister. I will tell you her name, the name that few know and those who know never speak. Billisi.

Billisi saw Dara's love for humanity and hated people, for she loved and desired Dara as a wife loves and desires her husband and not as a sister should love her brother. Jealousy swelled in her heart and she gathered those who hated people to her cause. Those who joined her were powerful. They knew the names of many things and could rip the hearts from the flesh of a person as easily as you might pluck an apple from its tree. They conspired and plotted to bring an end to humanity, for Billisi was jealous of Dara's love for them.

But Dara believed in people and thought that if He searched the earth, He would find one of pure heart who would set our minds to rest. So, He set about making His way from village to village in search of one of pure heart. He saw many wicked, sinful people and was fought, robbed and stoned in every village, for He appeared like a man in order to know the truth of your condition, but His skin was like dark honey and they had never seen His like before. Yet He did not give up and went from village to village, looking deep into the hearts of people.

Now there was a woman, her name was Jahmine. Pure of heart and though her life was hard, she loved Dara and walked in the Darani way. She cared for the sick, and though many died in her care – for she could not save them all – many too were spared. One day, Dara wandered into her village. He was robbed and beaten, and His robbers stripped Him bare and hanged Him from a tree, leaving Him to die.

But Jahmine came upon Him and cut Him down from the tree. She wept for Him, for she knew that He was in pain and though she had never known Him, she cared for

Him for she knew He had been set upon by wicked men. She took Him home and prayed for three days, not stopping to eat or to drink, and Dara heard her prayers and His heart was moved by her tears. On the third day, when life had nearly left Him, Dara reached out for His axe and became whole again. Though His axe brought death, it could also bring life, and when His hands touched the axe, His wounds were healed.

Jahmine knelt before Dara and saw that He was like no man she had ever seen, His hair was dark as the midnight sky and His skin was honey and mahogany, and when she looked upon Him she loved Him in a new way she had not loved before. Dara saw her heart and knew that He was loved, and when He looked upon her, He saw all the beauty in her kind. So, Dara lay with Jahmine and blessed her, and Jahmine's stomach grew heavy with new life.

When Billisi discovered this, she was consumed with a fiery rage, for she longed for Dara's seed.

And Jahmine bore twins that were a joy to look upon, for Dara and Jahmine held all the parts of beauty. The girl she gave the name Shirayo, and the boy bore the name Azuka. There was feasting and dancing in both worlds, for the children were as beautiful as Jahmine and as strong as Dara.

Dara, in His heart, knew the ways of man were crooked and He saw in Azuka and Shirayo the ones that would redeem humanity. Through them people could be reborn and washed clean of iniquity.

But Billisi plotted evil.

When it came Billisi's turn to present her gift to Dara, she gave Him a necklace that shone bright enough to shame the sun, with a crown as brilliant as the stars in the sky. Dara saw that it was finely made and thanked her and blessed her three times. But when Dara wore the necklace, He was bound up at His neck and confounded by His crown. He could not move to lift His axe. And Billisi loosed all manner of evil upon both worlds as Dara lay bound up, separating substance from shadow such that people could not be whole. Billisi's demons roamed both worlds freely and laid siege to humanity.

But Dara's power had no bounds and He broke His bondage, and when He did an almighty sound filled the air that sang songs of His vengeance and fury. When Billisi heard this, she looked upon the children for she knew Dara would not spare her if He caught her. So she stole Azuka and Shirayo from their secret place. When she looked upon Shirayo, she tore her to pieces for the child looked much like her mother Jahmine and Billisi's heart was heavy with jealousy. And she bound Azuka to her bosom and fled from the Higher World.

And Dara heard this and seized up His axe. He killed all those who had joined Billisi and pursued Billisi to the Lower World, His mouth filled with a promise of vengeance, for His sister had become an abomination unto Him.

But though Dara was strong, Billisi was fast and as thunder follows lightning, He could not catch Billisi. Everywhere He followed her He saw that she had left death and sorrow. Dara wept, for His own sister had brought this upon humanity. So everywhere He went He stole her names and stories from the minds of humanity, for He knew that Billisi had brought much pain upon them and their hearts were broken with grief.

But still Dara could not catch Billisi. He called upon the most powerful of us and sent us to all the ends of the earth so that we might alert Dara if we found His sister, and hold her long enough for Him to descend.

I waited for Billisi by the Brown Sea. A part of me wished I would see her, but a bigger part wished I would not, for we all knew it meant near certain death. I was not the first to see her; many had before and were dead before they could sound their horns or block her path. Billisi came to lay destruction beyond the Brown Sea and when I saw her coming, I sounded a horn, for I had the power of sight. Dara heard my horn and knew that she was upon us. Billisi came towards me with snarling teeth that were stained red with blood and eyes that had seen death and liked it. But I stood firm, and though I wanted to flee I could not, for my faith in Dara was greater than my fear of Billisi. As the heat of her fury burned my skin, the skies parted and He came, my salvation.

He descended upon Billisi so fiercely that the ground broke for Him to pass. He drove her deep into the depths of hell, binding her up with the necklace she had given Him as a gift. And when Dara saw her, He wept because Billisi was His sister, but she had done many evil things and had become an abomination unto Him. He pleaded with her to repent so that He could pass judgement and kill her quickly instead of executing the full judgement that she deserved.

But Billisi's heart was blackened to its core and when she answered there was no repentance in her voice. 'I love you, my brother, and I always will. But I have nothing to repent for. From the crooked wood of humanity, no straight thing was formed. I have done righteous things on my travels; I only wish I had killed many more, for they are like meat and drink to me. I have brought such sorrow upon this world, I have separated bone from flesh and substance from shadow and drunk blood to belly bursting. I have supped on babies and torn the hair and flesh from the heads of fathers and mothers. I have swallowed men and women whole and set fields alight with their limbs for firewood to dance a merry dance. All was gain. We shared a womb once, brother; share my bed now. Lay with me, brother, that you may have true knowledge of me and know the great things I have done. We failed with humanity once; let us try again.'

And Dara wept, for His sister had become an abomination. He threw her into the Hellmouth and bound her up, the gates never to be opened again.

When Billisi was bound He called upon His son. He was still only a boy but appeared like a young man, for he was the son of Dara and the strength in his arm was much. He told His son that he was to be the redeemer of humanity, and that through his death in the Lower World, they may live anew, connected to the Higher World forever. He told His son that he would hang from a tree for the iniquity of humanity.

But Azuka had seen all manner of things on his travels and had no love for humanity. He had seen people offer their children in sacrifice to Billisi when she came to destroy their lands and seen them kill one another trying to escape her fury. He had seen rich men and women lock their neighbours out, thinking their walls and gates would protect them and expecting all around them to die. He had seen things no child should see, not even the son of Dara.

So Azuka looked upon humanity as a stain upon the earth, undeserving of a connection to the things of the Higher World.

I was given charge of the boy to raise him up, to prepare for the day he was to hang from a tree and redeem the Lower

World with his blood. I looked upon the boy and saw the splendour of his parents in him, though his eyes had been darkened by the evils of the world. I taught him our ways; how to change his form, how to steal a piece of someone's mind, how to command a thing, how to wield the shadow. He learned quickly, for Billisi had already taught him many things. He could break a man from the inside and run faster than the wind as Billisi did. But he could do other things too, for he was the son of Dara: he could give a man long life by speaking it, or great strength, or beauty. I loved him as a son and gave him all of me, but it was not enough.

On the day that he was to redeem the world and give himself as a sacrifice to humanity, he refused. He spat in his father's eye and in the glare of all the Agbara said, 'The crooked wood of man will not be watered with my blood.' He chastised his own father and said that the love of people had weakened him, and he departed from the Higher World. Even I, who had helped raise him, wanted to end him, but the Skyfather loves without ending and would let no one lift a finger against His son. Had we known the child meant to release Billisi, perhaps we would have risked the Skyfather's wrath.

Dara let His son go, believing that if he travelled through the Lower World as He once had, he would find one pure of heart and see the wrong in his ways. But the son loosed Billisi. When she once again rose to break the world, Dara had to drag her back to the Hellmouth Himself.

This time He became the guardian of her gate and tender of her fire, for only He could sit in the heart of the Hellmouth. He entrusted his axe to the Agbara to bring back His son and to redeem humanity.

But the son was stronger than us all. He left the Higher World and no one could stop him. Many joined him; others fled into the Lower World waiting for their salvation. The son took on the name Palman and named himself the one true god. He stole many names from mankind, for he did not want them to pray to the Agbara, for that gave us our power. He set hunters upon the earth to kill all the Agbara who would not kneel for him, and he roams the earth in search of Dara's axe.

And Dara sits at the gates of the Hellmouth, tending the flame. Billisi cursed Him and offered herself and did all manner of things to stop Him, but He would not hear for she was an abomination unto Him and only He could sit in the Hellmouth and hold her there. The son seeks the axe, but the Agbara will protect it to the death and beyond, until the day it must be lifted again.

The Skyfather lies beneath, but his axe will rise again and we will rescue Him from the depths.

Rumi closed the book, his temple throbbing. It took a lot to stop himself from reading more. It was known by all Darani that death of the worst order came to those who stole the knowledge of the Agbara without instruction.

He went to the wrecked carriage and picked up a broken cut-glass. He dropped to his knees in the mud, right over the ground where Yami had died. Her essence would be strongest there.

He had no divination tray and no water to wash his hands, but he had a voice. He drove the cut-glass across his chest, opening a long line above the heart, and let the blood trail from the wound to pool in the forest soil. Yami had warned him against blood covenant, but prayer was not enough. Not for this.

As his blood dripped on his mother's grave, he didn't pray for wisdom or for strength. He didn't give thanks or ask for blessings. He prayed for vengeance. To feel the Priest of Vultures' blood on his hands, under his nails. He shouted, affirming his violence, petitioning all the Agbara of blood and war. *I will give my life to have my vengeance.*

When he finished, he found his fists clenched and his teeth gritted. He wouldn't die there; he couldn't. Yami had made a sacrifice. It had to count for something. He had promised an Agbara not to make a fool of her.

The wheelman and the Bishop of Basmine had both seemed intent on sending him the same message: *Palman reigns.* Rumi knew enough to tell coincidence from conspiracy. Those things were connected. They would pay in blood for that connection.

He had always thought himself strong, but when the moment came he had been found wanting. He was not who he thought he was. Never again. If he saw the Priest of Vultures again, he would be ready.

The word *shadowwielder* stirred in his mind. That was what Yami had been, a *shadowwielder*. Juju that made her fast and strong, black shadows teeming from her skin. He was certain that it was the same juju Ayeesha had spoken of him learning if he went to the Eredo.

With that sort of juju, he could kill them. He *would* kill them. The Priest of Vultures, the man with the iron eye and the Bishop of Basmine. All those who had brought him this pain would pay in blood. *Palman, son of Dara, I will learn if your godhunters can die. I swear it on my blood.*

He put the book in his oud case and picked up the prize purse from the Governor's Ball. It was fat with cowries that now seemed almost worthless. He would trade all the cowries in the world to have never gone to the Governor's Ball.

He buried the purse in his oud case and picked up the halberd, running his palm over the blade. It wasn't cold like steel. It had a faint warmth, like a tree, or a hillside. Something living.

He could not carry everything if he was to walk. He would have to forsake either the oud, the drums or the halberd. His choice was an easy one. He fastened the halberd to his back, summoned Kaat and left the drums and oud in the mud.

20

Strangers

ALANGBA

'Tea, anyone?' Alangba asked.

No one responded. Alangba shrugged and hooked his kettle over the iron handle above the cookfire.

The silence was near complete but for the crackle of wood under the fire and the slow-rising hiss of the kettle coming to boil. They had been on the road two days and Okafor had not caught up to them yet. Everyone was getting edgy.

'Who drinks tea in a country hot as this?' Princess Falina asked.

Alangba raised an eyebrow. 'You can never go wrong with tea, Omoba, no matter the weather.'

No Music stood away from the light, sharpening his knife in the shadow of a large mango tree. The man spent nearly all the time he wasn't killing preparing to kill.

Beside No Music, Maka Naki sat cross-legged watching the fire as though a wonderful theatre play was taking place in the flame.

'Okafor should arrive tomorrow,' Alangba said.

He had no real way of knowing for sure, but he had to break the silence to keep their focus on the road ahead. Silence had a way of teasing men back into the past and a soldier's past was naught but regrets.

The young ranger Phelix straightened. 'How do you know?'

Alangba frowned. 'You are Twenty-fourth Ranger, Phelix. Twenty-fourth.'

That was enough to put an end to the questions. Enough to say what barely needed saying. Phelix nodded and leaned back to stare at the stars.

No Music suddenly straightened and began to tap his foot. He gripped his knife with murderous intent. Maka rose to his feet too, sword in hand, studying the surrounding trees.

The kettle hissed in a great uprush of steam. Alangba glanced over his shoulder to his scabbard a few paces away.

Phelix stared at No Music. 'What is it?'

A dark figure came hurtling out from the night. No Music put a knife through him like he was bushmeat. Almost like he had been waiting for him to jump. Then came the shouts of violence. *An ambush.*

Somehow, Alangba had the kettle in hand. A man with night-dark skin shot towards him with an upraised spear. Alangba threw the contents of the kettle into the air, scalding the man. The man screamed as Alangba brought the kettle down on his skull with a sharp crunch. Another spearman moved into the light of the fire. No Music put a knife through him so quick that he moved three more paces before he knew he was dead. Alangba darted for his sword. A short spearman lunged for him. They collided and ended in a rolling tangle. Alangba gained the upper hand and started to strangle the man. He stared into the man's eyes and squeezed tighter, fingers crushing the man's throat stone. The man's eyes bulged and his pupils rolled. He scratched against Alangba's grip. The fighting behind them faded to soundlessness. All Alangba could see was the man's bulbous eyes.

When the man's arms fell limp to the side, Alangba let out a heavy breath and rose to his feet. The princess screamed as a spearman raised his weapon. Alangba moved as the spearman struck. He took the spear in the shoulder but rolled with the attack so the spear broke off at the handle. Alangba kicked the spearman back then snatched the spear-tip from his shoulder and buried it in the man's skull.

The princess's eyes widened as she looked up at him. 'You saved me,' she breathed.

Alangba met her gaze. 'Duty comes before death, Omoba. I would lay my life down for you a thousand times if it only meant you could live once.'

Her mouth didn't close as she watched him, her eyes wide with awe.

No Music watched with a face which – though festooned with blood – was completely inexpressive. Maka wore a solemn look as he pushed his sword into the soil. The ambush was over. A futile, ill-fated attempt. Alangba looked over the campsite. He counted eight dead including one of their own. Phelix lay lifeless with a spear protruding from his back. *Phelix*. Any smart betting man would have wagered his coin on Phelix being the first to die, but it still came as an unpleasant surprise. Their assailants were scattered dead around the still burning cookfire. You could tell No Music's work by looking. The man didn't pretend to be a clean fighter. Three had met death at the end of No Music's knife; stabbed in every unexpected place. Groin, armpit, eye socket. The idle handiwork of a savant in skulduggery. Maka's sword had taken care of the rest, save for the two Alangba had killed.

Alangba bit down on his lip staring at the lifeless corpse of the one he had killed. 'Serves him right.'

'Robbers,' Maka muttered. 'Not very good ones.'

He was right. They were all pointedly young. Barely a muff of just-begun chin hair between them. Armed with crude instruments of violence; sticks sharpened to killing points, stones flattened for clubbing.

Alangba waved Maka forward. 'Look around, make sure there aren't any more of them waiting in the bushes.'

Maka plucked his sword from the ground, saluted and back-tracked into the shadows.

'Everyone, into the wagon,' Alangba said. 'We will be moving soon.'

That left Alangba with No Music. Suddenly Alangba wished he had sent No Music away instead. Being alone with No Music was *awkward*. He gestured an instruction to Phelix's corpse and No Music knew what to do. Carefully dressing and wrapping the body, before placing it on the still-burning cookfire. They had expected casualties on this mission. In truth, with the delay in Okafor's arrival, it was a surprise it had taken this long for someone to die. All the same, it never got easy to look into a dead man's eyes when you had known him alive.

He muttered a quiet prayer for Phelix. *May the fire burn your sins away and the ashes burn evermore.* A plea for Dara to accept him into paradise. Phelix hadn't killed any young boys, after all; he had died with his hands clean. So, there was hope for him.

'Third Ranger,' Maka called, 'I found someone.'

Alangba glanced back. Maka led a young girl into the fire-light, her silver dress and leather farmer boots caked in mud and blood.

'We need help,' she snapped, heaving for breath as if she had been running hard.

'Calm down,' Maka said, 'the Third Ranger will hear you out.'

Alangba locked eyes with her. 'What is it, girl? What are you doing out here?'

'Our carriage ... was attacked,' she said, still panting. 'Demons and monsters ... we need to help my friends.'

'Slow down, girl. Catch your breath and talk to me.'

The girl steadied herself and sucked in a deep breath. 'Our carriage was attacked by a man with bleached white skin. Yami tried to fight them but she can't do it alone. My friend Rumi was there, too. We need to help them.'

Alangba shot Maka a curious look. 'A man with bleached white skin, you say?'

She nodded. 'And demon eyes. He wore—'

'Nothing but white cloth,' Alangba finished, 'stitched by the cleanest hands.'

She licked her teeth. 'Yes.'

Maka frowned. 'She's lying, Third Ranger. Trying to lead us into an ambush.'

Alangba walked over to the wagon and unlocked the latch to a cage which was built to hold a dozen prisoners. Ijere crept quietly out, extending his paws in a catlike stretch. 'We shall see about that. Take me to them,' Alangba said.

21

The Book of Gu

RUMI

The trail left by the carriage was faint, but Kaat had the way of it. The longer they walked, the more Rumi became aware of how deep the carriage driver had taken them into the Nyme. The trees stretched tall, shutting out the sunlight. Stories of the forest repeated in his mind. The Nyme: the Bush of Spirits in which no breed of animal was missing. Home to every vicious thing on earth.

Rumi should have been stricken with terror, but life becomes surreal when you have lost something as precious as your family. He walked in a ghostly haze, unable to think of anything but Yami's voice.

Day turned to night and the moon hung heavy in the sky. They rounded a large tree and Kaat's ears shot up. Rumi froze. Something had moved in the bushes.

He glanced over his shoulder and caught the glistening reflection of moonlight in two sets of bright yellow eyes.

Twin cats stared at him with all the attention of a surgeon stitching flesh. There was something unnerving about their gaze. He stamped his foot to scare them away, but they were unperturbed. Kaat did a better job of things. A low, rumbling growl and a flash of teeth sent the cats scampering away.

Rumi watched them disappear into the bush as he ran a hand through Kaat's mane. 'Good girl.'

Kaat gave a low, deep roar and Rumi gave a start. 'Kaat?'

The lionhound looked up at him and he realised the sound hadn't come from her. He stepped back from the bushes only a moment before a lion lunged forward.

Rumi raised the halberd in a desperate swipe but the lion hadn't come close. Rumi's heart thumped at the sight of it. Tall as a man and cut from thick muscle with radiant mane. The rightful king of the jungle.

'Lower your weapon,' came a deep voice.

A man stepped out from the bushes. He had dark, calculating eyes and a face that could have been carved from stone. He wore the scabbard at his waist as easily as one would a favoured shirt. Other men came into the moonlight. Every one of them had the stance and shoulders of those accustomed to violence and hard times. Faces like wolves, eyes like knife-slits. Rumi looked from the lion to the green-robed men and could not decide who was more dangerous.

'Rumi,' came a familiar voice.

Only then did Rumi see her. 'Renike,' he breathed.

It was like having the knife pulled back from your throat. An almost metaphysical relief.

Renike ran towards him and he gathered her into an embrace. 'Yami? Morire?' Renike whispered.

Rumi's silence was the answer. He closed his eyes. He could feel her pain like heat. Seeing the face of it would have set him alight and burned into his mind.

Her grip tightened on his ragged kaftan. 'Shege,' she breathed. 'I am … I am so sorry, Rumi.'

Rumi opened his eyes. She thought of him even at the centre of her hurt. He pulled her closer and let the tears loose. Violent tears; long buried emotions spilled out as the seams in his heart split open. But he was not alone, and that made it better.

The silence fanned out and stretched over them as they wept together. It was a long moment, before any words came. The killers around them didn't interrupt. They gave them their moment, respecting the silence.

When the tears were shed, the hard-faced man stepped forward and met Rumi's eye. 'Follow me,' he said. It was more a command than a recommendation.

Rumi followed until they came to a campsite fronted by two large wagons, each hitched to a tall, tacked up horse. He counted six people in the camp altogether, including Renike and the leader who walked with a lion.

'Get some rest,' the leader said. 'We will speak more of what you saw tomorrow.'

Rumi wanted to ask questions, but his throat was hoarse and his mind was riddled with sobering thoughts. After wandering idly for a few minutes, he found space beside Renike at the edge of the fire. Silently, he lay down his head to rest.

He dreamed of Gu, the Agbara of iron and war, the Eversmith. Resplendent with muscled arms and legs thicker than trees. In his right hand was a great warhammer; in his left, burning hot coals. His eyes were pearls of deep, endless, obsidian darkness.

I am the Eversmith, the first and the last, the noise in the engineer's machine. The furnace is hot, calling forth your iron. You must be remade. You have my instruction. Read the Book of Gu.

Rumi woke in a pool of sweat, his head throbbing from words that sounded in his mind and not his ears. *You must be remade.* The words rang in his head.

He fumbled in his oud case for the *Sakosaye* and turned to the *Book of Gu*. Then he started to read.

I was only a boy when Dara called me to forge the axe. I could fashion iron like no other. It was my gift, as the Eversmith. An axe fit for the Sky Father must be whole as He is whole, it must bring peace and war all at once, silence and sound at the same time.

The Eversmith was called to war; I knew nothing of peace. In my boyhood I knew only the breaking of nations and the hunting of great beasts. But the gift of design was also mine; of ingenuity, of creativity. These things must a smith have in great measure. So I sought out Elegi, the Wise one, for she had the answers to all things that had answers. She welcomed me with palm wine and agbalumo, as was her way, and I rested in her palace for six days before I made my petition.

'Elegi the Wise, where shall the Agbara of war find peace?' I asked.

She was quiet, for she had known my petition long before I made it. She saw things before they could be seen.

She told me that to find peace, I must find Ododo, the unending love. I had known the love of a woman through the wild heat of Itara, the scattering of seeds, the swift boil of blood. But I had never known the love of Ododo, the unending love that suffers any sacrifice. In war we called Ododo the folly of the bonobos, the surest road to slaughter. A warrior weds his weapon and none else.

I urged her to find me another challenge, a mountain to climb, a great beast to slaughter, an army to vanquish. She chased me from her palace.

And so, I set about on the search for Ododo.

My roaming led me first to the mountain lands where I

met the mighty Athena, strong of arm and broad of breast. As powerful as I, and as intelligent. She charged me to learn the dance of the Samai.

But I was no dancer; my ways were brutish and crude with no finesse. So I lived and learned with the Samai for a half score of years, learning to jump and bow and balance. With time I learned to leap from my toes and balance on the balls of my feet, to spin with the poise of a spider.

When I returned to dance for Athena, she clapped and laughed, but when the music was done, she could not love me, and I could not love her.

So, I roamed the earth again and came to the Sahar where the women are honey-brown with skin that sizzled at the touch. I met the great Shasha, fire in flesh, unmatched beauty, queen of cats and all the parts of seduction. She was every song written and more, the empress of the eye of man.

She held me under her spell for many years, teaching me things, showing me her art – the love of Itara. I was her willing muse in the cold wind of harmattan. When at the Great Banquet of Jebu, the Lord of Horns grew hungry for her love and sought to take it by force, I broke his leg with my hammer. She thanked me, for I had defended her, but in striking the Lord of Horns I had become a criminal to her people. She spurned me and sent me away, for she did not love me, not Ododo love.

I crossed the waters to where men made fire from powder and waged eternal war. There I met Billisi, wicked and wild, hungry for blood and brimming with adventure. She urged me to join her, to tear nations apart, break strong men and make sport of death. Though I found her beautiful, the delight of death did not warm me any longer. The breaking of man without cause now seemed to me an unfruitful exercise of rascality.

Billisi scorned me and scratched me and cursed me. I learned that hers was the lust of blood and the unholy love for the Sky Father. She made a mockery of my petition, damning me to hell and promising to scratch my tongue from my mouth should I see cause to speak to her. She could not love me.

When a generation had passed in my search, I returned to Elegi in disgrace, dreading the scorn of the Sky Father.

I had toured the world and failed. I had searched the ends of the earth for love and been found undeserving, discharged without merit. She welcomed me again with palm wine and agbalumo and I sat to tell her of all my failures, in hope that she would send me on a new quest. She listened silently to my story, to all the things I had seen and learned. For each failure I described, she asked me to demonstrate what I had learned. She saw that I could dance and play the harp and recite beautiful words.

On the third day in her palace, when I had told every part of my story, my eyes were laden with pain, but when I looked into the eyes of Elegi, she smiled.

She had seen me coming, the true smith of my story inspecting me after the forge. Only now would I be acceptable as a husband to her. We were iron and furnace, locked in unending love, renewing each other, burning impurities away. When we made love, I learned that there was a place higher and more precious than the Higher World, but we could only inhabit it for a night. We found peace, and from the furnace of our love bed two were born. Biku, the axe we forged of bone and bronze, and our son Xango, the first Alaafin. And so began Mgbedike, the time of the brave.

Rumi had heard many stories about the fabled love of Gu and Elegi and the making of Dara's great axe Biku, but he had not known that Xango was the son of Gu and Elegi. The story told him nothing of the Priest of Vultures or his connection to the Palman priesthood. He slammed the *Sakosaye* shut.

His heart drummed in his chest. The *Sakosaye* was the key to so many questions he had. To learn about the shadowless man; to learn about the Originate and of gods and godhunters. To find his brother. Those answers were all somewhere in the book. He gritted his teeth, fighting back the urge to read more. One way or another he would have his answers.

22

We Move

RUMI

Rumi cleared his throat, forcing himself to finish the story. 'And then—' He hesitated. 'And then I buried her,' he finished. It felt strange to say the words aloud.

Alangba studied the black halberd as he listened. 'This was her weapon?'

Rumi nodded. 'Yes, it was.'

His eyes darkened as though he had got a letter with bad news. 'And where did you get this?' he asked, pointing at the priestess's cowrie Rumi wore around his neck.

Rumi raised a hand to shade his eyes from the sun. 'A priestess gave it to me.'

A handsome but hard-faced man appeared at Alangba's side. He gave Rumi an appraising look and snorted his disappointment. 'Do you believe him?'

Alangba narrowed his eyes. 'I think I do, Maka.'

Maka shook his head with disbelief. 'This isn't what we bargained for, Alangba. None of it. We were only meant to bring one man back. First it was the lion, then the princess. Now this?'

'Calm down.'

'We cannot take them with us,' Maka said.

Alangba nodded. 'Yes, we can. We will if we have to. There

is providence in this,' he said, holding the halberd up to the light. 'This blade is shadowsteel. Do you not see who he is? What he is?'

'It does not matter, Alangba. I can take them back across the Neck myself. They can get a caravan to Alara from there.'

'He has that book. I have heard of only a few of those in existence – how many priestesses alive can write a *Sakosaye*? That alone is worth keeping safe.'

'Just take it then,' Maka snapped.

Rumi wrapped his hands protectively around his case with the book in it.

Maka smirked. 'You think you can stop us from taking anything we want from you?'

Alangba touched Maka's hand. 'Don't.' He turned to Rumi. 'We won't take anything from you and we won't take you anywhere you don't want to go.'

Alangba raised his chin and stared over at the woman sitting behind Maka. A stern-faced one, with royal tattoos across her neck. More than once, Rumi had heard them call her Omoba. *A princess. But of which tribe?*

Maka stepped close. 'What about the vultures? The boy said he had vultures after him. What sort of omen is that? We aren't sorcerers, Alangba. We are soldiers.'

'We are the Chainbreakers, Maka. That means we break *every* chain. For Dara's sake, look at the boy – he still has bloodstains on his clothes. Do you forget the day we met, Maka? Are you so quick to forget your own story?'

That made Maka wince and go completely still. 'I haven't forgotten,' he said after a long moment. All the frustration seemed to leak out of him as he gave a deep sigh. 'You are right. I just... everything seems to be happening all at once right now.'

Alangba nodded. 'Sometimes it goes that way.' He touched Maka's arm. 'But duty comes before death.'

Maka gave a deep sigh and touched his heart. 'Duty comes before death.'

Alangba watched him leave, then turned to Rumi. 'What will it be, boy? Do you wish to return to Alara or do you ride with us?'

Mention of Alara reminded Rumi of something that had once seemed so important. He reached into the oud case and pulled out the sack full of cowries. 'I need to get this to Alara somehow. To a woman called Mama Ayeesha.'

Alangba shrugged. 'Easily done. There is a town not far from here, with people we trust – I will be sending my letters there. If I send it, you have my word that it will arrive safely. That is, if you choose to come with us.'

Rumi raised an eyebrow. 'Come with you where?'

Alangba leaned forward, lowering his voice. 'To the Eredo.'

Mention of the word made the cowrie at his neck draw heat and Rumi's entire body bristled.

Alangba smiled seeing his reaction.

It wasn't just that so many had told Rumi to go there. That alone was enough. But there was something more compelling that made his answer irresistible. Something Mama Ayeesha had said. *Fighting with juju*. That was it – that was how he would do what needed doing.

Rumi cleared his throat. 'What is the Eredo exactly?'

Alangba seemed surprised by the question. He scratched his chin thoughtfully. 'It is a city ... but also a barracks.'

Rumi raised an eyebrow. 'A barracks for what?'

'The war that is to come.'

'With who?'

'The Palmaine.'

192

Rumi snorted. 'It will never happen. The natives are like oil, water and honey. We'd sooner fight ourselves than the Palmaine.'

'The Eredo is ... different,' Alangba said. 'They can make men into shadowwielders.'

Rumi's mind flashed back to shadow streaming from his mother's skin. 'How?'

'That, I do not know.'

'So you're not a shadowwielder?'

Alangba closed his eyes and drew in a sharp breath. 'I was too old by the time I came to the Eredo. They do not accept those above the fighting age of sixteen.'

'I'm seventeen,' Rumi said, frowning.

'Then you're too old,' Alangba said.

The vein at Rumi's temple throbbed. 'I *need* to become a shadowwielder.'

'I needed to once. Trust me, you get over it. You can be a sentry, or a guard.' He hesitated. 'Perhaps even a Chainbreaker like Maka and I.'

It wouldn't be enough.

Rumi shook his head. 'No.'

Alangba narrowed his eyes. 'The Shadow Order will not accept you unless you give them reason to make an exception.'

'What sort of reason?'

Alangba bit down on his lip as though deciding whether the truth or a lie was appropriate. 'I don't know.'

Rumi frowned. 'I had hoped you wouldn't say that.'

Alangba leaned forward. 'What is it about being a shadow-wielder that is so important to you?'

Rumi met his eyes. 'Have you ever done something you were ashamed of?'

'We all have.'

'Then you know how it eats at you. How every time you

remember you wince because you cannot believe you made such a pathetic decision. I watched a man attack my mother, beat down my brother, and when the challenge was put to me all I could do was piss myself and watch it happen. I'll carry that shame until my dying breath but I won't make a fool of my mother, I won't let her sacrifice be in vain. One day, the Priest of Vultures is going to come for me and I will look into those dead eyes again. When that day comes, I am going to make almighty amends. Becoming a shadowwielder is the only way I can do Yami right.'

Alangba's eyes didn't move and for a moment, Rumi thought the man hadn't been listening, then he let out a silent breath, reached into his pocket and produced a kola nut. 'I have a friend who might be able to help. I cannot promise you will be accepted but I can give you my word that I will do everything in my power to help you get into the Shadow Order.'

Rumi stared down at the kola nut for a moment, then he took it and broke it in half. 'A fair deal.'

Alangba nodded his affirmation and bit down on his half of kola nut before turning to Renike. 'What about you?'

She raised her chin. 'I go wherever he goes.'

Rumi shook his head. 'Renike, you cannot—'

'You don't tell me what I can and cannot do,' she snapped. 'You think you're the only one who carries shame? Every time I run and hide, someone dies. I am not running or hiding anymore. And I'm not letting you leave me, Rumi. Ever again.'

Her voice had no give in it and there was no sense in trying to convince her.

'All right,' he whispered, 'to the Eredo, then.'

Alangba spoke in a voice that carried to the whole camp. 'We move.'

★

A half hour later, they were on their way. Rumi was huddled in the wagon next to Renike and Kaat. Across from them sat the princess, her face solemn and serious. The last of them was the strange, sinewy man they called No Music. One look at the man's face and Rumi knew there wouldn't be much conversation on this ride. As the wagon rumbled on, there was silence.

Rumi watched the landscape change. They were driving deeper into the Nyme.

A few hours before sunset, the wagons slowed. Alangba called out for a halt and they came to a stop.

A bridge of woven grass lay ahead to cross over the river they called the Neck. Rumi narrowed his eyes; it was obvious their wagons were too wide to cross.

'Everyone out,' Alangba ordered.

They all dismounted, gathering their belongings as they climbed down.

Maka pulled the covering down from the second wagon, revealing a large, steel cage. Rumi had expected to see the lion in it, but instead saw a man.

Under normal circumstances, it would seem insane for a man to be locked in a cage while a lion roamed free, but the temperament of the two told the tale. The way the man strolled around the cage, one would think he was the governor in his parlour. Rumi had never seen anything in a cage remain so utterly unbowed. The man stood like a king at his coronation, resting his back against its iron bars as though he were a special guest. He had an overgrown beard and his once-princely clothes bore the marks of a hard journey, but he retained all the pride of a lion in the jungle.

There was something faintly familiar about the man, but Rumi couldn't quite make out what it was.

Maka led the prisoner out and threw a black sack over his head. He was bound at the wrist, ankle and twice around the neck. Whoever the man was, it was plain they thought he was dangerous.

When the wagons were empty, Maka set fire to them. They watched in wonder as the flame lapped up the wood. The wheels went black, broke apart and charred to ash in the flame. *There's no going back now.*

There were two horses, now cut free from the wagons. They whinnied and snorted their trepidation when faced with the lion but did not flee when they saw no attack was imminent. The first horse, Alangba gave to Renike and the princess. The second, he mounted with Rumi. No Music, Maka and the chained prisoner continued on foot.

They rode up to the front of the bridge. An open calabash, filled to the brim with stew and palm oil, lay idly by the side. Rumi's eyes widened. It was an old Darani tradition. *Food for the spirits.*

His mother used to hide bowls of palm oil, okra and bitter kola at crossroads. Crossroads, she had explained, were a juncture between the spiritual world and the mortal realm. A place of coming and going between the land of the living and the land of spirits. For the calabash to be displayed so openly told Rumi they were truly in the backwaters of Basmine.

Rumi turned to face Alangba.

Alangba gave him a questioning look. 'Something wrong?'

Rumi shook his head. 'No.'

It was plainly a dirty lie. Everything about this felt wrong but with Yami and Morire gone, nothing could ever really be right anymore.

Alangba gave him a blank, studying look then nodded.

They kept moving and before long, plumes of smoke appeared in the distance.

'A village?' Rumi said, his eyes fixed firmly on the smoke.

'It is called Korin,' Alangba said. 'The village of songs. I hope for us to pass the night there. Perhaps Okafor will finally catch up to us.'

A village in the Nyme. Who would ever have believed that such a thing could exist? But Rumi knew now that he had no idea what existed in the world.

Alangba closed his eyes for a moment and had a look he had seen Yami wear more than once. A breath later, the lion was at his side.

Rumi jerked back, his heart pounding at the sight of the beast. Neither Alangba nor the lion paid him any mind. Alangba leaned over to whisper something to the creature and its eyes narrowed in understanding.

Rumi let out a silent gasp.

The lion stretched, catlike against the ground, then strode almost casually into the bushes. Vanishing into the green.

Alangba made a hand signal to No Music. The wiry man nodded, took the prisoner by the neck and dragged him into the bushes too.

Satisfied, Alangba led the rest of them on.

They drew closer to the village and the aroma of roasting chickens and frying plantain wafted through the air. Rumi's stomach growled in awakening.

The village was fortified by a high, red-bricked wall that stretched out at least half a mile on either side of a silver metal gate. Narrow apertures lined the wall, big enough for an arm to pass through. *Arrowslits*.

As they approached the village, the steady tap of a talking drum sounded. Rumi knew enough about talking drum to know when the drumbeat was a call to violence. The villagers were readying themselves. Rumi's heart thudded in his chest as the gate shivered open just enough for a tall, gaunt man to step into view. He took a position at the front of the gate and barred their passage. The gate creaked closed behind him.

'Name yourselves,' the man said.

23

Special

RUMI

The man standing at the gate wore a red tunic decorated with decaying leaves. In one hand he carried a spear and in the other a kola nut. Rumi tried to decide what he was. He had dark brown eyes like Rumi, but was narrow at the nose with far darker skin. Dark as grapes. Not quite Odu; something else.

Behind the tall man, sets of small unblinking eyes peered through the arrow-slits. There would be bows nocked and ready to shower them with arrows if they did anything to the tall man's distaste.

Alangba climbed down from the horse and held two fingers up to the sky. Then he formed a circle with his thumb and forefinger and closed his hand into a fist.

'My name is Alangba Kashir,' he said with his close-fisted hand still raised.

The tall man inspected Alangba slowly, the corners of his mouth tightening before his eyes shifted to Rumi. Alangba nodded to Rumi, urging him forward to introduce himself.

'My name is Irumide Voltaine,' he said, stepping down from the horse.

Alangba stifled a laugh at that, but the tall man's face remained completely expressionless.

'Of what tribe?' the tall man asked.

'I am Odu,' he said.

The man's eyes widened as though Rumi had said he was the king of the Blackfae. He looked Rumi over again from toe to brow.

'Odu, you say?'

'Yes,' Alangba and Rumi said in unison.

The tall man smirked as though they had told him a wonderful joke. He looked back towards the eyes in the arrowslits and threw them a smile before he turned to Renike.

'What is your name?'

Renike blinked, taken aback by the man's sudden smile.

'My name is Renike Denaya of Odu,' she said. 'And who are you?'

Rumi smiled inside. A proper Alara girl, always pushing back.

The others introduced themselves, one after the other. When the tall man set eyes on the Omoba, his whole demeanour changed.

'Omoba,' he breathed, dropping to his knees and burying his face in the sand. 'May you live forever.'

Falina winced and looked away. 'Get up,' she snapped. 'I am no princess.'

The tall man looked up at her and gave her a curious look, then he straightened and turned to Alangba. 'A curious collection you have here. A princess who says she isn't a princess and an Odu who isn't Odu.'

Alangba gave half a smile. 'In this life, it is important to know the truth about yourself. It helps to resist the lies.'

Rumi straightened at those words. He had heard Tinu speak them so many times. He searched Alangba's face but the man lacked even a crumb of expression.

With a grin, the tall man turned to the wall holding up two fingers, then he raised his kola nut high, as though for the eyes in the arrowslit to see. He broke it in plain view and passed it on to each of them in turn.

'We seek passage through Korin,' Alangba said, 'and water, should you be so kind.'

'Our way and our water are yours if you come in peace. Have you any weapons?' the tall man asked.

'Yes,' everyone answered.

Rumi glanced at Renike. She shrugged.

The tall man raised a finger into the air and then made a shape with his hands like a bird in flight.

The gate stuttered open and two younger men carrying a large metal pan scurried into view. They dropped it on the ground in front of them and stepped back. The pan was long enough to sleep on, even for a full-grown man.

'Surrender your weapons. You will have them back when you leave the village,' the tall man said.

Alangba nodded. Rumi pulled his halberd free and dropped it in the metal pan. The shimmering sound of stone on metal rang out as it dropped. The tall man thumbed his chin, regarding the weapon, then nodded to Renike. She tossed in a small knife of her own. It seemed hardly sharp enough to cut stale bread, but it *was* a weapon. Alangba disarmed himself. Two swords, knives, shards of glass, small clubs and half-spears appeared from sleeves and cloth as though every article of his clothing was made to hold a killing instrument. The tall man watched the metal pan fill up with weapons and his smile grew wider with every clang of metal. When the last sickle blade had fallen, the tall man gave Alangba a devilish smile.

'Can never be too safe,' Alangba said.

'Of course,' the tall man said. 'My name is Toro Hoba, and you are welcome to Korin.'

'Thank you,' Alangba said. 'We hoped to pass the night here. We will be moving on at first light.'

'Where to?'

'A place not too far,' Alangba said.

'I don't mean to poke a finger in your soup. I only ask because this is the Nyme. There are parts of the Nyme where even the trees can kill a man. I could arrange an escort for you – for a fee, of course.'

Alangba raised an eyebrow. 'You are very kind. Thank you. But we will not be needing an escort. Only a place to rest our heads, and water, if you don't mind.'

Toro looked them over once more, this time with a hint of suspicion. 'A place to rest … and water. Not a problem.'

Alangba cleared his throat. 'One more thing,' he said.

Toro glanced back at him.

'We will need to exchange our horses,' Alangba said, 'for *special* horses.'

He put a strange emphasis on the word 'special'.

Toro smiled the deep, fraternal grin of a man who understands your private joke and nodded. 'That can be arranged,' he said, turning towards the gate. 'For a fee, of course.'

Alangba nodded. 'Of course.'

'Silekun!'

The gates stuttered open, just wide enough for them to pass two at a time. Rumi studied the gates as they walked through. They bore an inscription, written in each of the four tongues: 'We will sing again'.

Inside there were a dozen men and women putting arrows back into quivers. They all had the same purply-black skin as Toro, all tall and broad. Alangba and Rumi fit in with their height, but Renike was like a banana among plantain. She looked left and right as though trying to gather her bearings, surrounded by elbows.

The people greeted them with subtle bows of the head and hand gestures with touching thumbs as they spilled into the village. Not one of them said a word.

The village was like Alara in some ways. Mudbrick houses in clusters of five or six; open cookfires where men and women made dinner. At the centre of the town there was a podium made of stone, and on top of it there was a copper pot that looked as old as the village itself. There was music everywhere. The sounds of singing, drums, flutes, cymbals filled the air. *Music.*

Rumi went still as the sounds moved through him. When he'd left his drums behind at the wreckage, he couldn't have known the effect that loss would have on him. It was as though he had spurned the perfect lover in a fit of anger. He was desperate for her touch again and here she was having the time of her life without him. He was jealous, desperate and angry all at once. He gritted his teeth. *If it wasn't for music, I would still have Yami and Morire.* He forced the thought of music from his mind. *Those days are over.*

Toro directed them towards a large building down a grass-strewn path. 'Mama Toro will have you for the night.'

Alangba raised an eyebrow. 'Mama Toro?'

Toro smiled. 'Yes, she's my mother.'

'Supporting her business, I suppose.'

'It's our way here. He who shares the kola nut, shares the roof.'

'A good way,' Alangba said.

'The music,' Rumi said. 'Is that why they call this the village of songs?'

'No,' Toro said. 'There is a wedding tonight; Irigwe takes a third husband.'

Rumi raised his eyebrows. *A third husband.* Alangba gave him a quick look that said, *don't ask any more questions.* So he buttoned his lip.

'Let me show you to Mama Toro's.'

As Toro led them inside, Alangba touched Rumi's shoulder and lowered his voice. 'Come with me.'

Renike blinked and opened her mouth to speak but Alangba cut her off. 'He will join you soon. I will bring him to your shared room.'

Renike gave him a hard look then wagged a finger. 'Bring him back.'

Rumi followed Alangba down an alley silhouetted in shadow, where clothes sagged from wash lines above their heads.

Alangba gestured to a door marked with the sign of the crossroads and knocked once. The answer was almost instantaneous. A narrowed-eyed woman with oil-dark skin opened the door and stared up at them.

She rolled her eyes when she saw Alangba. 'You again,' she muttered as she turned to Rumi, 'and you've brought a friend.'

Alangba smiled. 'Good to see you too, Karima.'

Karima gave Rumi a questioning look. 'Name yourself?'

Rumi met her eye. 'Irumide Voltaine.'

She smiled and looked up at Alangba as she beckoned them inside. 'A friend with an interesting name. You know I love interesting names.'

They stepped inside and Karima lit a wall lantern at the far end of the room. It was a cramped, thick-walled room with a low ceiling. The only furniture was a single cabinet table with chipped wood along the edges. No chairs. No windows.

'How can I help you?' Karima asked.

'We have things that need delivering,' Alangba said, 'Letters to go ahead of me and cowries headed to Alara.'

She arched an eyebrow. 'How much in cowries?'

Alangba nodded to Rumi.

Rumi cleared his throat. 'Five hundred and forty cowries needs to get to a woman in Alara called Mama Ayeesha.'

Karima glanced up from her desk and gave Rumi a studying look. 'That's a lot.'

Alangba leaned on the table. 'I've done you a lot of favours.' He hiked his sleeve up a little. 'Hard favours.'

She sighed in exasperation. 'How long are you going to hold that over me?'

Alangba grinned. 'As long as I can.'

She made a sputtering sound with her lips. 'Fine.'

Alangba's grin widened. 'Always a pleasure working with you, Karima.'

'The pleasure is all yours,' she said with a snort.

He reached into his cloak and produced four folded letters with a single golden coin, then he nodded to Rumi.

Rumi pulled open his oud case and placed the sack full of cowries on the table.

Karima looked over the items with a scrutinising eye. 'Mama Ayeesha is it?'

Rumi nodded. 'Yes.'

Karima gave a knowing grin, then nodded her satisfaction. 'I'll make sure it all gets delivered. You have my word.'

She held out kola nut and they sealed it the old way.

Rumi wasn't sure if her word was enough, but Alangba trusted her and that felt as much as he could count on for now. If Alangba had wanted his money he could have taken it half a dozen times over in the days since they had met. The man was no thief, of that he could be sure.

They left everything with Karima and stepped back outside. When they turned down a different street, Rumi leaned in to ask his question.

'Why are you helping me?'

Alangba's face was expressionless. 'For many reasons. Because it gives me purpose. Because I am nothing without purpose – nothing good, anyway. Because your mother gave you a book that I believe is important. Because I don't believe in coincidences. Because I swore oaths deeper than hell to never turn my back on my brethren but most of all, because duty comes before death.'

Rumi looked up at the man, stunned by the casual, unwavering clarity of it all. Never had he encountered a man with such easy sincerity.

'Here we are,' Alangba said nodding ahead. 'Mama Toro's.'

He took Rumi inside and spoke in hand signals to Toro and Mama Toro.

Mama Toro was not what Rumi expected. She was a small woman with radiant grape skin and a bright smile. Even though there was age in the quiet corners of her face and the strands of white in her hair, she was full of life. Rumi wanted to ask exactly how old she was, but couldn't be sure that such a question wasn't an affront to Korin custom so he just gave a courteous nod. She flashed a wide, open-mouthed smile in return and Rumi noticed that she had no tongue.

It was a large house with an open-air courtyard at its centre and thirteen rooms set across three floors. The courtyard had a huge bloodwood tree and the entire house smelled of sweet burning incense and perfumes from lands afar.

Falina was given the largest room on the highest floor, all to herself – Mama Toro would not be persuaded otherwise. The rest of their party were given rooms across the building to share.

The room Mama Toro gave Rumi and Renike had round feather-beds covered in cushions of every size, and a cushioned cot for Kaat. The sweet smell of incense burned clean to ward away mosquitoes and give the room a fresh, comfortable air.

It was a room that made Rumi immediately aware of his own lack of cleanliness. He stepped into the bathroom and confirmed a copper tub and tank of water were available for a bath. He caught sight of himself in the mirror and it thumped his soul. Just a few days ago, he had looked into the mirror with all the pride of a bridegroom prince. Now he didn't like what he saw in it. *A coward.*

24

Nothing Wins Against the Sea Forever

FALINA

Falina traced her fingers over the balustrade and stared down at the courtyard that lay several floors below. The flowers seemed both an invitation and a warning.

Her sister, Adelina, would have jumped. Adelina had always been the brave one. That had got her killed.

Keep your head down. Survive. That had become her ethos.

She had promised never to set foot on this godforsaken continent ever again. Now she was back in the country where the nightmare had first begun. She glanced down over the balcony again. If she was quick, even Maka couldn't stop her. Her grip tightened around the handrail… *No, I won't. Who am I kidding?* She was the coward in the family, the only one alive.

'A cowrie for your thoughts, Omoba,' a voice said from behind her.

She turned. It was *him*. The one who'd dragged her back here. The mad man who walked with a lion. He had Maka Naki with him, too. There was a time when her hatred for Alangba had run hot but then he had saved her life. Put himself in harm's way to block her passage to an early grave. Her heart had softened since then. *Softened too much.*

'I am thinking about how to poison you, Alangba.'

'I love poison,' he said, smiling. 'A dry gin, or a wet brandy.'

'The sort I have in mind is stronger than that.'

He went silent. For a long moment, the only sounds were those of children running in the garden below.

'I see you, Omoba. I know the pain this journey must bring you,' Alangba said.

'You know *nothing* of my pain. You could have let me be; you could have told those men to forget they saw me and they would have obeyed. But you brought me here, for your pride.'

'For my duty.'

'Pride! Brought me here like a prize. Something to show your people.'

'*Your people*, Omoba. *Your* people.'

'They are not my people.'

Alangba was silent again for a moment, then spoke. 'I too once believed that my suffering was incredible and that I could never start again,' he said. 'Do you hear the music?'

Falina frowned. How could she not? It was impossible to avoid. The sound of singing, dancing and children running bare-foot. A people with the promise of a land they felt was theirs.

'You aren't listening to the story around you, Omoba. You see the tree and not the jungle; you're fighting a battle within that you cannot hope to win. Let the pain win and it will relieve you. Nothing wins against the sea forever. Let the waves wash you clean.'

'What the hell are you talking about?'

He smiled. 'Forgive yourself and think about what you could become if you saw the beauty in Basmine again. You are the last living remnant of royalty for a nation that has no king.'

'I have no interest in being a piece in your game of hate with the Palmaine.'

Alangba narrowed his eyes. 'We are guided by the hope in Dara, not the hatred of man. The only thing I hate is injustice.'

Falina smiled a mirthless smile. 'The word "injustice" is so light on your tongue. You speak of injustice when it was the Palmaine who abolished the slaving—'

'After being its chief beneficiary for decades.'

'They set up schools in your land, asylums, medicine houses.'

'And my father fattened his goats before a festival. It wasn't because he was a just man.'

'In Palmaine they have steam engines the size of a village, faster than a hundred horses. They will bring that to your land soon. The progress they bring...'

'Progress? You think they bring *progress* to our land? What a mercy on your soul that we rescued you from the tyranny of their story. I once heard a man refer to the days when our shores were full of slave ships as "the good days". Civilisation is a wonderful disguise for destruction.'

Falina scowled. 'You brought me here against my will; you're no different to me from the slavers you despise.'

Alangba closed his eyes, breathing from his chest as though stabbed. 'Can I ask you a question, Omoba?'

She frowned, but did not object.

'Did they let you use the same bath as they did?'

Her face fell to pieces, before she could think to remain composed. She tried to put her scowl back on, but it was too late. Her look had given Alangba his answer.

'I am no priest or scholar, Omoba, I am just a simple man – but one thing I know is that you can never be free in a nation that rides on myths that insist you despise yourself.'

He walked away, leaving Maka to watch her. *Idiot.*

Her stomach growled as the smell of salted beef filled her nose.

Maka heard it. 'Shall I arrange your dinner... Omoba?'

Maka was tall, with green robes tight around his arms,

shoulders and chest, and clean teeth that he had thrown into smiles one too many times for her taste. He was irritatingly handsome in the way some native men were, with unblemished dark skin. In sun like this, he shone like Xango himself.

'Yes,' Falina said.

The man smiled, dimpling his cheeks, and Falina felt the strange pull to smile back.

Maka was younger than most of the other rangers but his training showed with every move. He seemed to glide rather than step, and when he moved, he made no sound. He lived in a constant state of surveillance, taking inventory of everything around him, fingers twitching over the ida sword in his scabbard. Falina had caught him looking at her bottom more than once and decided there and then that if she caught him looking again, she would poke him in the eye.

Down in the courtyard, the children were running around like lizards. It sickened her in a way. Godsblood, they were in Basmine, not the Paradise Isles for goodness' sake. It was no place for children. They had no idea what Basmine really was.

'Maka,' Falina said.

'Yes, Omoba?'

'Is there salt beef?'

Maka smiled. 'There always is in Basmine. Will you want it with the pepper sauce, Omoba?'

She pondered. 'Yes.'

He smiled. 'I knew you were—'

'Shut up.'

When Maka had gone to find salt beef, she walked up to her room and waited for him to return. It was bigger than her quarters in Palmaine; enough to take six long paces in any direction. It was well furnished too – better than one would expect in a village such as this. At the corner of the room was an elegant chair, hand-carved from white wood and lacquered. It was the sort of thing that a Palmaine officer would have foamed at the mouth to claim as an exotic prize. She traced her hand over the woodwork. There was something very humbling about Mama Toro giving her – a stranger – her very best room.

A gentle knock came earlier than expected.

Falina gave a start before regaining her composure. 'You may enter.'

To her surprise a little girl's head curled around the door. She entered with slow, careful subordination and pressed her head to the floor in a bow.

'Forgive me, Omoba. I just … I just …' she trailed off.

Falina tapped her shoulder and the girl glanced up. 'You just what?'

The girl lowered her eyes. 'I just wanted to see if I could … see your face. I didn't expect you would be here alone.'

Falina blinked and then raised her hands. 'Well, here I am.'

A wide smile blossomed on the girl's face and she bowed her head again. 'My family will forever remember this as a day of pride. Thank you, Omoba, for giving us hope.' She rose to her feet and pressed a hand to her chest in salute. 'May you live forever.'

Falina snorted. 'That would be dreadful,' she muttered. The girl didn't catch it.

Just then, the noise from outside rose as the door slid open again. Maka stepped inside carrying an almighty tray of food.

'What are you doing in here?' he snapped, spotting the girl.

'Sorry,' the girl yelped, bowing low before she ran out from the room.

Maka frowned as he set Falina's food down. 'I am sorry

for that disturbance, your grace. I will make sure you are not bothered again.'

He made for the door, but Falina's voice froze him in place. 'Maka, stay.'

He turned slowly back towards her. Falina hadn't known why she had said it. True, conversation had been hard to come by in her time on the *Black Crocodile* but she was no stranger to being alone. Besides, what did she have to talk to Maka about?

As she looked up at him, he smiled and a soft tremor ran up her spine.

He bowed to *foribale*, the highest prostrate salute, with his forehead pressed to the floor. 'As you command, your grace.'

He watched her eat. A small smile quirked on his lips as she drowned her salt beef with pepper sauce. They hated the spiciness in Palmaine, but it was the one thing she had dearly missed about the land of her birth.

Maka had a hard face but he was a handsome man in a way that impressed itself stronger on you the longer you looked. If you studied his face for a while, you would see how the lines under his cheek gave his face a wonderful shape and how his eyes were like brown candlelight flame that captured the light and made it a prisoner.

Falina's smile faded a little as she saw Maka's face harden.

'How does it feel, Omoba?' he asked.

Falina gave him a confused look.

'To be such a source of hope to people?' he said. 'A rumour went round that you are the guest of honour at Irigwe's wedding. You should see the way they are dressed. The entire village must be out there.'

Falina frowned. 'None of that matters to me.'

He arched an eyebrow. 'Really?'

Falina nodded. 'Really.'

He narrowed his eyes. 'This isn't a perfect land, Princess, but it is ours. Just having this soil under my feet gives me a feeling I cannot explain. Don't run from what's yours.'

Falina scraped up the last of her salt beef and sucked in a deep breath. She glanced up at Maka. 'Thank you for the benefit of your company, Maka. You can leave now.'

If the dismissal had hurt him, Maka gave no indication. He simply bowed at the waist, picked up her tray and turned towards the door. 'As you command, Omoba.'

25

The Village of Songs

RUMI

Everyone else was at the wedding celebration, but Rumi wanted to be as far away from the music as possible. Renike wouldn't leave his side, so the pair set out to find something to eat. To their surprise, they found Mama Toro seated in the courtyard amongst the children. It was both a curiosity and a blessing that she had not joined the celebration, for it meant she was at hand to help them.

'I beg your pardon, Mama Toro, where would we find something to eat?' Rumi asked.

She smiled and gestured to a scrawny, pepper-haired boy who stood by her side.

The boy spoke on her behalf. 'We have the best beancakes you will taste anywhere.'

Renike straightened at the sound of one of her favourite foods.

As hungry as Rumi was, he would not be eating beancakes from someone that was not Yami. Not yet.

'Sorry, do you have anything else?'

Mama Toro frowned.

'Pounded yam with vegetable soup?' the boy asked.

'Perfect.'

'For me too, please,' Renike added.

Rumi appreciated her act of solidarity.

Mama Toro made a gesture to the boy with her hands.

'I'll send it right up,' the boy said, 'with bushmeat for your lionhound.'

Rumi bowed and touched his toe. 'Thank you, Mama.'

She smiled and nodded.

Rumi paused for a moment and asked a question at the edge of his mind. 'Why aren't you at the wedding, Mama?'

At that she smiled and made another gesture to the young boy at her side.

The boy cleared his throat. 'She said "it hurts too much to hear music I cannot sing to".'

Rumi's face fell as he glanced at her. Her expression was of the sort that made it clear she did not wish to elaborate. Rumi bowed again. 'I understand, Mama. Dara comfort you.'

She made the crossroads sign with her fingers in reply.

Rumi and Renike returned to their rooms and when the food came, they ate like savages. There was no one to correct or caution them. Renike grinned at Rumi with a mouth full of pounded yam and cheeks stained with soup. Rumi was not much neater. It was, in a way, liberating to eat like an animal, if only for a moment. They returned their bowls having licked the clay clean.

Renike fell asleep quickly, leaving Rumi with only his thoughts for company. Pounded yam could do that to you – send you to sleep quick as lightning.

The music outside died down before settling in silence. Before long, the village of songs was quiet as a tomb again.

Rumi tried to ward his mind against memories of the night of the Governor's Ball, but the more he tried to run from it, the more the images flashed through his mind. Morire's groan for help. Yami's split stomach. Ndebe's bulging eyes.

Abruptly, Kaat stirred and her ears shot up. Alangba burst into the room, his face grim and pitiless.

Rumi's eyes widened as he looked over Alangba. His clothes were stuck tight to his body and damp with sweat.

'We have to leave now,' Alangba said.

His voice was level, but there were flecks of worry in it.

Rumi sat up. 'Why?'

'Call it a feeling. Not sure I want to wait until first light to be sure it's just nerves.'

'So, you want us to steal out in the middle of the night?'

'Precisely.'

'How do we even leave without them knowing?'

'There's a mud road at the back of the village. The gatekeeper there won't be waking up till we're long gone; we can take that gate back out into the Nyme.'

'How do you know he won't wake up?'

'He won't.'

Rumi locked eyes with him. 'Talk to me, Alangba.'

Alangba stared at him and silently shifted a hand under his brownish green cloak. Something bulky ruffled the cloth as he fidgeted inside. Slowly he slid his hand out. He held the feet of a huge black vulture, with half its skin wet with blood. The carcass dangled from his fist like a disgusting prize. Without speaking, he slowly moved the vulture back underneath his cloak.

Rumi closed his mouth, then pulled Renike to her feet. She was limp in his arms for a moment until she found her bearings.

'We're leaving,' Rumi said as she woke.

Alangba left a fat purse of cowries on the bed and led them outside. They crept through the village in all the places the light did not shine. Alangba seemed to know the perfect route to leave the deathly silence uninterrupted.

Just as he'd said, there was a small gate at the village rear with a gatekeeper fast asleep. They walked past him, the sound of the creaking gate masked by his snores.

Outside the gates, Alangba led them down a crooked trail with a narrow rivulet to one side.

About a mile from the village, they found the others. By the look of things, Rumi and Renike were the last to arrive. Everyone else was already there. Rumi gave Alangba a studying look. *He got everyone out before us.* A subtle act of cold practicality – he had probably watched to see if Rumi had brought the vulture.

Metal clanged as Alangba kicked a pan forward. Rumi's halberd and Renike's small carving knife lay untouched inside.

'Take your weapons,' Alangba said.

They obliged and were led out towards a thick iroko tree.

Maka gave a low whistle and four large horses appeared from behind the tree. On second glance, they were more than horses; much more. Beasts built to pull chariots, not caravans or carriages. They were huge, with thick muscled legs, ink-black coats, and brilliant blue eyes. Visible puffs of air blasted from their noses as they purred and whinnied.

Rumi knew what these were; what they were supposed to be. Beasts of war known to trample men in the time of Mgbedike. He'd thought they were myths.

'*Shinala*,' he breathed.

Renike's mouth was wide open. 'What are these?'

Alangba put one foot in a stirrup and mounted one of the smaller Shinala, hoisting Renike on behind him with a single hand.

'This is Alaye,' Alangba said, stroking the fur of his Shinala. 'And that is Black Mother. They are Shinala. Only they know the way to the Eredo. If you ever see one of these without a bridle, don't even think about riding it.'

Rumi locked eyes with the Shinala in front of him and smiled. 'These are the *special* horses you asked Toro about.'

Kaat gave a low growl of what Rumi read as astonishment. In just a few days, even the lionhound looked transformed – though her pregnancy was part of that. Thicker, with a set to each step that spoke to Kaat's readiness for violence.

Alangba's face was pointedly blank. 'Who gave you the name Voltaine?'

Rumi raised an eyebrow. 'My mother.'

Alangba's lips curled in half a grin. 'Clever.'

Rumi frowned. 'What do you mean?'

Alangba hesitated for a moment than pulled a long iron file from his robes. It looked like the sort of thing a wealthy man might use to file his nails.

'They call this the Voltaine knife,' Alangba said, showing him the file handle. 'It is a weapon older than most languages.'

Rumi examined it. 'What is so special about it?'

Alangba smiled as he turned towards a tree. Without warning, he flung the file forward. It spiralled a dozen times and when it hit the tree it cut cleanly through, burying itself all the way to the hilt.

Alangba gave Rumi a speculative look. 'In the old tongue – Mushiain – the word "Voltaine" means "sharper than you think" or "more than meets the eye". A fitting name for you, I think.'

Rumi narrowed his eyes. 'She told me that was her grand-father's name.'

Alangba blinked. 'She lied.'

Rumi took a moment to process that information before he made his own bid to mount. The Shinala, seeming to sense his difficulty, lowered itself slightly for him to climb aboard.

Maka mounted with the princess only a moment before No Music appeared from the bushes with the prisoner in tow and silently climbed the last Shinala. The lion rumbled soon after, completing their party.

Rumi glanced back at the village, then to Alangba. 'Why do they call it the village of songs?'

Alangba narrowed his eyes. 'After the rebellion, when the Palmaine were hunting runaway rebels in the Nyme, the people of Korin sang songs to let the rebels know when the Palmaine were coming so they could hide.'

'So the rebels called it the village of songs?'

'No ...' Alangba frowned. 'When Lord Zaminu found out what the villagers were doing, he severed the tongues of every man, woman and child in the village and put them in a copper pot at the village centre.'

Rumi shuddered, remembering the pot they had seen.

'It was Lord Zaminu who called Korin the village of songs.'

'And they kept that name?' Rumi said.

'Yes, they did. They do not want to forget what was done to them. It is their story, and they will never lose it. That is the motto of their village: "We will sing again". They believe the day will come when they have their justice.'

Rumi's eyes widened as he realised that Mama Toro was one such victim. Only Toro and the children spoke for her. *Her tongue is in that pot.*

How many others? Alangba had spoken to Toro with hand signals and Toro had done the same with all the others. Looking back, Rumi realised that he had not heard a single man or woman of age speak a word to him. The most they had done was gesture with their hands.

Alangba glanced back at the village, then raised a flute to his lips. He lowered his head and started to chant. 'Make thee a flute of timber; of a whole piece shall you make it that you may use it for the calling of the assembly and for the journeying to the camps.'

He pressed it to his lips and blew. A long, winding note. At the sound of his music, the Shinala stuttered. Ears erect, muzzles lifted, necks arched.

They started at a trot and quickly moved into a gallop. Before Rumi could count ten breaths, the Shinala were racing like beasts possessed. They seemed to see obstacles before they appeared, barely slowing their stride to swerve around trees or leap over bushes. They knew the lay of the land intimately.

Kaat and the lion fell behind, but the lionhound would find the way back to them eventually. She had their scent.

The thunderous sound of hooves pounding the ground made it hard to hear anything else. Rumi clutched the reins tight and leaned forward as they rode. Renike wrapped her arms around Alangba like he was life itself. Alangba raised a hand and screamed in a language Rumi could not understand. An outburst of raw emotion so sudden and unexpected that Rumi's heart thudded in his chest.

He watched with open-mouthed awe as Alangba's Shinala pulled to the front of the riders, eyes fixed straight ahead. Rumi's heart pounded with the realisation of a man who has made a grave mistake. *What have I got myself into?*

26

Her

RUMI

The ride soon became a quiet, contemplative one. After an hour of hard riding, the pace slowed and only the soft pitter-patter of the Shinala and the thrumming flow of the thin rivulet that ran alongside them could be heard above the forest silence.

After the sun had long risen and was lowering to set again, the Shinala slowed to a stroll and Kaat and Ijere caught them up

Rumi palmed Black Mother's neck. 'We need to water them.'

'I know,' Alangba said. 'There's a village about a mile from here. We'll be stopping there.'

They had been riding side by side for a few hours. Alangba was a man of few words and fewer emotions, subtle in all things – he could convey fury with the mere raising of his brow or disapproval by a soft exhalation of breath. Rumi was learning to read his moves with every passing interaction.

'How many villages are there in the Nyme?' Rumi asked.

Alangba grunted. 'I would say four, but the taxman can only count the sheep he can find.'

Sure enough, cookfires appeared in the distance after another mile of travel.

'Tadjorah,' Alangba announced as they closed in on a small village. 'I hope to meet … a friend there.'

He gave the lion a curt nod and it moved to find its place in the bushes.

He reached into his side sack and pulled out bundles of dyed cloth. 'Men must cover their faces in Tadjorah,' he said, dressing his head in blue cloth.

Rumi wrapped his head in a red cloth, leaving a thin gap for his eyes. The village had no gate, but veiled men watched them suspiciously as they rode in.

The women wore no veils and their faces were reddish brown, and they had reddish brown hair. Certainly not Odu. Evidently, there were more tribes in Basmine than Rumi had known.

Alangba gave No Music wordless instructions and the man nodded his understanding, pulling his Shinala off to the side with the prisoner in tow and riding towards a weather-beaten shack of a building, which looked as though it might fall apart under a strong enough breeze.

He summoned Maka close. 'Take the princess to the lodging house. I will meet you there shortly.'

'What about Okafor?' Maka asked.

'If he doesn't arrive tomorrow, we continue to the Eredo.'

Maka nodded and moved off in some other direction. That left Rumi alone with Alangba and Renike.

Alangba dismounted and led the Shinala through the back of the village. After a few minutes, Rumi heard a sharp panting come from behind and glanced back to see Kaat, following along. The group came to what looked like a beer parlour, with a fat village strongman standing outside in a blue headdress. Alangba approached the door, reins in hand.

'Hashiyesi,' he said, lowering his veil. 'We need to water our horses and feed our dog.'

The strongman's eyes moved above the veil to Alangba, then to Rumi, then Renike, then to Kaat.

'Cowrie each,' the strongman snorted.

Alangba held out three cowries as though he had expected the price. The strongman took the reins and nodded for them to enter.

Rumi gave Kaat a nod of instruction and she followed the strongman in search of food. 'She's eating for two,' he explained and the strongman gave a wordless grunt.

The parlour was empty save for a short, stocky man polishing a table at the far corner. At the sound of the door, the barman's head jerked back with a nervous jitter.

Relief washed across the barman's face as he studied them. 'Can I help you?'

Alangba pulled his veil down. 'Firewine if you have it, palm wine if not. Water will do for the little one.'

Renike rolled her eyes at being called 'the little one'.

The stocky man nodded and disappeared behind a beaded curtain.

They took up a corner booth and sat in a wide semi-circle. Moments after they were seated, the door swung open. A tall man, thin to the point of skinny, wearing a green, high-necked kaftan, stepped into the parlour. His skin was almond-dark and did not quite match his greenish-grey eyes. He pulled his veil down to reveal a thin smile. As he approached, he touched his heart and pointed to the sky. Alangba responded in kind.

The man placed a kola nut on the table and stared at Alangba.

'My name is Ladan Anaiya,' the thin man said once they had eaten the kola nut.

Rumi and Renike offered their own names in return, which he accepted with nods. Ladan was an Odu name, but the man certainly did not look Odu.

'Where are you from, Ladan?' Rumi asked.

Ladan raised an eyebrow. 'I was born in Palmaine. My mother was Odu and my father was Kuba.'

Rumi wished he had not asked the question. Two-tribe children often did not like being reminded of the fact.

The stocky barman returned with a blue amphora of firewine, three footed cups and a jug of water. Alangba smiled as the man filled their cups with wine.

'One more cup, please,' Ladan said.

The stocky man sighed as he parted the beaded curtain once more.

Rumi observed as Alangba glanced up at Ladan. There was something tense and unspoken between the two. It was like watching two dogs walk past each other in an alley.

'It has been a long time, Ladan,' Alangba said. 'I wasn't sure if you would come.'

'Three years and thirty-four days, Alangba.'

Alangba blinked and gave a nod. 'A very long time. I am sure you are wondering why I asked you to come here?'

Ladan hunched his shoulders. 'When I got your letter, a part of me wanted to burn it but I decided I wanted to see you at least one last time.'

'I hoped—' Alangba began, but he cut his sentence off.

Ladan smiled. 'At least you've learned not to make promises you can't keep.'

If Alangba was offended by that, he gave no sign. He took a long sip of firewine and let out a breath. 'I need you to take some people to the Eredo,' Alangba said in a low voice.

'Is that what you asked me to come here for?'

Guilt flashed in Alangba's eyes only a moment before he drew in a breath. He put a hand on Rumi's shoulder. 'Rumi here wants to become a shadowwielder.'

Ladan gave Rumi an appraising look and wet his lips. 'What does that have to do with me?'

Alangba leaned forward and spoke low. 'He's above fighting age.'

The door creaked open as a lone woman entered the parlour. She had the taut gait of a fighter but she wore a scarf covering her face – so Rumi could only see her eyes – and a black sleeveless peplum over tight black breeches tracked with dirt from riding. She took up a seat just within earshot, but faced away from them.

She wore strength openly in her limbs. Arms like threaded rope with subtle bulges of muscle. Odu woman hips, wide like an embrace, and thighs like a camel racer, brimming with power. She glanced at Rumi and the flicker of light illuminated her grey-green eyes for an instant before she turned away. The cowrie seemed to warm up against his neck. Alangba inspected the woman cautiously before continuing.

Alangba gestured to the halberd. 'Rumi is ...'

'I can see who he is,' Ladan snapped, eyes fixed on the halberd. 'Don't think that changes anything. A baby with a knife is only a danger to itself. Adunola's shadowblade means nothing. The girl is young enough to squeeze through, but him? He's fighting age; they won't take him. Doesn't matter who he is or whose blade he carries.'

Rumi's eyes narrowed. 'How do you know my mother?'

Ladan gave him a confused look and ignored his question, turning back to Alangba. 'It's worse than I thought. He's an empty wineskin.'

Alangba leaned forward and spoke at a lower tone. 'There's something else, Ladan, the boy is in danger.'

'What sort of danger?'

Alangba leaned back on his chair. 'Danger of the darkest kind.'

Ladan drew back and hissed. 'Chief Lungelo hears he has something dangerous after him and he would have the boy chained to the farthest tree from the Eredo.'

'What has the Eredo become?'

'Afraid, Alangba, and you are a part of why. The last stray you brought nearly doomed us all.'

Alangba raised an eyebrow. 'About that... there are others.'

Ladan frowned. 'Besides these two?'

Alangba nodded. 'Maka is with one of them, at the lodging house. No Music is watching a prisoner for me, too.'

'A prisoner?'

Alangba nodded. '*The* prisoner.'

Ladan's eyes widened with understanding. 'It's never straight-forward with you, is it, Alangba?'

'You've always known that, Ladan,' he said with a smile.

Ladan gulped down the last of his drink and gave Alangba a long look. 'I'll take your people to the Eredo,' he said at last, rubbing his chin.

'And the Shadow Order, for the boy?'

Ladan shook his head. 'For that, there is no way. Trust me on this and forget about it.'

'Ladan, Ladan, precious Ladan,' came a soft, faintly familiar voice.

They all turned at once to the veiled woman. She rose to her feet and pulled her veil down slowly.

'There is always a way.'

Rumi stared at the woman, his eyes like saucers. He had seen her face a thousand times in his mind. *Nataré.*

27

Imagination

RUMI

Rumi stared open-mouthed as Nataré glided towards them. The light bounced off her dark skin, framing her body like a halo. Her face was much the same as he remembered from the Orchid House. Soft and dimpled; full, plump lips sculpted by Dara's hand to an eternal pout; a small gap in her two centremost teeth. Since he last saw her, she had added a shiny, golden nose-ring and a cluster of earrings to from her lobe up to the helix. Her grey-green eyes were like perfect drops of river water and her hair, once in flowing full locks, now danced around her head in a thick braid. Her eyes caught his and Rumi buckled completely.

Nataré didn't blink. 'Rumi,' she breathed with the thick relief of a cat narrowing in on a particularly elusive mouse.

Ladan glanced at her, then back at Rumi. 'You know each other,' he said.

Nataré nodded. 'We worked together once... A while back now. Before they found me.'

Rumi stared at her, blinking as though to clear his eyes and see the truth.

'What are you doing here, Kayalli?' Ladan said.

Rumi wanted to ask a similar question but could only manage silence. *Why is he calling her Kayalli?*

'I should ask you the same question, Ladan. A Suli like you should not be this far from the Eredo.'

Ladan crossed his arms tightly and stared at her.

'Another cup, please,' she said to the stocky barman.

The barman groaned. 'I'll bring two, just in case any more of you turn up.'

Alangba studied her as she took a seat. 'A friend of yours, Ladan?'

'She's a sentry at the Eredo, one of the best trackers we have.' He turned back to Nataré. 'How did you find us?'

She blinked. 'You literally just said I'm one of the best trackers you have.'

'I know how to watch my own back, Kayalli,' Ladan said.

Nataré knuckled her forehead. 'If you must know, it was the shege.'

'Excuse me?' said Ladan.

'Shinala. They leave massive turds. Imagine my surprise when I found three thoroughbred Shinala, being watered behind a beer parlour where the wine isn't worth a chewed-up cowrie.'

The stocky barman grunted as he dropped two glasses on the table. Nataré flashed an apologetic smile.

'A blind man could find you on a foggy, dark evening,' she said.

Alangba tapped his foot on the ground. 'What did you mean by "there is a way"?'

She sighed. 'There's infighting in the Eredo Council. They protect the Eredo at any cost. They don't take risks with letting people into the Shadow Order.'

'I know that,' Ladan snapped.

'Well, if he has the blessing of someone the Council respects, they might be swayed.'

Alangba leaned in. 'Someone like whom?'

Nataré reclined in her chair. 'Jarishma, the jungle mage.'

Ladan made a dismissive noise. 'The jungle mage is dead.'

'Not dead. In self-imposed exile, and I know where he is.'

Alangba sat up. 'Jarishma. Shadow Black himself. That could work. *Would* work.'

Ladan scrubbed his forehead. 'And you can find him?'

'Yes, I can.'

Rumi locked eyes with her. 'If that's the best chance of me being admitted to the Shadow Order, then I'm taking it.'

Ladan threw his hands up and let out an exasperated sigh. 'Where is Jarishma?'

Nataré blinked, then circled the mouth of her glass with her finger. 'Not far from here. Just give us your best Shinala and we'll be back in two days.'

'We?'

'Rumi and I. The only way this works.'

Alangba lowered back into his seat, eyes intent. 'Where is Jarishma?'

Nataré narrowed her eyes. 'In the Nyme... on the fourth level of Erin-Olu.'

Ladan slapped the table hard, causing froth from the firewine to slosh across the table. 'Erin-Olu?'

Nataré did not answer, her silence as sure as an affirmation.

Alangba wet his lips. 'Erin-Olu is too dangerous.'

Nataré frowned. 'You have no other choice. He'll never join the Shadow Order without an endorsement. With Jarishma's blessing, you have a chance.'

Alangba sipped from his cup. His forehead creased in consternation. He wore the look of a man forced to choose between death by hanging and death by longbow. He lingered in that all-encroaching silence until at last he took a conclusive sip from his cup. 'Two days it is, then.'

Renike perked up. 'I'm going too.'

'No, you bloody won't, and that's that on that,' Alangba snapped.

Rumi realised then why Alangba had agreed. The man had calculated that the vultures might follow Rumi and that his being away would give the rest of them a clean run to the Eredo. It was the cold, dead-handed logic of a good leader.

Ladan saw the fabric of the plan too, his eyes widening with recognition.

'Two days gives me enough time to take everyone else to the Eredo and prepare for your coming,' Ladan said.

Alangba nodded. 'You take the prisoner, the princess and everyone else to the Eredo, I will wait here for the boy.'

'As will I,' Renike protested.

Alangba gave her a hard look.

Renike's voice was low and steady. She sounded ten years older. 'You can prevent me from going with him, but you cannot force me to go on without him. I will wait for him here. With you.'

Alangba must have seen something in her eyes, for he did not argue, instead he turned to Nataré. 'Bring him back, Kayalli.'

She dropped a kola nut on the table. 'I will.'

Alangba took the kola nut and broke it. 'There's a lodging house on the east of the village with enough rooms for all of us – Renike and I will meet you there in two days.'

Nataré nodded. 'Agreed.'

Alangba ate in agreement, then he turned to Ladan and lowered his voice. 'I will be at my usual place. You know that my room is not barred to you.'

Ladan made a dismissive gesture with his eyes but the subtle glint told their own tale.

Nataré steepled her fingers on the table. 'Barman!' she called. 'I will take a vessel of wine to go.'

28

Into the Nyme

RUMI

The lodging house was as Rumi had envisioned: small, quiet, and adequate. The little sleep Rumi managed to catch in small bursts was filled with nightmares of Yami and Morire.

By the time Alangba came to his room carrying an ash-grey *buba* and matching grey trousers, Rumi had given up all hope of sleep.

'These were the best I could find,' he said, handing over the bundle of cloth.

They assembled for a breakfast of meat and yam stew in the lodging house common room. Nataré had her braid tied into a small bun and her veil covered all but her eyes. At her side was a slim black scabbard, and on her back there was an overhand flatbow with a dozen arrows in a quiver. Rumi reached under his veil to scratch his chin. All he had was a halberd he'd never used.

'You should start moving,' said Alangba, staring out the window.

Renike made a low, grumbling noise. Rumi thought of hugging her, but this was not the time for a ceremonial goodbye. Instead he gave her a soft, subtle smirk. It was a smirk that anyone accustomed to troublemaking understood: a precursor to mischief.

A wide smile curled on Renike's lips. Without warning, she gave his arm a playful thump. As good a blessing as he was likely to receive from Renike.

Nataré's sharp jolt from her seat read like a command – it was time to go.

With a quick word of goodbye to Kaat, Nataré and Rumi left the lodging house.

Black Mother was the Shinala of choice. Nataré took her by the reins and walked her out from the village.

Though Nataré held Black Mother's reins, it was not quite correct to say she led the Shinala. Shinala were not led in any complete sense. They were co-operative creatures, not submissive ones. Black Mother moved with all the subtle surety of a steed revered, each step a decision of her own. Rumi, however, had no such confidence. Out of the three, he was undoubtedly the one being led.

Walking with Nataré was surreal. He'd thought she was dead; mourned her, even.

He didn't realise he was staring at her until she turned to him and narrowed her eyes.

'What?' she asked.

Rumi fumbled for words. 'Nothing.'

Her frown deepened. 'Out with it, Rumi.'

Rumi swallowed. 'It's just... May I call you Nataré?'

Her mouth tightened at one corner. 'When we are alone.'

He nodded. 'I thought you were dead. I thought Tigrayin sold you to witch doctors.'

Her stare was fixed straight ahead, her expression unchanging. 'He did.'

'You escaped?'

'I was rescued by sentries from the Eredo.'

Rumi scratched his neck. 'Sentries?'

She sighed. 'Sentries protect the Eredo. Hunt for witch doctors. I'm one of them now.'

Rumi straightened. 'I see.'

A strange silence had its way again as they trudged deeper into the Nyme. It was a while before Rumi had the unction to say what had been bothering him.

'There's something I have to tell you.'

Nataré pulled Black Mother to a halt. 'Go on.'

He drew in breath. 'When I realised what Tigrayin did, I confronted him.'

Nothing changed but her eyes.

'Confronted him?' she whispered.

Rumi blinked. 'Yes.'

Her eyes thinned as she stared at him, then widened in understanding. 'Rumi ... I hope you didn't do that for me.'

He furrowed his brow and spoke with forced nonchalance. 'No, not for you.' He wasn't completely sure if that was true.

Her eyes softened as she looked at him, then she lowered her forehead. 'Good riddance to him, then,' she said, pulling Black Mother forward.

Rumi paused before he spoke. 'Good riddance,' he echoed.

Their agreement on that point came like the reprieve of an executioner. He realised, as he let out a sharp breath, that he had been taut as a bowstring. Hearing her put an end to the Tigrayin matter with such ease gave him a relief he had not known he needed.

She knew now that he was a killer, and here she still was. Cold as harmattan, but still here.

Perhaps one day she'd learn he'd been a coward the day his mother died. That he'd pissed himself like a child. Perhaps when that day came, she would rebuke him in the way he deserved.

But today there was no condemnation. Good riddance. Simple as that.

He let out another long breath and asked another question. 'Why are you helping me?'

She quickened the pace. 'Jarishma told me to.'

'Yes, but what's in it for you? What do *you* want?'

Nataré frowned. 'Right now, some quiet would be nice.'

Rumi clasped his hands. 'Quiet... all right then.'

He gave her quiet until the soil hardened underfoot and Nataré pulled Black Mother close. She removed several bundles of cloth from a side bag and wrapped Black Mother's hooves.

'We have to move quietly,' she said, tightening the cloth.

She mounted Black Mother with the aid of stirrups and stretched out a hand to pull Rumi up. Her hand was soft as a babe just born, but her grip was sure.

Black Mother trotted forward, her cloth-covered hooves making a soft sound on the hard mud.

'How long is it to the—'

'You ask a lot of questions, Rumi,' she said cutting his sentence in half. 'And impatience is an irritating travel companion.'

Rumi frowned. 'Nataré, I thought you were *dead*.'

She peeked over her shoulder, face blank as river stone. 'It's about half a day's ride to the foot of the waterfall, then a few hours to Jarishma's grove.'

Rumi snorted under his breath.

Nataré jerked her head back. 'Irumide, I don't know what brought you here, but we have a task to complete. We need focus.'

Irumide. He had forgotten she called him by his full name sometimes. It hurt to hear it. It reminded him of a time gone, never to return. He straightened before the memories could press down on him.

He raised his chin. 'I half thought you were lying about the whole Jarishma thing.'

'You thought I just wanted to get you alone in the forest?'

He tried to maintain a set jaw, but he could feel the undertones of red rising to flush his face. '...No.'

The whisper of a smirk flashed on Nataré's cheeks.

Sunlight grew sparse through the clefts and crevices in the ceiling of trees as they neared the interior of the Nyme.

Nataré glanced over her shoulder. 'We should pass the night there,' she said, pointing to a space between a cluster of trees ahead.

Rumi glanced up at the trees looming above. 'Why not there, beneath those trees?'

Nataré pointed to a large pink fruit on the forest floor. 'That's a bambanut. If one of those drops on your head from that high...'

'Goodnight, world,' Rumi said.

'Precisely.'

They rode forward before she threw a leg over the Shinala to sit sideways and dismount. Rumi helped her to undress the saddle and water Black Mother's back.

Nataré scooped up a fresh-fallen bambanut and peeled away the pink skin.

'Ever had one?' she asked, offering him the fine pink seed.

'No,' he said, examining it.

It took five ravenous bites to reduce the bambanut to an empty husk. Nataré smiled as he wiped his mouth clean and, for a moment, her eyes held his to a ransom he could not afford. Her dark skin gleamed where the light touched and caused a strange flutter in his stomach.

He glanced at her, trying very hard not to look at her lips. The effort required was inhuman.

'We can't sleep at the same time,' she said.

He was distracted as she slipped her peplum over her head, and his heart made to explode, but he realised to his relief that she was wearing an undervest beneath it.

'You sleep first,' he said. 'I'll wake you in a few hours.'

She formed a pillow with her peplum. 'Fair enough.' She pulled her sword free from his sheath and handed it to Rumi. 'This will be easier to use than that,' she said, pointing to the halberd.

Rumi nodded as he accepted the sword, the hilt cold in his hands.

She lay still and closed her eyes, though her pose still managed to be somewhat watchful.

Rumi felt the sudden urge to pass wind but held on for dear life. She was still awake.

One of the questions that had been sitting in his stomach crawled up, unbidden.

'Nataré?'

She cracked a singular eye open. 'Yes?'

'How did you ... cope all this time?'

She closed her eye.

An interval of silence passed. The only sound was the scurrying of bush creatures and the quiet whistle of the wind.

'One day at a time,' she said finally.

When Rumi was sure she was asleep, he seized his chance to pass wind. He let out a heavy breath as he did. A small trumpet in the night. Nataré's eyes cracked open at the sound. Rumi gasped. She locked eyes with him, blinked, then laughed. Rumi found himself laughing too. His laughter was not as it had once been. There was a bitter undertaste he could not completely ignore. The knowledge that happiness never stayed.

Rumi let the hours stroll by as she returned to sleep. He kept a vigilant watch, though he was unsure what he could do if anything dangerous did come their way.

When the night was at its darkest, Nataré suddenly screamed.

Rumi jerked back as she scratched furiously at thin air and reached for the empty scabbard at her side, swinging an invisible sword until she started to sweat.

He grabbed her shoulder and her eyes snapped open. Grey-green eyes like pinpricks on the canvas of white. Panic reigned for the faintest moment, then she jerked her head up and her calm, stoic countenance returned.

Wiping beads of sweat from her forehead, she stared up at the sky. 'You let me sleep too long.'

'I wasn't tired,' Rumi lied. 'I'll be fine.'

Her eyes narrowed. 'You'd better be.'

'What were you dreaming about?'

Her mouth tightened into a scowl, making her cheeks taut. 'I don't remember.'

They ate bambanuts, loaded Black Mother, and made sure no one stood a chance of discovering they had ever been there. Nataré went as far as to carry away any branches they had broken. Before sunrise, they were on the move again.

They had been riding for the span of an hour when the sound of rushing water thrummed through the silence. Black Mother stepped past a leaning tree into a scene from a poem.

Water ran over greenish rocks as butterflies of every colour danced in the cool mist. The gentle croak of frogs and chatter of crickets made a happy companion to the quiet. *Erin-Olu*. A waterfall of seven levels.

Rumi drank the scene in. Beautiful and terrifying all at once.

'Are you all right?'

'Yes, are you?'

'Yes, I am.'

But they were not completely all right. Rumi's heart pounded against his chest like a fugitive at the door of sanctuary. He could feel Nataré's heart doing the same as he leaned against her back. The damp, earthy scent of jungle seemed to grow stronger with each brush of misty breeze.

'Dara, Father of All, I will fear no evil for I walk in the refuge of your shadow,' Nataré muttered.

'We breathe out all our cares and breathe in your strength. May we walk under the shadow, where death wins no victory,' said Rumi, squeezing his arms tight around her as he completed the prayer.

Nataré's body tightened.

Of all the stories Rumi had heard about the Nyme, all the worst ones involved strange encounters at the Erin-Olu waterfall. Even Black Mother seemed to quiver and snort her distaste with each step. They rode up along the path towards the summit of the waterfall.

'We only have to get to the fourth level, right?'

Nataré nodded.

A distant sound broke the relative quiet.

Rumi straightened. 'What was that?'

The sound came again, clearer this time. It was the cry of a child; a baby.

Rumi glanced back like a rabbit caught in a bear cave.

'Bush baby!' Nataré screamed.

The words hit Rumi's chest like arrows. *Shege.*

She kicked Black Mother into a canter. The bush baby's wail grew louder, closer. Nataré kicked the horse twice. More speed.

240

The sound grew louder still. It was giving chase. Nataré gave Black Mother licence to use all means, and the Shinala complied. The trees seemed to blur as every line of muscle in Black Mother's body tightened with effort. Still the sound grew closer, metres behind at the most.

After a minute of hard galloping the bush baby's wail rang again, clear as a bell. Rumi could almost feel its presence on his back. Nataré slowed Black Mother down.

'What are you doing?' Rumi said.

She pulled down her flatbow and nocked an arrow, patient as death.

'It's faster than us,' she said, 'and yet it hasn't caught us all this while. Why do you think that is?'

Rumi's eyes widened. 'Pushing us into a trap.'

Nataré nodded and drew her bowstring.

Yami had told Rumi stories about bush babies. The spirits of abandoned children wailing in the bushes for their mothers. According to the stories, to look into the eyes of a bush baby was certain death. Travellers were lured by the sound of the crying child, only to die when they met its translucent, blood-shot eyes.

Rumi's heart thumped as they waited for the bush baby to burst into the opening. Its wail gave him gooseflesh; it was a terrible, heart-wrenching sound. Every moment took its time to pass. The wailing grew louder with each breath.

They were well and truly in Erin-Olu now. Hopping ghost frogs with milk-white eyes croaked deeply around them. Trees carved with the faces of men stared at them.

Nataré was taut as the string of her bow.

Without warning, she let loose her flatbow into the darkness. The arrow flew true and the cry came to a sudden stop.

She narrowed her eyes.

'Did you get it?' Rumi asked.

'I don't know.'

'So … do we … check?'

'Do you want to check?'

'No.'

'Then we sheg'in keep climbing.'

They continued upwards, speaking in whispers. They were tight against one another on the Shinala, Rumi's arms wrapped around Nataré's stomach and her elbows pressed close to his wrists to keep his arms there. His heart had not slowed; there was the lingering fear that the bush baby was waiting in ambush. The silence was so sharp he could hear his blood pumping.

In a valiant effort to fill the silence, he spun a story.

'Do you know why the cockerel crows in the morning?' he whispered.

Nataré turned slowly. 'Why?'

'It is to let his enemies know that the sun has risen,' came a dark, desolate voice from behind them.

Rumi looked over his shoulder and his heart dropped.

A giant of a man, nearly three metres tall, stood with a bloated black sack and a grin. The white markings on the man's face marked him as a witch doctor, with a swollen, tattooed balloon of a stomach. From his neck hung two heavy chains of copper. The first chain held a collection of dried bones and the second chain held a live tortoise, wriggling against his naked belly. Behind him there were two full-grown lions, but they nuzzled his knees like housecats, circling with slow obedience.

'Welcome to Erin-Olu,' the witch doctor said.

29

Ghost Stone

NATARÉ

Nataré's blade was in her hand. *Agbako.*

'You,' Agbako said, baring his teeth.

In her entire life, no one had ever crept up on her. *Ever.*

She stepped down from the Shinala and took a step towards him. Agbako stretched out an empty hand and a long sword materialised from air and black shadow in his grasp. Rumi dismounted and pulled his halberd free.

If it came to violence, they would die there. Nataré knew that, deep down. Agbako was the nastiest, most powerful witch doctor of them all. He would make sweatless work of them.

She lowered her chin. *You are the knife edge.*

'I did not come to fight,' Agbako said. 'Although you must know your trespass is an act of violence and intimidation.'

'Trespass? A witch doctor speaking of trespass?' Nataré spat.

Agbako snorted and held out his long sword in a gesture of surrender. 'I am not here to fight you. I am here to escort you to Jarishma. If not for me, you would be dead already, with a bush baby leading you into its den.'

When no one took his sword, he sheathed it and motioned towards the large sack hung over his shoulder. Nataré took in the awkward shape of the bulk in the sack and grimaced. So she had missed after all.

She made no move to sheathe her blade.

Agbako studied her stare and stretched out his hand. A lilac-brown kola nut rested in his open palm.

'I will do no violence; I swear it on my blood. You need me.'

Rumi lowered his halberd slightly, but Nataré stood firm.

Agbako stared at her. 'I know you see a monster, but I was a man once. A man driven from his home, his holiness condemned, stripped naked of his power. What is a man without power?'

'Still a man,' said Nataré.

'*Be-eni*, that I wish I had known before I bought power with blood. Now I fear I paid too much for a prize too low. Let me take you, *please*.'

The clouds groaned overhead with the heaviness of rain. Rumi glanced at her, awaiting her decision.

Her hands were shaking. *You are the knife edge.*

She turned to Rumi. 'This man is a witch doctor. He kidnaps people and uses their blood for sacrifice.'

Agbako narrowed his eyes. 'I have made peace with my violence. Dara's axe will come for me, but I will not be bloodied by *you* of ill repentance. You, who set Baron Saturday to sweat. You're a killer too. Your blood runs cold as a lizard; if I sacrificed you, the spirits would spit you back.'

Nataré craned her neck till she heard a crack.

Rumi touched her shoulder. He was a soft-spoken man, but when he spoke now, his voice had more edge than a sword.

'I don't think we should fight him, but if you think it best, then I am with you.'

Nataré blinked and thought back to Rumi as he had been back in the Orchid House, before she was taken. Blood rushed through her and her eyes watered a little.

'He could kill us both,' she whispered.

He looked at her and it was as though he'd taken a candle to inspect every dark corner of her mind. 'I thought so,' Rumi said. 'So, what do you want to do?'

Nataré drew in a long, exasperated breath. She rammed her sword into her scabbard with a soft *thunk*. 'When we are done here, I am back to hunting you down,' she said, snatching the nut from Agbako.

Agbako nodded and touched his heart in agreement. He held out two smooth stones with painted eyes. 'Put these in your mouths.'

Nataré and Rumi each took a stone. Nataré could scarcely believe her eyes. The stones were *aferi*: ghost stones. They allowed you to walk between the Lower World and the Originate, becoming completely invisible.

She placed the stone under her tongue. It crooned a song of energy in her throat, power gliding through her veins like water through pipes.

Rumi gasped, staring at the spot she had just been.

Agbako smiled. 'So long as you keep the stone in your mouth, neither you nor anything you touch will be seen or heard.'

Nataré removed the stone from her mouth and Rumi jumped back as though in fright. He stared down at the stone in his hand and then put it in his mouth. Within a heartbeat, he vanished too.

A real ghost stone.

A moment later, Rumi reappeared with a wide smile. 'Incredible,' he breathed. He took the ghost stone in his mouth again and touched Black Mother. The Shinala disappeared like smoke in a strong wind.

Agbako nodded. 'Indeed.' He stared at Rumi like a hyena in a hen-house. 'Tell me, why is Jarishma so interested in you? What is in you, boy?'

'Alara,' Rumi said, as though it was the most obvious thing in the world.

Nataré smiled. That was something she had always admired about him. The quiet pride of the martial eagle. Nothing to prove. Rumi caught her looking and nodded approvingly. That sent a strange flutter up her sternum. *Can he read my mind?* She heard they could do that, shadowwielders. But he wasn't a shadowwielder, not yet.

Agbako waved his lions forward and they led the way. He strolled after them as Nataré and Rumi rode Black Mother a few paces behind.

Nataré stole another glance at Rumi. He'd grown so much since she had known him as a boy. His once baby-round face had been chiselled to strong, rugged sharpness. His eyes were harder now. Nataré would wager that if his mood was foul, he would not lose many staring contests. He seemed to tower over her, too; while she had been riding between his broad shoulders, she had let the illusion of safety bewitch her. He'd always had a quiet fire in him. All that was still there, with more in reserve. He was a man, yet underneath it all she could still see that silent boy who adored his mother.

They made their way up the sloping rocks scattered alongside the waterfall. As they climbed to the second level of the waterfall, things thought fable named themselves true.

First was the Blackfae; winged men and women no bigger than a forearm, with skin the colour of night, flitting like butterflies around the forest singing and dancing in naked bliss. Capturing a Blackfae was said to bring good fortune, but to do so was to draw the ire of their secret kingdom.

'Can you see them?' Rumi asked.

'Yes,' she whispered.

'Look at that one,' Rumi said, pointing to a small childlike one with tiny wings. 'It's a baby.'

'Don't touch!'

He recoiled with a smile. 'Have you ever heard the story of the Blackfae king?'

'No...' She leaned back slightly so her ear was close to his mouth.

They were close now, tight on the Shinala. She could feel his hard chest on her back, her bottom on the insides of his thighs. *Am I leaning back or is he leaning forward?*

'Story, story,' Rumi said, waiting for her reply.

She wrinkled her nose, eyes fixed on the skies.

'I am not telling the story until you say it... Story, story...'

'Story,' she muttered.

Agbako chuckled ahead of them.

'His name is Obun. King of the Blackfae,' Rumi said. 'He's the reason men cannot see the Blackfae anymore.'

'Where did you hear that?'

'Don't worry about that,' Rumi said, turning his head slightly. 'Many years ago, a carpenter who had neither the means nor the talent to make toys for his children decided to kidnap the most beautiful Blackfae in the forest.'

Rumi pressed closer and she took in his leafy scent.

'So, the carpenter rode into the Nyme and waited in ambush at the foot of Erin-Olu, where the Blackfae bathe. In the dark evening he snatched Titi, the most beautiful Blackfae of all, with a net made of ugu leaves.

'His children danced and sang and clapped for their father, but in the forest, there was weeping and fury and oaths of vengeance. Obun, Titi's betrothed, had eyes red for blood. When Obun's father the king pleaded with him to still his sword, he struck his father dead and took the crown. He led the Blackfae army into the land of men to rescue his bride.

'But the Blackfae are not to be captured. Freedom and flight are their lifeblood. So it was that Titi, unable to freely fly, died in the carpenter's home.'

Nataré let out a breath as Rumi continued.

'When the Blackfae army finally found the carpenter's home, Obun discovered that his love had died. In a fury, he killed the carpenter and all his children but one, who he took back to the forest. Since that day, the Blackfae could no longer be seen by the naked human eye – save for the carpenter's son, who sings and dances in Obun's palace.'

'That is ... a dark story.'

'I know,' Rumi said.

'Now I can't look at them the same.'

'Almost every pretty thing has an ugly story,' Agbako said. 'We are at the third level of the waterfall.'

Rumi responded with a firm nod and in one small moment, all his boyish excitement was gone.

His jaw tightened as he closed the door on his inward smile and went deathly quiet. He still had that about him, that silence. That part of him he would never share. It was as though he lived in two worlds at once: in one he was the boy she knew, who she had grown up with and who had shared her deepest laughs. In the other, he was a wandering stranger who had nothing to share or receive. As they climbed, he slowly transformed into the wandering stranger again, silent as death.

She wanted to talk to him, to tell him things, but she always feared she would say something too true and get the silent Rumi when she needed the speaking one. So she went quiet too, listening to the forest as they climbed.

A sudden ripple in the water sent all the creatures running. Even the Blackfae brought their bathing to a halt. Agbako stopped their party with an outstretched hand, bidding them be still as he used a ghost stone of his own. He gestured to his lions and they backtracked into the bushes.

A giant red lizard, bigger than any house, with a giraffe-like neck, leathery wings and a beak like two conjoined spears erupted from the deep. There was a horrible silence as the creature moved, water dripping from its blood-red scales. It was at least thirty feet long, its eyes the colour of lemon.

Nataré nearly swallowed her ghost stone as she gulped back saliva. *You are the knife edge.*

She did not look directly at the thing. It was better to keep the lie that such things did not exist. *A kongamoto.*

The kongamoto spread its wings and the forest was covered by its shadow as it took off into the evening sky.

Nataré held her breath as she watched it fly away.

When the coast was clear, Agbako spoke. 'That was a close one.'

Nataré held her hand to her chest, trying to slow her heart-beat. *Knife. Edge.*

She could feel Rumi's heart pounding. She leaned into him a little, trying to calm him down – at least, that was the reason she gave herself. They were close, as one. The soft brush of his shaking breath touched her ear and neck. She pulled her elbows in closer.

Agbako shook his head, staring after the kongamoto. 'Now imagine coming here without a ghost stone.'

A few metres ahead stood a giant tree with vines draped like curtains over its branches. The tree had been carved apart to make a house, and a large round calabash lay at its door.

Agbako smiled. 'Welcome to the fourth level.'

Twin cats, black with bright yellow eyes, seemed to watch them. Unlike the other creatures, the cats were plainly aware of them.

Nataré watched the cats until a voice made her jump.

'The Kukoyi! Here at last.'

A man stepped out from the tree house. He was bare to the waist, with a woven raffia-cloth skirt. His entire body from the neck down was decorated with Darani tattoos, and on his chest was the clear imprint of two large eyes. Agbako fell prostrate on the floor, his nose pressed to earth in obeisance.

It was him. *Jarishma.*

Rumi leaped down from the Shinala and threw his shoulders back. He closed in on the tree and seemed to slip on a leaf, but when his foot came down, it fell not on earth but water. Nataré screamed as his body disappeared in the splash.

'Leave him,' Jarishma said, glaring at her. 'He wrestles with the pool of shadows.'

'You said you wanted to help him!'

'If the Agbara favour him, he will live. If they do not, he will die. If he is really Adunola's son ... He will have my blessing.'

30

The Jungle Mage

RUMI

Rumi tumbled forward, sinking into a watery abyss. Those were not leaves; they were bloodleaf frogs.

He thrashed at the water as he fell, but it was near impossible to swim through a bloodleaf frog pond. They would swarm you and drag you down until you drowned, then make a feast of flesh with their fangs.

Swathes of red painted the water as he bludgeoned and slashed the frogs, but his motions were slow and there were too many of them. The stone flew out from under his tongue and frogs swarmed over him as he became visible. He tried to scream but all he did was shoot out bubbles and drink in water.

He saw the darkness, waiting for him, triumphant. A deep gargle of laughter echoed in the back of his mind. He saw the face of Saturday, his gold-toothed smile, wiping down his shovel.

I'm not done yet. He gritted his teeth and swung his halberd. There was only a moment's reprieve before the frogs were dragging him down again. He fought with every fibre of his body, slashing, kicking, biting. *I will take them all to the grave with me!*

With death at his throat, he heard a voice. A voice like a wave crashing against a mountain. A voice that sounded not in his ears, but in his mind.

'Say the words!' came the voice.

Rumi shouted with all that remained in his lungs, the first words of prayer that his mother had ever taught him. '*Awon mimo Alaini!*'

There was a flash of white light, then a crash of thunder, then a hissing sound like oil in a hot pan. The frogs floated dead to the surface like real leaves. He was free.

With the last vestiges of his strength, he swam to the top of the pond. He hauled himself up and someone grabbed him under the arms. *Nataré*. He wrapped his arms around her back as she wrestled him from the pond, and they flopped together onto the forest floor.

Water came out from his mouth in green streams as he choked and fought to breathe.

'Rumi...' Her voice was breathless, but firm.

He tried to say something but only coughed up more green water. She pressed down on his chest as he retched.

It was a while before Rumi could sit up. Then a longer while to wash the wounds and swelling from frog bites.

Rumi forced his eyes open. Jarishma stared down at them as though noticing a blemish in the mirror.

'It took you long enough to get here,' Jarishma said. 'Now you are committed again, my blessing is yours.'

He gave Rumi a necklace, near identical to the priestess's cowrie he already wore. 'With this, they will know you have my blessing.'

Nataré grabbed his shoulders, her voice soft as cotton. 'Breathe. Just breathe.'

Jarishma stepped close. 'Tell the Council that Jarishma said you are to join the Shadow Order. School of the shadow-wielders.'

The word echoed in Rumi's mind. *Shadowwielders.* He could almost hear Kamanu's ocean-deep voice. *You are of the old blood ... Born to be a shadowwielder.*

Breathless, he forced a question out. 'What *is* a shadow-wielder?'

Jarishma smiled and whispered something under his breath.

Clouds gathered to dominate the clear night sky. A flash of lightning was pursued by the guttural groan of thunder. Jarishma blinked and his shadow morphed into a mist of black, shrouding him.

Rumi wanted to shout, but it felt as though his stomach had fallen out.

Jarishma raised a hand. A spear of black shadow coalesced in his palm. His eyes leaked black mist.

'This is a shadowwielder!' he roared, arms outstretched.

He threw the spear to the sky. It came back in a bolt of thunder to echo his voice. From the mist, Jarishma formed the image of a snarling lion, then a charging bull, then an antelope, hopping on a field of shadow.

'This is the old blood!' His voice crashed like ocean waves against the rock face as he went nose-to-nose with Rumi.

The shadow bristled his skin, like spiders crawling over him.

'This is the power of the ancestors, Rumi!'

He pressed his hands together and the mist commingled into a lump of congealed black. The clouds dissolved into the night sky. The shadow floated in the air, pulsing like a thing alive.

'Touch it,' Jarishma said.

Rumi's heart was in a dog race. His hands shook with pure black terror.

'Touch it!'

Gritting his teeth, Rumi reached out and touched the shadow. It was solid as stone.

Jarishma threw back his head and laughed. The shadow fell to the ground and returned to its normal shape; the mist vanished. Where the shadow had struck the ground, the earth was cracked.

It was the same power that Yami had used, except Jarishma's strength in shadow seemed tenfold what Yami's was. With that sort of power Rumi would have his vengeance and more. *Then we will see who is nothing.*

'Teach me,' Rumi said.

Jarishma raised an eyebrow. 'That is what the Order is for.'

'They will teach me to do that?' He pointed at the cracked earth.

Jarishma's face was calm as sea breeze. 'Much more than that.' He turned his gaze to Nataré. 'The forest will not harm the boy so long as he carries my blessing, but you must use the ghost stone.'

She nodded.

He narrowed his eyes. 'The ghost stone is a powerful thing, but also a dangerous one. It will make you invisible to some, but to those who can see the other realm you will stick out like a flame in the darkness. Throw it into the river before you enter the Eredo.'

'I understand.'

She fixed her eyes on Agbako and her face hardened. 'We will meet again, Agbako.'

He nodded. 'I know.'

Abruptly the priestess's cowrie flared up with heat, sending a pang of pain through Rumi's neck.

Jarishma glanced at the sky and his eyes narrowed to thin slits. 'You must go. Now!'

Rumi did not wait for Nataré to understand. He mounted Black Mother and pulled her astride.

With two steady kicks, he urged Black Mother into action. The Shinala responded. In a blink they were at the third level, moving with frantic, desperate speed.

Behind them, Rumi heard a hissing sound. A sound like a kettle coming to a full boil. It was faint at first, but within moments it was a cacophony.

He looked over his shoulder. In the skies there was a cloud of black wings and feathers. *Vultures.* There must have been two dozen of them, swooping low in the open forest.

The priestess's cowrie was white-hot, scalding his neck. He kicked Black Mother to run faster still, but the hissing grew louder.

He heard Tinu's voice in his head. *There is a time to run and a time to stand.* The darkness seemed to taunt him. *Just like when she died, you're running scared.* He glanced at Nataré. She deserved no part of this.

All rational sense fled from him. Not allowing himself to think, he drew rein, slowing Black Mother to a stop, then slid off her back.

Nataré stared at him incredulously. 'What are you doing?'

'You go ahead!' he snarled. He shoved Black Mother with the flat of his foot and she took off at a canter.

He turned towards the flying mass, halberd in hand.

Two dozen had been a poor guess. There were more than fifty vultures in the cloud of black, with wide muscled wings and bloodstained beaks. They hissed with hate and blood-hunger as they swarmed towards him.

Rumi took a deep, everlasting breath and tightened his grip on the halberd, staring at the sky as the horde approached.

There was a loud screech and one vulture fell to the ground, barely a metre in front of him. He froze. The vulture's neck was pierced with a black arrow, blood painting its feathers. Another fell with a heavy thud, an arrow in its breast.

'Rumi!' Nataré said from behind him. 'Get back here!'

A vulture dived for him and Rumi turned it to flesh and feathers with a slash of his halberd. He turned to Nataré as she whirled Black Mother to a stop beside him. He grabbed her arm and leaped onto the Shinala. Within breaths, Black Mother had kicked into a full gallop.

Nataré fired three arrows in quick succession behind them, each one striking true. Muscles coiled tight under the strain of the draw-weight, she loosed a fourth and the vulture nearest them screeched. With the organisation of a veteran battalion, the remaining vultures stretched out their wings and fell back, abandoning the chase.

'What did you think you were doing?' Nataré snapped.

'He's back,' Rumi said, breathing desperately as they galloped. 'He was coming.'

He wanted to retch. What he had done was foolish, very foolish. The Priest of Vultures would have killed him. He was not near ready to face him, not even close to ready. He had to be stronger, be a shadowwielder.

They rode on in silence, close enough to whisper.

Rumi's heart was like the talking drum. He knew Nataré could feel it beating against her back, but somehow, she protected him from shame. She pretended his heart wasn't thumping at all.

31

The Eredo

RUMI

Rumi and Nataré entered Tadjorah with their veils drawn, making their way to the lodging house common room.

'Rumi!' Renike darted towards him as they stepped inside. Alangba followed close behind.

'Did you find him?' asked Alangba.

'We did,' replied Nataré. 'Jarishma blessed him.'

That drew smiles to every face but Rumi's.

'We should leave right away,' Rumi said, locking his eyes on Alangba. 'Birds may not be far behind.'

Alangba blinked and nodded. He seized up the side-sacks and satchels with their belongings.

'To the Eredo then.'

They loaded Black Mother and Alaye. Nataré rode with Rumi, Alangba rode with Renike. Kaat trotted patiently behind. Rumi never saw the lion but he knew it was trailing after them too, lurking under the cover of shadow.

For a while, they followed the rushing rivulet that bordered Tadjorah.

Alangba pulled up beside Rumi. 'When you get to the Shadow Order, don't forget that you were a boy once. One who loved his mother and his brother.'

Rumi stared at him, somewhat confused.

'That was why she didn't want you going there so soon,' he continued. 'She didn't want you to forget that.'

'I see,' he said. He didn't see, not completely, but he figured it would make sense one day. For now, he only needed not to forget.

After an hour or so of riding, they came to a conflux of two water bodies. A thin rivulet merged with a thicker vein of water flowing from the west.

The conflux formed a barrier to the edge of a deep ditch; behind that ditch was a wall that stood at least two hundred feet tall. If they wanted to move forward, they would have to overcome three deathly perils: the current of the conflux; the depth of the ditch; the height of the wall.

Renike gasped, pointing up at the wall. Rumi inclined his head.

There was a massive black figure at the top of the wall. From a distance, it looked like a giant dog. *A fourth peril.*

The wall was utterly impenetrable. If you gave twenty good bowmen a barrel of good ale, you could survive a siege of a ten-thousand-man army and litter the ditch with bodies.

'What in Dara's name is that?' Rumi said, staring up at the silhouette of the beast atop the wall.

'A distraction,' said Alangba, his eyes fixed on the stream.

Nataré nudged the Shinala into the stream and they all followed. The water climbed to the soles of their feet and Nataré drew rein. She unbuckled her sandals and stepped into the water.

'By Dara, creator of all things, you say when the four tribes are gathered, you are in our midst. Shuni, mother of the water, your children seek refuge. Who shall dwell in thy holy river? Protect us from the trap of our enemies, from the fire of their weapons in the day and their eyes that watch in the night. By precious Jahmine we plead.'

A faint image erupted from the water. It was Shuni, the Agbara of sweetness, water, beauty and sensuality.

Rumi's breath caught in his chest as her body rose from the stream, drops of water trailing over her brown flesh. She wore a golden headdress which draped over her body, turning her into a portrait of gold and brown.

All the poems and stories Rumi had heard did no justice to her ineffable beauty. She was an Agbara. It was like seeing the sun for the first time.

'Do you know the words, my child?' she said in soft Odu.

Her voice was like music, a voice that could turn a single word into a poem.

Nataré reached behind her neck and unlocked her thin rope of gold. She bowed as she raised it towards Shuni, dropping it carefully in the water to let the tide carry it away. Then she spoke words in a language Rumi could only halfway understand.

Shuni arched her back with a smile and dived into the stream, disappearing as soon as her skin touched it. The earth stirred and the water parted like a curtain. Rumi watched with bulging eyes as the water gave way to moist earth. A curved interlacing arch over a tunnelling staircase appeared in its wake.

His mouth dropped open. The conflux was a crossroads of sorts, if you saw it true. A juncture between the spiritual world and the mortal realm.

Nataré stepped forward.

'The stone,' Rumi said, softly.

Nataré raised a brow at that, then reached into her pocket. A moment later he heard the splash of a stone in the water.

The tunnel was tall and wide enough for the Shinala's to enter side-by-side.

They travelled down quarter of an hour before the tunnel flattened into a stone landing. They came to a large metal double-door that had no handles, lined with a bamboo portcullis.

Nataré stepped down from the Shinala. The rest of them followed her lead.

'Do we knock?' Rumi said, reaching for Nataré's hand. He didn't realise he was doing it until their palms touched. She blinked, turning to him.

The sudden blast of a horn made Rumi jump. He clutched Nataré's hand tighter. She took it in her stride, eyes expressionless.

A sprinkle of dust filled the air as the portcullis was raised. The doors stuttered open, revealing a room with high ceilings and built-in stone benches moulded into the ground. The walls were ornamented with icons, masks and figurines that harkened back to times long forgotten.

Five men stood in front of them. Two, on either side of the door, held the ring pulls that kept it open. The fifth man, who stood taller than Alangba, was wickedly handsome, with a thick beard, a truly magnificent moustache, and stony brown eyes.

At the sight of the man, Nataré dropped Rumi's hand like it was a too-hot beancake. The way the man narrowed his eyes, it was plain that he had noticed it.

All of them were armed with spears and moved with the experience of using them. Rumi had seen enough fights to know how killers moved. These men moved like a pack of wolves encircling their prey, every step invested with the predetermination of a clean kill. Not one smile amongst them. If they wanted to, they could skewer Rumi and his companions before they had the breath to shout.

Rumi slowly dropped his halberd to the floor and took a step back with upturned palms.

'Kayalli,' said the bearded man. 'We feared you were lost to the witch doctors.'

Nataré stepped forward. 'I'm not so easily lost.'

Her voice had adopted a cold, hard timbre.

The bearded man nodded and glanced past Nataré, his eyes darkening at the sight of Rumi. 'Who are these…'

He left the sentence unfinished, as though not finding the words to classify Rumi and his companions. The man's look was that of a prize-fighter glaring at his opponent before the bell.

Alangba stepped between them, eyebrows arched as though asking a question. He fixed the bearded man with a glare of his own and kept all the quiet of a crocodile waiting for the antelope to get thirsty. They held their stares for what felt like forever.

Eventually Alangba produced a kola nut, which the bearded man took and broke.

'I am Alangba Kashir, Third Ranger of the Chainbreakers. I am no stranger to this place.'

'Strogus Ebele,' the bearded man barked, 'and you're a stranger to me.'

His voice was sharp and snappy. Like the sound of a door slamming.

Nataré brushed across and put an easy hand on the bearded man's chest. Her hand seemed to douse the flame and he simmered still.

'Ladan will be here any moment for them. They are expected,' she said softly.

'Godsblood! Always the heavy man, Strogus,' came a sharp voice.

Ladan stepped into the room with all the timing of a master showman. He was dressed in a brilliant purple *agbada*. So far, he was the only person Rumi had seen smile.

'Welcome to the Eredo,' Ladan said, clapping Rumi on the shoulder. He turned to the bearded man. 'Strogus, please let your men see to their—' He hesitated, noticing the full-grown lion standing beside Alangba. 'Their animals. I am to take them to Lord Mandla immediately.'

Strogus's face convulsed in a stare that was equally incensed and incredulous. 'What does Mandla want with these...'

The words eluded him again. Plainly, the man wasn't skilled with words.

Ladan gave him a winning smile. 'Should I tell Lord Mandla you need to know?'

Strogus straightened, seeming to choke on his own breath. 'No... of course not.'

'Their lionhound is expecting,' Ladan said, as he beckoned them forward, 'treat her with care.'

Strogus grunted as they all made to follow Ladan's lead. All except Nataré.

Rumi's head snapped back to look at her. Her stare was stone. 'You're not coming with us?'

'No.'

Rumi wanted to ask why not, but from the joyless note in her stare and the satisfied smile on Strogus's face, Rumi could read the storybook.

'All right,' he said.

The jarring pang of rejection washed over him. He forced himself towards Ladan, doing his utmost to take it in his stride.

Nataré nodded and, without looking back, walked away with Strogus and the Shinala.

Ladan's smile was an earnest effort to ease the tension. 'Follow me.'

The Eredo was an engineering marvel, a city almost entirely underground. Ladan led them through a short, tunnelling corridor into a massive hall filled with more people than Rumi had imagined possible. The high ceilings were decorated with intricately carved stalactites, supported by fine columns of coloured marble. The air carried the smell of food, fire and perspiration. Men and women carried books, baskets of bread, fresh fish and goods of all kinds. The people were every shape and constitution, all the colours of Darosa.

It was just like the market, a constellation of activity that had its own rhythm, but if you studied it carefully there were subtle reminders that you were in a strange place. For one, tall lionhounds were poised like statues at every corner and crevice, heads rotating to study the scene. For another, martial eagles wheeled around the ceiling, watching the life below.

If the market told you anything about the size of the place, the Eredo was more a city than a town and a large one at that.

'The Council is expecting you,' Ladan said.

'I am here to join the Shadow Order,' Rumi said.

Ladan raised a brow slightly. 'Well, you're late. The Bleeding is done. They have anointed new Seedlings into the Shadow Order.'

'I have Jarishma's blessing.'

Ladan raised his eyebrow even further. 'A great boon. Even so, you need to be tactful. Do not rub their noses in it, and only use it if you absolutely have to. A gentle touch is what you need.'

A gentle touch.

Ladan turned towards a small, weathered door and twisted

the creaking handle. They followed him into a domed octagon of stone with painted stalactite carvings on the ceiling.

'Please wait here a moment,' Ladan said before leaving the room.

Alangba had been near silent the entire walk.

'How many people are here?' Rumi asked.

'Thousands. Tens of thousands now, I'm sure,' Alangba said.

'No Palmaine though.'

'Of course not. This place is for children of the soil. It is an ancient sanctuary, hundreds of years old. A place people came to hide from the Palmaine. They do not speak the Common Tongue here, either. Ever. So only speak Odu.'

'What is this place?'

The door creaked open and Ladan led an elderly looking man into the room. Behind them stood a giant of a man holding an even taller spear.

'This *place* is war and it is peace,' the elderly man said, smiling.

His voice was like the bass drum, eyes a dancing fire. He wore a woven raffia headdress over his storm-grey curls. The headdress extended all the way to his waist with dried straw. In one hand he held an old wooden staff and in the other an unlit golden torch. He favoured one leg when he walked, supporting his other with his staff. His attire was as good as a proclamation of what he was. *An aminague.* Now Rumi was the son of a storyteller. More than a hundred times he had heard the tales of the aminague. In old Odu mythos, the aminague were great priests who could commune with ancestral spirits when they visited the realm of the living to balance the destiny of man. They were feared and obeyed. That was a long time ago. On festival day in Alara, men would sometimes wear the costume of an aminague and dance for a few shells or a plate of food. The man Rumi saw now was no streetside performer.

Upon closer inspection, the man was not *really* elderly. His face was smooth and unwrinkled, but his eyes had the weathered fire of age. When his gaze settled on Rumi, his eyes seemed to bypass skin and search to the bone.

'Welcome,' the aminague said, 'my name is Mandla Xhosi.'

Alangba bowed low. Rumi quickly followed suit, and Renike bent her knees in a crude attempt at a curtsy. The enormous bodyguard behind Mandla had knuckles like rocks. If the aminague had a face moulded from clay, his bodyguard's face was made with hammer and anvil. The sort of man who guarded the doors to great, forbidden treasures in storybooks. A man to do violence, break things and stop nonsense.

Rumi cleared his throat. 'My name is Rumi, of Oduland.'

Mandla regarded Rumi with a faint smile. 'Just like Griff,' he said, '*and* Adunola.'

Rumi straightened. 'Who's Griff?'

The room hardened in cold silence. He had spoken in the Common Tongue.

The bodyguard's mouth tightened at each corner. Mandla narrowed his eyes.

'I'm sorry,' Rumi said in Odu.

Mandla lifted his chin. 'There is no need to apologise. When the spoon no longer stirs the soup, the soup holds its swirl for a while. Within a week, the Common Tongue will fall from you like broken shackles. We speak in the native tongues here because the Common Tongue was given to us by other people. It contains lies that we cannot avoid. To speak and think in it requires our tacit cooperation; you must agree that things are what they say they are. When we think and speak in our native tongues, we can have certain feelings that are characteristically Darosan, but when we use the Common Tongue, we cannot have those feelings. And how can one find himself if he cannot express himself?'

Rumi scratched his neck. Though his Odu was not perfect and his accent and pronunciation needed much practice, he resolved in his mind to make it his own.

'Who is Griff?' he said in Odu.

'Your father,' Alangba said, 'the one they call the darkman.'

The words hit Rumi like a slap. He let out a heavy breath and realised that Mandla's words had made his fist curl around the halberd. 'I don't have a father,' Rumi whispered.

Mandla caught the look on Rumi's face and narrowed his eyes. 'Only Dara has no father. Ladan, summon all the chiefs and bring them to the hall.'

Ladan nodded and bowed. Mandla tilted his head slightly, then was quickly out of the door. His bodyguard trailed after him like a long, wide shadow.

'What's going on?' Rumi said.

'They are preparing for a full hearing,' Alangba said.

Ladan knuckled his forehead. 'A full Council is not good.'

'Why?'

'It means they will be extra careful,' said Alangba.

'What do they need to be careful about?'

He sighed. 'The Palmaine. They have their spies. Weeds sown amongst the wheat.'

Rumi glanced at Alangba. 'I thought you said there were no Palmaine here.'

Ladan rolled his eyes. 'You can't tell a Palmaine by the colour of their skin. There are men who look just like you and I who are as Palmaine on the inside as one is likely to be. You made a good start when you said you were of Oduland and not of Basmine, but that's only the small part of it. In an army, every recruit must be vetted and trained. You don't give a man a gun until you're sure he won't shoot his comrades in the camp.'

Before Rumi could press for more, there was a knock at the door.

'It is time,' Ladan said, straightening. 'Leave all your belongings here.'

Ladan led them through the door and into a new corridor bounded by stone walls. Rumi tried to memorise the turns they made and the doors they entered, but to no avail. The Eredo must have been designed to prevent that very thing.

Lionhounds patrolled the corridors. Rumi counted eleven in the space of a minute's walking.

They came at last to an imposing pair of doors guarded by two magnificent wood carvings of fierce lionhounds, each singular fang carved to perfection. Rumi fought the desperate urge to touch them. It was masterful work, but he dared not venture too close. He had seen too many strange things.

The doors groaned as they were opened from inside. Alangba unbuckled his sandals and gestured for the others to do the same, stepping into the room barefoot.

The room had all the markings of a grand palace reception. A gorgeous stalactite canopy overlooked a large table shaped in the crescent of a slim moon. In front of the table was a clearing of black marble covered in sand. The floor was a mosaic made of tiny coloured stones to form a lizard, its tail encircling the crescent-shaped table.

On the wall, there were a dozen or so paintings. The nearest depicted a towering figure in black, wearing a wide-sleeved *agbada* robe embroidered with patterns of stars. Across his chest he held a huge cutlass and had a hard, uncompromising stare. The face was deeply familiar. The name on the crust of his lips.

Madioha Alaye. The Raging Flame. He had seen his picture once before – at Mama Ayeesha's home.

The next painting showed a young woman wearing a high-necked, egg-shell white boubou that covered everything but her face. Her hair fell to her shoulders in thick red curls and her eyes shone an emerald green. Her skin was almost Palmaine fair, but her features were decidedly Darosan. She seemed to stare disapprovingly down at Rumi. He shifted his eyes to the next painting and froze.

He was staring at himself. *No, not quite me.* Older and harder-faced. A chain of cowries hung from the neck of the man in the painting, and he held an iron-hilted ida sword with an upward-curving quillon.

In the middle of the room was a curved table, where people were already seated. Lord Mandla occupied the seat at the centre. Behind him, as though there to massage his shoulders, stood the hulking bodyguard.

Ladan led Alangba, Rumi and Renike into the full glare of the table and took a hasty leave.

There were five at the table. The eldest, save perhaps for Mandla, was a frail woman, with flowing silver-black hair and oak-dark skin. She had a distant, untouchable grace about her. She was Darosan, but certainly not Odu – at least not entirely. He could not be sure what she was.

The man next to her was the youngest at the table, and he wore a scowl so deep that Rumi feared his cheeks might burst. His dark moustache framed a disgusted frown as he stared down at Rumi. Again, Rumi could not quite place his tribe.

There were two other men on the other side of Mandla. One with a short, neat beard of snow-white and the other completely hairless. There was a symmetry to the two men; like two different sides to the same cowrie. The bald one inspected

Rumi with all the silent concentration of a seamstress threading a needle.

The door made a creaking sound and a tall, muscled man with a seamless black tunic stepped into the room. He had red eyes, the likes of which Rumi had never seen. The truth struck Rumi as he spotted the long-curved blade fastened to his belt and watched him take a seat. *A Kasinabe bloodgeneral.*

He looked around the room again. *Shege.* All six of them were slightly lighter in complexion than the Odu, with curlier hair and redder eyes. They were all Kasinabe. Different clans, but doubtless Kasinabe. Six Kasinabe in one room. Each wearing their rank in their air and manner. Some wore white caps, which told Rumi what they were: war chiefs.

Rumi's eyes bulged. It was said that the Kasinabe and Odu were different branches of the same tree. In terms of both language and religion this was true, but in appearance Rumi saw it was a dirty lie. The Kasinabe were a tall, fierce people with an imperious air that the Odu could not match; it was like watching an older, more accomplished brother enter the room.

'You are late, Gaitan,' Mandla said, his voice strangling the room into silence.

The Kasinabe bloodgeneral, Gaitan, bowed apologetically. 'Double hundred apologies, Lord Mandla. I was … distracted.'

The bloodgeneral took a seat next to the woman and attention returned to Lord Mandla.

Mandla motioned Rumi and Renike towards the sand circle at the centre of the room, then smiled. 'We begin.'

32

The Last Chiefs

RUMI

'Chiefs of the last clans, nobility of this great Council,' Mandla said.

'Awani!' the five chiefs shouted back as one.

Mandla nodded, satisfied, and stared out to the circle. He fixed his eyes on Renike. 'Who speaks for the young lady?'

Alangba began to step forward.

'I speak for myself,' Renike said.

The Kasinabe bloodgeneral leaned forward, smiling.

'Good,' Mandla said. 'May I know your name?'

'Renike Denaiya of Odu.'

'And what is your petition?'

Renike glanced at Rumi before she spoke. 'To stay here . . . Lord Mandla.'

Mandla broke into a slight smile. 'Well, I have no objection to that. Are there any objections to her admission?'

An interval of silence marked their acceptance.

'This Council accepts Renike Denaiya'. Mandla gestured to his bodyguard. ' Telemi, please show this young lady to the dining hall. I am sure she must be very hungry.'

The bodyguard Telemi gave a low grunt of acceptance.

'I'm not going anywhere without him,' Renike said, moving to stand in front of Rumi.

'I like her spirit,' said the Kasinabe bloodgeneral.

The woman at the table leaned over with a kola nut. 'Renike, you have my word that your friend will not be harmed, my promise.'

Renike raised an eyebrow and eyeballed each one of them at the table, then she hissed and took the kola nut from the woman.

'No harm,' she said as she broke the kola nut.

Telemi led her out and the eyes settled on Rumi.

'Young man, please step forward,' Mandla said.

Rumi took a small step forward, lifting his chin slightly to look at the Council. *A gentle touch, Ladan said.* They stared at him like alley cats at a mouse.

'What is your petition?' asked Mandla.

Rumi straightened. 'To be admitted to the Shadow Order. To become a shadowwielder.'

A chorus of whispers flared up from the table until Mandla spoke up, cutting a black trail through the noise.

'I will have decorum,' Mandla said coolly.

Silence returned.

Mandla looked at the others. 'This man is the son of Griff and Adunola. Do we have any objections to his petition?'

The hairless man raised a hand to speak.

'How old are you, boy?'

'I'm ...' Rumi paused. The rainy season had come and gone; that meant his birthday had gone by. It had gone by and he had not even noticed. He bit his lower lip. 'I'm eighteen.'

'As I thought,' said the hairless man. 'We do not accept men or women past fighting age, except in exceptional circumstances. Anyone with eyes can see that he is Griff's get, and yet I see nothing exceptional about him. He is an untrained youngling and one amongst ten thousand.'

Rumi forced back a grimace.

Mandla nodded. 'Your objection is noted, Chief Kwesi. Do you have any rebuttal, young man?'

Rumi let the dice rattle in his head as he picked his next words. *A gentle touch.*

'I do not, as the Palmaine do, make a judgement of a man's character with the things I can see. I am certain that Chief Kwesi also does not make such foolish leaps to judgement. So, I would enquire how the good Chief Kwesi has gathered that I am unexceptional.'

They might have looked at him like a mouse in the alley, but he was more a street rat. Wily and elusive, with a knack for finding the holes and crevices they couldn't reach. He figured that likening Chief Kwesi to the Palmaine was akin to an act of violence in this room, but Chief Kwesi had already showed his hand. Sometimes you fire a shot in the air to lure the real bandits out.

Chief Kwesi glared down at Rumi.

'Look at his eyes,' said the bearded man, 'flush with stubborn pride. I wager that any one boy of fighting age in the Eredo would beat him at any test. He does not know our way. It is a waste of the Bloods.'

'I would match your wager,' Rumi said.

The bloodgeneral slapped the table and laughed.

To wilt in the face of the chiefs would have made their decision easy. He needed them to know he was no festival goat.

'Lord Mandla,' the woman said. 'If I may?'

Mandla nodded. 'You most certainly may, Chief Karile.'

Chief Karile narrowed her eyes and settled them on Rumi. 'You speak Odu?'

'*Ini*,' Rumi said.

'Saharene?'

'*Sipho.*'

'Kuba?'

He paused. 'No.'

'Why not?'

He weighed his words a moment before he answered.

'I don't like their language very much.'

Gaitan, the bloodgeneral, exploded with laughter. His huge frame shook the table with each bellow.

The woman continued. 'What about Mushiain?'

Mushiain was much like Odu, but it was a Kasinabe dialect inflected with many strange Kasinabe words and diversions in grammar that made it near unintelligible when spoken by a native. There were no natives to learn from in Alara, perhaps not even in Basmine. Only old Kasinabe songs showed how Odu and Mushiain had lives of their own.

'*Diyin*,' Rumi said. It meant, just a little.

The woman looked at him for a moment then turned to Mandla.

'He can be taught.'

Mandla nodded in agreement and turned to the bloodgeneral. 'Chief Gaitan?'

The bloodgeneral stirred. 'What do you know about the Kasinabe?'

Rumi knew a great deal about the Kasinabe. It was said that, on the battlefield, one Kasinabe farmer with a stick was more dangerous than two trained soldiers with horses and spears. Before today, he had believed on good account that the Palmaine had annihilated the Kasinabe. It had not quite sunk in that they were a real, living people.

In the end, he returned to a story. Stories always hit the hardest. He could almost picture Yami saying the words.

'Death comes but once. Do not die before you are dead.'

Chief Gaitan smiled. 'He is not an empty vessel.'

Mandla nodded in satisfaction, turning to the man that wore the hardest scowl Rumi had ever seen.

'Chief Lungelo?'

Lungelo turned to Rumi and his scowl morphed into a grin. 'What is your name?'

The room fell into a strange silence. Plainly, there was more to the question than it seemed. Rumi raised an eyebrow, unsure of what to say. What else could he say?

'Rumi Voltaine,' he said.

Alangba's head fell. Lungelo smiled and steepled his fingers as though his work was done. Chief Kwesi and Chief Kovi laughed like young boys.

'The caterpillar does not know it will fly until it bursts from the darkness,' Mandla said.

His voice was like rocks falling from the high places. Kwesi and Kovi choked back their laughter as though they had been strangled. Lungelo spoke again.

'Whatever his parentage, he is already of fighting age and has not been taught our way. I need not remind you that the enemy will sow weeds in the wheat. Look at him: he has no control. He rides the unbridled Shinala; his shadow looms over him, hungry for release. He aligns himself with the traitor Alangba and stands in our hall with all the pride of a pig in the mud. We should wash our hands of this stain *now.*'

Alangba nodded to Rumi. *Time for the boon.*

'Jarishma told me to send his regards to you, Lord Mandla,' Rumi said.

His words made Mandla's eyes light up. Pulling Jarishma's cowrie free of its thin rope, Rumi stepped forward and placed it at the centre of the table. Murmurs took over the table as the

274

chiefs studied the cowrie. Mandla, who had seemed completely expressionless, suddenly seemed on the brink of tears.

'Where did you get this?' he said.

'From Jarishma. He said to tell you that I am to join the Shadow Order, that I have his blessing.'

Lungelo looked as though he'd found a nest of worms in his food.

Karile smiled. 'We need not have gone through this had we known you were blessed by the jungle mage.'

'No one asked me if I was,' Rumi said, feigning surprise.

Mandla cleared his throat. 'Any further objections?'

Silence.

'This Council hereby accepts Master Rumi Voltaine to the Shadow Order as a Seedling. He will be ordained with the Bloods tonight.'

'So much for a gentle touch,' Alangba whispered.

Mandla tapped gently on the table. 'Well done, Alangba. This is a wise thing you have done, bringing him here. We will speak more of the others you have brought through Ladan.'

'Traitor,' Lungelo hissed. Loud enough for everyone to hear.

Alangba stopped in his tracks, then glared back at him. 'My name is Alangba Kashir, and you would be wise to speak it carefully, Lungelo.'

'Suppose I choose folly. What then, traitor?'

'If you said that outside this room, it would be the bravest thing you have ever done.'

'My sincerest wish is to rattle your jaw,' Lungelo said.

'Any man can taunt a lion when it's in a cage. Let me have the Bloods and you can earn your wish.'

'Can't say I'm not tempted.'

'Enough.'

Mandla's voice was quiet, but it still brought death to nonsense.

Lungelo rose to his feet as though to start a fight.

'What have we become? Look at him. Black with anger and pride! The unfruitful works of darkness!'

Mandla's voice swallowed the room. 'And who were you before you saw Dara's mercy? Where was your heart? Or do you think you have climbed so high as to question Jarishma's blessing? Is that what you think, Lungelo?'

Inflected with anger, Mandla's voice was like a punishment. Even the bodyguard glanced up as though the ceiling would start to crumble.

Lungelo slunk quietly back into his seat and bowed his head. 'I apologise, Lord Mandla.'

Alangba bent forward and pulled Rumi close enough to whisper. 'Do not tell anyone but Mandla about everything that happened to you.'

The bodyguard appeared behind Alangba, plainly to escort him out. Rumi nodded to Alangba, then touched his heart and pointed to the sky. Alangba responded in kind before being escorted from the room.

'We must confer, Lord Diviner,' said Gaitan. 'To give him a new name.'

'The work is already half done,' Karile said. 'The boy does not know his true last name, so there is no reason to hide it. He can keep the name Voltaine.'

Mandla nodded. 'He will continue to bear Voltaine. For his given name, he will have Ajanla Erenteyo.'

Rumi raised an eyebrow. 'Ajanla Erenteyo? What does that mean?'

Mandla blinked. 'It means a lot.'

Dissatisfied with that answer, Rumi opened his mouth to

protest, then closed it. He had asked enough questions as it was and could see that was not expected here. *A gentle touch.*

When Rumi didn't complain, Gaitan smiled and lowered his head. 'Ajanla Erenteyo … it works, Lord Mandla.'

Mandla turned to Karile. 'Will you see to the young lady? I would like to have a word with young … Voltaine.'

'Yes, Lord Mandla,' she said.

Mandla gestured with a brush of his hand. The chiefs filed out, one after the other, until they were left alone.

'You come with me,' Mandla said.

Rumi followed him out into the corridor.

'Tell me, do you believe in spirits, Rumi?' Mandla asked.

Rumi laughed. 'I don't think I have a choice with what I have seen.'

'Ah but our learning cannot achieve maturity until we begin to discountenance the testimony of our eyes. Have you ever seen a real spirit?'

He paused, considering the question for a moment.

'Yes,' he said.

'How do you know?'

'Excuse me?'

'How do you know you saw a spirit?'

'Because I remember seeing it.'

'Memory is such a curious thing, though, isn't it?' Mandla mused.

Rumi raised an eyebrow at the man. 'I suppose it is.'

Mandla grinned and put an arm on Rumi's shoulder. 'How did you get here?'

Rumi opened his mouth to answer, then stopped. He could not quite remember. He narrowed his eyes to focus.

It was the most obvious thing he had ever tried to recall, and yet it eluded him, like a mosquito in the darkness. He trawled through his mind, retracing everything that had happened on this incredible day, but came up with nothing.

'How did we get here?' Rumi whispered quietly to himself. *I know this. It was just … We went through …*

Mandla's expression did not change.

'I can't remember,' Rumi said finally, feeling stupid as he said it.

'You can't remember?' Mandla asked incredulously. 'You've been here barely an hour and you cannot remember how you got here?'

Rumi ran his hand through his hair and sighed. 'No, I don't remember.'

Mandla's lips curled into a mirthless smile. 'Incredible, isn't it? How such simple details can be stolen from our minds? How is it that you have forgotten something so simple, so recent, so obvious?'

Rumi did not prepare a response.

'I ask again, how did you get here?'

This time the answer came without thinking. He was answering before he even thought seriously about the question.

'We came on Shinala. I rode Black Mother through the Nyme. A tunnel under a river crossing,' he said.

Mandla smiled. 'Would you believe me if I said that I stole that memory, and if I never wanted you to have it back, you would never remember how you got here no matter how long you tried? Would you call me a liar if I said that you have seen demons, spirits, even gods before, perhaps even several times, but you will never remember them because they do not want you to? That almost every dream you had was stolen in this same way?'

Rumi's cheek twitched. 'Tell me more.'

'No, you tell me. What is your name?'

'My name is... is... is...' His mind was barren again. 'Stop it,' Rumi snapped.

Mandla smiled like a troublesome mother playing with her child's food. 'The mind is a good servant, but a poor master; do not forget that. Any half decent shadowwielder can enter a person's mind by touching them with only their name. In the Eredo, we give one another false names; it is a tradition that began long ago. A stolen first name in the hands of a wicked thief is more dangerous than a knife in the chest, but if an enemy has your full name, then you might as well prepare your grave. To tell a man your first and last name here is to say, "I am a foolish idiot".'

'So Mandla isn't your real name?'

He smiled. 'It is, but if anyone entered my mind, they might find it a dangerous place.'

Rumi raised an eyebrow. 'So, everyone else here uses a fake name?'

'At first, yes, until they have broken kola nut. Names are protected where kola nut has been broken.'

'I see,' Rumi said.

'To tell the roundtable what you thought was your real name was a demonstration that you knew nothing of the Eredo way. It was a cruel jibe.'

Rumi bit down on his lip. 'From now on my name is Slaps then.'

'Why Slaps?'

''Cos I am going to slap Chief Lungelo one day.'

Mandla smiled and looked forty years younger. 'You are definitely Adunola's son.'

The sound of his mother's name made Rumi wince, but he remastered himself. The surprise of learning Mandla knew his father had withered away and curiosity had blossomed in its place.

He considered for the first time in a long while: what if his father wasn't a coward after all? What if he had some noble mission that led him away? What if he had wanted to come back? He turned to Mandla. 'My father. What was he like?'

'He can tell you himself,' Mandla said.

Rumi raised an eyebrow. 'Excuse me?'

They came around a corner to the foot of a tall door of tilakia stone. Mandla knocked once.

'I'm coming,' came a soft voice.

He's still alive.

33

Griff

RUMI

The wheels beneath the sliding door groaned as it was pushed aside. The man who opened it was close to fifty, with reddish-brown eyes and a thick beard that covered his chin and neck. He was tall, his shoulders broad, arms thick with muscle.

He glanced at Mandla, then Rumi. His eyes stayed with Rumi.

'Griff, this is your son,' Mandla said.

He looked just like Rumi, only with a full beard and thirty more years of life. The same broad shoulders, the same sharp lines and arched brow with slim slits for eyes.

Without thinking, Rumi slapped the man across the face. Perhaps because he was confused, probably because he hated him, but almost certainly because he already felt he might come to love him in a way he did not deserve. Where was this well-groomed man when his mother fought tax collectors in the open market? Was he shaving his beard while Morire and Rumi scrubbed floors for cowries?

'I suppose I deserve that,' Griff said, massaging his cheek.

Rumi frowned at the sound of his voice. *Godsblood, how did I get my voice from this man?*

He stepped aside. 'Please, come in.'

The room had a large bookshelf at the far wall and a domed,

painted ceiling. A small round table surrounded by carved wooden chairs took up space at the corner of the room. There were paintings on the wall and clear glass bowls with fish swimming in them. On the walls were paintings of ancient Odu tribes; on the floor, the wide, sprawling coat of a vanquished lion. Rumi's stomach churned as he looked around. He forced back tears.

'Cry if you must. It is human,' said Mandla. 'To be supple and tender is to live. Even the great iroko must have its sway, lest it challenge the wind and fall. Let the pain have its way; there is no strength in denial.'

'Lord Mandla, your words are rain,' Griff said, bowing, 'but perhaps it would suffice to say, "it is okay to cry, Rumi".'

Mandla raised an eyebrow. 'It is okay to cry, Rumi.'

Rumi struggled to stop sniffing.

'I would imagine you want to know where I have been all your life,' Griff said.

Rumi set his jaw, unable to speak.

Griff sighed deeply. 'When I met your mother, she was training to be a priestess. She had gone through her isolation in the forest and was under the care of the diviners. I was a ... a—'

'He was a plantain hawker,' Mandla said. 'Say it as it is.'

'I was a plantain hawker in what was then Oduland. This was before the Palmaine came.'

Rumi retained his silence, drumming his thigh as Griff spoke.

'We met in the market. She came for the plantain, but came back for my story. Every time she came, I would tell her the sliver of a story, just enough for her to return for more. She would listen as her plantain roasted and I would stretch the story out to hold her attention for as long as I could manage.'

Rumi bunched his hand into a fist. 'Did you love her?'

Griff gave a start. 'I did. I really did. *Ododo* love... But you see, your mother was a gifted young priestess-to-be, and I was...'

'A plantain hawker,' said Mandla.

Griff frowned. 'Everyone in the market loved her, but I loved her more than all of them conjoined. They would tease me about it in the market, but I didn't care. By the time my story was close to its end, your mother was a young woman and had been roasting plantain with me for seven years. I was a young man. I could lift ten sacks of plantain at once, I could strike down trees with one axe blow. I was a fool, so I said foolish things. I told her I would fight anyone who stood between us and the marriage cup. It was a foolish boast. Her attendants told the diviners, and they dragged me out in the market square. They asked if it was true that I loved her; I confirmed it. They asked if it was true that I promised to fight anyone who opposed my love; I confirmed it. Before I knew what was happening, your mother came out in the market square dressed in the full garb of a bloodgeneral.'

Mandla gave a wry smile. 'She asked him to name his weapon.'

'We duelled with koboko.'

'He doesn't know what koboko is,' Mandla said, prodding Griff with an elbow.

Griff raised an eyebrow. 'Koboko is a sort of stick-whip. A tree branch stripped of its leaves so that it bends and whips in the air. In times past, every mother had a koboko for the errant child.'

Mandla interjected. 'Now, in all this, you must remember that though Griff was a plantain hawker, he was still Kasinabe with old blood. Blood that harkens back to the very men who built the Kasinabe tribe. But your mother was something else: patient, disciplined, practiced. She had grown up in the house of diviners among old, leathery women who did not suffer the foolish or feeble.'

'I didn't take her seriously at first, and I paid dearly for that. She whipped me bloody before I knew what I had walked into.

'The longer we fought, the more intense it became. Every strike of koboko was thrown with more venom than the last. We fought until it was too dark to fight, and when the sun rose, we picked up our koboko again. It was on the third day that your mother finally threw her koboko to the ground.'

Rumi tapped the table. 'Then what?'

'Well, we accepted, as we had always known, that we were in love. But I was still...'

'A plantain hawker,' Mandla said.

'He gets it,' Griff snapped. 'She was a soon-to-be priestess, and a gifted one. The diviners respected me, but to allow a marriage was too much. The Lord Diviner tried keeping her away from me in the hope that it would suffocate our love. It did not. Then the Palmaine came.'

'Everything changed after that,' said Mandla. 'Of the four kingdoms, only two declared war against the Palmaine.'

'The Odu kingdom and the Kasinabe kingdom,' Rumi said.

'So you know some history,' Griff said. 'The Saharene surrendered; the Kuba... enlisted.'

'Almost like they knew it was coming,' Rumi said.

'They did not know anything was coming. They are victims of the Palmaine in the same way the Odu and Kasinabe are!' Mandla snapped.

'Well, Lord Mandla, I wouldn't say in the *exact* same way,' Griff said. 'What did King Olu used to call them... "profiteers of a violent theft"?'

Mandla glared at him and his voice adopted that bubbling menace. 'There is no place for that divisive chatter here.'

Griff's smile vanished.

'Anyway, the war changed it all. The Palmaine were killing everything. Killed the Lord Diviner. Killed half her teachers. Killed her mother. Burned everything we loved; everything we held sacred. Your mother was wild with grief. She berated me for not doing more, not fighting, letting her sisters die. I still loved her.'

'I suppose you think it noble. Loving a woman in her grief,' Rumi said.

'Be still, Rumi,' said Mandla.

Griff closed his eyes and pressed his fingers down on his eyelids. 'She was pregnant with our second child when she gathered what was left of the Kasinabe and Odu armies. You. A full three years had passed since they had torn down our flags and broken our palaces. Given old lands new names. The battle was lost. I pleaded with them. The consular guard, the Palmaine... They were too strong. They had guns that tore down ten men in a minute. We had no answer to that.'

Now it was Griff who had tears on his cheeks.

'King Olu of Kasabia lost his son to the Palmaine. He was ready for war and ready to die. Nasir Neverkneel was there too. You know his words?'

'Die in defiance,' Rumi said.

'Another fool, spoiling for death. But there were many of us who knew it was a suicide pact and saw wisdom in accepting Palmaine rule, at least for a season. Even Walade the Widowmaker had fear in his eye. When someone as bloodmad as Walade says to consider peace, you know that to fight is madness. But your mother would not hear it. She donned Kasinabe red, pregnant and all. When she joined her voice to King Olu and Nasir, the die was cast. You know the bloodgeneral's words?'

'Until the last Kasinabe heart stops beating, we ride,' Rumi said.

'And so they rode.'

'And you let them ride? You left your pregnant love to ride to her death?'

'It was her choice; she wouldn't listen to me. She made a mockery of me in front of all the bloodgenerals. She called me a coward half a hundred times. She... she stole my name from me. Do you know what it is for a man not to know his own name?'

Rumi's glare was colder than ice. 'You make a mockery of yourself. Even now, you do not deserve your name.'

'I wasn't to know she survived. I would have come back. I would have come back.'

'When did you find out she survived?' Rumi asked.

Griff went silent at his question. Still as stone.

'When did you find out she survived?'

'That's enough, Rumi,' Mandla said.

'You are no father of mine. The yellow in your soul is clear as glass. It's no wonder Yami left you behind. Look at you! A man who abandons his partner and their children. I am glad you weren't a part of my life. Thank Dara for Yami – if not for her, perhaps I'd have grown to be an empty scabbard like you. She was the only one I ever needed.'

'Was?' Griff said. 'She's gone?'

'What do you care? You left her to die.'

Griff swallowed hard and for a moment Rumi read the tale of turmoil in his eyes. His lip quivered as he drew in breath and he seemed unsure of what to say. When the words finally came they were a staggering disappointment.

'Did she tell you? Did she ever tell you what my name is?'

Rumi narrowed his eyes. 'Why would she ever tell me any-thing about you?'

'You don't know what it was like in those days. We were being strung up from trees. The things men had to deal with in our lives...'

'What *men* had to deal with? What would you know about that? What Morire had to deal with. What I did. All because you couldn't stand up. You abandoned us when we needed you the most. Honestly, how do you live with yourself?'

'Enough, Rumi!' Mandla snapped.

'That's what this place is, isn't it?' Rumi said, staring at Mandla. 'A hiding place for all the Kasinabe who chose not to fight. Not to ride with your king.'

Mandla's face was impossibly blank. 'When the martyr's spear falls, there must be those who can sharpen it again. Our nation was not strong enough then, but will be when the time comes again.'

He turned to Griff, placing an arm on his shoulder. 'I'm taking him to the dining hall. This will get easier.'

Griff nodded.

Mandla led Rumi back out of the sliding doors.

Outside, Mandla spoke in hushed tones. 'She did not tell you your name? Your true name? Or the name of your father?'

'Irumide Voltaine.'

'Voltaine is not a name. Your true name is far older than that. Ancient Mushiain words.'

'She did not know it.'

Mandla was quiet for a while at that. 'She did. If she did not tell you, then she has given you the means to reveal it.'

34

Rice and Beans

RUMI

Mandla's bodyguard Telemi, handed Rumi over to Ladan with instruction to find him food.

This time, as they moved through the corridor, Rumi did not try to memorise their path. Instead he looked for markings. A prominent inscription or an ornate door handle. Anything that would give him a sense of where exactly he was in the endless labyrinth.

'How does anyone find their way around these corridors?'

'Part of our training is to master them,' Ladan said. 'If you get lost, you can let a dog lead you back to the market and start over.'

Rumi sucked his lips into his mouth and studied the walls. *I've joined a merry collection of madmen.*

As they travelled down the corridor, the aroma of stewed beans and fragrant rice wafted to fill it. They came to a set of doors bordered by stone columns and a triumphal arch. Ladan pulled the doors open with a jerk.

The dining hall was large, with rows of tables and chairs sparsely gathered in clusters. At the front of the hall was an arched opening where the sounds of pans, pots and sizzling oil rang loud and clear. Ladan motioned towards a cluster of chairs.

Strogus, the bearded doorkeeper who had left with Nataré, appeared from the opening. Rumi's jaw tightened at the sight of him.

'Hello,' Strogus said, approaching their table.

He placed a kola nut gently on the table and pushed it towards Rumi. 'I suppose we didn't start out on the best terms. Forgive me, I am the doorkeeper here. It's practically part of my job to be harsh to strangers.'

Rumi's stare softened. He took the kola nut and broke it. 'Where I am from, we say you shake with a man while you still have hands.'

'I like that,' Strogus said.

Ladan rose to his feet. 'I'll get us all some food.'

He darted towards the kitchen and a moment later returned with a tray of food. A pot of steamed rice, a bowl of king's beans and a larger pot of stewed venison.

Rumi washed his hands clean in a water bowl and sized up the meat. Strogus moved his hand towards a plate, stopping short as Ladan murmured, 'He has guest rights until he's admitted.'

Grunting, Strogus passed the plate to Rumi.

Unwilling to deepen his enmity with Strogus, Rumi scooped up the smallest of the three cuts of meat. Ladan and Strogus had no such modesty, each commandeering frankly ridiculous helpings of rice and beans.

Rumi watched them eat for a moment before making a start. His experience with calabash shards was limited. The curved wooden shards were no longer used in Alara.

Ladan raised an eyebrow. 'Would you like a knife and fork?'

'No,' Rumi lied.

Ladan nodded. 'Palmaine cutlery is so violent. They butcher their food all over again on the plate. Barbarous.'

Rumi shakily raised a mound of food to his mouth.

The first bite was a lesson; fall-apart tender with soft undertones of seasoning. He instantly regretted not taking the bigger piece.

'This is good,' he said.

Had he been at his mother's table, she would have reprimanded him for speaking with a full mouth.

All shyness fled as he set to clumsy work with the shard. When the meal was done, he sat in silent marvel. If they ate like this at every meal, he would stay forever.

'Well, I'll be having some more,' Strogus said, rising to his feet. 'And you brothers?'

'Yes, please.'

'None for me. Nothing beats the first batch,' said Ladan, rubbing his stomach.

Strogus trudged once more towards the kitchen.

Rumi watched him go. He was what most would describe as a rough man, but inarguably handsome. Rumi could see how Nataré might have been drawn to him, the way some women are drawn to leafy huntsmen and seafarers who always smell like the sea. He found himself trying to measure in his head how much taller than him Strogus was. *Not that much, a few inches at most.*

'I bet you're wondering what he's about,' Ladan said.

'Not really,' Rumi lied again.

Ladan smiled. 'Strogus worked three years as a maicer before he was rescued. He takes everything as an insult and holds grudges longer than the Agbara. Hard to blame him, really. Damn good doorkeeper though. Used to be shadowwielder too until they stripped him of the shadow a few years back.'

Rumi's eyebrows rose. 'Why did they strip him?'

Ladan shrugged. 'I don't know. He doesn't talk about it.'

Rumi had heard about maicers – enslaved people for rent. Sometimes used for brutish physical work, other times to kill or maim people. Occasionally, there were much darker stories about what they were forced to do.

Rumi dared not imagine what stories Strogus had to tell. When he strolled back, carrying a refilled tray of food, Rumi thanked him warmly and encouraged him to serve himself first.

They did sweet justice to the venison and rice. Rumi sighed as though breathing out all his troubles. It had been days since good food had passed through his lips. Now he just wanted to sleep and to do nothing of consequence.

'I wonder who will train you to shadowdance,' Ladan said.

'With any luck he'll get Xhosa, but I'm holding out hope for Zarcanis the Viper,' Strogus said.

Ladan sniggered. 'You want to kill him? The Viper doesn't train Seedlings.'

'A shadowwielder can train anyone they want. If a personal request is made, the Council will listen,' Strogus replied.

'In that case, Rumi, better stay away from the lower levels. Believe me, you don't want Zarcanis taking an interest in you,' said Ladan. 'Who was the last shadowdancer to train under Zarcanis?'

'Yomiku,' Strogus said.

'Godsblood,' Ladan muttered. 'Tell you what, I'd rather fight a Suli or a Truetree than fight with Yomiku. That lad is a monster. Why is *he* still a Seedling?'

'He got into some nasty business after his first Bleeding,' Strogus said, picking food from his teeth. 'Should have gone down for conduct unbecoming, but they put him through the Arakoro instead.'

Ladan leaned forward. 'What exactly goes on in that place? The Arakoro, I mean.'

Strogus shrugged. 'How in Dara's name would I know? Nobody that knows ever talks about it. Yomiku weren't the same after. Then the chiefs put him in the Viper's hands and said he has to wait the full five years before becoming a Suli.'

'How many years has he done now?'

'Almost four, and I reckon he can already beat every one of the shadowwielders, except the Viper.'

'No way Yomiku beats Xhosa, there's no way,' Ladan said.

'I'd wager my last cowrie on Yomiku making light work of Xhosa with any weapon. Don't get emotional, boy.'

'Xhosa puts Yomiku on his back any day of the week!' Ladan rose to his feet.

'Oh, I've heard she puts men on their backs. Not in the arena, though. Like teacher, like student, I suppose,' Strogus said, also standing.

'What did you just say?' Ladan glared at Strogus.

'You heard me. Your shadowwielder is a pretty thing who knows more about bedding than she does about bleeding, and you are a boylover.' Strogus's cheekbones shifted like sheets of metal, inflecting his words with uncompromising malice.

Ladan didn't even hesitate. He let his fist sing through Strogus's chin.

Rumi moved to get between them, but he was stopped by a voice that sounded like a hammer beating rocks.

'Unacceptable.'

Strogus stepped back from Ladan, his eyes alight with rage. Ladan fell to one knee and bowed his head.

It was Mandla.

'Now you remember your manners,' Mandla said, slapping Ladan across the back of his head.

He turned to Strogus. 'And you, the things I just heard you say ... Simply unacceptable. Xhosa will hear of your tales today. The Ghedo tournament is in nine months and you will defend your claims in the fighting pit. And Ladan, raising your fist in anger to a man at least five years your senior, you will serve a punishment for that.'

Mandla split his stare between the two of them, managing to strike a balance between sweltering anger and steady calm.

'I'll deal with you both later. Get out of my sight.'

Rumi tried to stand, but a low 'not you' from Mandla kept him in his seat.

Ladan and Strogus streaked from the room like rabbits from a cage, leaving Rumi and Mandla completely alone. It was quiet, save for the distant clang of iron pots and clay from the kitchens.

Mandla drew in a long breath before speaking. 'I feel it might be beneficial for you and I to speak frankly. When you begin in the Order, we might not get the opportunity again. I have some questions, and I am sure you have half a hundred questions of your own.'

'I do.'

'Well, I will tell you all that I can. It is not long before we are interrupted.'

'Perhaps it would be faster if you just read out the questions from my mind and answered them yourself,' Rumi hissed.

'To enter one's mind is not something to be done without reason.'

'Making me look stupid seemed reason enough, only a few hours ago.'

Mandla's face was stern as a blade. 'That was an important lesson you won't soon forget. I have no desire to enter your mind again. The little of it I saw was ... enough. We must focus; our time is at a canter.'

Rumi would never get used to the way Mandla spoke.

'Why did Lungelo call Alangba a traitor?'

Lines formed on Mandla's forehead. 'Alangba has a deep empathy for those who have lost family. Sometimes it leads him to make ill-considered decisions. He once brought a man here called Kojo. A freed slave who became a brother to us. One day, Kojo had a disagreement with the chiefs and left the Eredo to write books in Basmine. Books which many believe led to the first and only attack we have suffered.'

'How could anyone possibly attack this place?'

'Every strong tower has a back door. Praise be to Dara, our sentries caught them in the woods, so we settled the matter there, but we lost thirty-two people.'

'And that was the end of the attacks?'

Mandla nodded. 'There's a damudamu charm all around the Eredo. Only the Shinala know how to find the way here. Anyone else who tries will find themselves roaming in circles. It took three years to steal every memory of Kojo's book from the people in Basmine. Another year was spent on an excursion to the Ethiope and the Paronesian continent, tying up any loose ends we could find. Another year we spent robbing Kojo of his own knowledge. We left some things there, but not much. His mind is like a bookshelf with no books. One day we will face another attack, but they will not find us easily.'

'Why did the man write the book?'

'He always believed that the Eredo should not be kept secret from the natives. He wanted to force our hand to war.' Mandla glanced at the door. 'Our time is dying. Tell me ... How did you get this?' He pointed to the cowrie necklace, despite it being beneath Rumi's leopard-skin scarf.

Rumi massaged an eyelid with his thumb. Alangba's parting words flashed in his head. *Only Mandla, he said.*

'Let's keep it between us,' Mandla said, producing a kola nut.

Rumi glared at him. *Is he reading my mind?*

'I'm not reading your mind,' Mandla said with a grin.

Rumi frowned, knuckled his forehead. He told his story

entire. It hurt to retell it. Losing his family, seeing it happen. Even so, he managed it without tears. He withheld only the Priest of Vultures' name.

When he was done, Mandla picked up a glass of water from the table and took a generous gulp. 'Did his vultures follow you here?'

'No … at least not that I saw. I think I would feel it if they did.'

The sound of voices from the corridor startled Rumi. Mandla glanced at the door.

Rumi seized his chance before the interruption came.

'What do you know about him … about the Priest of Vultures?'

Mandla stared through Rumi.

'Palman has six High Priests. The Accuser is one of them. He is the oldest.'

'There are others?'

'Oh, yes. Pretty Yelloweye, Priestess of Cats; the Lord of Horns, whom they call the Broken One; Ntanga, whom they call the Laughing One; and two others whose names I do not know.'

Rumi gulped back saliva. 'What do they want?'

Mandla's eyes darted towards the door.

'To wipe all our gods away.'

'Why?'

He frowned. 'There is a … disagreement amongst the Agbara. The Son and his followers believe that mankind is a failed creation; that the world must begin anew. Those who still follow Dara's word believe that mankind can be redeemed. Therein lies the conflict.'

'Who is winning?'

Mandla furrowed his brow again and rubbed his chin, but did not answer.

'Do the Priests of the Son have anything to do with the Palmaine and the Palman priests? Like the bishop of Basmine?' Rumi asked.

Mandla blinked. 'If the Priests of the Son are the tree that Palman planted, the Palman priests are its fruit.'

'So they are connected?'

'In the same way the abattoir is connected to rats. The Palman priests are revellers in the same great sacrilege.'

'Would it be forward of me to ask for a yes or no answer?'

'Yes, it would... but yes, they are connected.'

'How are they connected?'

'For that, I'm afraid, I do not have a simple answer. I suppose it is in the same way as if you say the lizard is connected to the kongamoto.'

Rumi furrowed his brow. He sensed his window was closing. He did not have the time to ask the man to translate. He pressed on. 'What about the Palmaine?'

Mandla smiled. 'Well, that connection is easier to explain. The Palmaine believe they are the chosen people of Palman. They are the sainted and we are the damned. They say they do the work of God, conquering nations, recreating the world in Palman's image. One true world under one true god. The perfect world for the followers of the Son to inherit.'

'And what of those who choose not to follow Palman?'

'Their scripture says the Son shall cast them down, erase their names, their seed in the land.'

Rumi's mind regurgitated the smell of burning flesh and the sight of vultures ripping flesh from bone. He had heard those words before.

'Enough for now, Rumi.' Mandla rose to his feet. 'Everything has a season, even the knowledge of things has its time.'

Rumi stretched out a hand towards Mandla, willing him to stop. 'The *Sakosaye*. How do I get the Agbara to let me read it?'

Mandla laughed so suddenly he snorted. '*Get* the Agbara? If you find a way to *get* the Agbara to do anything, you would be as good as an Agbara yourself. There is only one way to read a *Sakosaye*: waiting until you are told to do so.'

Rumi frowned.

Mandla turned towards the door. 'Goodbye for now.'

Rumi stumbled out of the dining hall after Mandla, but there was no sign of him. He took two turns in the corridor and found himself lost in the constellation of paintings and inscriptions on the walls and ceilings.

Wandering alone, he let his mind unfurl and his imagination stretch. An hour passed with only the odd passer-by or patrolling lionhound for company. The Eredo, in corridor alone, was a wondrous place.

A small, waist-high carving of a martial eagle in flight drew his attention. As he paused to admire the work, the soft beat of drums made his eyebrows shoot upwards.

Something shifted in his chest. He followed the sound like a hunting hound to the scent.

He came to a door that was slightly ajar and eased it open with his toe.

There was a drummer, a flautist, and a singer, too deep in their music to notice him.

The sound rattled him. The sound of the soul, of defiance. Eloquent Mushiain words, both foreign and familiar. For a moment, he looked into the singer's eyes. The man was operating from the only place a man can be truly fearless.

With effort, Rumi stepped back and slowly closed the door. Music had no place in his life now. If he had never given time to music in the first place, he would not have been in that carriage on that night. That, soft, supple side of himself had to die.

He let out a heavy breath.

'Incredible, isn't it?' came a cold, still voice behind him.

He spun.

A woman with red hair in thick curly ringlets and dark green eyes met his stare. She looked to be a touch above thirty, tall, with a high-collared dress covering her neck entirely. Her eyes were gentle, but her face was hard as paving stone.

'Yes,' Rumi said.

'The only real form of communication, I feel.' She extended a hand. 'You must be the new iron to be hammered. Griff's son. I hear you are joining the Shadow Order.'

Rumi met her eyes. 'So I'm told.'

He shook her hand.

'I thought they didn't allow men of fighting age into the Order?'

'Exceptional circumstances.'

She rubbed her lower lip as though trying to solve a puzzle.

'*Exceptional circumstances*,' she repeated. 'Dara guide you.'

'And may his way be yours.'

Rumi watched her leave. The Eredo was an intriguing place. In Basmine, Rumi had often felt like a man wearing an ill-fitting, centuries-old cloak tailored by a malevolent seamstress. In the Eredo, he felt like he was walking naked. He wasn't yet sure which he preferred.

35

Things Forgotten

RUMI

Ladan and Strogus broke into relieved sighs when they found Rumi in the corridor. It had not been long since they had come to blows, yet they were walking with their arms locked at the elbow.

'Where did you go? Everyone is asking about you.' Ladan placed a hand on Rumi's shoulder.

'I needed to clear my head,' said Rumi. 'News spreads fast here. I met a lady just now who asked about me joining the Shadow Order.'

'Already meeting ladies! Maybe you *are* a fast learner,' Ladan teased. 'What was her name?'

Rumi frowned. 'I didn't ask for it,' he replied, empty-handed.

'Too stupid to ask a pretty girl her name? Definitely not a fast learner,' said Strogus.

'I didn't say she was pretty.'

'If she wasn't pretty, then why did you say it like she was the first woman you ever met? *Oooh, I just met a laaaaady!*' Strogus lifted his voice several octaves too high.

Ladan smirked, slapping Strogus on the back as a dog walked soundlessly by.

Rumi rolled his eyes. 'What is it with this place and dogs?'

'Haven't you ever seen a dog barking and snarling at nothing?'

said Ladan. 'They see what we cannot see. In the old days, people believed that if you rubbed the water from a dog's eye on your own, you would see the spirits like they do for a short while.'

'Ever tried it?'

'Why would I want to rub manky dog eye–water on my eyes? I don't even *want* to see spirits.'

'Fair enough,' Rumi said, thumbing his lip. He looked to Strogus. 'Where is Kaat, my own lionhound?'

Strogus arched an eyebrow. 'The pregnant one?'

Rumi nodded.

'She is being taken care of; ask for me after your Bleeding and I will take you to see her,' Strogus said.

Ladan touched his chin. 'There will be shadowwielders at your Bleeding, watching everything you do. Try to be friendly; Xhosa likes friendliness. That should keep the Viper away from you, too.'

Strogus hissed a disgusted noise. He unlocked his arm from Ladan's. 'You should get him ready; they'll call for him soon,' he said. 'I've got somewhere I need to be.'

Ladan nodded and they diverted down different teeth at a fork in the corridor. Ladan led Rumi into a room and Renike shrieked as they entered.

'Rumi! This place is wonderful! The food, the rooms! Look at this!' she said, pirouetting.

Rumi glanced around the room. It was, lest he lie in the matter, wonderful. There was a feather bed with two identical wooden cabinets either side and a small iron lantern sitting on one of them. Rumi pressed his palm against the mattress and smiled. His side sack and oud case were there with all his belongings, save for the halberd. Ladan studied him, taking in his wonder.

'You won't be sleeping like this in the Seedling dorms,' Ladan said. 'These are the guest quarters.'

Rumi turned. 'These names – Seedling, Suli – what do they all mean?'

Renike seemed to perk up at that and sat still to listen.

'They are the levels of training in the Shadow Order,' Ladan began. 'We all start as a Seedling to learn the basics. How to fight, how to mindwalk. If you demonstrate the required level of skill within five years, your trainer may elevate you to Suli to learn the art of war. Less than two in ten Seedlings will ever progress beyond Suli to become Truetrees. It is for those with an aptitude for leadership. Truth is, most people don't want to lead; they want to follow, and there is no shame in following. If you become a Truetree, you can challenge any trainer to become a Shadowblack – a full shadowwielder.'

Kamanu's words flashed in Rumi's head. *Born to be a shadowwielder.* The way Ladan told it, it seemed a long journey.

He looked to Ladan. 'What level are you?'

'I am a Suli.'

'And did you take five years to make it to Suli?'

'Three, but that was based on good performance at the Ghedo and because I have a special talent.'

'The Ghedo?'

'It's a tournament that comes about every five years. The best performers at the Ghedo are often elevated faster.'

'And what special talent do you have?'

'I … Well, I see things. It is an advanced form of mindwalking called spiritsight.'

'You see things?'

'Yes. I can see things that may happen.'

'Like a fortune teller?'

Ladan's face darkened. 'I suppose. Have you ever heard the saying "a man's hands tell his story"?'

Rumi raised an eyebrow. 'Of course.'

'Well, there is a great deal of truth in it.'

Rumi glanced at his hands, then held them out to Ladan. 'What do my hands tell you about me?'

Ladan pushed his hands down. 'If you were playing a game of *seraiye* and discovered you could not win, you would abandon the game.'

'So what?'

'If I tell you your future, I might destroy it. Sometimes spirit-sight can steal the joy in things.'

'Not me.' *They stole my joy already.*

Ladan raised an eyebrow. 'If I told you that one day Kayalli's lips would turn to rotting worm food, should it make you any less likely to want to kiss them today?'

It took Rumi a moment to recall that Nataré called herself Kayalli.

'Kiss Kayalli?' Renike chirped.

'Who said I want to kiss Kayalli?' Rumi said.

'I see ... So we are just lying to ourselves today?'

Rumi snorted. 'So, you just see people's futures and don't tell anyone?'

Ladan furrowed his brow. 'It isn't as clear as you think. It's like watching shadows: you can get the outline of a thing, but you miss the details. It's not as clear as seeing face to face, and the longer you leave it without telling it or writing it down, the more it drifts from your mind. Like painting a picture of a man you only saw once and from a distance.'

'So tell me what you see, even if it's just the outline.'

Ladan fixed Rumi with a flat, dark look and suddenly grabbed Rumi's wrist. His grip was tight as a snake on its supper.

'You sure?' he asked.

Between the hollow glint in Ladan's two-coloured eyes and the noose-tight grip on Rumi's wrist, there was, all of a sudden, something very unsettling about the whole affair. Whatever it was, though, it wasn't enough to douse the fire of Rumi's curiosity.

'I'm sure.'

Ladan laughed and let his grip slacken, eyes adopting a far-away cast as he spoke. 'I see all sorts of things. Strongest of all, I see a dog, chased by three black shadows in a field of white sand. I see a broken crown and a four-point star above your forehead.'

'That it?'

Ladan nodded.

Rumi snorted. 'What a crap prophecy.'

'You're the one who asked,' said Ladan, releasing his wrist.

'Do mine,' Renike said, holding out her hand.

Ladan hesitated, then frowned and took her hand. 'I see a goblet filled with... with blood. I see four small shadows and one big one. I see you kneeling before a tree.'

Renike drew her hand back when Ladan was finished. 'I agree with Rumi. Crap prophecy.'

Ladan shrugged. 'If you say so.'

'Tell me something,' Rumi said. 'What do you know about the Priest of Vultures?'

Ladan's eyes nearly popped from his skull. He clapped his hand over Rumi's mouth, his eyes darting across the room as though a bat had flown in.

'A name is a powerful thing, Rumi. You do not call all names without care, especially not a name like that one.'

He formed the sign of the crossroads with his forefingers.

'Is that his name? It sounds more like a title to me. I know his mother didn't call him "The Priest of Vultures".'

'Stop it,' Ladan snapped, still holding up the crossroads.

Rumi sighed. 'What do you know about him?'

Renike's eyes hardened as she listened.

Ladan cleared his throat. 'Well, I know not to go shouting that name about, that's for starters. He is one of the Godsbane. The hunters. Priests of the Son.'

'What else?'

'That's all I need to know about such a thing. Makes my skin itch. Go ask Lord Mandla.'

Rumi didn't press. He didn't want to lose Ladan's company. He still had much to say, and much more that he would like to hear. He had never mastered the art of keeping friends, but Ladan was a window to understanding.

'How did you end up here, Ladan?'

'The Chainbreakers rescued me.'

Rumi raised an eyebrow. 'What are the Chainbreakers exactly?'

'They are like good pirates. They are led by a man called Okafor Blaise and rescue enslaved natives from land and sea.'

'Earlier today, Strogus called you a bo—'

'A boylover.'

'Yes… I'm sorry he sai—'

'There's nothing to be sorry about, Rumi. We put no shame on it here; this isn't like the rest of Basmine. I *am* a boylover. Well, more of a manlover.'

'Strogus seemed to—'

'Strogus is half a fool and half a warrior, not fully dispossessed of the times he was owned by a Palman priest. You have to learn to ignore him half the time. Our history is filled with men and women like me; it was the Palmaine that taught natives to hate us. Why do you think they called King Kosi the King of Men?'

Rumi shivered with laughter. 'I always wondered why they called him that. I mean ... they were *all* kings of men. Why did he get a special title for it?'

'Because when it came to men, he was king.'

Rumi chuckled.

'I hope you have no problem with it, though if you do, I can see you in the fighting pit any time. I don't care who your father is. If you have a problem, speak it now and we will settle it the old way.'

'I don't have a problem with it.'

'Good,' Ladan said with a smile.

Rumi flashed a smile of his own and held out an unbroken kola nut. 'Seal it with a promise.'

Ladan beamed, broke the kola nut and they ate.

'You should get ready. There is a bathroom and a fresh kaftan over there,' Ladan said, pointing. 'They will send for you any moment.'

'Thank you, Ladan.'

The kaftan was indeed fresh. It was dark blue with gold threadwork and tiger-eye buttons. He looked like a prince.

When he stepped out from the bathroom, Ladan was gone and three men holding spears were in his place. The one at the centre wore full leather armour with an ironwire vest, his helmet moulded in the shape of a snarling bear.

'It is time,' he said.

36

The Bloods

RUMI

Rumi followed the armoured men down the corridor to the hall with the moon-shaped table. Over a dozen men and women were seated as he stepped in. Their muttering gave way to silence as the attention of the room turned to him.

There were six gourdlets of different colours on the table, along with a large, empty calabash. Lord Mandla sat at the centre with Telemi behind him. To his left sat Chief Karile and to his right sat a tall man Rumi did not know. He had a long, black beard that likened him to a jungle bear.

There were others he did not know. The man sitting next to Chief Lungelo was bald as a chief in wartime with fiery brown eyes and such an obvious, unrelenting fierceness to his stare that Rumi was almost certain he was the Viper. The man deserved the moniker.

The woman from the corridor was there too. Her fiery red hair shone brighter in the light. She smiled and Rumi smiled back. *Be friendly.*

These must have been the trainers. The rest of the chiefs were also in attendance.

Mandla raised his hand. It was a gesture with all the practiced nonchalance of a conductor coaxing a chorus from the orchestra; except that when Mandla raised a hand, he brought silence, not sound.

'Come forward,' Mandla said.

Rumi shuffled forward.

'He looks just like the darkman,' said one man, gliding his mortar-sized fist across the table.

'I like him already,' said another man with receding hair.

'He looks scared to me,' said the man Rumi guessed was the Viper. 'Are you scared?'

'Not this very moment,' Rumi said.

Be friendly.

'We may exchange kola nut,' Mandla said.

A ceremony ensued. Some of the men and women chose to introduce themselves after that. The man with mortar fists gave the name Domo Ayebere; the dark-haired woman was Xhosi Odunife, the thick bearded man was Kairobi Naya and the man he thought was the viper gave the singular name Admar. The rest had not given names.

'We begin,' Mandla said. 'Son of Odu, do you accept the Bloods?'

Rumi stepped forward. 'I do.'

'Do you promise to keep the immortal secrets of the Bloods and all its manifestations?

'I do.'

Mandla nodded with a grim satisfaction and picked up a gourdlet.

'Blood of the leopard,' he said, pouring the contents into the calabash. Thick red blood painted the bowl. 'Blood of the bull.' He took the second gourdlet and poured in the same manner. 'Blood of the eagle ... Blood of the lion ... Blood of the tree.'

He was hesitant with the last gourdlet, glancing at the others before he poured. 'Blood of the Agbara,' he said. The mixture of six bloods filled the calabash. His eyes flashed white and he spoke in Mushiain.

'Drink,' he said offering the calabash to Rumi.

'All of it?'

'Yes.'

He looked into the purply red bowl, then he drained it. Nothing changed.

Mandla whistled and a small white dove flew into his outstretched hand.

'Eat this,' he said, offering the white dove.

'Excuse me?' Rumi said, flinching at the thought.

'Eat the bird,' he said.

Rumi took the bird in his hand, looking at it carefully. It was alive. *I will not eat a live bird.* He looked back to the table. All eyes were fixed on him, expectant. They were serious.

He looked back at the bird, nestled in his palm. The creature was almost small enough to disappear in his closed fist. *Do I start with the head or with the feet?* The thought made him shudder.

'Eat the bird,' Mandla said. It was a command, not a request. *If this is what it takes to become a shadowwielder.*

He pressed the bird between his palms and crushed it. It trembled feebly in his hands, making no attempt to fly away, resigned to its fate. He started from the top. The blood was hot in his mouth, the feathers dusty and strange to chew. He was thrown by the hardness of the bone. He wanted to retch. Blood, bone and feathers spewed from his lips as he chewed. He glared at them with each bite. *Why did they make me do this?* He swallowed what was left whole, crushing bone, flesh and feathers between his teeth.

Mandla produced a final vial of purple red blood. 'Drink,' he said.

Rumi did not hesitate to throw the blood back and lick his teeth clean, spitting bone.

'It is done,' said Mandla.

There was a strange interval of silence. Then, in the half-blink of an eye, the room grew cold. Rumi's shadow flew around the room like a kite in a crazed wind. His eyes raced after it, but it moved with blurring speed. It came back to him, stretched out, and turned to billowing smoke. Power shot through his body. His eyes bulged. It was like waking up after eternal slumber.

Wisps of shadow leaked from the pores of his skin. The thrum of his heart slowed to a patient crawl, like the slow drip of water from a half-closed tap. His skin tingled and his breath came in short, light bursts.

The power within groaned for him to act, to spill blood. He wanted to go after those he owed vengeance. The Priest of Vultures and his iron-eyed companion. He saw them in his mind. Searching through the forest. He wanted to run to them, to seize the blood from their insides. He closed his eyes.

'The fugitive from death,' he heard a voice say. A voice that was like an oud out of tune. Music with no melody. 'So you think to touch the shadow?'

The priestess's cowrie sizzled against his neck. Rumi was suddenly somewhere far from the Eredo.

The Priest of Vultures sat cross-legged, watching a fire. Whatever was burning there was dead and vile. Rumi could smell it, he could feel it on his skin, corroding hair and flesh. He averted his eyes,

'Do you think you can hide from me? Do you think I can be resisted?'

'I will find you and I will kill you,' Rumi said.

'Find me? Is that what you believe? Surely not. No, you cannot be so foolish. I am the one who hunts. I will come.

I will break you beyond repair, twist your neck until you see your backside, make you envy the dead. Deep down you know it – you burn with the turbulence of a forshortened future, a story to end in bleeding and screams.'

The Priest of Vultures stirred for a moment. 'I suppose I could spare you. If you give it back to me … Yes, if you do that, there would be no need for death and mourning. Yes.' The slither in the word 'yes' lingered on his tongue as though he had figured out something wonderful. He turned to Rumi and his eyes burrowed to bone, strangling breath. 'Speak my name and I will spare you. My true name, the one you know. Speak it to me.'

The name burned in Rumi's mind, the one his mother had used. If he had lived a thousand years, he could not forget it. Rumi recalled the way the Priest of Vultures had reacted when Yami said it – it was the only thing he had seen that gave the Priest of Vultures a moment of fear.

'Return my name!' the priest snarled.

Rumi's lips moved, the name on the brink of falling from his lips. Suddenly an icy cool touched his skin, like a cloak of ice being draped across his shoulders. This was smooth, delightful. There were more voices.

'Defy him.' It was Kamanu's voice, clear and sharp, like funeral drum. 'Defy him.'

'The riding hammer will be the breaking of you, Accuser. The Dancing Lion will break every bond.' That was another voice. A voice with a scratchy husk and commanding pitch. The voice of Gu.

'Defy him,' Gu repeated.

Rumi stretched his hands up to the sky. It was a movement as unwitting as breathing. He opened his mouth.

'I defy you.'

'So ... you mean to challenge me,' spat the Priest of Vultures.
Rumi stared at him.

'Look,' said the Priest of Vultures, pointing at the fire.

Rumi froze at what he saw.

'Look!'

It was Yami, her flesh charred black. He turned away from
the scene, pursing his lips to forestall vomit.

'If it is defiance, then look well. You will meet the same end.
If the tree will not bend, then it must be broken.'

The world flashed black. Rumi blinked and found himself
back in the great hall. The Chiefs and Shadowwielders sat semi-
circled around him, watching him as though he was a child
juggling knives. There was vomit on the floor. From his pores
there was still simmering shadow.

No sooner had he raised his fist than his shadow came back
together, falling in place like conjoined drops of water at the
floor of a gourd. The power was gone, the names forgotten. He
choked, coughing blood.

Karile came to his side, placing a hand on the small of his
back.

'Breathe,' said Gaitan.

His heart pounded against his chest.

'A good first try,' said Karile. 'He drew a lot of the shadow.'

'A strong binding,' said Gaitan.

'What was that?' Rumi said.

'The first fellowship of the substance and the shadow. The
first taste of your power. You'll understand it better with time.
The shadow is the part of you long forgotten, an untapped
well of power.'

'Now the small matter of who will train him,' said Karile.

Mandla rose from his seat. 'All the shadowwielders have
expressed an interest in taking him on, but one argument has

311

compelled me.' He looked to the fair woman with the curly fire-red hair. 'Zarcanis the Viper, you will train him.'

The woman smiled. *So, she is the Viper.*

Rumi knuckled his chest as the coughing stopped. 'Is it normal to hear voices?'

Gaitan started. 'Yes, that happens sometimes. The mind is a feeble thing.'

'Whose voices?' said Mandla.

'Gu. Kamanu.' He did not dare to mention the third voice he had heard.

The room fell still and silent.

Mandla's voice was cold enough to quench fire. 'Leave us.'

The Chiefs and Shadowwielders dispersed.

When they were alone, Rumi met Mandla's gaze.

'The Bloods,' Rumi said. 'That was blood sacrifice.'

Mandla's stare was hard as stone. 'It is our only way to contact the Higher World. Our back door. The Son was supposed to die so that we could have free access to the Higher World, but here we are.'

'So you use blood sacrifice?' Rumi spat. 'That is against the Darani way, the scriptures say so.'

Mandla frowned and drew a finger over the exact line of the long scar on Rumi's chest. 'You are above the use of blood?'

Rumi shuddered. 'That's different.'

'So you agree that there are different kinds of blood sacrifice. We are not witch doctors; there is still some *art* in what we do. An Agbara gave his life for the Kasinabe. His blood gives us access to the power from the Higher World, the Originate.'

Rumi pinched the bridge of his nose. 'Is that where the voices came from? The Originate?'

Mandla rubbed his barren chin, his eyebrows arched to frame his unwrinkled face. 'Everything that happens in the Originate has a resonance in our world. It is the place where all things become things.'

'So why did I hear voices?'

'Strange things happen sometimes. Have you ever thought you heard your name but then when you looked around, no one had called you?'

'Of course.'

'That is the Originate touching our world. If you hear your name like that again, don't answer. You were touching the Originate somehow. It is not unheard of. Our part is to teach you the eternal arts of the shadowwielders. Shadowdancing, conjuring, mindwalking, dominion, bloodlettering and shadow's tongue. You will learn the first four as a Seedling. Karile will train you in mindwalking, Gaitan in dominion, and Zarcanis in shadowdancing.'

Rumi frowned. 'This wasn't just a strange voice. I saw it clear. Heard the words. Why?'

Mandla's eyes hardened as he wet his lips. 'Because someone from the Originate wants you dead.'

37

Dark Words

ALANGBA

Alangba discarded his sandals at the foot of the door and walked into the room. He stared up at the stalactite canopy as he entered. It had been years since he'd had the pleasure of seeing it.

Lord Mandla was seated at the centre of the moon table with Chief Karile and Gaitan either side of him. A man with cobalt cuffs and a black sack over his head knelt in the sand – beside him was the First Ranger Okafor, arrived at last. A woman with curly red hair stood just to the side. From the stubborn set of the kneeling man's shoulders, Alangba knew the cuffed man was Governor-General Zaminu but the woman – to his surprise – was Zarcanis the Viper.

Zarcanis ripped the sack from Zaminu's head.

'Remember me?' she said.

Zaminu squinted, as though trying to puzzle her out, not a hint of recognition on his face. 'Am I supposed to?'

Zarcanis snorted and shrugged before moving to the table with Lord Mandla. Okafor nodded Alangba forward and he stepped into the sand.

Mandla's eyes fixed on him like a hawk on a house mouse. 'Is it true that you found him performing blood rituals?' Mandla asked.

Alangba bowed low. 'Yes, Lord Mandla. He was with a Palman priest. They had a divination tray and a candle, and had already offered two men as a sacrifice.'

Mandla's stare hardened. Zaminu smiled.

'You broke the law first but Palman has revealed all your little tricks. The New Covenant has been sealed. Palman reigns, the Son reigns,' Zaminu said as he raised four fingers.

Okafor thumped the back of his head. 'Do not speak unless spoken to.'

Mandla's stare settled on Zaminu for an extended moment. 'Zaminu Shangala.'

Alangba raised an eyebrow. That was not Zaminu's name and everyone in the room knew it. Shangala was a commoner name in Palmaine.

If it was a provocation, it worked. Zaminu's manacles rattled as he shook his fists at Mandla. 'My name is Governor-General Zaminu Elha Shangria! My rank remains, even in chains.'

He spoke the name with a heavy, aspirated inflection that seemed to send a ripple of distaste across the room. A name that stood in infamy.

A smile prickled on Mandla's lips. 'Governor-General Zaminu Shangria, you were arrested for the crimes of murder and theft, and now you are charged with the crime of blood ritual. How do you plead to the charges brought against you?'

Zaminu's face contorted into a scowl. 'Everything will burn. When the Palmaine find this place, down to your cattle, you will die. They will set upon you and drive you deep into gutters for graves.'

Mandla stared blankly at him. 'I will record a plea of not guilty, then.'

Zaminu seethed. 'The children of the Coldlands are a peculiar treasure—'

'Unto the Son above all people. Spare me, I know your scripture,' Mandla said, cutting him off. 'Funny thing is, that isn't quite what was said, if you read the early translation. You fight for a past you neither lived in nor understand.' He gestured to Okafor. 'First Ranger, see to it that the governor-general is specially accommodated in our dungeon. He will stand trial as soon as we have gathered testimonies.'

'Trial?' Gaitan said. 'We know this man's work.'

'We do not sentence a man without trial, even men such as him,' Mandla said.

Okafor moved to drag Zaminu away. As Zaminu was led out from the room, he began to chant.

'And the Son shall cast them down, erase their names, their seed in the land.'

Mandla's nostrils flared. For a moment, Alangba was sure Mandla would order the man dead, but the moment passed. Mandla's expressionless stare returned.

Alangba turned to follow Okafor but was stopped by Lord Mandla's voice.

'A moment, Third Ranger.'

Alangba froze, then backtracked into the sand.

Chief Gaitan turned to Mandla. 'The fool gave you his whole name, just as you said. What did you see?'

Mandla scratched his chin. 'It is worse than I feared. His mind had all sorts of dark sentimentalities.'

Gaitan leaned in close. 'What was the worst of it?'

'The Palmaine king has entered into a blood covenant. They are building an army.'

Gaitan grunted. 'They already have an army.'

'This is different,' Mandla said. 'They know about the Bloods.'

Zarcanis steepled her fingers on the table and worked the kinks out of her neck. 'Can they ...?'

The question lingered in the air unanswered.

Mandla stiffened. 'I don't know.' He turned his expressionless stare to Alangba. 'Third Ranger, when the trial is over, we will need you to return to Palmaine. I have a mission for you.'

Alangba bowed. 'Your man is loyal, Lord Mandla.' He didn't need to know more – wherever he was needed, he would attend.

'Thank you.'

'Will that be all, Lord Mandla?'

Mandla sucked in his lips. 'Not quite yet, Third Ranger.'

The door shifted behind him and a woman with a long spear led Princess Falina into the room. She wore a gold woven iro skirt with a matching gele headdress that likened her to a queen from storybooks. A sanyan *iborun* shawl was draped over one shoulder and with her free hand she waved a white *irukere* fly-whisk made from the tail of thoroughbred Shinala.

'Omoba,' Alangba said, dropping to one knee.

All the chiefs were on their knees, too. Falina strode towards the table looking straight ahead. Her chin lifted to an imperious angle, the *irukere* dancing in the air like a sceptre. She had become, before his eyes, every inch the royal from ages past.

Mandla vacated the seat at the centre and pulled it out for her. She smiled and politely curtsied. *The perfect show of humility.* Alangba smiled.

'We welcome you, Omoba, to this Council of the Chiefs.'

She nodded as she took her seat. 'I am grateful for your welcome.'

'We understand you were rescued by the Third Ranger and his Chainbreakers.'

Her jaw tightened for the briefest moment at the mention of the word 'rescued'. It was a subtle thing, but plainly she was still not quite agreed in seeing it as a rescue. As though to confirm her position, she said, 'I was taken against my will.'

A few of the chiefs gasped but Mandla's expression did not change.

'I know,' Mandla said. 'You found peace in Palmaine that you have not found here, but I believe with time your view will change.'

'What are the conditions of my stay here?'

'I am merely a Lord Diviner. You are an Omoba. Our precepts say that you are under the protection of the chiefs until you become queen.'

'And when am I supposed to become queen?'

'You are the last of your line. You will become queen as soon as the Council arranges your coronation.'

'And if I refuse?'

'Then we will make arrangements for a ship to take you back to Palmaine.'

She lowered her chin and narrowed her eyes, opening her mouth to speak.

Mandla raised a hand. 'I would ask, Omoba, that you consider your decision. We do not intend to arrange your coronation until after the trial of the governor-general. Perhaps that would give you time to think on it. You may still change your mind.'

She licked her teeth. It was the first indelicate thing she had done since stepping into the room. 'All right. After the trial.'

Alangba followed her out, quickening his pace to fall in step with her and Maka. 'I greet you, Omoba,' he said.

She glanced at him and her face softened. 'I greet you, Alangba.'

He gave a start. It was the first time she had not threatened to poison, strangle, or stab him in the back. He'd had a comeback prepared.

Alangba drew in breath. 'I know you have a difficult decision ahead.'

Her head jerked towards him. 'But I am sure you are here to tell me all the ways I will be letting my nation down if I refuse to be its queen.'

Alangba cleared his throat. 'No matter what you do, you will not be letting your nation down.' He drew closer and spoke low. 'Your nation let you down. Let your father down. You owe us all nothing.'

Her glare softened and she narrowed her eyes as she glanced at him. 'Then why should I do it, Alangba? Why should I serve the people who once sold me into slavery, just to save themselves?'

Alangba straightened and bit down on his lip. 'We all have our convictions, Omoba. Stories we tell ourselves that go to the very centre of our being. Now, I do not know what you believe. I do not know what your stories are. But if your life is to mean anything at all, there must be some deep-rooted value that is your light in a dark time such as this. I believe that this nation is worth fighting for, not for what it has done but for what it is. I choose to harken back to one simple rule and that is what makes me vital. Makes me brave. When you find your rule, you will have your answer.'

Falina regarded him with a cold calculating stare. 'And what is your rule?'

Alangba hiked his leather armour back, rolling his shoulder so she would see the scabbed-over wound where he had taken a spear saving her. Then he met her gaze. 'Duty comes before death.'

38

The Shadow Order

RUMI

The lantern light in the corridor gave everything a yellowish cast as Rumi trailed after Ladan. He thumbed the new marks on his arm that marked him a Seedling. The image of a seed sprouting; the beginnings of life.

He quickened his step to keep pace with Ladan. 'If I wanted to find Kayalli, where would I look? Not saying I want to, just so I know.'

Ladan gave a small laugh. 'She would likely be in the Thatcher.'

'What's that?'

'The Thatcher is the Eredo's ... backyard. Where we farm our crops, tend to horses, rear our cattle, that sort of thing.'

'Is that where Kaat is too?'

Ladan nodded. 'More than likely.'

Rumi's eyebrows perked up. Strogus had promised to take him to see her, but there was no better time than the present to check on something you love. He cleared his throat. 'How do I get there?'

'Seedlings aren't allowed into the Thatcher without a witness and a good reason. It is the most exposed part of the Eredo. Shuni the Agbara of water guards the river door, but we only have dogs and sentries to guard the Thatcher.'

'Can't you be my witness?'

'Why would I do that? If anything happens to you, I would be held responsible.'

'Nothing is going to happen to me.'

'I won't do it, Rumi.'

'Ah ... I should have known. You're a rooster.'

'Excuse me?'

'You make a big show of adventure, but deep down, you can't fly.'

Ladan's lips tightened. 'Godsblood, Rumi. You don't need to get a rise out of me to manipulate me to do things. I was believing we would be friends, and here you are already acting like your story is the important one. Don't become one of those people. That's the problem with this place – the Bloods turn cankerworms to gods.'

'Am I the cankerworm?'

'It's a figure of speech.'

Rumi scratched his chin. 'I apologise.'

Ladan drew in breath and narrowed his eyes. 'Let's get you ready for the Shadow Order.'

★　★　★

A tailor stretched his tape rope across Rumi's back, taking his time to get the exact measurement.

'Any particular style you want?' the tailor asked.

'Keep it simple,' Rumi said.

The tailor nodded and gave Rumi an earthen brown kaftan to wear. The halberd had been given back to him and he was getting used to having it in hand.

'Seedlings wear brown,' the tailor said matter-of-factly. 'Sulis wear green and Truetrees may wear what they please.'

'So I'm stuck with this?' He thumbed the brown kaftan.

'Until the Ghedo tournament,' said Ladan. 'Then you can wear some other colour. If you do well.'

The tailor left the room in a wind of tape rope and thread.

Renike tapped her foot impatiently as she watched him prepare. 'Will I see you soon?'

'I hope so.'

She frowned. 'I hate it when people say "I hope so".'

Rumi crouched. 'I think this place will be good for us, Ren.'

Renike chewed her lip and pulled Rumi's wrist, locking their arms at the elbow. 'I hope so.'

They said their goodbyes and Ladan led Rumi into the corridor. They came at last to a large assembly hall with high ceilings drooping with intricate stalactite carvings. Unending rows of wooden benches criss-crossed around the hall to face a large stone lectern.

There were well over a thousand people in the hall. Perhaps double that. They sat in huddles and filled the room with conversation and laughter.

'You will have three knowledge days with the other seedlings and three fighting days with your trainer each week,' Ladan said.

'What do I do with the other day?'

'If you are wise, you rest.'

Rumi nodded and glanced around the room.

'Seedlings sit over there,' Ladan said, pointing. 'Sulis sit over there.'

'So this is where you leave me?'

Ladan nodded. 'Yes. The Order can be ... difficult. A lot of people believe you shouldn't be here; that you don't deserve it. That you are too old. And the Viper, she has ... a reputation. But you will learn a great deal here. Don't give up.'

Rumi nodded. 'Thank you.'

'I'll see you,' Ladan said, walking off towards the Suli cluster.

322

Rumi considered the room. The order of the jungle was clear. The Sulis wore vibrant green kaftans with the straight-backed gait of men and women who commanded respect in the Order. A line of rogue unoccupied benches marked the boundary between Suli and Seedling.

He glanced past the Sulis and stiffened. If the Suli were the princes and princesses of the Shadow Order, then the Truetrees – with their fine silk kaftans and tattoos of rank – were the kings and queens. They wore battle weapons and did not need to sit together to show their strength, peppering the seas of brown and green with spots of colour.

Rumi made his way to the Seedlings at the furthermost corner of the hall. A hundred or so young men and women regarded him with calculating stares as he claimed a seat.

It was like the first day at a new school, or his first day with the players at the Golden Room. Almost all of them were Kasinabe. Some had the focused stares of eager warriors-to-be; others had the shifting gaze of anxious novices. While the rest of the room bubbled with chatter, the Seedlings sat in silence. Everyone inspected him, some examined his halberd too.

Soon after he had taken his seat, Lord Mandla strolled into the hall, taking his place at the lectern.

'Good morning,' Mandla said. His voice filled the room, overpowering all other noise. 'To our new Seedlings, I say welcome and congratulations. You are in the Order now: you have been given names and you are welcome to the family. Listen to and respect your teachers; it will profit you in this journey. Life in the Order is difficult – some of you will not make it as far as you hope, but we all have a part to play under the shadow of the Skyfather. If you do not make it to Suli, take it as joy. Not everyone can lead and it is an honour to have even been given the Bloods. Remember these words and you will make a great story here. To those who are not new here, I ask a question ... how do we make tomorrow come?'

The crowd answered in one booming voice. 'We build it today!'

Mandla saluted. His eyes searched across the room and his attention quickly settled on Rumi. This brought many other eyes Rumi's way.

'We all know why we are here,' Mandla said. 'We know what happened to our brothers and to our sisters; we know what is happening to us. They are butchering us. Not only with guns and cannons, but with books and doctrine. Progress has become a measurement of how much you can become like them. I say that is no progress at all!'

The crowd cheered.

'It is easy to make light of their occupation. Some think that the battle is over because they do not see the smoking gun or the blood-wet bayonet, but we must make no mistake: the object of their occupation has always been *genocidal*. They tried to wipe us out. If you are not Kasinabe, you can ask any of your Kasinabe brothers and sisters. They know. They know the violence of the enemy's lies.'

Shouts of agreement filled the hall.

'They burn down our places of worship, cast down our monuments, steal our masterpieces, set us against one another. And all this with our compliance! But we are here because we will not sit still! We are here because we know that our fathers are not beasts of burden and our mothers are not playthings! We know that a beauty higher than their queen is available to our daughters, that civilisation is not theirs to give and take. That there was once a nation and it was better than this! New stories start today! May the hand of the Skyfather write them!'

The noise was deafening. Even the dogs howled in cheer.

Gaitan entered the room in full armour, his face visible through the mandibles of a lion's head helmet.

'All new Seedlings, with me,' he said.

Rumi and a dozen or so other Seedlings rose to their feet. They trailed after Gaitan into the corridor and through an arched open door. Rumi had to turn his halberd to one side to fit through.

They arrived in a room that carried the stench of sweat, coal dust and molten iron. The clang of a hammer dominating iron rang through the air and the heat of a furnace drew slow sweat. *A smithy.*

A tall, broad-shouldered man with a horseshoe moustache appeared beside Gaitan and whispered something into his ear. Rumi could tell by the hammer in his hand and his large, muscled arms that he was a blacksmith, and a seasoned one at that.

Rumi had known a few blacksmiths in Alara. It was the work of grit and grace, not easily learned. The marks of smithy work were always plain to see on blacksmith bodies: powerful arms, blackened palms and squinting eyes too accustomed to the dancing, white-hot flame of a furnace.

Gaitan turned to the blacksmith. 'Jidey, see to it that they all have all the armour and weaponry they will need.'

Jidey bowed low and turned to the Seedlings. He led them one by one into a room with a broad black door. They emerged with helmets fashioned in the image of beasts, leather armour covered in riveted ironwire and crude, ink-black weapons.

Rumi's turn came and he followed Jidey through the heavy door. It opened into a room lined from floor-to-ceiling with metalworks.

Jidey smiled. 'I have just the helmet for you.'

He climbed a short ladder to retrieve a gleaming metal helmet from the uppermost row of armaments. The image of a fierce, slit-eyed lionhound glistened in his hands. It reminded him of Kaat. Rumi had to check on her as soon as the opportunity came.

'Ajanla Erenteyo,' Jidey said, handing over the helmet.

Rumi raised an eyebrow, taking the helmet in his hands. 'What does it mean?'

'It is Mushiain. It means the old dog still barks. Your mother's words.'

'You knew her?'

'Not personally, no. I just know her story. Some of it, at least.' The man had a hint of pride in his eyes.

Rumi pushed his head through the helmet's opening and slammed it shut with a sharp *clink*. Through its snarl, the room looked different. Everything had a different focus about it now, as though the helmet sharpened his vision.

'Fits you perfectly,' Jidey said, smiling. He gestured to the halberd. 'Usually, we make Seedlings forge their own shadow-steel, but this will serve you well. Many will be jealous of this. Marvellous work.'

Rumi raised an eyebrow. 'Shadowsteel?'

Jidey nodded as he pulled a sickle blade from the shelf. 'When you forge weapons with iron and conjured shadow, you get shadowsteel.' He stretched his other hand out and a small, pulsing circle of shadow coalesced in the air, coating the blade. 'It is one of the first things you will start to learn: conjuring. It's not easy when you first try. Like drawing with your wrong hand. You will be shaky at first, but with practice, repetition, and oneness of mind...' He smiled as the blade shifted from silver metal to glistening black. 'The result is harder than any blade;

will cut through near any substance. Unbreakable. Impervious to rust.'

Rumi's eyes bulged as he stared at the tar-black blade. 'Incredible.'

Jidey smiled. 'Only the best, most talented conjurers are able to make things that will endure. The longer you want the conjuring to last, the stronger your command of the shadow must be. The very best Seedlings might be able to keep a conjuring for a few weeks, months, perhaps. But a truly gifted conjurer can make something that lasts for years.' He ran his finger over the halberd. '*This* was the work of a master conjurer. You carry legacy with this weapon. It may be one of the oldest in the Eredo.'

Rumi removed the lionhound helmet. 'I will carry it with pride.'

Jidey smiled. 'Dara guide you.'

'And may His way be yours.'

Back in the smithy, the other Seedlings studied Rumi as he emerged. Gaitan smiled the way a fisherman does at his child's first catch.

Soon all the Seedlings had their armaments. Seven-foot shadowsteel-tipped spears, crooked ida swords and crude double-axes swished through the air in practice.

'Your weapons will be kept here,' Gaitan said. 'You collect them on fighting days. There are six hundred Suli, three hundred men and three hundred women. This year there are only seventy-four Seedlings. We are counting on you to stay the course, but accept that many of you will drop out from the Order before making it to Suli. Tomorrow, your training begins. Give it your all and don't slack off. Any one of the chiefs can announce a snap test at any time to check your aptitude in any of the three disciplines you will be starting with. Always be ready.

Rest well tonight, for this is the last time you will find anything easy for a while.'

Rumi followed the procession of new Seedlings to a room filled with wooden storage lockers. He pushed the halberd into one of the narrow storage compartments and pushed it shut.

'I hear you are being trained by the Viper,' came a voice.

Rumi clicked the padlock shut as he turned. A small-boned, bespectacled Kuba boy stared up at him holding a helmet fashioned in the shape of an owl, with holes through the large eyes.

'So it would appear,' Rumi said.

The young man offered Rumi a kola nut. 'I would like to share my real name with you.'

Rumi stared down at the kola nut in the boy's outstretched hand. *Spear's length away.*

'Your given name will do,' he said, pushing his hand away.

If the Kuba boy was offended, he did not show it. Not even a flicker of disappointment touched his face. 'Call me Ailera.'

Rumi frowned. The name meant 'weakling' in Odu and in Kasinabe. A terrible name to have in a place where students could smell something to terrorise. He understood why the boy wanted to share his real name.

'Ajanla Erenteyo ... Voltaine,' he offered in return.

'Thank you for not laughing,' the boy said. 'Where are you from?'

'Alara.'

The Kuba boy scratched his chin. 'A village in the South, if I'm not mistaken?'

Rumi raised an eyebrow. 'Yes. Have you been there?'

'I'm afraid not. I'm from the Agede peninsula, in the east.'

'A fishing village?'

'Yes.'

Rumi's eyebrows darted upwards. 'I didn't know there were Kuba in the fishing villages.'

There was an interval of silence before the boy spoke again. 'I was thinking…There are only a few of us softborn. It might be wise for us to, you know… stick together.'

'Softborn?' Rumi said.

'It's what they call us,' said another new voice.

Rumi turned as a young man stepped forward. At first glance the young man looked like a very pale Palmaine, but a second glance marked him true. A tall, rangy albino with thick yellow hair in foamy clumps on his head. He had large eyes that didn't settle and a wide, flat nose.

'They call those of us who are not full Kasinabe "softborn".'

'I see,' Rumi said.

The albino lad stiffened. 'He's right. We *should* stick together, at least for now.'

Rumi eyed them one after the other. 'I appreciate the offer, but I'll be fine on my own,' he said, turning away from them.

They came at last to the Seedling hostel. There were five dormitories, and at the front of their dorm was a triple-layered tray with bundles of brown cloth marked with each person's given name. Rumi lifted a bundle marked 'Ajanla Erenteyo' from the tray and walked into the dormitory.

Inside were twenty or so beds arranged in two parallel lines. Some of the beds were already claimed and dressed in fresh linens or guarded by older Seedlings. Rumi claimed a bed at the corner of the room, as far away from the others as possible. He dressed the bed quickly with fresh linens and placed his new clothes in the cupboard.

Somehow, the Kuba boy found a way to take up the bed closest to his and the albino boy managed to negotiate for the bed on the other side of him.

'A happy coincidence,' the Kuba said, smiling.

Rumi rolled his eyes.

The dormitory quickly filled and soon the sound of chatting and laughter could be heard above the opening and closing of cupboards.

Rumi did his best to ignore the voices of the Kuba boy and the albino as they became pointedly acquainted with one another, but they seemed to be doing their very best to force every point of interest into their conversation.

Sudden as a baby's cry, he was struck by a sharp pang of unmistakable alarm. He jerked upright and glanced up at the ceiling. The cowrie was hot on his neck. It was as though someone was calling his name from far above. He walked as though in a trance towards the door.

The albino boy gave him a sharp look. 'Need to go some-where?'

Rumi ignored him and continued to the door.

The albino boy fell in step with him. The Kuba followed too.

'Maybe we can help you find where you need to go,' offered the Kuba boy.

Rumi's heart thumped as he pointed to the roof. 'What's up there?'

The albino boy gave him a curious look but the Kuba seemed to understand. 'You must mean the Thatcher.'

Rumi straightened. That must have been it – where Nataré was. He nodded. 'Yes, the Thatcher.'

The Kuba boy gave him a long, stern look. 'Would you like me to take you to the entrance? We aren't allowed in yet but I know where it is.'

If there was one thing Rumi hated more than asking for a favour, he had yet to find it. And yet the pull to go up there was irresistible. Besides, he did not like how things had ended with Nataré. He wanted to see her, to talk to her, at least.

He let out a long breath. 'Yes, I would like you to take me.'

The Kuba boy smiled a small, triumphant smile as he held out an unbroken kola nut. 'I guess we should get to know one another then.'

39

The Thatcher

RUMI

Rumi watched carefully as the Kuba boy led them through the corridors. His name was Sameer Mabalo and he seemed to know his way around. He had a book in his hand, making notes as they walked.

'How did you learn your way around?' Rumi asked.

'A great deal of time and desire,' he said, trailing a finger over the inscriptions on the wall.

The albino, who had given the name Ahwazi Tilewan, placed a hand on Sameer's shoulder. 'What are you going to do about the doorkeeper?'

'I'll figure it out,' said Sameer, squinting at the inscriptions.

After a few quick twists and turns through the corridor, they were at the foot of a thin, spiralling staircase.

Sameer led the way, one step after the other. For someone with such short legs, he set a truly merciless pace. By the time they came to the top of the everlasting staircase Rumi was short of breath.

Ahwazi gave him a wry smile. 'Need a moment?'

Rumi straightened and scowled. 'I'm fine,' he lied.

A large door was attended by a tall Kasinabe man with an eight-foot spear. Sameer approached the doorkeeper with exposed palms in greeting. The doorkeeper spoke first, scattering words in heavily accented Mushiain. Rumi tried to decipher the language, but the doorkeeper was speaking too quickly for him to understand anything more than a stray word.

Sameer waited for the doorkeeper to finish, patient as death. His head bowed slightly in deference. Then he replied. His Mushiain was so musical and polished that Rumi was content with just catching the melody, making no attempt to decode the words. The obstinacy drained out from the doorkeeper and he nodded. Plainly, Sameer was a wordsmith.

Abruptly, the doorkeeper stepped aside for them to pass.

'Dara guide you,' the doorkeeper said to Rumi in simple Odu.

'And may His way be yours.'

They came up to a trapdoor made of thatch and streams of dry hay and climbed up to emerge on a vast garden shaded by tall palm trees with dozens of dogs in patrol.

'What just happened?'

'He asked where I was taking you.'

'And?'

'I told him that you needed to pray in the old way, under the trees where our ancestors' blood was shed.'

Ahwazi stared incredulously at him and Rumi raised an eyebrow. 'And he just let you through?'

'I also promised him some homebrew whiskey, when next I come up.'

Ahwazi laughed. Sameer certainly had some mischief in him. The nighttime breeze was delightful as they walked.

'Sulis can come up here whenever they like?' Rumi asked.

'Yes,' Sameer said.

'And they can leave the Eredo through here too?'

'With permission, yes.'

Rumi took a step forward and Ahwazi put an arm across his chest.

'Yahya is passing by.'

Rumi raised an eyebrow. 'Yahya?'

Ahwazi only smiled, looking into the distance. It was a moment before Rumi followed his gaze.

A giant lionhound about a hundred metres or so away was herding a group of cows.

Rumi went completely still. 'What is that?'

Ahwazi grinned. 'That's Yahya. King of Dogs.'

Rumi watched the dog with open-mouthed awe, statue stiff as it walked by. His ink-black fur coat had patches of silver-white piebald spotting on its chest, and his blood-red eyes patrolled the peak like a landlord. He commanded the herd of cows with a strong, assured bearing. It was the same beast Rumi had seen as they approached the Eredo. Up close, the sight of Yahya turned his heart to a kettledrum. Stocky as a merchant's last moneypurse, cut with lean muscle. Rumi had never seen anything so big. The dog seemed to pay them no mind but they gave it the respect of waiting till it was well out of distance before they moved.

'So, what did you want to come here for?' asked Ahwazi.

Rumi remastered himself. 'I'm looking for—'

Just then, something moved at the corner of his vision. Before he could turn or move, it careened into him. He fell back, clutching at air as he hit the ground. Something sharp scratched his sides as he realised what was happening. Kaat licked his face and let out a low, excited yelp.

'Good girl,' Rumi said with a smile, as he pitched up on his elbows. 'Good girl.'

Kaat seemed to have grown in the few days since they had

334

come. Thickened with the promise of a new whelp. Her fur lush and full.

'I missed you,' Rumi said, as the lionhound nuzzled against his forearm.

'She's yours?' Sameer asked staring down at him.

Rumi got to his feet. 'She was my mother's.'

Sameer nodded. 'I see. Is that why you came here?'

Rumi hesitated. 'I was also looking for a sentry. Kayalli.'

Ahwazi cracked a smile at that and Sameer wore a slight smirk. Rumi could guess at what they were thinking.

'Let's ask,' said Sameer.

Ahead, they spotted a spearman wearing black overalls. Sameer approached and spoke in Mushiain, gesturing with his hands. The man's face stiffened as he pointed towards a dim light in the near distance.

Kaat followed along as they passed armed sentries and patrolling dogs, fields where rice, maize and cassava rose from the soil in legion and pens where cattle of all kinds gossiped and chewed their cud. At the far end of the Thatcher was a giant black iron gate, barred three times across the middle. *A true fortress.*

The sharp *click-clack* of a crossbow made their entire party stop in their tracks.

'Who's there?' shot a voice from the dark.

Sameer turned, raising his empty hands. 'Ailera. I am a Seedling.'

'Awaji, a Seedling,' offered Ahwazi.

'Ajanla Erenteyo, a Seedling,' Rumi said.

The sentry stepped forward, his face spotlighted by the lantern above his head. He was young, Odu, with dark brown eyes and hair. One of the few Odu men Rumi had seen in the Eredo.

'What are you doing out here? It's late.'

'We're looking for Kayalli,' said Sameer.

'What do you want from me?' came Nataré's voice.

Ladan and Rumi glanced up into the tree next to them. There she was. Her stony grey-green eyes drank in rays of moonlight as she looked down at them, crossbow at the ready.

Rumi's voice was low. 'I wanted to speak to you.'

She jumped down and landed like a jaguar, crossbow still in hand.

'What about?'

Sameer and Ahwazi turned to Rumi. The sentry turned to Rumi. Everyone was staring at him.

He had no real answer. He had nothing specific to say, especially not in front of all of them.

'I wanted to ... say thank you, for everything in the forest.'

She stared at him with a stranger's indifference. 'You're welcome.'

Rumi fumbled for a sentence. 'I'm in the Shadow Order.'

'I know.'

'Will I see you there?'

Sameer tugged at the back of his kaftan. A warning. The unknown sentry wrinkled his forehead and spat derisively at the ground.

'Sentries aren't allowed into the Order quarters.'

Rumi wanted to ask why, but Sameer tugged at his kaftan with calculated viciousness.

'Well, I hope I see you again soon.'

'Hope is good,' she said.

She turned away from them and took up a position behind the tree. Sameer tilted his head slightly, gesturing that it was time for them to go. Rumi wanted more – he wanted to talk to her alone, to look into her eyes and make sure they were all right.

'I wanted to talk to you, alone,' he said.

'I want many things also, but I cannot always have them,' she said.

He rounded the tree and locked eyes with her. 'Please.'

Her eyes flickered.

'We can walk to the marula,' she said, pointing towards a tall, crooked marula tree at the edge of Rumi's vision.

They set off for the tree, leaving Ahwazi and Sameer behind. Nataré fiddled with her earring, her eyes fixed on the moon.

'The man at the door. Strogus. Is he your...'

'My what?'

'Your... man.'

She smirked. 'Far from it. Doorkeepers and sentries, we tend to look out for one another, that's all.'

'Oh. I thought perhaps...'

'No.'

Rumi found himself smiling. 'Do you still sing?'

She gave a start. 'What?'

'You used to sing... in the Orchid House.'

She shut her eyes. 'That was a long time ago.'

'Not *that* long ago. You should sing now; there's no one around.'

'You're getting a bit annoying now.'

Rumi smiled in an effort to repair things. 'Sorry.'

She let out a long sigh and rested a hand on her hip. 'What do you want, Rumi?'

Rumi's smile faded. 'I wanted to make sure we were okay. After everything in the forest.'

'You came all this way for that?'

He wet his lips. He could almost feel himself about to say something stupid, but he was talking before he could stop himself.

'When I was a boy, I used to think about you all the time. It was a distraction, sort of, from all the things I was going through. It made me ... happy, sometimes.'

She tilted her head, eyes seeming not to blink.

Rumi had turned the tap and now he had to let it have its flow. Stupidly, he kept talking.

'When you disappeared, I realised that I never really *understood* you. I just had this idea of you which, deep down, I knew wasn't real. I didn't know you at all, and it hurt when I thought I could never know you. My memory of you was really a memory of me, not you. It's just ... Since you showed up again, I thought maybe I *could* know you, this time.'

Nataré's steady calm fell apart like a quiet pond that had a stone thrown into it. She lowered her head, eyes far away in thought. 'You should go back to your Order friends.'

'Nataré—'

'Please, Rumi, go.'

She clasped her hands behind her back and pulled away from him.

'I'm sorry, I didn't mean to—'

'Go!'

He nodded. 'Goodnight.'

She gave no response. Rumi waited in the uneasy silence for long enough to feel an upswell of shame. Then he turned back to Sameer and Ahwazi.

He left Kaat in the company of the other lionhounds, knowing she had found her kin as they left the Thatcher. As they started back down the stone staircase, Rumi turned to Sameer. 'Why aren't sentries allowed in the Order?'

'The Bloods do not work on those with shallow blood.'

'Shallow blood?'

'This is the land where the first man trod. The deeper your blood runs to the first man, the stronger the likelihood that you have the inborn ability to harness the Bloods. Hardly anyone not born Kasinabe is given the Bloods.'

'Why not?'

'Think about it. If you were the Kasinabe and you watched your nation burned to the ground, how would you behave if you were trying to rebuild it?'

Rumi drew in breath. 'Like a cat in the doghouse.'

40

One Great Chapter

NATARÉ

Nataré watched Rumi walk away. A part of her wanted to tell him to stop, to talk with her a little more, but that was the foolish part. A remnant from before she had become the knife edge. The other part, the wiser part, knew it was time to let him go.

She had found him to be a dangerous distraction. The way he looked at her... Well, it was one thing to be looked at, but quite another to be seen. Rumi was in the business of seeing. Riding with him in the Nyme, a part of her had thought such stupid thoughts. Even the way she slept, deep and carefree, in the shegin' Nyme. After her kidnap she had become the knife edge, hard as any rock, but in Rumi she had glimpsed the space to be soft sometimes. A very dangerous distraction.

She pinched the bridge of her nose and closed her eyes, letting the breath out. *Rumi Voltaine, a shadowwielder.* She trampled on the dream and reached deep into her pocket. Better to leave the story unfinished than continue to the miserable end.

Life had taught her the pains of being a two-tribe woman. A thing to be desired, but never loved all the way through. Her story didn't have many pages left. She closed her fist around the deathly cold ghost stone. *But now, I will have one great chapter.*

Now she knew the whereabouts of the witch doctor's lair, and with the ghost stone she'd kept in secret she could strike at the very heart of it. She had considered telling the sentry captain, but the man was too cautious. He'd send at least two scouting parties before ordering an assault, and she didn't trust any of the other sentries to scout the lair unnoticed. The witch doctors knew the forest too well for that. If she let the sentry captain know, it would be too loud, too official; even if he did succeed, he would parade the witch doctors as prisoners for trial.

A trial was out of the question. If she was going to do this, she had to do it herself. It had to be quick, quiet, and clean.

She had been practicing with the ghost stone, learning how it worked, stalking in the night with a sword drawn. With it, she could sneak through the Thatcher gates with the sentry captain none the wiser.

She touched the stone again. *Godsblood, what if I die out there?* She balled her hand up into a fist, washing that thought away. There were worse ways to die.

She sheathed her ida sword and fastened a quiver of fresh arrows to her back.

The stables were empty, save for a young golden Shinala. She mounted the Shinala and moved at a slow trot through the Thatcher, eyes in constant motion. She wasn't completely sure that the dogs would see her with the stone, but she wasn't going to test her luck. On those rare occasions she did find luck, it was never all-the-way good. The sort of luck where the cut misses an artery but the rust gives you tetanus. Bittersweet.

'Where are *you* going?' came a sharp voice.

Nataré nearly jumped from the horse. She glanced over her shoulder as a tall man approached. Her hand instinctively moved to her sword hilt.

Strogus stepped into the sprinkle of light and quirked an eyebrow. 'You mean to use that?'

'Strogus,' she said, letting out a long breath. 'You startled me.'

He brushed her comment aside. 'Where are you going?'

She narrowed her eyes. 'Out on patrol.'

'Is the sentry captain aware?'

'What is your concern with sentry business?'

'I'm a doorkeeper. All goings in or out are my business.'

'Are you going to drag me back to my post, O' mighty King of Doors?'

Strogus let out an exasperated breath. 'Where are you going, Kayalli?'

'I am going to kill some witch doctors,' she said.

There was a long interval of silence. Strogus just stared at her. Stared like he was watching a masquerade dance.

'Let us go then.'

'Us?'

'Yes,' Strogus insisted.

'I ride alone,' she said.

'Not tonight you don't.'

She frowned. 'Fine. I won't leave the Eredo tonight.'

'Then we will go and explain whatever you were planning to the sentry captain.'

'What do you want from me?'

The man narrowed his eyes. 'Last time you left the Eredo, you returned with Griff's son and a known traitor. I've been doorkeeper long enough to know to watch the people who like to bring strays back. I want to see what you might find this time. You either go with me, or we go to the sentry captain.'

Nataré glared at him, then let her blade fall to the side. 'Get me through the gates, then.'

41

The Lair of the Jazzmen

NATARÉ

Nataré brushed the debris from the bludgeoned tree bark, revealing the shape of an eye.

'They are here,' she said.

At the foot of the tree there was a short trail of red on the forest floor. It was unmistakable: steady droplets of blood. Strogus's face convulsed.

'Blood ritual,' she said.

He squinted. 'What do you want to do?'

She rolled a kola nut around in the palm of her hand. 'Kill all of them.' Despite the seriousness of her suggestion, she found the tone of her voice to be remarkably smooth. 'You can come with me, or you can wait here. I'm going now.'

Strogus snatched the kola nut. 'I'm coming.'

She nodded. 'We move quiet. In and out quickly. There is no complication in this.'

'There is always complication in death.'

The thought came to argue with that statement, but her focus was on the killing. 'If fighting starts, use that thing, or run,' she said, pointing to Strogus's sword. 'They won't moralise before using theirs.'

Strogus nodded. The man was no longer a shadowwielder, but he could swing a good sword if it came to that.

She led the way down a path of half-dried blood and pink and yellow flowers till they came to a building of bricks. Her heart tapped urgently at her chest. Bricks way out in the Nyme. Only black-hearted conspiracy could lead men to carry bricks this far.

She ripped the sleeves from her garb, freeing her arms. Then she drew her sword from its scabbard.

She fumbled in her pocket and closed her fist around the ghost stone. 'Are you ready?'

Strogus clicked his neck and swung his sword around in an arc of practice. 'Yes.'

She nodded and then put the ghost stone under her tongue. Power swelled within her.

'Kayalli?'

To him she was invisible, but this was not a time for lengthy exposition about the stone. She threw herself at the door, shoulder-first.

A bare-chested man in the first room made to rise to his feet, but she perforated his stomach and he sank back into his seat. *One dead.*

Strogus gasped.

She hurtled through the next door. There was only a sliver of light, but it was enough to show the smeared walls and the mouldy, gaping hole in the corner of the ceiling.

In the darkness something stuttered to life. She flashed forward, her forehand slash sending the man directly to the spirit realm. He tried to scream but the sword was through him before he could manage a groan.

She stepped towards the next door. Behind her, Strogus followed. He held his sword in low, trembling hands. Perhaps that moment of brief observation gave her the silence she needed to hear the ever-so-slight creak of wood from the door ahead.

344

She snarled and thrust the sword through the flimsy door. A man screamed. She kicked the door open and the man slumped dead to the side. *I know all of your tricks.*

Upturned drums littered the room. There was a slim walkway carpet on the floor, dark blue and speckled with blood. It led to an open courtyard.

The spray of moonlight illuminated a scene from a nightmare at the centre of the courtyard.

'Godsblood,' Strogus exclaimed.

Two young Kuba girls in perfect white dresses were chained to a tall stone pillar. Their wrists were bloody where the chains bound them, and they had sunken, bloodshot eyes. One of them rested almost on the floor, as though dead. Limp, but for the chains that held her wrists up.

Nataré plucked the stone from her mouth and the power receded. Strogus jumped as she became visible again. 'You need to let me know before you do that,' he snapped.

One of the girls rose to her feet. Her gaze was as good as a promise of violence. She had an eye-shaped scar on her cheek that could only have been the work of someone with a blade, time, and no conscience.

'We will not hurt you,' Nataré said.

The girl's eyes softened, but the lines at the side of her jaw betrayed no surrender. She turned to Nataré, holding her gaze.

Nataré crouched low, speaking in a low, flat voice. 'Is there anyone else here?'

The girl nodded, her teeth too clenched to speak.

'Where?' Nataré asked.

The girl pointed with her eyes to a door on the other side of the courtyard.

'How many people?'

345

The chains rattled as she forced two fingers up. Nataré nodded and crept towards the door, Strogus a half-pace behind her, sword raised. She leaned in to press her ear to the door.

A voiced barked from inside. 'You may enter.'

She kicked the door open and it slapped the wall with a low *thunk*. It was a small room with round open windows on the far wall allowing a gentle breeze. A man stood away from the light. Tall, broad-shouldered, and bare to the waist. He had two chains of copper around his neck and a third ornamented with the husk of dead fruit. His face had white markings, his eyebrows shaved bare. In one hand he held a bunch of pink and yellow flowers, in the other a calabash of palm wine. His eyes shone a stony grey and he showed more interest in his palm wine than their intrusion. He barely lifted his gaze as they barged in.

'You are too late,' the man said, gesturing towards the corner of the room.

There in the darkened corner lay a dead girl in a slowly spreading pool of blood. Burned down candle wicks were arranged in a circle around her body.

Nataré hardened her grip on her sword. 'I will kill you.'

Her words came out quiet, as though not meant for anyone to hear.

'Really?' the witch doctor said, raising an eyebrow. He wiped the foam of palm wine from his lip and raised a hand. The door behind them slammed closed. The windows jammed and the stonework floor groaned as if being pulled apart. Nataré's feet left the ground. Blocks of stone erupted from the floor. The uprooted stone flew around the room at breakneck speed, like a colony of crazed bats.

Nataré jerked her head as a block of stone nicked her ear on its flight past. Her sword clattered uselessly to the ground as she fought against the force lifting her into the air.

Strogus snarled as a flying stone caught him flush in the face. He too lifted into the air.

With a strained, trembling effort, she raised the ghost stone to her lips. A welter of blood filled her mouth as she bent her arm at the elbow to bring the ghost stone up.

The witch doctor seemed uninterested, too focused on his lovely parlour trick with the flying bricks. Nataré brought her arm halfway up and found she could not bring it any further. With a strained effort, she tossed the ghost stone towards her mouth, caught it. Tucking it under her tongue, she vanished.

The witch doctor's eyes bulged. 'Impossible—'

The power of his magic slipped away as soon as she used the ghost stone. She was no longer in a realm he could control.

'Show yourself!' he snarled.

Nataré appeared at the witch doctor's side and slashed from stomach to shoulder. The man slumped forward. She pulled the sword back and forced it through his chin until she found the brain. Blood fountained as the corpse fell.

Strogus fell back to the ground with a heavy thump, along with all the whirling stone bricks.

Nataré touched the back of her head and her hand returned wet with blood.

'What was he doing?'

'Sacrifice,' Nataré said, spitting at the witch doctor's corpse. 'They sacrifice human beings to the Agbara, to draw from their power. The sacrifices are most powerful if it is a loved one ... or a virgin.'

Strogus stared as the young dead girl in the corner. 'We have to bury her, so she will find rest.' he said, lifting the girl in his arms.

Nataré blinked, then nodded in agreement. They walked back into the courtyard where the two girls were in chains.

347

There were gasps and sobs when they saw Strogus carrying the lifeless body. The girl with the scar on her cheek strained against her bonds. The sound of chains rattling made Nataré wince. *You are the knife edge.*

'Don't touch her! Get your hands off her!' the scarred girl snarled, trying to pull herself free of the chains.

Nataré turned to the girl. 'It's all right, he's not—'

'It's fine,' Strogus interjected. He lowered the girl's body to the floor, placing her down gently. 'I am sorry about your friend. The men who killed her were … evil men. I won't touch her again.'

The scarred girl's mouth levelled into a grimace, but she stopped fighting.

'Can you break their chains?' Nataré whispered to Strogus.

He nodded, glancing at the bolt on their manacles and the chain that held them to the stone pillar.

'I'm going to free you,' he said to the girls, raising his sword.

The scarred girl glowered at him but made no sound. With an overhand chop, the metal parted and the chain was broken. He crept in closer to remove the small bolt which bound the metal at their wrists. While trying to remove the scarred girl's bindings, Strogus's finger brushed ever so slightly on her wrist, and she recoiled as though burned by the touch. Once free, she staggered to her feet and looked up to the moon from the courtyard as though striking off a debt owed.

The other girl had an unkempt thicket of dark hair. She didn't move. The scarred girl walked over to her.

'Leave me,' the bushy-haired girl said.

Strogus stared at Nataré as though to ask 'what do we do?'.

Nataré narrowed her eyes and gestured for him to watch the girls.

'Get up, Toshane!' shouted the scarred girl. 'Get up!'

She kicked the bushy-haired girl, not hard, but with urgency.

'Leave me, N'Goné. I am not strong like you! Just let me die here!'

N'Goné's face softened. She crawled beside Toshane, hugging her close. She wriggled against the embrace, but did not break free. Nataré watched silently.

Eventually N'Goné's whispers seemed to work, and the bushy-haired girl stirred to life.

'Only for Sanu,' the bushy-haired girl said.

'Only for Sanu.'

N'Goné, the girl with the scar, allowed Strogus to carry their dead friend, Sanu. With help of the bushy-haired girl Toshane, they buried Sanu beneath a tree, away from the house of bricks. In a place where flowers might grow. The girls wore brave faces but cried as they lowered her into the ground.

'A fitting end,' a man's voice said from behind them.

They whirled as one. A lean-muscled man with a rope in hand, dressed for riding, stood watching them. He was the catcher. Nataré knew all about catchers. They were the ones charged with snatching victims up for sacrifice.

N'Goné's heavy breathing grew louder as she stepped towards the man, her eyes wide with a faraway resolute look. She snatched a stone from the ground and charged at him. The catcher did not retreat, nor did he try to defend himself – he stretched his arms out wide as though she was running to embrace him.

'Though I may die, I have fed the Agbara well,' said the man.

Nataré shouldered N'Goné aside, sending her toppling to the ground.

'You don't want to carry that, N'Goné. Trust me.'

The girl looked up at her.

'Close your eyes!' Nataré urged.

N'Goné stared for a moment, eyes wide and fist clenched, then she did as she was told. Nataré stepped towards the catcher with a steady, dead-eyed focus.

'Ah, a righteous young woman, here to condemn me. Tell me, when will you accept that the things you despise are part of you, part of us? When will we embrace that? Sacrifice is our tradition and has been so since even before the Palmaine ever broached these shores.' His eyes locked in on Nataré. 'You would have wed many years ago if the four kingdoms still stood. Virgins were always a thing for sacrifice. It was a necess—'

His body hit the floor.

'They always have something they want to tell you about in the end,' Nataré said, staring at the body. 'It's like they want you to know why they did it, give everything some sick context. Not today.'

Nataré pulled N'Goné to her feet. 'You are not an easy mark. You are not helpless. You are strong. Always remember that.'

N'Goné lifted her chin slightly and nodded.

Kayalli fixed her eyes on Strogus. 'We found them alone in the forest.'

It wasn't a suggestion; it was a command.

'Alone in the forest,' he confirmed.

A vulture flew into the jazzmen's lair as they rode towards the Eredo.

42

The Viper

RUMI

Rumi sat waiting in the hall for the Viper to appear, massaging his head.

He had got into a fight at breakfast with a Suli over bread. Ladan had brought an end to it, but Rumi had lumps on his head for souvenirs.

There was an itch somewhere inside his leather armour that he couldn't reach, and his arms ached from carrying the helmet and halberd. Most of the other Seedlings were long gone with their shadowwielders. Rumi was left alone with one other.

The Seedling had black Darani tattoos all over his neck and torso, and a thick black mane of hair. Strapped to his back was a massive *tuaragi* shadowblade. The sight of it alone would cut a man's bravado in half. The man's dark red-brown eyes were framed by round spectacles that would give any other man a scholarly air. This man, with his arms thick with muscle and monstrous blade, did not look like a scholar. He wore his Kasinabe heritage like a cloak. The man would not be out of place in a hero's tale from the age of Mgbedike. A face from folklore. The very notion of a Kasinabe warrior. His forearm was tattooed with nine thin, black, parallel lines.

Rumi reached in his pocket for a kola nut and pulled it out. 'Spare me,' the man said, refusing the offer.

Rumi put the kola nut away. They sat in an uncomfortable silence for a while longer before Zarcanis the Viper finally strolled in.

Her fiery hair bounced on her shoulders as she walked. Her one-piece tunic, tailored to perfection, covered her entire neck. She seemed to always cover her neck. It was as though she was trying to hide her tattoos. *Why would she do that? Everyone has tattoos here.*

She looked quickly from Rumi to the other man. 'New moon, new opportunity. Yomiku, you know what I expect.'

The man with the tuaragi blade nodded and rose to his feet. *So he's Yomiku.* The Seedling Strogus and Ladan believed could beat a shadowwielder.

Zarcanis's eyes settled on Rumi. 'Forget everything you have heard about me. I am probably worse.'

Yomiku mumbled in agreement.

Zarcanis smiled. 'Let's go.'

She led Yomiku and Rumi into a wide corridor. They entered a dimly lit room partitioned such that it was two rooms in one. The larger part had books and wooden chairs, the other weapons on the walls and a large fighting circle at the centre. Yomiku unstrapped his tuaragi blade and walked into the part with the weapons.

'Relax... take a seat. I won't bite,' Zarcanis said. She took a seat and nudged out an empty chair.

Rumi took the seat in front of her, leaning back a little to keep some distance.

'Do you know anything about fighting?'

Rumi scratched his head. 'A little. Bobiri mostly.'

'So not a complete novice. Bobiri is good. Have you ever killed someone before?'

Rumi hesitated. 'Yes.'

'Do you think you could kill someone again?'

'If I absolutely had to.'

'Do you think you could kill him, if you absolutely had to?' she said, pointing towards Yomiku in the next room.

Rumi lowered his eyes.

'Kubani!' she yelled.

It was a Mushiain approximation of the Odu word Kubano, which could mean angry bull or stupid bull, depending on the context.

Yomiku approached, breathing heavy. From the look on his face, it was plain he did not appreciate being called Kubani.

'This young man thinks he could kill you,' Zarcanis said.

'I didn't say that!'

'You didn't have to,' she said.

Yomiku glanced down at Rumi like a cat with a mouse in its paw. Then he made a disgusted noise in his throat and turned back to the other room.

Zarcanis slapped a book down on the desk between them. 'You will have to read this.'

Rumi picked the book up. *Lessons from the Sea* by Kuda Kamo.

Zarcanis leaned forward. 'So, tell me, who are you?'

'Who am I?'

'Yes, tell me.'

'I'm ... from Alara. I used to play music. I fought Bobiri for a while. I try to be a good person.'

'You are certainly *not* a good person. There's no such thing as a good person. It is important that you understand that. We are what we are. Dancers in the great masquerade, ants on the great wandering rock, crawling through the cosmos in a place where there is neither up nor down, good nor evil.'

Rumi raised an eyebrow. 'What do you mean there is neither good nor evil?'

'You disagree?'

'I do. My mother was a good person. She protected people, fought for people. My brother, too, was a gentle soul, a good person. The one who took them from me was evil.'

Zarcanis rolled her eyes. 'I knew your mother when she sacrificed ten men to appease the Agbara of war. Your brother, I gather, was a half-wit with no good sense to decide whether he wanted to be good or evil. Some would call their killer a saint for what he did to your family.'

His blood stirred but he pinched his mouth shut, rubbing his thumb slowly across his forefinger.

'Am I making you angry?'

'I would prefer if we don't discuss my family.'

'You brought them up. Funny you didn't bring your father up. Perhaps because he abandoned you the first chance he got. Wisdom.'

Rumi rose to his feet. 'Watch your tongue, woman!'

'There it is! That is who you are! The unacknowledged shadow. The unconscious truth. Not a good boy, but an angry, angry man. Something complex. You even reminded me that I am a woman, too. Tell me, of what relevance is that for you to remind me? Where did *that* come from? Do you think of women as less than you?'

'Where is Mandla?'

'He can't save you,' she said, rising to her feet. Rumi noticed she overmatched him for height. She had broad shoulders too.

'It's just you and me until I'm done with you, Zarot.'

She drew her head back and head-butted him with such force that his legs buckled. Rumi could feel blood rolling out

354

from the broken flesh on his forehead. He jumped back to his feet and stepped close.

'You came into my domain with entitlement,' Zarcanis said, stepping forward. 'Lose that. I will not suffer your petulance when your entitlement is compromised. You are here on my terms.' She raised her chin in thought. 'The man who killed your mother and brother, is he alive?'

Rumi nodded, still standing with his fists tightly clenched.

'I suppose that's why you're here. You want to go kill him, don't you?'

Rumi did not answer.

She smiled. 'Yes! I can see it. How terribly predictable. Little boy wants to get revenge on the wicked man who killed his mother, so he goes to become a warrior. Where have I read that before ... oh, *everywhere*.'

Rumi rubbed blood from his brow with his forearm. 'And how wonderfully unique your story is, lonely older woman head-butting young men to get back at the handsome bastard who broke her heart once.'

'You wound me! I am hit! I am hit!' she said, laughing. 'Now that we know ourselves, we can begin. I want you to acknowledge all your deceptions. I want you to smile at the mirror because you know that there is a world of difference between what goes on inside and what goes on outside. If you want me to train you, you will have to learn to walk in the dark places. No good man can learn to beat people until they can no longer stand. If you are working with me, drop the mask. I know you've killed before; I can see it in your eyes, in the way you answer my questions. I know you think everything you do is right, because someone somewhere did you terribly wrong. Follow my lead and I will turn you into a dangerous bastard. Perhaps you will get your revenge along the way.'

Rumi forced back a smile. A dangerous bastard was precisely what he needed to become and he was past the point of caring who helped him become one.

Zarcanis touched his chin. 'How will your story go? Will you be defined by your scars or by your healing? This is the question you will need to answer here.' She pushed him back gently. 'Now, go down into a split as low as you can.'

'What?'

'You are too straight. Clenched too tight. I need you bendy.'

Rumi went down at a split until he was a few inches off the ground. Zarcanis took up a position behind him and wrapped his arms at the shoulder.

'Stretching is the first part of your transformation.'

She slowly leaned her weight onto him, forcing him lower to the ground. His legs trembled.

'Lower,' she said, forcing him down.

Rumi screamed.

'Scream if you must, but I need you lower,' she said, forcing him down.

He felt as though his body would be ripped apart at any moment.

'Keep breathing. If you stop and tense up, you will hurt yourself badly.'

She pushed him down further. No matter how much he screamed or begged her to stop, she held him true and he was powerless to stop her. Finally she let him fall flat on his back. His cheeks were wet with tears and his thighs were trembling.

She glanced at his gleaming halberd. 'Does it have a name?'

'What?'

'Your blade. Does it have a name?'

'No.'

'Oh, you must give it a name. All the good stories have a weapon with a name. Come, let me show you mine.'

She pulled him up, limp-legged, into the other room. He winced at each footfall, his thighs ready to tear at any step. On the far side was a wall of weapons.

'Every shadowdancer must master at least two weapons,' she said, plucking a black long spear from the wall. 'This is Iron Maiden, a spear. The spear is the primary battle weapon. Three shadowddancers with spears like this and a good formation can kill a hundred swordsmen, if they know to control the distance.'

She stepped forward and pulled down a thin, ugly, shadow-steel sword with sharp protruding ridges. 'This is Silence. If a man manages to get inside the reach of your spear in a melee, you better have a sword or a knife to shut him up. Swords are more *romantic* weapons; sometimes a man gets close enough to kiss before a sword does its work.'

She shuffled forward again and Rumi's eyes bulged as she pulled down a massive black greatsword with an iron crossguard.

'This ... this is Widowmaker, the self-same blade of Walade the Widowmaker. A two-handed greatsword. More dexterous than a spear, but longer than any normal sword. With this, Widowmaker defended the Kasinabe gates against—'

'Fifty-six men,' Rumi said, staring at the massive sword.

Zarcanis raised an eyebrow. 'You know your history, then. My load is lessened.' She pulled a cabinet drawer open. 'Your weapon is a work of art. Well-balanced, wicked spike. It can thrust like a spear and cut like an axe ... You're not worthy of it yet.'

'Sorry?'

'Drop it in here.'

'Why?'

She frowned slightly. 'Are you always this prissy?'

'It was my mother's.'

'Oh dear, so you're one of *those*.'

Rumi scowled, then dropped the halberd into the drawer.

She slammed the cabinet shut, nearly snapping Rumi's fingers, and turned towards the room with the books.

'Now, as I was saying, nothing is completely "good" or "bad". Even the Palmaine are not "bad" in any real sense; anyone who has interrogated themselves knows that. They just can't help themselves.'

Rumi gave a small smile.

Zarcanis reclaimed her seat at the reading table. 'There is a beautiful balance in all the great oppositions. Equality and inequality, reason and passion, obedience and rascality. All conflict has its resolution in fellowship, and none is perfect on its own. And in that same way, your being is completed in the fellowship of substance and shadow. I presume you know the story of Dara and Billisi?'

'Yes.'

'Then you must understand what I mean to say. There is no greater name than Dara, but there is also no greater name than Billisi.'

Rumi formed the crossroads symbol with his fingers.

Zarcanis snorted. 'When the Palman priests came from Palmaine, determined to spread their religion, they needed a great opponent. A great evil like they have in their religion: a devil. So they cast Billisi in that role. A devil is essential to their teaching. That is the only way one can assert divine correctness, you see, by making things black and white. But "The Way" is not so ... primitive. Divine correctness is for the extremists. There are no absolutes in the Darani Way. To truly become whole, one must integrate the evil. Only with balance can there be perfection.'

Rumi found himself leaning forward as she continued.

'You see, Billisi is not the devil. Malevolent, yes; wicked yes; but she is not pure evil, because it is impossible to be so. In fact, there are some Darani who worship Billisi.'

Rumi formed the crossroads again. 'Worship her?'

'Oh yes. Billisi is worshipped because she brought the best out of Dara. His bravery, his love, his sacrifice. Dara is the Great Old King, but He was blind to Billisi's malevolence, wilfully ignorant of it. Billisi was full of violence and death, but she loved Dara, always. Only by throwing Billisi into the Hellmouth could Dara find his true balance, good confronting evil. It is a symbiotic relationship; an eternal contest. You cannot understand the meaning of good unless you understand the meaning of evil. Even in the village play, you cannot have a hero without a villain and you do not jeer the villain after the play. He is an actor playing his part.'

'That is ... either interesting or blasphemy,' Rumi said.

'I go with interesting,' she said. 'We do not confront our enemies because we are good. We do it to restore balance. We are a people whose nature has suffered a great intrusion, but suffering does not ennoble a man and we cannot fight with hate. Trust me, I have tried.'

'So how do we fight?'

'By learning who we are,' she said, gesturing to the book, *Lessons from the Sea.* 'The Palmaine are a people of engineering, and the objective of the engineer is to correct nature. They work against nature, paying no mind to the price for this interference. Gods are a reflection of people and so it comes as no surprise that the Palmaine worship a god that moralises. That may work on the Paronesian continent, but that has never been our way here.

We are the people of music; we understand the world by singing a song about it. That has always been the beauty of our people.'

'What good is music when the engineers have gunpowder?'

'We made absolutely fabulous war songs. But you are making my point for me. There must be balance.'

Rumi was quiet. The Viper was a little mad, of that he was sure, but she was also wise. *If she's the one to make me a shadow-wielder, then so be it.*

She leaned back in her chair and placed her palms on the table between them. 'The shadow is the true beginning of knowing yourself. It is the place where every unexamined emotion finds rest. A well of power, as deep as the strength of your emotion. The deeper you draw from it, the more you will be confronted by the emotions you keep locked away. To control it requires a submission to truth: coming to terms with the darkness that is part of you and embracing that emotion. Think of the shadow as your twin brother, with twenty times your speed and strength, and imagine how your twin brother would behave if he was beaten, neglected, and fed iron nails his whole life. That is the challenge you face. If you find a way to work with the shadow, your power is infinite, but if you don't, it will consume you. You must know what it is capable of by knowing what *you* are capable of. You understand me?'

'Not really.'

'Good; that is the beginning of your learning. Tomorrow we will talk more of these things.'

She lifted her sleeve, baring a series of thin black lines tattooed on her forearm. Rumi had learned that they indicated her level of strength in the shadow. He stopped counting at nineteen, but he was sure that the black line tattoos ran at least to her shoulder.

'How many lines am I?' Rumi asked, noticing the black lines on her other arm.

She quirked an eyebrow up. 'Well, let's see.'

With that she moved through a short choreography of stances to get his body acquainted with how he was expected to move. The movements were sharp, taxing manoeuvres that asked a lot of his knees and forearms and sore thighs in particular. After three good hours of choreography the Viper left him with a simple instruction.

'Chest on the ground, arms extended out, palms down... and hold... and count to a thousand. When you are done, start reading.'

She placed the book in front of him and left the room.

'Hello?' Rumi called, but she had left him on the floor alone, stretched out like a bird in flight. At the count of three hundred, his arms trembled. By three-fifty they gave way entirely. He did not have the strength to push back up. So he lay there, reading the book. His arms and thighs burned with pain.

The book was about the life of an enslaved Kuba man aboard a Palmaine ship bound for Paronesia. A harrowing read.

The sudden sound of blades clashing made his head jerk up. He rose and peeked into the other room. There they were, in the fighting pit. Yomiku and Zarcanis.

The scattered energy of Yomiku's shadow flittered about him in a misty froth. Zarcanis's shadow was purply-black, draped over her shoulders like a cape. Her shadow was not like the others Rumi had seen; it was not scattered and messy, but calm and disciplined. The perfect synthesis of motion and stillness.

The power of shadowwielders was demonstrated in them. Neither of them wore helmets, despite carrying real blades. They were unbelievably strong and fast. It was like sword-fighting at inhuman speed, with the ability to form solid shadow constructs while doing it. Yomiku slashed with otherworldly speed, half a hundred hacks of his blade in the blinking of an eye. The Viper danced around his strikes like a fly dancing around the swipes of a cook. They moved in black blurs.

Zarcanis spotted Rumi and called out. 'Watch the forms, Ajanla.'

Rumi leaned forward, trying to keep track.

The Viper exerted her dominance. Yomiku struck left and she leaped over his blade, smashing the back of his head with the flat side of her sword. Yomiku hit the ground hard but rose immediately to his feet. Zarcanis bounced back, inviting him on. He charged at her with his blade held high. She sidestepped and rounded on him, hammering his back with the hilt of her blade.

'Do you yield?' she asked, stepping back.

'No.' Yomiku rose to his feet, spitting blood.

She glanced over her shoulder at Rumi. 'What emotion is he feeding his shadow?'

Rumi raised an eyebrow. It was obvious. 'Rage.'

She smiled for a moment then darted back to lead the dance. She struck for Yomiku's thigh and he anticipated it, leaping over her blade. It was a less graceful imitation of her earlier counter. Mid-leap, Yomiku brought his hand down and even as he did a blade materialised from shadow in his grip. He was going for her head. In the half-blink of her eye the Viper unveiled the trap. She conjured a solid block of shadow to protect her back and grabbed Yomiku's ankle. His conjured blade shattered against her shield and with a two-handed grip, she slammed him to the ground. Rumi flinched at the impact. It was a manoeuvre she had shown him just that morning. *Puppet snatches the strings.* Ten times she had shown that particular manoeuvre to him.

The thought crossed his mind that she had choreographed the entire exchange to show him the form in action.

Yomiku lay there broken and bloodied, one eye open as she stood over him. His shadow fell apart and congealed into a black pool of tar on the floor.

'Not rage, Ajanla,' Zarcanis said, peering over her shoulder at him. 'Fetch him a botanical. Third door on the right, quickly.'

Rumi rushed out of the room. Through the door, a man and woman in white kaftans stared at him. At the centre of the room was an iron-wrought staff.

'I need a botanical,' he said, panting.

'The Viper?'

He nodded. As they rushed back to the room and carried Yomiku away, Rumi thought of the fight he had just seen. Yomiku had been trying to kill her, that much was obvious. He had swung for her head with no pause, no hesitation. Had she not flipped at the perfect moment he would have split her head in two.

'He could have killed you,' he said when they were alone.

'If that were the case then I would be dead.'

'He swung for your head.'

'A man fights at his best when he faces death. I would be thoroughly impressed if he had killed me. Thoroughly impressed.'

'Were you trying to kill him?'

'Of course not. Where would that leave me? With no sparring partner? How tedious.'

'What if his blade had broken your shield?'

She laughed. 'My shields are not easily broken. The strength of one's conjuring is tied to the strength of their emotion. I have tapped into an emotion stronger than you can imagine.'

'He hates you,' Rumi said.

'And he loves me. The great oppositions. There are few I would rather have by my side in battle. That is where I want him to show his love – protecting my unguarded side as I protect his.' She smiled. 'Anyway, that is enough for one day. Go do whatever you Seedlings do. Your novelty is wearing off faster than I'd hoped.'

43

Bloodlines

RUMI

After a month in the Eredo, Rumi had adjusted to the loose routine of fighting days. More than once he'd tried to check in on Renike but there were strict rules for Seedlings in the Order. She was under the care of Chief Karile and doing well, he was told. He barely had the time to leave his dorm outside of his lessons.

The Viper would often start their sessions with a strange question or a statement.

'So, do you believe in Dara?' she asked, settling into her seat at the reading table.

Rumi thumbed his chin. He did believe in Dara. In the existence of him. He had seen his mother call down thunder in Dara's name. But he did not believe in the Dara his mother had told him about. The Skyfather, the Defender of the Defenceless. That Dara was a lie. Only a cold, loveless god would let his Yami die the way she had. Not a father.

He realised he was taking too long to answer.

'Yes, I do believe in Dara,' he said, leaning back as he took a seat opposite her.

'Why?'

Rumi considered the question. 'I have seen some incredible things done in His name.'

'I could do some incredible things in my own name. Would you then believe I am a god?'

'It's not quite the same.'

'It is precisely the same thing. If your belief is based on the knowledge and experience of others, what good is it?'

'You don't need to jump into the fire to know that it is hot,' he said.

'Well, someone had to jump in it, at some time, to really know. You will never know how hot it is until you touch it. They pamper Seedlings in the Order these days. That is one thing I hate. I won't be responsible for another self-serious zealot, thanking Dara when they find two yolks in an egg.'

'So how do you see Dara?'

She ran a hand through her fiery hair. 'You should see Dara as being a part of yourself. You are not separate. To unravel Dara's mystery does not belittle him; it enlarges him. His power does not come from being something distant – it comes from being just like a man, having a story.

'In Mushiain, the word for human being is *yenina*; it means "the Chosen Ones". The Palman priests say man is not allowed to think he is god. The Darani say man is god in disguise. Any man can become a god, an Agbara. And many gods were once men. It is the worship that turns men into gods, the stories. Our goal on earth is to move from being worms to gods, writing our stories in the hearts of men. That is the Darani Way.'

'That's the second time someone here has called me a worm.'

She tilted her head. 'Well, your body is sort of long…worm-like. If I were to pick one animal, I would opt for a dog, but a worm is—'

'Zarcanis!'

She shook with laughter. 'I joke. Don't worry, I'm sure some of the little Seedling girls will take a liking to you.'

Rumi smiled. 'So, you mean to tell me that if enough people *worship* me, I can become an Agbara?'

'It is the Way ... worm.'

Rumi smirked. 'Have you ever been in love, or wanted a family or a position?'

'I was in love once, yes.'

'What happened?'

'I had to leave him.'

'Why?'

She frowned. 'Women like me are easy to despise.'

Rumi laughed, then realised that she wasn't laughing along. The smile melted from his face. He wanted to ask more questions, but Zarcanis's temper was unpredictable.

'What about you, have you ever been in love?' she asked.

'No ... well, I don't think so.'

'I'm surprised. Spry little hero boys like you often find some poor girl to love in some fierce way before they touch twenty.'

'I'm not a spry little hero boy. Especially if I never get to use the halberd.' He gestured pointedly to the black tattooed lines of shadow ranking on her arm. 'When do I begin to earn my own lines? I hear there is a tournament coming. The Ghedo?'

'Forget getting any lines for now. Forget the Ghedo. As far as I'm concerned you should still be on the teat, with all the learning you have ahead of you. You do not know your own name, your shadow is far too dark, and you are unable to subdue it.' She rose to her feet. 'Working with an unnamed shadow is no easy task. I want you to see what is wrong for yourself. I want you to want my change.'

'What change?'

'Letting yourself go, so you can become something. If the actor believes he is the character he portrays, then he is trapped in a story already written. See and accept your true nature.'

Rumi stared at her blankly, waiting for more.

Zarcanis sighed. 'Go down into a split as low as you can.'

Always the same pattern; questions, then stretching to the point of near death. Within weeks, Rumi found himself seeing the forms in his dreams. He learned there were two distinct aspects to combat with the shadow. The first was shadowdancing, which involved weapon battle and mastery of the forms. The second was conjuring, which involved moulding the shadow into solid constructs such as a shield to block an attack or a staircase to run up a wall.

After long fighting days, Rumi would join up with Ladan, who would throttle him with questions about Zarcanis. He answered as much as he could, but there was a lot that was beyond explanation. The Viper had a way of terrifying you and intriguing you all at once. Like being too close to fire; you know it is searing your hair and skin, but the warmth is irresistible.

Besides Rumi, Sameer and Ahwazi were the only Seedlings that were not Kasinabe. The Kasinabe treated the three of them like sickly dogs, and so they were stuck with one another.

In his fifth week at the Eredo, Sameer returned from fighting day with his arms and legs strapped with weights. Ahwazi, on the other hand, returned with a thick black tattooed line on his forearm, a swollen eye and a serpentine swagger.

After that, whenever fighting days came, Sameer moved with palpable apprehension and Ahwazi walked with a slow, quiet confidence. They would return with Sameer studying the floor and Ahwazi enraptured in the euphoria of a fighter's high. It made Rumi even more anxious to start his own sparring.

He had learned a great deal about fighting from Tinu. How to roll a punch, how to protect yourself when you dodge, how to run while walking. Sparring with the shadow, however, was an entirely different matter.

Everything in the Order was an opportunity for competition. The dinner bell was the signal of a full-pelt race to the dining hall. Weapon collection on fighting day was a pageant for all the fighting forms. A stubbed toe or a brushed shoulder could easily degenerate into a fist-fight and the shadowwielders would take their time to stop it. Most competitive of all were the black tattooed lines of shadow ranking. Each line was as precious to a Seedling as a babe to its nursing mother.

Rumi thrummed with the lust for sparring in the shadow but all Zarcanis did was make him stretch and answer strange questions. The day came when even Sameer had earned his first line tattoo and Rumi seemed to be the only one in the entire dormitory who had earned no shadow rank. He satiated his hunger for competition with games of *seraiye* with Sameer and Ahwazi.

'You always win,' Rumi said one day, dropping his leopard stone in defeat. 'Even when I have more stones, you find a way to win.'

Sameer was near expressionless. He had a way of keeping his face completely blank, even when Rumi could tell he was grinning underneath. In *seraiye*, Sameer had humbled Rumi near a hundred times and his nonchalance made the defeats so much worse.

'You always find a way to lose,' Sameer said casually.

'Teach me,' Rumi said, studying his formation.

'I can't teach you anything,' he said. 'You know most of the best openings; I've seen you weave complex formations around me more than half a hundred times. You're no goat on festival day.'

'What is it then? What am I getting wrong?'

Sameer massaged his temples as though he had gained fifty years in age. 'You play the man and not the position.'

'What is that supposed to mean?'

Sameer sighed. 'My mother used to say *seraiye* tells you more about a man than his words do. Look at this.' He moved his hyena stone in a quick line to demonstrate. 'This was ... this was brilliant. You surprised me.'

'I knew I had you!'

Sameer had barely flinched when it happened, but that move had hurt him. The hyena was a dexterous piece to those initiated in *seraiye*; surprise attacks like his worked well with the hyena.

Sameer smiled. 'You surprised me, but I knew that *you* knew you surprised me. When you find a weak link in the chain you always run to break it.'

Sameer moved a leopard stone to the rear of Rumi's lion stone with a quick diagonal step. 'You always harry when you should hold. It's like you can't wait to prove you're better than me; you don't want a minute to pass without it being known, and in doing so ...' He moved another monkey stone in a small triangle. 'You leave your backside unguarded.' He struck Rumi's lion stone from the board as he spoke. 'I am a dubious player and you know it, but I stick to the plan, I play my position. I watch. You ... Even in *seraiye* you play the hero.'

'You *dominated* me.'

'Oh, yes ... oh, yes, I did,' Sameer said, letting his lips curl as he sashayed his leopard stone in rehearsal of the game. Striking Rumi's stones one after the other. 'But I think you wanted that ... To fail spectacularly. Maybe you think it will make your eventual victory sweeter. But I am no goat on festival day either.'

Ahwazi threw his head back and laughed.

'I am never playing *seraiye* with you again. Next thing you know you'll be telling me why I don't wash my underarms,' he said.

'You don't wash your—'

'Oh, shut up!' Ahwazi snapped.

They all laughed together.

After two months in the Order, Rumi had – to his silent frustration – not received any divine instructions to read the *Sakosaye*. He had, however, read *Lessons from the Sea* twice from cover to cover.

It was a difficult read. The beauty of Basmine sometimes made it easy to forget the violence of its birth. *Lessons from the Sea* reclaimed the canvas and uncovered the bloodstains.

The harrowing account of death and disease on the Palmaine ships made his heart hit his stomach. The book spoke of how the Palmaine were careful to keep men of the same tribes apart: Odu were chained next to Kuba to ensure that they could neither communicate nor conspire. They gave the Kuba larger rations of food to foster infighting. Everything was deliberate.

The book's closing remarks didn't leave his mind:

I find that the Paronesians in all respects remain committed to overlooking their indignity. They have fallen and do not know it. We must learn from their fall, lest we make the same mistake. We must never think ourselves incapable of doing unto others that which has been done to us – that is a lie without profit.

He chewed on those final words often, not completely sure what they meant. It seemed an irony on a grand scale to think natives of the Darosa continent were in any position to make Paronesian mistakes.

When curiosity had overpowered his reluctance, he asked Sameer about it.

'I think it means we shouldn't feel that we are righteous only because we have been wronged. There must be more to us,' Sameer had said.

It stayed with him. Even here, hidden away from all Palmaine influence, the wounds of the natives still ran deep. But the wounded man who seeks only to wound in return has learned nothing. He found in that moment the confidence to ask another, more belly-scraping question.

'Sameer, tell me, what do you know about spirits?'

A bright smile spread across Sameer's face. He gestured towards the corner of his bedspace, obscured from view by his wardrobe. Once out of easy sight, he threw himself to the floor to pull aside a loose board under his bed.

Rumi watched with a quirked eyebrow as Sameer carefully reached down and returned to his feet holding a large clear bottle of transparent liquid.

'I must say, I am a wine man myself,' Sameer said, 'but I do find time for a good, earthy gin.'

Rumi couldn't stop the laughter from spattering out. 'I didn't mean alcoholic spirits.'

Ahwazi too scattered into a rolling, skittering laugh.

Sameer blinked. 'Oh ... oh dear. You meant *spirits*, as in other-worldly things?'

Rumi nodded and Sameer slowly lowered the bottle.

Ahwazi snatched the bottle from him. 'Well, since your secret is out,' he said, fiddling with the cork, 'you can answer while we drink.'

Sameer brushed his palms down on his kaftan. 'Spirits ... erm ... Well, spirits are all the things that can enter the Originate. Ancestors, Agbara, masquerades. Every bloodline has a connection to the spirits.'

'Even I know all that,' Ahwazi said, passing the bottle to Rumi. 'And my father says I have less upstairs than a bungalow.'

The fumes from the bottle shot up into Rumi's nose. He took a sharp swig and scowled, then threw back another.

'Slow down, Ajanla,' Sameer said chuckling. 'What if one of the chiefs comes in for a snap test?'

Rumi wiped his mouth clean. 'What else do you know?'

Sameer rubbed his chin. 'Well, if you can tell me about your bloodline, perhaps I can tell you more.'

Rumi narrowed his eyes. 'Do you know anything about Griff Voltaine?'

Ahwazi nearly choked, spraying gin as he coughed. 'The darkman is your father?'

He said it like it was an accusation, voice all loud and scratchy.

Rumi frowned. 'Apparently.'

'Why didn't you mention this before?'

Rumi glared at him. 'I didn't know I owed you anything.'

Ahwazi swallowed and wiped the gin from his wet lips.

Sameer quickly cut through any tension. 'Griff was easily the best shadowwielder when he was active. He trained Zarcanis. He holds nearly every record of note in the Ghedo tournaments.'

Rumi sat up. 'He trained Zarcanis?'

'Yes,' said Ahwazi.

Griff trained Zarcanis.

'Why isn't he a shadowwielder anymore?'

Ahwazi swallowed. Sameer avoided his eyes.

'What is it? Tell me!' Rumi said.

'When you don't know your last name, your shadow eventually leaves you and you cannot recall it. The darkman was drawing his shadow with blood and one day it stopped coming.'

'How long?' Rumi asked.

Ahwazi raised an eyebrow. 'What?'

'For how long was he able to call his shadow?'

'Five years,' Sameer said. 'I'm sorry, I cannot tell you anything about your bloodline, about your spirits.'

Rumi nodded. *Five years. Five years to become strong enough. Five years to find and kill them.*

Sameer's eyes carried a sincere pinch of sympathy.

They were a strange trio, Sameer with the wisdom beyond his years that came from having no friends, Ahwazi the quiet contrarian with a penchant for fighting. In truth, Rumi had come to like them both – inwardly, of course.

He only had five years to do what he had sworn in blood to do. He could not afford to like them outwardly. Not now.

44

A Trial

RUMI

Breakfast the next day was interrupted by the blast of a horn. One horn meant someone important had arrived, two in quick succession meant that an assembly was called, three blasts meant the Eredo was under attack. After the first two blasts, there was a patient silence. Just two blasts. An assembly. The dining room erupted. Ladan's eyes bulged. He dropped his shard and joined the throng of people moving for the corridor.

Sameer touched Rumi's shoulder. 'We need to get good seats,' he said, before running off.

Rumi had barely made good work of his breakfast. He hissed, then took another bite of yam.

He caught up with Sameer and Ahwazi as they moved past the open door of the Order. Before long, they found themselves in the grand entrance hall with the massive dais at its centre.

The crowd formed a wide circle around the dais. All the chiefs were there, sat in a crescent around a man with a dark sack over his head. Rumi instantly recognised him as the prisoner the Chainbreakers had brought.

A lean, wiry figure stood beside the man. He held his sword almost casually to the side as he watched the room fill up. *No Music.* It dawned on Rumi, as he regarded the man, that they might be there to witness an execution.

No Music ripped the sack from the prisoner's head and the crowd reacted with gasps of surprise.

The cowrie on Rumi's necklace ran hot as he stared at the prisoner.

'What's that on his neck?' Ahwazi asked.

Rumi squinted. The prisoner wore a collar with a black stone at its centre, tight around his neck.

'It's an Odeshi,' Sameer said. 'The quartercuff.'

Ahwazi's eyes widened. 'Dara's might.'

Rumi scratched his chin. 'What's an Odeshi?'

Sameer had seen the question coming. 'It's a collar made from cobalt. Takes away three-quarters of a shadowwielder's power. I've never seen one actually used before.'

'Can a Palmaine man be a shadowwielder?' said Ahwazi.

'No,' said Sameer. 'Must be some sort of precaution.'

Rumi looked at the man again. For a man like that, it was wise to have precautions.

'Is that who I think it is?' Sameer said, narrowing his eyes. He gave a sharp gasp. 'It is.'

'Who is it?' Rumi asked.

Sameer's voice took on a hard edge. 'That is Governor-General Zaminu.'

The priestess's cowrie flared up at the mention of that name. Recognition flooded him. Rumi had seen that face in one of the paintings at the Golden Room. His overgrown beard and rundown hair were different but those proud eyes were still the same. A man responsible for more death in Basmine than anyone alive.

Rumi let his gaze leave the man and scanned for Nataré. Just to see her. Just to check she was all right. She didn't have to like him, but he needed to know she was all right. At least, that was what he told himself as he craned his neck around the room.

'What are you looking for?' he heard from behind.

He didn't have to turn to know who had spoken.

'Nothing,' Rumi said, his face crumpling at being caught off guard.

'Really?' Nataré said and turned him to face her.

She smiled and a bolt of blood surged up his veins. He smiled back, stupidly.

'I am ...' He paused to consider his words.

Her face darkened. 'Let's not,' she said, putting a finger on his lips as though to silence him.

He buttoned his lip and nodded. They had begun, it seemed, to speak a sort of private language. Every word pregnant with hidden meaning. Every pause a sentence of its own. All the freedom of the Nyme was gone.

She stepped close and spoke low. 'The last time we spoke in the Thatcher, you said you wanted to get to know me.'

'I do.'

She met his eye, her voice still just above a whisper. 'All right. What do you want to know?'

Rumi gave a start, surprised at the opportunity. He fidgeted with his inner pocket. 'Umm ...'

She frowned. 'Isn't there anything you actually want to know about me?'

Rumi cleared his throat. 'I wanted to know,' he began, 'what activity makes you feel the most joy when you're doing it?'

She narrowed her eyes and gave him a considering look. She opened her mouth to speak then closed it again. 'I quite like smelling the soil after it rains,' she said at last.

Rumi arched an eyebrow. 'Really?'

She nodded. 'It's delightful. You should try it one day. After it rains.'

He laughed. 'That is … not what I expected you to say.'

She formed a line with her lips. 'What's your answer? What makes you feel the most joy?'

The answer came easily to Rumi. *Playing music.* But that was an old incarnation of himself. The one he had abandoned with his drums at the wreckage. He searched his mind for a more fitting answer. 'Sparring,' he lied.

The sharp flash of disappointment on her face was the certain indication that he had answered incorrectly. 'I thought you would say music. I remember how you used to play the drums.' Her eyes seemed to drift away. 'You were so talented,' she whispered, almost to herself.

Rumi formed a thin line with his lips. 'A lifetime ago.'

'Do you still play?'

'No,' he snapped. It came out with more edge than he had intended.

Her eyes narrowed to slits. 'I should go find a seat.'

Rumi immediately wanted to apologise but couldn't find the words to put it perfectly. She turned away from him as he fumbled for a sentence.

In two breaths, he'd lost her in the crowd. 'Shege,' he hissed.

As he turned away, he met the gaze of Griff, his father. He frowned and hissed for good measure, but the man did not look away.

Someone slapped him hard on the back.

'Rumi!'

His face moved from a glare to a grin. He took Renike by the shoulders.

In just two months, she had undergone an incredible metamorphosis. Her arms were not quite so spindly anymore, and

378

her shoulders were broader. But the transformation was more subtle than that. Rumi could hear it in the inflection of her voice, see it in the set of her lips, in her eyes.

The twinkle of joy in her eye had been replaced by stony, purposeful resolution. She had crossed the line from believing the world was a delightful place into seeing it for what it was. She had lost her father and left home young. She had lived amongst a people preparing for war. Renike was not like him; she was a girl who simply wanted to love. *Why did we bring her here?*

She saw the way he was looking at her and shrugged. 'Puberty,' she said, smiling. 'Chief Karile says I will join the Order soon if I work hard.'

Rumi imagined her training with Zarcanis and flinched. 'You don't want—'

'Yes, I do,' she said. 'I want to be a shadowwielder, like Yami was. Like you will become.'

Rumi drew in a long breath and looked her in the eye. She put her hands on her hips and raised her chin.

They both broke into smiles and she pulled him into a tight embrace.

'I hope so,' Rumi whispered.

Just then, Mandla rose to his feet and cleared his throat. The room fell into an almost instantaneous silence. Mandla stepped up to the prisoner, took him by the shoulders and turned him for all to see. 'This man stands accused of murder, grievous mutilation, theft and blood ritual,' Mandla began. 'Chief Karile, what is the proper punishment for these crimes?'

Karile rose to her feet. 'For a conviction of murder and unauthorised blood ritual, the convicted shall be sentenced to death by arrowfire,' she said with an air of recitation. 'For a conviction of grievous mutilation, the convicted is to be subject to at least a year of imprisonment, and for a conviction of theft, the convicted shall be lashed at least forty times across the back and pay a fine amounting to three times the value of the materials stolen.'

Mandla nodded. 'Thank you, Karile.' He turned to Zaminu. 'And how do you plead?'

Zaminu hissed out a gob of bloody spittle. 'The elephant does not answer to the parliament of baboons.'

Mandla's face gave barely a hint of expression. 'Enter a plea of not guilty.'

Karile nodded.

The trial played out as one might expect, witness after witness stepped forward to testify of Zaminu's crimes. Mutilation was the least of them. Were the old governor-general to write a book of his crimes it would span several volumes and overrun any modest library.

The crowd was tense as they listened, awaiting the moment when Mandla would pass the Council's judgement. After the tenth witness, Mandla raised his hand.

'I think we have heard quite enough,' he said, his eyes narrow with rage. 'Do you have any response to these testimonies, Zaminu?'

The man shot Mandla a disgusted look and scowled. 'I wish I had done worse. I wish more of you were in unmarked graves. You are an abominable people and deep down you know it too.'

Mandla's eyes didn't move. 'Well, in that case I move to pass the judgement of the Council.' All the other chiefs rose. 'Zaminu, you are pronounced guilty. You are hereby sentenced to death by arrowfire under the watchful eye of the Almighty.'

The prisoner cracked a broken, raspy laugh. 'Pathetic.'

Mandla nodded to No Music and the thin man pulled the

sack tight over Zaminu's head once more. 'Take him to the dungeons. His day of death is not far ahead.'

No Music dragged Zaminu out, with all the consideration one might give a dirty rag. The crowd watched him go. A death sentence was an act of great mercy.

Mandla narrowed his eyes, then shifted his stare to the tall doors at the far end of the room.

The doors flew open and a dozen spear-carrying Chainbreakers appeared, draped to their toes in their brown-green robes. They formed a corridor of killers, standing one on either side with a pathway down the middle. An honour guard. A young woman strode forward, looking straight ahead, imperious in dress and bearing. Though she wore no beaded crown, the golden *iborun* shawl draped over a shoulder and the Shinala tail *irukere* fly-whisk in her hand, were as loud as a proclamation. The woman was a queen, in every inch and strand.

Mandla smiled. 'I present to you the Golden Eagle, Princess Falina Almarak, rightful heir to King Olu Almarak of the Otaru clan, blood of the ancestors and rightful ruler of our nation. *Ka-Biyesi O!*'

Every person in the room lay in *foribale*, the highest prostrate salute with foreheads pressed to the floor. Even the dogs seemed to bow their heads.

She nodded and spoke in perfect Mushiain. '*Ejide.*'

At her command, men and women rose from their bows. Rumi glanced up at her as she looked across the multitude, plainly overwhelmed by the show of allegiance.

'Omoba,' Mandla said, 'we, the Council of the Eredo, have called this congregation to ask you under the eye of the Almighty, will you be our queen?'

Omoba's shoulders shook as she heaved in a breath, then another. There was silence as every eye in the room fixed itself on her direction. She glanced at Alangba, and he gave a single nod of encouragement.

She closed her eyes bit down on her lip. 'Yes, I will be your queen.'

The crowd exploded.

45

Mindwalking and Pain

RUMI

Chief Karile beat a wooden ruler against the rock wall. The soft *twack twack* of the wood on stone produced an echo through the acoustics of the domed stalactite canopy.

'Today we will learn about the doorways to the mind,' said Chief Karile.

Chief Karile's lessons involved a great deal of history, centring also on the importance of names and how to use them. In three months they had learned how a loose tongue could give someone the power to sneak into your mind, quick as a rat up a drainpipe. How the names of all men are written in the Originate, and how a name is a source of power to those who know how to use it.

They sat cross-legged on the raffia floormats. On the walls there were paintings of places that looked like Alara; villages with cookfires and clusters of life.

'Mindwalking,' Karile said. 'If you have been a thief before, then you may know a part of it. How to make a friend of silence and focus. To travel light. The mind is ordered in three distinct parts. The foremind is the first, it rules over our immediate awareness, thoughts, and feelings. The dreamscape is the second. A level deeper. It holds our remembered experiences, our tendencies and predispositions. Deepest of all is the shadowmind, which holds everything that drives who we are. Our pain, anxiety, our faith and fears.'

She looked over them one after the other, strolling through the centre of the class.

'You,' she said, pointing right at Rumi. 'Call your shadow.'

Rumi stirred for a moment. Of everyone in the class, he was the only one who hadn't started sparring yet – he did not know how to call his shadow; didn't even know if he still had one. He squeezed his eyes shut, willing his shadow to come, but it gave no answer.

'Struggling?' Karile said.

Rumi nodded, avoiding the eyes settling on him.

Karile took a few steps towards Rumi and leaned in. Then her hand moved with a slash and a line of red appeared on his arm. He jerked back as the pain flashed through him.

'Lick the blood,' Karile said.

Rumi stared at her with raised eyebrows, then he licked the wound clean. A moment passed and power filled him. Wisps of black smoke surrounded him as though something burned within. *The shadow.* He drank deep on the shadow. A taste like the first bite of fresh baked bread.

Karile smiled. 'Good. Now I want you to release your shadow.'

Regretfully, Rumi let his shadow depart, the sweet energy seeping out from his pores like sweat.

'Good,' Karile said. 'Hold my hand.'

Rumi took her hand.

'Can you feel that?'

He *could* feel it, like heat radiating from her hand to his.

'The knowledge of shadows is a gateway to a great many things. It keeps the secrets you refuse to admit exist. Your shadow calls to mine and you can feel it. Close your eyes.'

Rumi closed his eyes.

'Can you see it?'

He could see it, her mind. An endless expanse of space, with small floating orbs of crystalline blue and a long, winding road that encircled three giant pillars. Foremind, dreamscape and shadowmind.

'I can see it!'

'Good, now forget yourself entirely and find that which connects us. Think as I would think.'

Rumi fixed his mind on history lessons.

Karile laughed. 'So, is that what you think I spend my time thinking about?'

Rumi focused on her voice, on how it trembled when she spoke about the rebellion, on how she carried pain somewhere there.

'Good, very good. Now, I want you to steal a thought from my foremind.'

Rumi narrowed in on one of the floating blue orbs and chased after it. It fled from him, with agile, unpredictable movement. He doubled his speed, floating with no body in another person's mind. Every time he thought he was closing in on it, the orb would slip by him. It was like chasing a chicken in a field when your hands are oily. And you have no fingers.

Eventually he relented, his mind trembling from the effort of chasing orbs he could never catch. As he floated in her consciousness, resigned to defeat, the orbs floated around again, this time disabused of the notion that he was there. Rumi understood. He waited, like a thief. Silent and unmoving. Before long, a small blue orb floated to him and he reached out with his mind to make contact.

A sudden flash of light made him jerk back. He saw Karile with ... with Yami, riding side by side on two beautiful Shinala adorned with war saddles and reins formed of heavy-linked gold chains. Their faces were solemn and determined. Yami carried the halberd while Karile held a wide ida longsword. They rode like mentor and apprentice, reflecting one another in a way. They saw something in the distance, something on fire, and he saw Yami coil her legs into her stirrups.

'Yami,' he breathed wistfully.

That seemed to get her attention, Karile's too. They turned on him, weapons drawn and suddenly he was in very real danger. He tried to stumble away but he was running on wet ice. His mother threw the halberd back and brought it down to split his skull. He screamed.

The blue orb exploded and he found himself with eyes shut in the classroom again.

'Excellent,' Karile said.

Rumi opened his eyes. Everyone was staring at him. His heart pounded like a war drum.

'How ... how long was I ... in your mind?' Rumi said.

'Only a few moments. For you, perhaps it felt like an hour.'

Rumi wiped his forehead, which was wet with sweat. 'My mother, she ... She tried to kill me.'

Karile nodded. 'A mind will always defend its integrity. It will only allow you to stay if it thinks you are cut from the same tree.'

'What would have happened if she split my skull?'

Karile shrugged. 'Better not to find out.'

'What did I see?'

'One of my memories, but it could just as well have been my imagination. You will learn with time how to tell a true thought from a lie.'

'You let me have it?'

'Oh yes, I don't want you seeing anything too juicy. Besides, when a person is awake it is especially difficult to steal thoughts.'

'The giant blue sphere at the centre of it all. Was that—'

'The shadowmind. It is the connection that every one of us has to the Originate. We wouldn't want you getting anywhere near that.'

The class was abuzz with questions.

'Can you enter a mind without touching?' someone called out.

'If you have the person's true name, then yes, you can sneak into a mind with a name just by looking at the person.'

'What about the dead?' Rumi said. 'Can you commune with the dead in this way?'

Karile frowned. 'We are skipping chapters now. You will learn a lot more before you start to answer those questions.'

'Can you make your own memory vanish?' he asked instead.

She smiled. 'Now *that* is a crucial question.'

After the lesson, Rumi approached Karile. He was convinced that in mindwalking, he would find answers to many of the questions that kept him awake at night. The power of knowing a person's true name in particular was of interest. There was one true name only he knew.

'I would like to learn more … about mindwalking.'

She raised an eyebrow and studied him. 'Why?'

Rumi was not prepared for the question. He fumbled for an answer. 'Because I … know it will help to become a Suli.'

She frowned. 'I have an hour immediately after dinner, where I train interested Seedlings and Suli. You are welcome to join us.'

Rumi nodded. 'Thank you. I will be there.'

Gaitan's lesson came next. He was teaching them what he called 'the Preparations'. The Preparations covered every one of the preparatory steps to war and combat: everything from hair-braiding to horsemanship to charms and meditation. He taught them how to tell by muscle mass what Shinala to ride in a chase down and what Shinala to ride in a spear melee. How to oil and sharpen their weapons every day to keep them kill-sharp. That was the essence of dominion: control and co-existence with the world around you.

Gaitan was an affable man, with a booming laugh that set the room alight with giggling. His room was a reflection of him. Paintings of men and women at war hung from the walls, and all around his lecture theatre were plants that gave the room a rainbow of colour. At the back of the room there was a door fastened shut by a heavy metal-link chain.

'We learn today about using the shadow to embrace pain,' Gaitan said.

There were a few murmurs of surprise or excitement.

'Pain is a part of our lives and we cannot escape that. It is important, if you are to last in the Order, that you accept that you will suffer. You will feel some pain. Make your peace with it now if you have not already.'

Rumi leaned forward on his chair.

'Lord Mandla once said, "pain and suffering are the stones in your shoe as you tread the distance to your desire". Some think he means that pain and suffering are a distraction, a sort of chronic frustration, but I think he means that pain and suffering are an ever-present, a part of the journey.'

Sameer raised a hand.

'Yes, Ailera,' Gaitan said.

A ripple of giggles always followed when they called Sameer that name.

'Are you saying that we will suffer and feel pain in our lives until we … die?'

'That is one way of it,' Gaitan said, smiling. 'But that is not the Darani Way. There is another way. A way to make a friend of the stones in the shoe.'

He rose to his feet and walked towards the chain-bolted door.

'When I was a child, my father had a pair of white slippers. I will never forget those slippers. He would playfully chase me around the house with those white slippers and I would cry with laughter when he caught me and scored my bottom with them. The white slippers were a thing of joy.'

He stopped at Ahwazi's chair and rested a hand on his shoulder.

'One day I brought a dog into the house. When my father came back from the farm, he found the house decorated with turds and dog piss.'

Ahwazi burst into laughter.

'When my father saw the house, he went for his white slippers again, except this time there was no joy in his eyes. After he scored my bottom, I cried myself to sleep. After that, whenever I made mischief, my father went for his white slippers. Before long, I started to cry before the slippers even touched my bottom. The slippers had become a thing of pain. Now, my father used precisely the same force when he spanked me in jest as when he spanked me in rebuke, but the mind has a way of ascribing pain based on the context of your experience. Just in the same way the word "Zarot" has a special violence from the lips of a Palmaine man, tears of sorrow can become tears of joy depending on the context. Now, imagine if I could feel the joy of the jest when my father spanked me for letting a dirty dog loose in the house.'

Gaitan reached the door and unfastened the heavy, metal-link chain. The sound of links touching the ground made a soft chime. Gaitan pointed at a second-year Seedling called Dasuki.

Dasuki was the sort of man that made veteran soldiers smile

and nod, a tall tower with arms like Gu carved from the hardest rock. Next to Dasuki, even Gaitan looked unimpressive.

Gaitan put the end of the chain in Dasuki's hand and ripped his armour from his torso, exposing his bare chest and back. He called his shadow and a thick, viscous fog engulfed him.

'I want you to stripe my back with that chain, Dasuki.'

Dasuki raised an eyebrow. 'Chief—'

'Stripe my back,' Gaitan repeated.

Dasuki shrugged and wrapped a part of the chain around his forearm, collecting the rest in his palms. He swung sidewise and the chain thrashed Gaitan's back. The sound of metal hitting dull flesh made Rumi wince as he looked away.

'Again!' Gaitan said.

Dasuki swung again and blood splashed back at him.

'Again!'

Dasuki swung hard. The sound was horrible.

After the third swing Dasuki dropped the chain and stepped back.

Gaitan turned around, still oozing shadow. His eyes were steady focused, and incredibly, there was a wide grin on his face.

'With the shadow, you can embrace the pain. Pull it close until you find the joy in it.'

Sameer raised a hand.

'Yes, Ailera,' Gaitan said, wiping down his back.

'How does it work?'

Gaitan's smile widened. 'Ailera, you are from the Agede peninsula, am I correct? The fishing villages?'

'Yes, sir.'

'Are you familiar with the word *tesara*?'

Sameer's cheeks swelled and his eyes studied the floor. 'Yes.'

'Could you tell us what *tesara* is?'

Sameer's wandering eyes said 'I'd rather not' but he licked his lips to speak.

'In the fishing villages, *tesara* is the belief that the very highest form of arousal comes when a needle is buried in the flesh.'

'Buried in the flesh?' Gaitan repeated. 'I thought they were very specific about the bottom?'

The room erupted in laughter.

'Thank you, Ailera,' Gaitan said. 'You see, the mind is a strange thing. Pain can be … blissful if you learn to cooperate with it. The shadow is a mediator; with it, you can change your attitude to the experience of pain and suffering. After all, the same knife that stabs the heart also carves beauty into the slab of wood.'

'What about pain of the mind?' Rumi said. 'I can see it for needles in the bottom, but what about suffering here?' He pointed to his skull.

The laughter lost its edge and Gaitan's face hardened.

'Ah, pain of the mind … That is a more delicate matter. Have you ever had to pick beans before?'

'My mother was a market woman,' Rumi said.

'Good. So you know how utterly frustrating it is to pick beans, separating the good beans from the bad ones, the sand, the weevils, ants and every other unwanted thing. Hellish work.'

'Worse than any stone in the shoe.'

'You refuse to lie!' Gaitan said, smiling at Rumi. 'Pain of the mind must be addressed in the same way you address the picking of beans: one bean at a time. If you focus on the unpicked sacks full of beans, you might kill yourself. So, you pick the beans, one at a time, doing the best you can and somehow, you find the joy in picking. Forget the sacks unpicked entirely and pick each bean, knowing that each bean is like an agbalumo fruit: when you pluck it, you must drain all the bittersweet juice from it and discard the skin. Each time you feel the pain, you must go to the source of that pain, understand it, then you must get rid of it, after you have taken everything useful from it.'

He put a hand on Rumi's shoulder.

'That is the eternal battle for which the shadow cannot mediate. One day, you will find that all the sacks have been picked.'

46

Call Your Shadow

RUMI

When the time for Zarcanis's next lecture came, Rumi had mustered all the courage he needed to make an important statement.

She sat cross-legged on the floor, reading a book when he entered.

'Griff trained you,' Rumi said.

In his head, he had imagined saying it more artfully than that, but Zarcanis's stare had a way of shattering eloquence.

She glanced up at him. 'Someone had to do it.'

'And you didn't think to mention it before?'

'It isn't important.'

She was avoiding his gaze. Usually she had no problem with confrontation. *Why is she being elusive?*

It struck him like a thrown stone.

'You loved him,' Rumi said.

She stared up at him with blank, inexpressive eyes. 'We start sparring in an hour. Limber up.'

Godsblood. I'm a fool, aren't I?

Rumi spent the hour stretching and practicing the spear forms. He tried to focus, to revive something inside, stir up that serene chaos like he had seen Tinu do before he stepped into the cornerbox. His hands were slick with sweat. *She won't kill me ... will she?*

Zarcanis walked into the room and beckoned him forward.

'I thought of a name for your blade,' she said, smiling. 'Epilogue.'

Rumi stared blankly at her.

'Epilogue ... like end of a story, get it?'

Rumi retained his expressionless gaze.

She sighed. 'No time for banter, I see. Waste of a great name. Straight to business, then.'

She grabbed two safespears and threw one at Rumi. 'What are you waiting for? Call your shadow.'

He tightened his grip on the safespear and closed his eyes, lines of tension sprouting at the sides of his head.

Zarcanis raised an eyebrow. 'What are you doing?'

Rumi concentrated, gritting his teeth.

'Godsblood. Of course, you don't know your full name,' she said, massaging her cloth-covered neck. 'I almost forgot. Come with me.'

She led him out of the room down a path he had not trodden before. They came to a door guarded by a white lionhound. Zarcanis pulled the door open.

Rumi stepped in and froze.

Just a few steps into the room, the ground disappeared. It was a cliff edge. At least a thirty-metre drop. His heart rattled in his rib cage. Whatever came from a fall from that height would be permanent: death or paralysis.

Zarcanis stepped up beside him. 'Are you afraid?'

Rumi tried not to look down. 'No.'

Zarcanis shook her head. 'You still have a lot to learn. We confess our fears here. That way we can use the energy of

394

the lies.' She drew in a long, deep breath. 'I'll join you down there.'

Rumi stared at her. 'Excuse me?'

'I said, I will join you down there.'

'Are you ma—'

She pushed him before he could finish his sentence. He lost his grasp on the safespear as his insides jumped to his throat.

The ground pulled him down, every item of clothing fluttering like bed linen in the breeze. It all happened so quickly. He heard a soft sound, like the buzz of a mosquito in his ear, and then his shadow came. It coated him as he fell, the power surging through him like fire setting wood aflame.

He landed like an anvil, his knees flexed, and absorbed the impact. The ground split where he landed, but there was no pain. Only the sweet power of the shadow.

Zarcanis landed like an acrobat beside him, barely caressing the ground. Rumi's shadow swirled like smoke smothering burning refuse. Hers trailed neatly in the wind like a cape.

They were alone between two rock ridges. In the distance there was a tunnel carved into the wall. From the chalk markings on the walls of stone, it was plain someone had once had plans to turn the place into something grand, but for now it was just a sunken place between two cliffs. *A fighting pit.*

'So, you do have a shadow after all,' Zarcanis said, tossing her safespear from one hand to the other.

Rumi stared upwards at the cliff. 'What happened?'

'I had to get your heart pumping hard enough to make your shadow wake up. Danger seems to rouse it. Well, danger and blood.'

Rumi stared at her. 'What if it hadn't appeared?'

'Then I'd probably have some cleaning up to do.'

Rumi scowled as he picked up the safespear from the ground.

With the shadow it was weightless, as much a part of him as his arm.

'Attack me with everything you have,' Zarcanis urged. 'Nothing held back.'

Rumi nodded and drew deep on the shadow, filling himself with it. He charged at her, thrusting the safespear at her thigh. She leaped over his swing, smashing her knee into his chin. His teeth rattled as he hit the ground.

'If you hold back again, I will kill you,' Zarcanis said, in an almost casual tone.

Rumi gulped back saliva and thought back to his lessons with Tinu, how to defeat a superior opponent with suddenness. He charged again, drawing deep on the shadow until his insides burned. If she thought she would embarrass him, she was wrong. He faked to swing, then threw his elbow at her nose. She dodged at the very last moment, slinking under his elbow. Before he could turn, her safespear cracked down on the back of his skull. He hit the ground again. Blood sloshed around his mouth as he pushed himself back up to his feet.

'Better,' she said, taking a step back. 'You don't close your eyes when you strike. I like that. What emotion are you using? I can't really tell.'

Rumi stepped forward, spitting blood. 'Anger, irritation.'

She frowned. 'I'd hoped for something less predictable.'

As their weapons clashed she called out the forms before demonstrating. *Monkey climbs the tree, snake crosses the valley, lion snatches the impala.*

She was so much faster, but Rumi could tell she was holding back just enough. Her strikes were precise, missing his vitals, but scoring his flesh. Her control of the shadow was seamless. She was one with it, nothing out of place in her movements. A walking, living treatise of violence.

When he was slack, she struck down with deadly force. *Leopard speeds through forest* flowed into *fox enters the hen-house* so smoothly that he could not see her coming.

After they had gone at it for some time, he was drenched in sweat and half-dried blood. Zarcanis was fresh-faced, her clothes still dry.

'How long does the shadow last?' he said, blowing like a fish.

'As long as you can hold on to it. Why, are you tired?'

'No,' he lied.

Truth was, he was so exhausted that he could barely lift his safespear. She came at him. He tried to parry but she spun around his defence and nearly broke his clavicle with *eagle snatches the heart.*

'Do you yield?'

That irked him a bit. Having to yield. He tightened his hand around the safespear and the shadow's power swelled as he rose to his feet.

'No!' Rumi yelled.

'Then fight.'

He was panting like a dog in the desert. His vision was blurry from bloody sweat. If she struck him again, he felt like he would die.

He charged at her again using the form he knew best, *rhinoceros rages.* Her eyes narrowed. Rumi aimed for her neck. She always covered her neck, was always so protective of it; he could use that. He brought the safespear midway through the air fixing to smash her throat. She preempted it as he had expected, her spear rising to block. As soon as she moved, Rumi switched to *snake shoots venom*, his spear shifting to strike her stomach. She saw it too late; her stomach was his. She had a sliver of a smile as he struck.

He struck the space where her stomach had been, but she bent back and sucked it in. His safespear struck air. He had paid too steep a price for the strike, leaned into it too much; now he was exposed. She swept his left leg with a brush of her shin and his neck fell into her waiting grasp.

'You're better than I expected.' She lifted him from the ground by his neck and squeezed. 'You were taught Bobiri well.'

He squirmed in her grip, like a fisherman's fresh catch.

She looked up at him. 'You are relying on all the wrong things ... I need you to understand what it means to start from scratch.'

With a brush of her arms, she threw him against the stone with such force that his body bounced from the impact. He screamed as bones shattered inside.

He tried to stand but his body forbade him. He heard something snap and pain flashed across his back like the lash of a whip. His ribs were cracked to pieces.

She crouched low, staring at him. 'You don't have to do this. You don't have to be here. Say the word and I will have your memory flashed. As much of it as you want, all the pain.'

Rumi drew in breath. He considered it, back to Alara with no memory of Yami or Morire dying, to the Golden Room perhaps. The Priest of Vultures would doubtless find him but at least he'd forget the pain. It was tempting.

He forced the word out. 'No.'

He'd made a vow. An oath in blood. He owed Yami vengeance.

Zarcanis looked at him for a long moment, then she smiled and stretched out a finger, drew a half line of shadow rank on his forearm. 'From now on, we will have to use your blood to call the shadow. A poor substitute, but it will serve for the time being. Your shadow is at its strongest when it answers its own name.'

Half a line. *Half.* It was worse than nothing at all.

Zarcanis glanced over her shoulder. 'I will send a botanical to come fetch you.'

47

Recovery

RUMI

Rumi woke to the press of soft, cold hands on his face. His eyes stuttered open. A botanical stared down at him, face indifferent. The right side of his body felt like one long, continuous bruise.

'He's awake,' said the botanical.

Rumi tried to move. Pain flared across his body.

'I... can't move,' he whispered.

'You have some broken bones,' said the botanical.

Another flash of pain sprang up his spine.

'Will I walk again?'

'Oh, come on. Don't be dramatic,' said another voice.

Zarcanis came into view at the corner of his eye.

He was in the botanical ward. A glass of water rested on a small cabinet to his side and a bright oil lamp burned overhead.

'Let him drink it,' said Zarcanis.

The botanical nodded and tilted his head back to help him drink.

Rumi had intended to spit it all out, but the moment it touched his tongue, all stubbornness fled. It wasn't quite water – it was sweeter, with a soft, metallic undertone. He gulped down every drop.

Almost immediately, he could feel the drink start to work on his body, pushing the pain away.

'What is this?' he said, looking up.

'Water from the source of the Erin-Olu waterfall,' said Zarcanis. 'A master pain-reliever.'

Zarcanis leaned in closer. 'You'll be good as new in a week. Tell me, what did you do wrong today?'

'I'm not strong enough yet.'

'Quite the opposite. You rely too much on your strength, on your body. You needed to see that a body can be broken; your mind will win you more battles than your body ever will.'

Rumi wanted to curse her for putting him through such pain, but he was a slave to her learning. As besotted with it as a lickhead to agbo.

She stretched out a hand and a black flame sprouted from shadow. Rumi's eyes widened as he watched the fire dance in her hand.

She closed her hand and the fire winked out. 'There is a lot I have to teach you.'

Rumi leaned forward. 'I'm listening.'

She smiled. 'Stretch your hand out.'

He did so and Zarcanis drew a thin line of blood across his forearm with her nail.

'Lick it,' she said.

Rumi hesitated, then licked the blood. The shadow's black effervescent mist steamed from his pores, forming a shroud around him.

'Good,' Zarcanis said. 'Start with a simple ball of shadow.'

A ball of solid shadow materialised in her hand as she demonstrated. 'Use your mind to flare the shadow, then mould it like clay.'

Rumi narrowed his eyes and tried to focus. He pulled from the encircling shadow, trying to make it bend to his will. The shadow resisted, maintaining its shapeless form. The crystal-clear image of Morire's caved-in skull flashed in his mind. He groaned, shutting his eyes.

'Remember, your shadow is part of you,' Zarcanis said softly.

He gritted his teeth, trying to pull the shadow together, sweat trickling down his cheek. Yami's face blossomed in his mind. She stared into his eyes, blood leaking from her stomach.

Rumi realised he was growling from his throat. The wisps of shadow rotated faster around him.

'You cannot dominate it. Accept your nature. You have to honour your most difficult emotions, honour them and you can draw more from the shadow.'

He fought against the shadow and felt it start to win, to overpower him. He pushed back. Tinu's image welled up in his mind. He was in a slumped, pathetic pose in an Oké-Dar gutter, his eyes wet and glassy as milk-white agbo drooled from his mouth. Rumi pushed the memory aside. He felt his inner rage, his hunger for violence, for revenge, start to overrun him. He felt his shadow standing alongside the darkness, goading him to join them. He clenched his free hand into a fist.

The smallest, most pathetic ball of shadow formed in his hand. Small enough to rest on a fingertip. It swirled for a moment above his palm, then it broke apart into scattered shadow. Rumi gasped, letting the shadow go.

Zarcanis shook her head as she rose to her feet. 'We have a lot of work to do. The past is still your puppeteer.'

'You know nothing about my past,' he snarled.

She blinked and looked over him. 'Well, I mean ... I suppose you are right about that.'

Rumi let out a slow breath, surprised by her concession.

She scrubbed her forehead thoughtfully. 'Perhaps it's time we take off our masks.'

She shuffled in her seat. 'I was born in Guyarica, across the Brown Sea.'

Rumi blinked. 'Across the Brown Sea?'

'Look, I had a parrot once. You don't want to go the way he did.'

'Understood,' Rumi mumbled.

She nodded. 'I'll spare you the story of my childhood, but by seventeen I was, by most accounts, a good killer. Guyarica was a place where the Odu slavers came often. They took my cousin and my brother. Later they took my father. Our village was small. All we could do was run, hide, and pray. All our strongest were dead or stolen; we were easy pickings. The elders in our village went to Altani, the witch doctor, the one who knew how to muster power. He told them to bring him an untouched virgin.'

Rumi winced. 'They brought you?'

'I had no father or mother to fight for me, no siblings to protest. They didn't even convene a village meeting before they offered me to Altani.'

She squeezed her chin and pulled her long-necked dress almost to her lips. 'But Altani had other plans for me. He worked me like iron, bending me in heat to his will. I grew taller and stronger in those first two weeks than I had ever grown in any year. He gave me vials to drink that made my focus so potent, my concentration so polished, that I could hear a blade of grass break in strong wind. He made me the best. By the time he sent me back to the village, much had changed. The consular guard had arrived, saving us from the slavers. The village had long forgotten me and found other heroes. There was a Palman temple in the middle of our town square. Nicest building in town. Full to bursting every market day.'

Rumi scowled.

'Blissfully simple religion to follow. No sacrifices, just one god, only one day of worship a week. Nice and easy. Brilliant expansion strategy.'

She gulped down a sip of water. 'So there I am, in my twenties, with all this violence in me and nothing to kill. So what do I do?'

'Fight the Palmaine?'

'Are you crazy? They had guns! I'm no fool. I joined the Palmaine armed forces. I was Lord Zaminu's first native captain.'

'Before Zaminu became governor-general,' said Rumi.

'Correct,' Zarcanis said. 'The Palmaine forces weren't too different from this place: men who killed for purpose, men who killed because they were told to, and men who killed because they liked the idea of it. Heroes and cowards in good measure. Make no mistake, though, they were seasoned in the business of killing. Far more than the men here.'

Rumi glared at her. 'So you joined the Palmaine to kill natives?'

Her face was expressionless. 'Yes, a lot of them. In my time I killed more natives than the sleeping sickness.'

'You say it like you are proud.'

She narrowed her eyes. 'I am not proud of it at all, but I must remain conscious of the darkness that is within me. The great—'

'Oppositions. I know.'

She smiled. 'That's right. We must encourage one another to confess our darkness, so we can overcome it. Anyway, as I was saying before you got prissy. When the rebellion began, some grey-haired Palmaine twit had the grand idea of saving Kasabia for last. An unqualified moron. If I have learned one thing about the Kasinabe, it is that when you give them an opportunity to prepare for war, you must also give yourself an opportunity to prepare to die. When we marched for Kasabia, they had burned everything within twelve days' ride. Nothing but burned crops and rotting cattle for miles before their city walls. We found ourselves a dozen days from Kasabia and as far as the eye could see there was nothing but black earth. I knew we did not have enough supplies to sustain us for the whole journey, but Zaminu ordered us to ride on. He was a proud man.'

'A difficult ride,' Rumi said.

'It was. Horse hooves sink in burned earth; it made the going slow. By the third week, half the horses had died. It was nearly impossible to find clean wood to roast the horsemeat. People started to fall by the fourth week, the horses left were too weak to ride, and the horse blood we had been drinking made us sick. When we found an abandoned village three days' ride from the city walls, it seemed almost too good to be true: fruit on trees; barns full of maize; a well with water clear as glass. Men drank and ate till bellies were swollen round. When the singing stopped and we realised that everything had been poisoned, it was too late. King Olu rode down on the village and did the kind of slaughter that made him a legend in his youth. There was no escape for us. Those not dead from poison were ridden down by Kasinabe cavalry. Somehow, in my youthful, resilient way, I clung to my shred of life long enough to see Zaminu ride away on a camel and leave us to die.'

'And the Kasinabe found you?'

'It was the Kasinabe who first called me the Viper. They said I was touched by poison. They could have killed me, but King Olu spared me. Walade begged for my blood and he refused. He would not kill a native. He spared me and I will never forget it. When even Palman had not spared me, King Olu let me live. I was one of them after that and I still am.'

Rumi squirmed uncomfortably onto his side to speak. 'King Olu...Yes, I see it. Look at you, smitten even now. Yes, that's why you broke my back. A vendetta against men.'

Zarcanis gave him a smirk that managed to be friendly on the surface and unfriendly underneath. 'I am glad to see you haven't lost your sense of humour. A wise man once said that if you are going to tell people the truth, be funny or they'll kill you.' She squeezed his shoulder until he cried out, and rose to leave. 'Keep practicing. Acknowledge your emotions, let them have their say. When your body is right again, I want to see what you have learned.' She placed a thick tome on his bedside table. 'In case you get any inspiration.'

Rumi narrowed his eyes. It was the *Sakosaye*. 'Know I won't forget this,' Rumi said gesturing to his condition.

'Don't be so emotional. It is your story to suffer, you know that. The smoothest pounded yam must suffer in the mortar.'

48

Confrontation

RUMI

It took Rumi twelve days to fully recover. He had a few visits in that time: from Ladan, Sameer, Ahwazi; even Chief Karile and Renike. No word from Nataré, though he had not expected any. They brought gifts, goodwill, and gossip in equal measure. Griff came once too, but Rumi had pretended to be asleep.

At night, Rumi took time to practice. His pillow and chair had become his night sparring partners.

He worked on his conjuring, too, which was always a small terror. Zarcanis needed only to raise an eyebrow and the shadow would rush to obey her, but Rumi had to grit his teeth and bunch up his fist and scratch his skin just to conjure a finger-width of shadow. The strain was made worse by the memories and emotions that pressed down on him whenever he tried. All in all, it was the most unpleasant part of his training.

He had, however, made some progress. He had learned how to form truces with the shadow over some emotions. The first truce had come with his acceptance that he had been a coward on the night his family were killed. His agreement with the shadow was to never be so powerless again, and whenever he focused on that agreement, he had small levels of progress. The second truce was his devotion to vengeance. He agreed that he would go to any length to have his revenge. That was a surer, more accessible route to the shadow's power. The more he could embrace the truths that terrified him – his loneliness, his depravity, his cowardice – the stronger his conjuring was.

He dripped with sweat after managing to conjure a solid rod of shadow. That had been his greatest feat in all his time bedridden. Caught in the pithy euphoria of a threshold crossed, sleep took him unawares as the shadow slipped away.

He shivered from a distant cold as a voice called out to him. 'Heed the message of the messenger.' Rumi glanced up at the one who stood before him. His eyes were dark as soot with no trace of white and he wore a cap that was red on one side and white on the other.

'The Agbara of the crossroads,' Rumi said.

The Agbara nodded. 'Some call me the Trickster. You have my instruction. Read my book.'

Rumi bolted upright as sleep fled. He reached out for the *Sakoye* and flipped through pages until he found the page he was looking for.

Of all the hunters in all the world, there were three most revered. Oshosi, the hunter with the single arrow; Aja, who some call the night huntress; and Akiti, who runs with the leopards. I was given charge over them with one impossible task – to find the Son. He who knew not the view from a noose.

Now, the Son was still young in the knowing of things but he was the blood of Dara. Under the eye of the Skyfather there was no greater power than the Son. To catch him was not to be an act of strength, it was to be an act of stealth and cunning. That was why they chose me – they said that I was cunning; that I knew the turning of things. It takes a snake to catch a snake, they said.

Though I hated my commission, I accepted it. I am much more than a trickster – despite what the stories might say. I gathered the hunters to devise a plan and when I saw that the plan was good we set to work.

We spread a message across all the land and all the sea: Gather one and every priest, prophet, diviner or jazzman at the summit of the Mount Darman so that it may be known once and for all which god is the most powerful.

And so came the prophets of Kurusha from the nation of the monsoon and the High Priests of Pyat from the desert dwelling North and all the great diviners of Oduland and the Ethiope and places where they prayed to ice or trees or the sun. For a whole year men and women came until the mountain was overrun with people of great power.

I searched amongst them for those who would proclaim themselves priests of Palman but I could not find them amongst the multitude. And so I took on the shape of man, for I have the gift of turning, and told all gathered to demonstrate the strength of their god.

Some spun gold from clay and named it the handiwork of their god. Others commanded rain to fall and the clouds obeyed. Some even commanded a tree to sprout from a seedling and it too did sprout.

Though these things did amaze, I was not moved, for I knew the turning of things and the secrets of the Son's heart. No matter what any priest did, I knew the Son would not allow the sun to set on any proclamation that a name stood taller than his own.

Just as was my prediction, an hour before the sun would set, a man stepped forward. He was dressed all in white and about his neck he wore a chain with a pendant bearing the four-point star. His skin was bleached white and his eyes were the desperate dark of a man who sees not through eyes alone. He was the first Priest of the Son and he proclaimed Palman was the one true god, Lord of All.

There was an uproar at his proclamation, for though others had rested on the strength of their god, no one else had named the other gods false. To most, the priest's words were the height of blasphemy.

One of the prophets of Kakalkun raised a sword in anger but the Priest of the Son did not fear. He spoke two words and the prophet of Kakalkun was struck down for vultures to eat his flesh. Others spoke out against him but they were struck down also.

Seeing the truth of his power, some knelt before the Priest of the Son and proclaimed that Palman was the one true god. They were spared the wrath of the Son but all others who stood against him were struck down. All but three priests – for they were not priests, they were hunters.

And as the Priest of the Son considered the battle won, Aja commanded the sun to turn to night, and it obeyed. Akiti ran with the leopards, encircling the priest, and Oshosi, whose arrow has never missed, aimed his bow. And the priest called for them to be struck down, but they still stood. For they were touched of Dara the Skyfather and could not be struck down by word alone. As they bound the priest I called out atop the mountain, so that all may know that Dara lives.

The Priest of the Son stared up to the heavens and shouted, 'Will your servant be forgotten?'

And the earth rumbled, for the Son had heard the cry of his Priest. He passed from the Originate into the mortal realm and came to the aid of the Priest. Only then did we set the teeth of our trap against him, for we had drawn a circle about the Son and when he tried to cross the line of the circle, he found he was blocked by something solid as stone.

And I clapped, for I had succeeded in catching the Son. But Palman was not done yet. And though we were four and he was one we were no match for his power. He struck us down, one after the other; broke our wards and saw that we were hunters. He drew around the circle on the floor until it became an eye, then he pulled the Priest up and blessed him.

'For you were faithful, no longer will you be hunted but you will be hunter unto false gods. The glove through which my hand is felt.'

And to all the other priests who had knelt in supplication to the Son, Palman gave new names and blessings, so that they may be hunters also.

And though we had trapped the Son, he walked free, for he was the blood of Dara and we ran through a gateway to escape his fury. Until this day Mount Darman is called the God-Eye mountain for there the eye of the Son was drawn and there is his essence found.

Rumi's heart pounded as he came to the end of the chapter.

A cough sounded ahead and he glanced up.

Nataré stood in the doorway looking directly at him. 'You look like you've just seen a spirit.'

Rumi closed his mouth and shut the *Sakosaye*. 'Something like that.'

The voice of a botanical sounded from outside the door. 'You cannot be in here.'

Nataré shrivelled the botanical to near mist with a single glare, then she turned back to Rumi. 'How are you feeling?'

Rumi turned to his side. 'A lot better than I was last week.'

She smiled and he saw the small gap between her two

centremost teeth. Her skin glistened under the light. Brown gloss lined the lilt of her lips and her eyes shone a sharp greyish-green. This close, he could almost taste the scent of leaves on her.

'I had meant to come earlier when I heard the rumours but getting here was … difficult.'

'It's okay,' Rumi said, 'I am glad to see you.'

'I'm glad to see you too.'

There was an interval of silence. Sitting at the edge of his bed, she put a hand behind his head and scratched the base of his neck. A jolt of electricity shot through him. It was unnerving to be so easily set alight. He locked eyes with hers, there was barely a handspan between them. He could feel her thigh against his shoulder. *Is that on purpose?*

The scent of her intoxicated him. It felt like a dream. He wanted to go somewhere with just her and stay there forever.

'Nataré,' he began.

She leaned forward and put a hand on his arm.

He fixed his mouth to speak.

'There she is!' shouted a botanical.

Rumi turned; the botanical stood pointing, flanked by two men.

Nataré squeezed his hand. 'Save a dance for me at the Ghedo.'

Rumi gave a start. 'I will,' he coughed. *Too eager.*

'I mean it, Rumi. I've heard the way they giggle in the corridor. Half a hundred girls have plans for Ajanla at the Ghedo. And the older ones wish they still had youth enough to make plans of their own.' She lowered her voice to a whisper. 'If only they knew he whistles when he's on the chamber pot.'

His mouth fell open. 'What?'

The botanical reached the door and she turned to follow them without protest. As Rumi watched her walk away, she whistled a tune he'd thought no one knew.

He lay there for a moment with a stupefied smile, allowing all the hard truths of the world to be stilled by a beautiful dream. Then his smile faded and he called his shadow again.

On the day of Rumi's discharge from the botanical ward, someone was whistling in the corridor. He recognised the tune immediately. It was a farmer's song: *When the old dog died, we dug a hole and the whole farm cried.*

He suppressed a smile. *Zarcanis.*

She stuck her head through the door.

'Good morning,' she said, grinning. 'You're ready today. I can smell it.'

Rumi shifted his left leg to his right side and in one fluid movement he sprung from his bed.

Zarcanis's smile widened. 'I knew it. When I saw the new marks on your forearm, I knew you had been cutting yourself. You've been practicing.'

Rumi set his jaw and stared at her.

'Come,' she said.

He followed her back to the fighting room, walking with pursed lips and arms folded behind his back.

'Are we going to spar?' Rumi asked when they arrived.

'Patience,' she said.

She lowered him into a split and pushed down. The stretching was easier now – he still screamed, but he did not cry. He made a good show of stretching, taking his time to touch his toes, extend his legs and slide into an effortless box split.

'Are we going to spar?' he asked again.

She threw him a safespear, not meeting his eye.

He caught it in one hand. 'I want to use real steel.'

Zarcanis kissed her teeth loudly, pointing to the wall. 'Over there.'

413

The halberd glistened in the lantern light. He touched it and his whole body stirred.

'Feels good, doesn't it?' Zarcanis held her long, ridged sword. 'You know I've always loved this blade. The ridges, the way it's all twisted and misshapen. When you pull it free it does more damage than going in; it cuts you in ways a straight blade just can't. You don't get that kind of character in blades anymore. Everyone wants a big sword like King Olu.' She was shifting the blade between hands. 'In the right hands, this is a better, more punishing instrument than a straight blade.'

'I don't need to enjoy violence.'

She smiled. 'I love the game you play. It's a good one. You pretend, even to yourself.' She leaned close to whisper: 'But deep down, you're not that different to me.'

'You fought with Palmaine,' he said. His neck made a popping sound as he worked out the kinks. 'I would never fight with Palmaine.'

She sighed as though she had come home to a sink of unwashed dishes. 'Let's see it then. Show me what you've been practicing.'

With the nib of his halberd, he made a small line in his skin and licked the oozing blood.

Black mist exploded from him. He gasped as the power pulsed through his body.

Zarcanis called her own shadow, securing the high-necked collar of her leather armour to keep her neck concealed. Her shadow draped down from her shoulders like a king's cape.

Her eyes thinned to slits. 'Nothing held back. I want to see if you've been working on your form, like I was working on mine.'

Rumi leaped forward. He thought to overrun her, but she was ready for him. She moved with a different cadence to anyone he had ever seen. Like the music playing in her head was different to what everyone else could hear. She danced around his lunge with a nonchalant pirouette and set her leg to trip him up. He stumbled forward like fool in a village pantomine.

'Nothing held back,' she said.

He lunged for her.

Whenever he thought he had gained an advantage, he found she had set a trap. They sparred until he could no longer hold the shadow and it came to a merciful end. Their bodies told the story entire. He was bruised and bloodied. She was daisy fresh.

'You learned a tiny bit,' she said, scratching her elbow. 'Get rid of those big overhand swings. This isn't a storybook. Use the halberd like a spear; thrusts more than swings. You try to look good while you fight, too, and that's just bone daft. The last thing you should think about in combat is your pride. I need you to be a thinking fighter. *Think*. There will always be someone stronger, faster. Learn the forms, learn them so well that they become part of you, then take them apart and create your own forms.'

With a brush of her finger she completed the half-formed tattooed line on his forearm and added a second full line. Two lines was approaching respectable. The most respected Seedlings had at least five, but three seemed the happy threshold.

He was gasping for air and had no strength to respond.

Zarcanis wet her lips. 'In a real battle, you don't have the time to show how fast you are. The forms will fall apart. Instinct is what matters. Precision. Time spent with a weapon in hand always tells. You are obvious when you conjure, too; your conjuring should be sudden and unexpected. When I see you squeeze your face like you're on the chamberpot, I know you're cooking something. No subtlety. No surprises. Focus on the forms for now; you're not ready to conjure while shadowdancing.'

She picked his halberd up and examined it. 'You haven't earned the privilege of using this, either. Not even close. There is a consistency to this thing. This is everyday work – not just the good days, not just the fighting days; this is everyday work. An owl at night and an eagle in the morning. They give Seedlings five years because this work takes time.'

Yomiku poked his head in and glanced at Rumi. His eyes carried the look of a slaughterman regarding a growing calf.

Zarcanis turned to him. 'Kubani, what do you think? Think he can hurt you?'

'Not a chance,' said Yomiku.

'Well then, I guess you two can spar on our next fighting day.'

Rumi bared his teeth. Hours of practice, days of pain. She'd made him look like a fool. A part of him hated her and another part had immense respect for her. He could not imagine a finer, more elegant fighter. In her he saw that there is nobility to be found, even in violence – like language it can be crude and coarse or it can be eloquent and refined. Rumi was a child, only at the beginning of learning words; Zarcanis was a master orator and a poet. If he could learn from her, take all she had to offer, then maybe he would be strong enough. Maybe he would have his revenge.

It needed to come fast. He could not afford to lose the shadow like Griff. *Everyday work.* He thought he had pushed himself to his limits in the Golden Room; he now knew he would have to find new limits.

He was ready for it; he swore to himself he was. No more games, he would give it everything. Never would he yield to anyone in the fighting pit again. He would show Zarcanis, show Yomiku, show them all the meaning of work.

★　★　★

Back in the dormitory, Sameer and Ahwazi gave him a drunkard's welcome. Sameer had unearthed a small bottle of syrupy brandy and the faraway look in Ahwazi's eyes suggested he'd had a few good gulps.

'People are starting to talk about you,' Sameer said. 'Used to be you had the longest odds in the Order for the Ghedo tournament, but your odds are starting to improve.'

'People bet on the Ghedo tournament?' Rumi said.

Ahwazi smiled. 'Of course they do. There is food, drink and dancing, and we compete in everything from shadowdancing to horsemanship. It's a gamblers' paradise.'

Sameer nodded. 'No softborn has ever won a single competition at the Ghedo.'

'How many Ghedo tournaments have there been?'

'Thirty-four,' Sameer said. 'The Ghedo goes all the way back to the Kasinabe kingdom before the Palmaine.'

'And in all that time, no softborn has ever won a single competition?'

'No,' said Sameer, 'but this year will be different.'

Ahwazi cackled. 'You think you stand a chance of winning something, Sameer?'

'Yes.'

The look in Sameer's eyes was one of absolute certainty. It was not a suggestion, it was an affirmation.

49

The Old Dog and the Kubani

RUMI

Rumi wiped the sweat from his forehead. 'An owl at night and an eagle in the morning,' Zarcanis had said. He practiced the forms, one after another.

By the time Zarcanis stepped into her training room, Rumi had been working the forms for hours.

She smiled when she saw him. 'A beautiful day. The Kubani and the old dog; just like the old days, this is a story writing itself.'

Yomiku walked into the room shortly after her, his tuaragi blade in hand and eyes locked on Rumi, his clothes darkened with sweat.

'How long have you been holding the shadow?' Zarcanis asked.

'What does it matter?' Yomiku replied, rippling with effervescent black mist.

'You could burn out, Kubani, you know that.'

Yomiku sneered. 'A softborn cannot push me hard enough to burn out.'

Zarcanis raised an eyebrow. 'Let's get to it, then.'

They walked towards the fighting circle slowly. Rumi tried to avoid Yomiku's stalking gaze.

He trusted Zarcanis, in some small way, not to kill him. He

could not trust Yomiku in that same way. Rumi had promised himself he would not yield to any man. Now he wanted to renege on that promise. Anyone who looked in Yomiku's eyes would know he was a man typecast for violence.

As they lined up, Yomiku licked his lips with all the anticipation of a groom waiting for the bridal tent to fall.

Zarcanis gave them each safespears and stepped between them. 'No conjuring. Rumi isn't skilled enough for that yet.'

That was a small mercy. With conjuring, Yomiku would make short work of him. Without conjuring, likely still short work, but not quite so short.

Yomiku grunted impatiently.

Zarcanis stepped aside. 'Rumi, call your shadow.'

Rumi sliced through his forearm with a small blade, drawing blood. He licked the blood and shadow teemed from his skin like vapour from the kettle's spout.

'Engage!'

Yomiku closed the distance quickly with three sharp steps and raised his safespear into *leopard watches the fire*. He tested Rumi with a lean of the shoulder. Rumi parried easily.

The man's eyes were framed by dark circles. Plainly he had been holding the shadow for a long time. If Rumi could hold him out long enough, perhaps he *would* burn out.

'What are you waiting for?' Rumi said, taunting Yomiku.

He immediately regretted that. Yomiku charged forward, his safespear at a killer's angle. Rumi dodged and the strike glanced his shoulder. It was only a glancing blow and still he felt like a blacksmith had taken a hammer to his bones.

Yomiku darted forward again, spinning around Rumi's defence. Rumi dodged the thrust but Yomiku brought the backswing in a jagged arch, opening up a cut on Rumi's side.

He drew deep on the shadow to embrace the pain as blood trickled down his hip.

'Do you yield?' asked Yomiku.

Rumi answered with his safespear, flowing into *rhinoceros rages.* Yomiku danced out of range. The man was fast, but he was no Zarcanis. There were holes in his footwork.

Rumi moved to corner him, stepping forward to close the angles of escape. The idea was to overwhelm him. An ill-conceived idea. Yomiku jumped back and pushed himself up off the wall. His safespear struck Rumi's nose with such virulent force that his feet left the ground. He went down hard and tasted the metallic pang of blood.

'Don't you ever think yourself my equal! Ever!' growled Yomiku, leaning over him. 'When she says you should spar with me, you beg on hands and knees to do something else.'

Rumi coughed up blood on the floor, helpless.

Yomiku crouched low, speaking softly. 'I am of the old blood. The Widowmaker, the Special. Neverkneel. I am born from the same broth.'

He raised his spear high, muscles at his trapezius taut and thick, veins flaring. 'I don't lose to the softborn.'

He started to walk away. Rumi stared up at him. It was over. Yomiku had torn down his pride brick by brick. His breath came in short gasps. Zarcanis glanced down at him, her face empty of emotion.

He wouldn't let it end that way. He couldn't.

Slowly, gingerly, he rose from the ground.

Yomiku glanced over his shoulder at him.

Rumi spoke in a low rumble. 'I did not yield.'

Yomiku turned. 'What did you say, boy?'

'I said ... I did not yield ... *Kubani.*'

Yomiku narrowed his eyes and raised his safespear. Rumi

shifted his weight, poised for a counter strike. Yomiku barrelled into him, leaving no space for one.

Bubbles of coloured light blurred Rumi's vision as he tried to suck in air. In the ensuing tumble, Yomiku emerged the victor. He climbed on top of Rumi and brought his fist down so hard Rumi thought his skull would crack. Through his blood-blurred vision, he saw Yomiku raise his fist again before it fell with godly force. Ladan had described him as a monster. It was apt.

Rumi raised a hand to protect himself but the blows did not stop. Bone mortars pounded his head. Yomiku's wide-eyed gaze and full-toothed smile told him that the man had every intention to pummel him to dust.

'Do you yield now, softborn?'

It was a good time to surrender; a wise time. But Rumi was good and tired of surrender. If he was going to die, he would do it with his pride.

He stared up at Yomiku and locked eyes. As he gritted his teeth, small bubbles of blood formed in the crevices. 'No!'

Yomiku stared down at him. He looked genuinely overjoyed. 'So be it.'

He brought his fist down on Rumi's head again. The sound was like that of a butcher tenderising meat.

I really am going to die. The shocking truth of it hit him harder than Yomiku.

His vision blurred to near blackness as the blows continued to rain down. At the edge of his vision Zarcanis moved to stop the fight. She could still make it on time. He cracked an eye open to look up at Yomiku. He froze. It was no longer Yomiku on top of him, but a man with translucent white skin and sharp teeth. *Him.*

'*Always remember you are nothing.*'

Something within snapped. Like the gates of the Hellmouth

had broken open, filling him with fire and sulphur. Like someone had cranked the tap of his anger all the way open and let the tank of rage within spill all the way out.

He pulled violently at the shadow with fury unimaginable, drinking it in deep, taking in more than he had ever done before. The priestess's cowrie was a smouldering coal on his neck. His entire body pulsed as images from the darkest recesses of his consciousness flashed across his mind.

'I will kill you,' Rumi snarled.

A flush of strength returned to his bloody, beaten body. Pain retreated and the blur in his vision was replaced with shocking clarity. It was Yomiku's face again. The man tried to strike, but Rumi caught his upraised fist and flung his head forward in a head-butt.

Yomiku jerked back with a grunt. Rumi snatched up his safespear and rose to his feet. Black mist teemed from his eyes.

Zarcanis was expressionless as she watched, frozen at the edge of the fighting pit.

'Come,' Rumi said.

Yomiku's eyes went wide, then narrow. He charged with all the abandon of a bull at the height of vim. Rumi stood with his safespear held to the side. Something was different. He could count Yomiku's footsteps; he could see the beginning, middle and end of the blink of his eye. He was burning out of the shadow. With a smooth motion, he sidestepped Yomiku's charge then threw the safespear upwards into his chest with *eagle stands amongst cockerels*. Yomiku stumbled back. If they had been using real spears, Yomiku would be dead.

Yomiku's eyes bulged, touching his ironwire vest where he had been struck, then he moved forward again. Rumi smashed Yomiku's neck with the side of his safespear, then he struck the underside of his chin. There was blood.

'I said come, Kubani!'

Yomiku raised his spear to parry but it was futile. Rumi struck with a hammer blow between neck and shoulder. Yomiku stumbled, barely breaking his fall. His safespear skittered across the floor. His shadow trickled away, pooling on the floor like rainwater.

'Oh dear,' Rumi said, kicking Yomiku's safespear aside. 'Your shadow is gone.'

Yomiku tried to rise but Rumi prodded him down.

'I barely ever heard you talk before today. Moments ago you could blather like a market woman. Now you've gone all quiet again. Do you yield?'

A smile seemed to colour Yomiku's face.

'Do you think,' he said, flecks of bloody spittle spattering Rumi's face, 'I would ever yield to a softborn?'

He rose gingerly to his feet. 'I figure this is as close as we can get to an even fight – me with no shadow, you full of new brass. Come.'

A prideful man. A pride he would die before letting go. No matter his skill as a fighter, without the shadow, it was no match at all. It was admirable in a way. But in his mother's words, *if you're going to beat an egg, beat it thoroughly.*

Rumi darted forward with *rhinoceros rages.* It was a ruse to fix Yomiku's feet. At the last moment he flowed into *eagle snatches the heart* and drove his safespear at Yomiku's chest. Despite the dull edges, the blow pierced flesh. Yomiku staggered back, holding his chest. Rumi smiled – but that small candle of triumph lasted only a moment. Yomiku was smiling back.

He glanced down at his safespear. Yomiku had broken more than half of it off, leaving him with nought but a useless stump. The other, more dangerous end was clutched in Yomiku's fist.

Confusion morphed to resignation. Yomiku was the better fighter. Far better. Even without the shadow, he was still the bigger threat. It was a sobering realisation. Yomiku, evidently having come to the same conclusion, lunged at him. Deadly and fast with *fox enters the hen-house*. The safespear thudded into Rumi's side and brought a slap of pain.

'Enough,' said Zarcanis, stepping into the fighting pit.

'Why would you interfere?' snarled Yomiku, his bloodied face a picture of disgusted malice.

Zarcanis fixed him with an inexpressive stare.

He snorted like a bull, then stalked off, trying to disguise his limp.

Rumi met Zarcanis's eye. 'I could have beaten him.'

She looked at him like he was a pup barking at her heels. 'I suppose you didn't embarrass yourself, but he was toying with you. And he lost his shadow.'

'But I still could have beaten him.'

She shrugged. 'Sure you could.'

He took a step forward and the shadow winked out of him. He tried to pull it back, but his hold on it dissipated as it pooled and shapeshifted into his silhouette.

The bite-back of pain was instant. Every bone and muscle sang with the story of a godawful beating. He fell to one knee.

Zarcanis stepped closer. 'The shadow can numb your pain, but when it goes your pain returns. You must be hurting a great deal right now.'

Rumi wailed.

Zarcanis glanced over her shoulder, looking around, and her face fell in disappointment.

'I guess I have to be the one to fetch the botanical,' she grumbled.

50

The Night Army

SABACHI

The Priest of Vultures, in creaseless white, stood above Aja, the Agbara of the forest. The wild wind herself.

Aja's skin was the colour of wet leaves, her hair like vines and long grass, and teeth a perfect, snarling white. Sabachi smiled as he hammered the nail through her palm, pinning her to the tree.

She was known as a fierce huntress and protector of the wilderness. Powerful enough to more than rival Oshosi, the hunter of the single arrow. *Look at her now, broken and powerless.* His Master had ripped her name from her. He loved it when his Master revealed their names to him. It seemed to break them to know Sabachi knew their names.

'I fear for you when Dara rises,' Aja said, her nose bloodied, her eye swollen from blows. 'Justice always prevails in the end.'

His Master laughed. 'You think you are on the side of justice? Dara polluted himself with a woman, doing as the sons of men do. You taught men things too sacred. Bloodmagic and human sacrifice? What were you thinking? Man is a parasite; they feed on one another and feed on the land, adding no value except to themselves. We are the true justice.'

'In the old days I would have torn you apart.'

'I have heard that so many times. I have killed so many that

425

have told me about the old days. Don't you ever consider that the Son chose Billisi and not Dara?'

'A child misled.'

'Perhaps he wasn't misled at all. Perhaps he saw through your hypocrisy. The condemnation of Billisi was the very grain of hypocrisy. You know it too. Man is not worth fighting for; certainly not dying for. The heart of man is wicked. He is a failed creation, the work of a monster.'

'We did not create them; quite the opposite. We are connected in the same way that the flower is connected to the bee. Without us, there is no them and without them, there is no us. Their praise is our lifeblood. We find our strength in their worship, their sacrifice.'

'And soon they will praise and make sacrifice to the one true god. One true power. How it should always have been.'

'The Skyfather is lightning in the clear sky. He is everything sudden. Palman is but a stone on the path.'

Sabachi slapped the good sense out of her, snapping her head back. 'Shut your filthy mouth, demon!'

Aja glared at him. There was a time that her glare would have turned a man to ash, but those times were over. The Agbara were fruit for his Master to pick now.

Sabachi drew his hand back to slap her again but his Master raised a hand. 'I suspect I know your answer but it is my solemn duty to give you a choice. If you kneel for the Son, I will pardon you and you will be accepted as a saint under the authority of the one true god. So many others have chosen the light – you need not die, only serve.'

Aja's jaw tightened as she shut her eyes, then she started to sing. 'The Destroyer of Chains is coming again. Oh, how you will burn, when he makes his return.'

426

The Master narrowed his eyes as though in bitter disappointment, then he spoke two words gently. 'Igima Kusibe.'

It was Sabachi's favourite part. The vultures coalesced like
a thick cloud, blackening the sky. Hundreds of them, moving
as one.

They descended and began the business of tearing flesh from
bone. To Sabachi's surprise, Aja did not scream. She kept singing,
even after her tongue was ripped out.

Eventually there was silence. When there was nothing left of
her but palms nailed to the tree, Sabachi's Master raised a hand.
That was how it had been, since that boy and his wretched
mother. There was a time his Master revelled in their work, but
something had been lost. Their hunting now was done with the
spirit of a chore.

'I praise you, Master. Another stain has been wiped away,'
Sabachi said.

'Praise belongs to the Son, Sabachi. We are merely the glove
through which his hand is felt.'

'Praise be to the Son, Master.'

His Master stared at the nails in the tree. 'Why do we do
what we do?'

'I beg your pardon, Master?'

'Why do we hunt them?'

'To purge the stains from the land and remake the nation.'

'Why do we seek to lead them to the Son? Why not just...
kill them?'

'That would be an unfruitful work of anger. We have a purpose.'

'Precisely... and yet.' He pulled his hand into a fist. 'And yet
you slapped an Agbara because she made you angry.'

The blinding pain was sudden and incredible. Sabachi's hands
went to his throat, but that was not where the pain came from.

It was like being strangled from the inside and set on fire. Blood filled his mouth and every hair on his flesh sang with burning. He screamed, begging for death.

'Please, Master, it was … it was … it was an error, a foolish remnant of my tainted blood. They insulted you, Master. I just, I hate them so much.'

'Vengeance belongs to the Son! You disgrace yourself! A servant of the Son, slapping an Agbara in anger? Do you forget why we do what we do?'

'Master, please, let my death be swift! A swift death for your servant. Please!'

Blood gushed from Sabachi's nose in a thick stream.

His Master stared at him, opened his palm and the burning stopped. 'If I killed you, you would have no opportunity to learn.'

Sabachi's pain subsided.

'We do not embrace our emotions as the shadowwielders do, Sabachi. We have been cleansed of those feelings and we must maintain that holiness. Even the Skyfather was brought low by emotion. The Son shows us that truth and reason rule over emotion.'

'Yes, Master,' Sabachi said breathlessly.

'Next time an Agbara insults me or insults you, you must remind them of the truth you now know.'

'Yes, Master.'

'The truth within you is more powerful than anger; more powerful than vengeance.'

'Yes, Master.'

'Good. I did not want to hurt you, but I have learned that pain can be a teacher. It taught you, after all. Or have you forgotten?'

He could still faintly feel his lost eye.

'I remember, Master.'

'And what is the truth of the heretics?'

'A nail's purpose is to be hammered; all else is a corruption.'

'And what will become of those who do not kneel?'

'The Son shall cast them down, erase their names, their seed in the land.'

'Who do we serve?'

'We serve the Son; He who knew not the view from a noose. The hope of the world.'

Sabachi's Master nodded in acceptance, a satisfied line across his mouth as he turned away.

'We will find the youngling with my name. He may not be the Son of Despair but he could become a thorn in our side if left unattended.'

'Yes, Master.'

'There was a moment I felt him in the forest. He was using a ghost stone.'

'Where would he find one?'

'I do not know. But all those who can use such power will be known and felt by me, eventually.'

'Master... with your name the boy can enter your—'

'Remember who I am, Sabachi. You know my work, you know who I command. Or have you forgotten?'

'I have not, Master.'

'Who do I command?'

At the sound of his voice, shadows in the shapes of men formed around him. Men and women in chains carrying swords and spears and axes, shadows in the form of men with no pupils in their eyes. Sabachi blinked and there were hundreds of them.

'You command the Night Army, Master.'

His Master stared up at the sky, eyes wet with reverence. 'We serve the Son. He guides us. You have seen for yourself how the mighty tremble at the whisper of His Name. He is the Last Sufferer. Preserver of Truth. The Unfailing and Ever-Victorious Battle Lord. The Roaring Waters and the Whispering Palms. Worthiness Incarnate and Light in the Darkness. He is God.'

That last declarative name sent Sabachi to his knees, face pressed prostrate in the soil.

The Priest of Vultures knelt down beside him. 'Gather all our forces. We will find the boy, lure him out of whatever hole he hides in, and I will have my name again.'

51

The Brown Sea Burning

RUMI

'Ajanla Erenteyo?' Karile said, snapping him out of his thoughts.

'Sorry?' Rumi said, blinking. He often forgot to answer that name.

'I said, what do you think? Of the nation; do you think we can remain as one?'

'Basmine?'

She nodded.

He pondered the question for a moment. 'No.'

Karile touched her chin. 'Why not?'

'Basmine is a Palmaine creation. Four nations forced to become one for the sake of Palmaine trade and exploitation. Even the name Basmine is not our own. There is no *real* nation here. Kuba and Odu have been waving spears at each other since the age of Mgbedike.'

'And why do you think that is?'

'The same reason that the mongoose fights the snake.'

'You believe there is some great difference between the Kuba man and the Odu man?'

'In some ways, yes.'

'What ways would that be?'

'The Odu are fighters; they are brave, and they are proud.'

'The Kuba are not?'

Rumi heard a chair shuffle behind him.

'Sit down, Ailera,' Karile said.

Sameer made a gruff, disgusted noise.

Karile scratched her neck. 'I disagree with you, Voltaine. I think the Odu and Kuba man are more alike than you could ever imagine. I think the Palmaine love the fact that the Kuba and Odu remain at odds.'

'We have been at odds long before the Palmaine. Look at the Brown Sea Burning,' he said.

She frowned. 'Tell me about the Brown Sea Burning.'

'The Kuba burned a ship with a hundred innocent Odu on board.'

'And who told you that the Kuba burned that ship?'

Rumi gave her a puzzled look. 'Who else would have done it?'

She let out a long breath. 'You are a very clever young man, Ajanla, but in this I have found you to be woefully blind. The time has come to put childish things aside. Do you think we have a chance of resisting Palmaine rule if we are not together?'

Rumi furrowed his brow.

Karile continued. 'Even if I accept that it was a Kuba plot – which I do not – there is a generation of Kuba long before you and I that will point to the Tiwele village massacre and tell you that no Odu man has good conscience. There are the thousands captured and sold as slaves by raiding Odu clans who will call you a demon, and there are Kasinabe here that see a traitor in every Kuba face.'

'So we should just forgive and forget all these wrongs?'

'No; that is impossible. Every wound must be dressed, compensated, and allowed to heal. I'm not saying we must ignore.

I'm not even saying we must forgive. But the time must come when we decide to stop hurting one another.'

Rumi's eyebrows darted upwards.

Karile's lessons were always like that. They left him feeling like a bespectacled man that had finally cleaned muck from his eyeglasses. She forced them to think incisively about every aspect of their history. To put themselves in the old, forgotten shoes of men and women from ages dead. She took a hammer to every preconception and forced them to stare at the truth beneath.

For the rest of that day, Sameer refused to speak to him and every time their eyes met, Sameer's glare was pure venom. It was deserved.

Something Karile said had stayed with him: 'The time must come when we decide to stop hurting each other.' He saw now what she wanted him to understand. The way the Kasinabe treated softborn was not far from the way the Kuba treated Odu.

Even in the Eredo, a place for the natives with no cause for disunity, they had found a way to inject poison and prejudice. He recalled a line from Kamo in *Lessons from the Sea*: 'Our affliction has become both the break in the bone and the crutch upon which we stand. How easy it is to love the brother and hate the other'. It rang true. That was what Basmine was, what the Eredo was in part: crabs quarrelling in the cookpot, oblivious to the slow boil. Kuba or no, Sameer had been nothing but a good and loyal friend to him these past five months. The Shadow Order had accepted Rumi, but only Sameer and Ahwazi had embraced him. In return, Rumi had insulted Sameer's people for reasons he did not even truly understand. He had to be better than that. They all did. Ahwazi and Sameer had made him part of

433

the softborn clan. It meant something and they were all part of a greater clan, a nation. One day, they would have to face the Palmaine; an enemy that understood the importance of unity, of being one nation.

In the end, it was Belize, the master poet, who watered the ground between Rumi and Sameer. Rumi caught Sameer alone on his bed. In his hands was a small brown book, with a beaten cover and faded gold lettering. Rumi's heart skittered with the tingle of recognition. *Belize's Dialogues.*

'What dialogue are you reading?'

'Nineteenth,' Sameer said, not looking up from the book.

'One of my favourites,' Rumi said.

Sameer turned the page with an irritated jerk.

Rumi let out a small breath, cleared his throat, lifted his chin and spoke in deep Odu:

> *'No closer kin than haste and hate,*
> *Each day of life an angel's kiss*
> *Learned this truth at the Hellmouth's gate—'*

''Tis no bliss, to die un-missed,' Sameer said, finishing the verse.

A moment of silence passed between them. It was the sort of moment that passes between a child when he sees another child near his age. An isthmus between kinship and indifference.

'You can recite the dialogues?' Sameer asked.

Rumi nodded. 'It was one of my mother's favourite books.'

Sameer's eyes brightened. 'What are your thoughts on the last song?'

Rumi smiled. Anyone with any familiarity with *Belize's Dialogues* knew that discussing the last song was an exercise among friends. It was Sameer's oil-slick way of saying 'I accept your apology' but it also carried an under-message: 'Show me the same respect I show you'.

And so the great debate of Belize's last song began. An argument that drove them closer together, rather than further apart.

The next day was the last fighting day of the week and thus the toughest. They all returned to the dormitory exhausted.

They had barely settled into any form of comfort when a sharp voice shot through the room.

'All Seedlings come with me.'

It was Chief Lungelo. The chief who had named Alangba a traitor and resisted Rumi's admission.

He walked with an almost unnaturally straight back, and when he spoke, he angled his head slightly so he would always be looking down on you. They formed a single file and followed him to a small lecture hall with a low hanging ceiling.

'Snap test,' Sameer muttered, glancing around the room.

Right on cue, Lungelo cleared all doubt. 'To walk in the corridors of the mind, you must have control over your emotions.' He fixed his eyes firmly on Rumi and raised his eyebrows in disgusted surprise. 'Some of you may have trouble doing that. You are puppets to your emotional extremes, blood boiling at the flicker of a candle. This is, as you may have guessed, a snap test. I will be testing your mindwalking.'

He pointed at Sameer. 'You.'

Sameer stepped forward. He was a confident mindwalker. Steady and stealthy.

'Enter my mind,' Lungelo ordered.

Sameer closed his eyes and called his shadow. Rumi watched as the black fumes of Sameer's shadow dissipated, signifying that the connection was made.

Lungelo closed his eyes. 'Strength in shadow is connected to the strength of your emotions and oneness of mind. To be a skilled mindwalker, you must counterbalance your strongest emotions with surety of purpose and oneness of mind.'

Sameer dropped to one knee, his right arm shaking as he raised it to his head.

'What happens when you enter a mind with stronger emotion than you, with a more powerful sense of purpose?'

Drops of blood spilled from Sameer's nose as he tried to stand.

'You must embrace stronger emotions, show your willpower. When you enter a battle of mind against mind, only the strongest will and emotion will survive it.' Lungelo glanced down at Sameer. 'I was told we were building warriors. Surely you are stronger in the shadow than this.'

Sameer drew in a whimpering breath.

'Stop it,' Rumi said, 'you're hurting him.'

A tremor of shock rippled across the room like a plucked oud string.

Lungelo did not open his eyes. 'I do not encourage speaking out of turn at my testings.'

Sameer bunched up his fists and gingerly rose to his feet, trembling with the effort.

Ahwazi placed a hand on Rumi's shoulder but Rumi threw it aside, stepping towards Lungelo. 'I said stop it.'

Lungelo's eyes snapped open. 'Ah, Ajanla Erenteyo.'

He released Sameer and shifted his shoulders so he was faced up to Rumi. 'Do not believe I will indulge your blustering pride as others have. I still maintain you should never have been admitted to the Order. We are raising warriors; there is no room in our ranks for Zarot petulance.'

436

Rumi's fist flew through the air before he knew what he was doing. It was instinct. At the point of contact, Lungelo called his shadow and it threw him aside. There were gasps across the lecture hall.

Rumi bit down into his forearm until he tasted the hot blood on his tongue. A heartbeat passed, then another. The shadow did not come. Lungelo loomed over him with one foot either side of his stomach.

'Like a deer in a snare,' Lungelo said, effervescent shadow misting from his pores. He motioned in his shadow and it pinned Rumi to the ground. He stretched out his hand and a long, thick whip coalesced from the darkness.

Rumi struggled against the shadow, but it was futile. Lungelo had him. He gritted his teeth.

Lungelo stared into his eyes. 'No ... No, I will not beat you, youngling. I see it in your eyes. You're a striver. You *like* the pain; you think it proves you are resilient.'

Lungelo turned towards the others in the room. 'I brought you here to test you, but instead I see an opportunity for a lesson. We will learn today the importance of control.' He rounded on Rumi. 'This man rides an unbridled Shinala. It should not be so.'

He held his shadowwhip by the edges and stretched it out sharply, so it made a snapping sound. Then he wrapped it around his fist. 'When we give in to our passions, it is often others that pay the price.'

He struck out at Sameer. The sharp whip crack made Rumi shudder. Of all the Seedlings, Sameer was – on account of his small-boned frame – the least equipped to withstand strokes like that. Lungelo struck again and the lecture hall gasped collectively.

Rumi watched in helpless horror as Lungelo went to bloody work with the whip. When the strapping was done, Sameer's light blue kaftan had dark patches of blood across his back.

Lungelo tilted his head back and wiped sweat from his brow. 'This is the price you pay for letting your emotions have control. Do not let it happen again.'

He recalled his shadow, freeing Rumi, and left the room.

Rumi darted to Sameer's side. 'I am so sorry.'

Sameer groaned as he raised a hand. 'It's all right.'

He helped Sameer to his feet.

'I will have my vengeance on that man,' Sameer murmured, more to himself than anyone else.

Ahwazi appeared beside them. 'You are a madman, Ajanla. A lucky madman. If you had called your shadow on him they could have done you for conduct unbecoming, even sent you to walk the Arakoro for that.'

Rumi scowled. 'I tried to call my shadow on him. It didn't work.'

Ahwazi gasped. 'Dara's might!'

'He probably blocked the call before you ever tried it,' said Sameer.

'They can do that?' Ahwazi said.

'Strong mindwalkers can, but they have to see you coming.'

Rumi snorted. 'And he saw me coming from a mile off.'

'Like a deer in a snare.'

'The block, how is it done?' Rumi asked.

'You separate the shadow and you throw it down the throat. It works like a gag. A strong mindwalker can hold on to his own shadow while blocking another, but if you aren't strong enough, you block yourself too.'

★

No further punishment came from the snap test, but Rumi's shame and guilt was punishment enough. He would face the mysterious peril of the Arakoro if it meant not having to see Sameer wince every night when he lay down to sleep or wake up through the night to groan. *I am a fool*, he decided.

52

Yield

RUMI

Rumi lay flat on his back, soaked with sweat. He wiped his forearm across the top of his head to dry it with his hair, then cleared the sweat from his eyes. Zarcanis stood above him.

'I yield,' Rumi said through heavy breaths. Pain makes a pygmy of your pride. More than once he had broken his promise never to yield – but Zarcanis was, of course, specially gifted in the breaking of things; promises and bodies both.

She helped him to his feet and put her hand under his chin to snap his neck one way and then the other.

'You are improving.'

He glanced down at his forearm. Wrist to elbow was criss-crossed with scabs and scars, the cost of calling his shadow day after day and night after night. Even Yomiku couldn't outwork him.

Zarcanis had once made him frog-jump to the Thatcher as a punishment; now he made that the first routine of the day. In his seven months in the Order, he had become a complete servant to the improvement of his craft. Building for the day he would expunge his disgrace and face the Priest of Vultures.

Zarcanis pressed a shadow-strewn finger to his forearm and gave him a third line of shadow rank.

He glanced up at Zarcanis, trying not to smile. 'What do you think? Will I be a Suli soon?'

'Soon is a terribly relative term. But I suppose to you it would not be soon at all.'

'Where do I need to improve?'

'Your control, your accuracy and every single other part of shadowdancing.'

'My control *has* improved.'

'Not even a little. I know more than anyone the danger of the unacknowledged shadow. Your heart is filled with anger of the worst kind. The anger that wears the guise of righteousness. That kind of anger is destructive because it is pandered to, justified. You worship your hurt feelings. Every time you embrace your shadow, you lose yourself in it. Why would I ever make you a Suli after one Bleeding?'

'There are so many crazy things about what you just said, but I'll just take it as I need more practice.'

She glanced at Yomiku. 'How many years have you been a Seedling?'

'Four,' he spat.

'That doesn't count,' said Rumi. 'He's a Seedling as punishment.'

Zarcanis pinched the bridge of her nose. 'To become a Suli is not about being hard. It is about being dependable, ready to go through pain for others.' She glanced at Yomiku. 'Does this boy know pain? Is he ready to face *real* pain?'

Yomiku shook his head silently. 'No.'

'You know nothing about my pain,' Rumi found he was right up in Zarcanis's face, a hard edge to his voice. 'Who are you to judge me?'

Her eyes went narrow. 'I am not here to judge you, I'm here to set you free.'

'Then help me become a Suli!'

'I will make you an offer, then,' she said, stretching out a hand. 'Conjure a spear, five feet long. Do that now and I will make you a Suli tonight.'

Rumi blinked and then licked the open wound on his forearm. His shadow flared like steam from a spring, filling him with its power. He gritted his teeth and stretched out a hand. A finger-thick bar of shadow formed in the air. He bunched his free hand into a tight fist and the bar stretched out to about half the length of a forearm. Dark images pressed themselves on his mind as he drew deeper into the shadow, trying to lengthen the bar.

His fist grew marbled with veins as the bar stretched to about two feet. Zarcanis's eyes widened ever so slightly. Rumi roared as he let the shadow swell within, trying to force the bar to grow longer. His mind had begun a full assault. Sweat blurred his vision as he tried to focus. He stamped his foot on the ground and squeezed with all his strength. Then his shadow whimpered out.

A bar of shadow less than two feet long clattered to the floor and returned to his dark silhouette.

Zarcanis turned her back to him without saying a word and started to walk away. 'Not even close.'

Rumi reached out towards her. When he spoke, he found his voice had lost its edge.

'I'll lose it one day,' he croaked, 'just like Griff did. The shadow. Five years, maybe less. I don't have ... time like everyone else. I need to learn *quickly*.'

Zarcanis glanced over her shoulder, face expressionless. 'Why? So you can have your precious revenge? Tell me, after you get your revenge, what more is there to you?'

442

Rumi was silent.

Without looking back, Zarcanis's hand shot out and a solid spear, stretching from the floor to the stalactite canopy above, coalesced at once.

Rumi gasped.

She hadn't said a word, hadn't shown a hint of strain, not even a sign of her calling the shadow. It was effortless.

She locked eyes with him. 'There are no shortcuts in the Way. Your journey does not end because you think you have arrived.'

'The Ghedo is less than a month away. If I show I have improved then, will you make me a Suli?'

'Highly unlikely,' she said. 'I *will* be watching, but adjust your expectations.'

That night Rumi considered Zarcanis's words as he made his way back to the dormitory. *Filled with anger of the worst kind.* How could anyone not be filled with anger after dealing with Zarcanis? Yomiku was the very notion of anger. If anger was a man, it would tell Yomiku to calm down. And she liked him. *Who is she to tell me about anger?*

He pushed the dormitory door open and strode over to their corner. Sameer had a large piece of paper sprawled out in front of him and was drawing from the instructions in his notebook.

Rumi squinted. It was a map of some sort. A labyrinth on seven levels, separated by ladders and staircases. The blueprint of a place where one could play an everlasting game of hide and seek. The corridor.

'What are you doing?' Rumi said.

Sameer stopped scribbling and glanced back. 'I told you I would have my revenge on Lungelo.'

Rumi dropped to a knee to inspect the map. 'I thought you had forgotten about that. I thought you were being the bigger person.'

'You thought wrong. My philosophy in life is to be a tiny person, a miniature if you will.'

Rumi thumbed the map. 'Tell me more.'

Sameer blinked. 'I have been working, for quite some time, on a map of the Eredo.' He traced his hand over the drawings. 'It was built to be the ultimate maze, impossible to navigate. There is barely a room within the Eredo without a false wall or a trap door, and the staircases are arranged so they don't lead to the levels you expect.'

Ahwazi appeared at Rumi's side. 'I heard they mind-wiped all the architects who designed each floor.'

'It is true,' said Sameer. 'No one completely knows their way around, except maybe Lord Mandla.'

'So what do you plan to do?'

Sameer allowed a slight smile. 'The chief's rooms are on the sixth and fifth floors,' he said indicating on the map. 'Lungelo's room is here.'

He pointed to a large rectangle on the sixth level of the map.

'How do you know it's his?'

'A deduction, I suppose. It's the most well-hidden, over-protected room of all the chiefs. The room of a man with vicious paranoia.'

'Fair enough,' Rumi said.

'Solid reasoning,' added Ahwazi.

'So what do you plan to do?'

Sameer rubbed his palms and retrieved a small wooden box from under his bedframe. Inside was a small, black ball formed of conjured shadow.

'What's that?' Ahwazi asked.

Sameer stared at the ball like a she-wolf at its first get. 'I've been working on it for a while now. It contains the very worst,

444

most foul-smelling things I could find, all encased in a ball of clay and conjured shadow. Once broken open, this beauty emits a catching smell that will make you run for cover.'

He picked the ball up and held it close. 'I call it, the stink bomb.'

Almost at the exact same time, Rumi and Ahwazi burst into laughter.

'What?' Sameer said. 'It is simple but effective.'

'For all the sophistication of your planning, your end game is surprisingly crude.'

'The smell would last for at least a month. Even his clothes will reek; all those agbadas and kaftans.'

Rumi grinned. It was a frightfully clever bit of conjuring. 'How do we help?'

Sameer raised an eyebrow. 'The risk of—'

'I'm helping,' Rumi said, cutting him off.

'I'm in too,' Ahwazi said.

Sameer's lips curled into a devious smile. 'So, here's what I'm thinking.'

Night had well and truly fallen by the time they had the plan. Black riding trousers and shirts buttoned at the sleeve was the designated attire. They crept into the corridor.

Sameer led the way, wooden box in hand. They moved at first to the empty dining hall, where they found a false wall behind one of the tables. A firm push saw them in a large room with low-slung stalactite carvings on the ceiling. Sameer led them through another door that revealed a large man-hole with a ladder for descent.

'You weren't kidding. Lungelo does this every day to get to his room?'

Sameer nodded. 'Getting in isn't even the tricky part. When we drop the bomb, we have to take a different route out. That's where I need you guys, you have to go ahead of me and make sure the coast is clear all the way back to the dorm.'

'Got it,' Rumi said.

They took their sandals off to tread through an ankle-deep pool, and walked in a single file through a narrow tunnel. They came at last to a palatial room with large circular chairs and satin cushions.

'His room is through there,' Sameer said, pointing. 'The stink bomb takes ten minutes to completely set. I would like for us to be safely in our dorms when it does. Ahwazi, you go ahead now. Rumi, you follow in three minutes exactly; I'll be three minutes behind you. If anyone gets caught on the way, scream like a baby and we will know to improvise in the corridor.'

They all nodded.

'Let's go.'

Ahwazi took off in one direction and Sameer in another. Rumi counted silently. His heart pummelled his chest. He fumbled in his counting at least twice, but maintained a rough approximation of the time spent. The third minute was the slowest of all. If anyone caught him, he was doomed on sight.

The minute ended and he took off after Ahwazi. He had memorised the path, but Ahwazi had marked it out for him. Doors left open and trap doors slightly ajar were reminders. Before long, he found himself in the dining hall again. He slowed to a stroll, making a good effort not to breathe too hard.

Back in the dormitory, Ahwazi was on his bed. His chest heaved from the running, but he did a good job of not looking guilty. A minute or so later, Sameer strolled in, fresh as a daisy. No eye contact was exchanged; if their eyes had met, they would have all exploded in laughter.

A few moments later, there was an almighty shout that disrupted all silence. Someone, somewhere in the Eredo was cursing up an absolute storm.

Sameer peered at Rumi over the top of his spectacles and that was the spark. They all exploded in laughter.

53

The Ghedo

RUMI

Rumi wore a deep red kaftan with plumes of grey at the collar. In a fight, Tinu had said, showmanship was as much a weapon as a spear. The colours channelled the Odu warriors of old, who had defended their homeland for over a hundred years before the Palmaine.

Ahwazi wore a brilliant yellow kaftan with sand-coloured sandals, and Sameer wore a long, black, high-necked kaftan. Dangerously businesslike. Together, it struck him, they would look quite grand.

'Are you nervous?' asked Sameer.

'A little.'

'My heart is beating like an angry slaver,' said Ahwazi.

'What kind of joke is that?' Rumi said.

'I don't know, I heard someone say it once. I'm sorry. I'm nervous.'

Rumi was nervous too, but nerves had a way of announcing themselves when least expected or approved. He walked with a straight back and a lifted chin as they sauntered through the corridor.

They arrived at the giant sunken theatre. It was a sight to behold. A great bowl, circled with terraced viewing platforms and stepped seating along the sides. The central ground of

the theatre looked big enough to host hundreds of people all
at once.

Stone icons of the old Agbara were placed among the crowd
as though they too were attendees at the Ghedo. The floor was
littered with flowers of every colour and there was a sharp,
unmistakeable sound. A sound that made Rumi's heart leap. The
soft patter of palms slapping a drum hide.

It was music from within, no artifice to it. Emotion tran-
scribed by drumbeat. There were singers, too, singing old native
songs that had meaning. Like rays of sunshine on a flower. It
had been so long since he had heard music of this kind. This . . .
this was liberation.

Rumi dared not ask the drummers if he could touch their
drums. These were real musicians. To men such as these, to use
their instrument was as intrusive as sharing their bed or kissing
their child.

He patted the air in gentle appreciation, knowing he looked
stupid. One of the drummers seemed to understand and nodded
with encouragement as he watched Rumi's hands. 'May I have
a dance?' came a voice from behind him.

The trance was broken. A young woman with a smile like
the smell of a bakery stared an invitation at him. Her skin was
midnight dark and her smile radiant white. Rumi had grown
up around market women and in that, he had listened to and
learned the sing-song of flirtation. He could almost tell by
inflection when a woman was proposing marriage, even if all
she had told a man was the price of tomatoes. It was a subtle
art, and though he had learned to understand the language, he
had never learned to speak it.

He smiled awkwardly back. 'I can't . . . I mean . . . I promised
my first dance to someone else.'

'Who's *that* lucky girl?'

He wet his lips. 'Kayalli.'

The woman's smile rumpled slightly. 'Kayalli has no interest in dancing, I'm sure of it.' She touched his arm.

He jerked it back like her fingers scalded him. He was a mess at this. An utter mess.

'Perhaps not, but I would hear it from her … if you don't mind.'

The woman's smile was gone. 'She'll probably be where the wine is.'

She was right. At the far corner of the theatre where there were decanters of wine, Nataré stood in conversation with a tall man in Chainbreaker robes. In her hand there was a clear glass of ruby-red firewine.

Rumi waited until there was a pause in their conversation before he interrupted.

'I promised you a dance,' he said.

She tore her eyes away from the Chainbreaker and looked at him. When their eyes locked his heart dropped. She looked … *incredible*. She always did. Did she even know she had that effect on him?

Her eyes were a window to her power. They moved from playful to serious as easily as the lioness through the prairie. They narrowed at the sight of danger, knowing she was the type to act. They carried a sweetness that made no petition; that was not cloying. Whether he liked it or not, she had him. Had him like the nectarine flower has the bumblebee. Her eyes watched his and she smiled with silent satisfaction. He was more enchanted then than he had been when he heard the drummers. He closed his mouth and blinked.

'You look …'

'I look what?'

'I don't have the words. I would say beautiful, but so many things are called beautiful and they are not like you.'

He wished he had not said that, but he was running mad, all sense had fled.

She pinned him with her eyes. 'Are you flirting with me, Ajanla?'

A stutter materialised from mist in his voice. 'No ... I mean, not that I wouldn't ... you're a very ...'

'A very what?'

'A very ... good person.'

She snorted, then took hold of his hand. 'Let's dance.'

Her skin was dangerously soft. His arm was going limp in hers as she led him to the centre of the theatre where people were dancing. Rumi recognised some of them; Ahwazi and a pretty Seedling, Ladan with Alangba, Gaitan with a reluctant Karile, Griff with some woman too young for him. His heart thumped with each step. The Priest of Vultures couldn't be more terrifying than the thought of letting her down as a dance partner. Rumi rehearsed moves in his mind, but his mind was a mess. He was woefully unprepared.

'I'm not a great dancer,' Rumi mumbled.

She smiled. 'Don't worry, I'm used to leading you.'

She rounded on him and moved. If his heart had beat for her before, watching her dance he could not be sure whether the thrumming sound came from the drums or his chest. She moved with uncommon grace, her bare feet caressing the floor with twists and turns. Rumi moved as carefully as he could, trying not to embarrass the pair of them. She urged him on with a smile, daring him to take more risks. He moved his shoulders one way then the other and she nodded in encouragement.

There was no shame with her. They had seen so much of one another from childhood; there was an understanding they shared that no one else in the Eredo would understand and if he looked stupid dancing with her, she would not care. She had seen him look stupid many times and here she was still, smiling at him.

So they danced, close and smooth. He felt watching eyes as they got closer, but he paid them no mind. She leaned into him, her head resting on the underside of his chin. Warmth shot through him from inside. The music slowed and she wrapped her arms around his neck, her eyes fixed on his. There was barely a naked inch between any part of their bodies.

When the song came to an end, he did not want the dance to stop. She filled his cup in a way he did not know he needed and by Dara's might, it felt good.

She smiled and then she was laughing, freely and fully. 'I thought you said you couldn't dance.'

He looked at her, smiled and tucked a loose braid behind her ear. 'I just followed your lead.'

She stiffened and he realised they were well within kissing distance. There was a moment, a small piece of eternity where time seemed to present him an opportunity. His chin sagged. He could clash spears with Zarcanis, but had nowhere near the boldness to kiss her.

She eyed him carefully, and in the flickering of a lantern, she suddenly looked as though she would cry. Her lip quivered and her eyes drooped.

'What's wrong?' he said.

She looked up at him, dragging the top of her forearm across her brow.

'Nothing,' she said, her eyes now fixed and determined. 'The Ghedo will soon begin. Go and join your Order people.'

'My Order people?'

'Yes. The ones who look like I'm stealing their favourite shoes.'

Rumi glanced over his shoulder. Ladan's eyes were the size of saucers and Ahwazi chewed his bottom lip like it was food. Even Griff was staring at him.

'They will be all right,' he said, turning back to her.

She placed a gentle hand on his chest. 'You should make sure.'

Rumi raised an eyebrow in surprise. She was flitting away from him like a Blackfae. He reached for the words to keep her, just for a moment, but they didn't come.

She flashed him a troublesome grin, and then he was watching her walk away.

'She really is something, isn't she?'

It was Ladan's voice.

'She is,' said Rumi.

'If you make it to Suli tonight, you would be able to go and see her out by the watchpoint. Alone. It's beautiful up there.'

Rumi thought about it and it made him a little warmer at the top of his chest.

'Have you kissed her yet?' Ladan asked.

Rumi's face flushed and he quickly tried to correct it. He raised his brow as though to suggest that kissing was no big deal.

'No, I have not.'

Ladan studied him carefully. 'Have you kissed anyone yet?'

Rumi flushed again. 'Of course I have.'

Ladan called his bluff. 'Who?'

'This girl in Basmine,' Rumi said, not meeting his stare.

Ladan smiled from near ear to ear. 'Speak no lies, Ajanla. If you lie to me, I cannot help you.'

Rumi studied the ground. 'I just ... the moment never came. I worried I would ... get it wrong. I don't know.'

453

'You worry too much. When the music plays—'

'It is better to dance than to stand still. My mother always used to say that.'

'A wise woman.'

Rumi swallowed. 'She was.'

The promise he had made seemed to tug at his neck. 'What would it take? To make me a Suli?'

Ladan stroked his chin thoughtfully. 'Zarcanis would have to petition.'

'And how do I get her to do that?'

'Impress her. What are you good at?'

'Shadowdancing,' he said without thinking.

'Everyone thinks they are good at shadowdancing until they have blood in their eye. You can forget impressing her with that; all the other Seedlings have been sparring for at least five bleedings. You have barely seen two.'

'Whoever I step up against – Seedling, Suli or Truetree – will meet a challenge.'

Ladan raised an eyebrow. 'I suppose they will.'

A drum sounded and people moved to viewing platforms. There was an order to things: first there would be a tournament involving those vying to become Seedlings, then a tournament for the Seedlings, and it would proceed to Sulis and eventually to the Truetrees.

The action began with younglings by the dozen trying their hand at *kiwinje*, a competition that required two people to face off on a thin bench with the aim of one person knocking the other off with the assistance of a harmless club of straw. One of them they called N'Gone made that straw club harmful, somehow. She knocked off boys double her size, swinging the club with accrued malice.

'That one will be in the Order before the year is done,' said
Ladan, watching her topple another opponent with a sharp
swing of the straw club. 'She's like a wildcat freed from a cage.'

He was right; she was alive with motion, instinct, and un-
faltering focus. What did she carry inside that gave her such
angry vitality?

Renike competed too – not with the ferocity of N'Gone, but
with a resolute determination not to be overcome. In the end,
Renike and N'Gone were both beaten by a bigger Kasinabe
boy, clearly better trained than either of them. With time, they
would plainly both make short work of boys like him, but for
now he wore the wreath of victory with boyish pride. There
were other contests among them; Rumi was proud of Renike's
determined performance in all. *She will be in the Order soon.*

The Seedling contests began after that. Fire walks, spear
throwing, a bread-eating contest, even a test of speed. Rumi
watched patiently. He had only come for one.

He watched Ahwazi lose the footrace to a lean Kasinabe man
with calves like tubers of yam. Looking at his legs, it was no
disgrace to finish a distant second behind him.

When the test of speed was done, they announced a contest
of music. Rumi's mouth immediately felt bone-dry. His fingers
itched as he watched young Seedlings pick their instruments
and start to tune them. Something roared inside him at the
sound of the first drum.

I'm out of practice. I cannot win. I have no drums. As he watched
the Seedlings line up, he felt a pair of eyes settle on him. Rumi
glanced over his shoulder.

A hefty Kasinabe lad, stood clutching a brass Florinian flute.
'So you play?' the flautist said.

Rumi blinked. 'How do you know?'

'Your fingers,' he said.

Rumi noticed then that he was tapping out melodies on his thigh, in silent preparation. *A man's hands tell his story.* He smiled and straightened his right hand, burying the other in the cloth of his kaftan.

'Call me Stake,' said the flautist, extending a hand.

Rumi took it. 'Ajanla Erenteyo.'

Stake smiled. 'Do you need to borrow some drums?'

Rumi drew in a long breath. 'Yes.'

54

When the Music Plays

RUMI

Rumi watched the players take their turns. There were no music sheets or rehearsed symphonies here. It was an instinctive thing. Players playing the music that came to them. A thing as familiar and delicious as Yami's beancakes.

They were marvellous players, Stake most of all. He played with such furious freedom that there was a pulsing in the vein at Rumi's neck. He smiled when he played too. An uncanny thing; you could see the curl of his lips at either side of the flute.

Even if Rumi could not match his performance, it would be enough to leave knowing that they were thought of as peers. When he walked past him, Stake nodded with gentle encouragement. But there was an undercurrent, as if he wanted to say, 'You cannot win today'.

When Rumi's turn came he felt no pressure, just an opportunity to speak. When his fingers touched the drums, he had much to say. He spoke of things he had seen; he spoke of gratitude, of fear and of expectation, each beat of the drum speaking without the need of words. It was more personal than anything he had played before, and the crowd seemed to appreciate it. There was a reverent silence while he played.

When he was done, there was vibrant applause. Perhaps someone else would wear the wreath, but he had said his piece.

Tears washed his cheeks. The theatre had given him something he had neither the means nor the ability to repay. Ladan was right; playing brought him a kind of clarity and peace.

In the end, he did not win the wreath, but he had certainly won the crowd. When he was announced as first runner-up, the crowd responded with salutes and a spattering of cheers with words that were hard to hear over the applause. He got the gist of it.

'That was ... beautiful,' Ladan said when he saw him. 'You have a gift, a real gift. You should have won; if you weren't softborn you would have won handily. If you shadowdance as well as you play the drums, you will win a wreath for certain. There are no biases in the fighting pit. Win that and you have a great chance at Suli.'

'He surely will,' said the flautist, appearing at his side. 'You have blessed hands. Specially blessed. Where did you play before you came here?'

A shot of emotion ran through him and his voice cracked as he spoke. 'I played at the Golden Room.'

The flautist raised an eyebrow. 'What a great rescue you were given. Your hands were not made to dance to an audience that could not nourish you. An audience that would only debase your gift. They would have chained you in that place. My goodness, you would have loved the chains too. What a great rescue.'

He smiled at Rumi as though he had seen a king cowrie on the floor and picked it up before anyone noticed. 'I will come to find you soon. You should join our players' circle.'

Rumi thought on the words. *An audience that could not nourish you.* He thought of Tinu and how much he'd despised the audience at the Orchid House.

When the flautist was gone, Ladan, Sameer and Rumi returned to a discussion about shadowdancing and the impending contest.

THE DANCE OF SHADOWS

'You know the Seedlings to watch out for?' Ladan said.

'Anyone can be dangerous with the shadow,' said Rumi.

'Too true, but even so, there are some who might have *advantages*.'

'There's this big fellow, shoulders like a bridge...'

'Dasuki,' Ladan said.

'Yes,' Rumi confirmed. 'I've seen him lift a Seedling off his feet with one hand.'

'Dasuki's always been strong. Even before he was a Seedling, Sulis would tread carefully around him.'

'I'll watch out for him then.'

'What about Yomiku?'

Rumi drew in breath. 'Yomiku? He's not a true Seedling.'

'Technically he is. He's never fought at the Ghedo as a Seedling; he qualifies.'

'That isn't fair,' said Sameer.

'It isn't,' Ladan agreed. 'I'd say if you meet him in the fighting pit, yield quickly. There is no shame in that. A man like that is out to make a name.'

'Thinks he's bloody Walade Widowmaker reborn,' spat Rumi.

'Good reason to steer well clear.'

'Shege.'

That was an almighty dollop of elephant dung to his plans. He closed his eyes and pressed his fingers against them. *Just make an impression.*

As if to put death to small talk, a bell rang, signalling the beginning of the shadowdancing contest. Ladan put a hand on Rumi's shoulder. 'Dara's favour be yours.'

'Let it be so,' Rumi said.

The cluster of shadowdancers was bigger than that of any of the contests before. Almost all Seedlings were there, whether male or female, short or tall. Rumi imagined that to abstain from shadowdancing was to mark yourself out for mockery in the Order. Even if you were no good at it, you had to show appetite for the fight; that was the Kasinabe way.

Sameer stood nervously in the cluster. He was not a fighter, nowhere close, but he was a proud man and he had pinned his hopes on winning a wreath at *seraiye* later in the day.

The umpire explained the rules. Bouts were to last ten minutes and would be decided on surrender, incapacitation or strikes landed. As they drew names for the first bout, Rumi's heartbeat quickened.

The first two bouts ended with quick surrenders, size and strength proving enough to turn the tide in favour of the two bigger fighters. The next bout was more even, swirling wisps of shadow in a dance of elbows and safespears. Rumi watched carefully. It was remarkable how you could tell who had trained a shadowdancer by watching their bouts. Jenna's fighters were precise and highly technical. Domo's fighters had a casual air that belied a wonderful poise and a knack for finding openings.

Rumi watched Yomiku's first bout. He gritted his teeth as Yomiku took to the centre of the fighting pit. As always, his footwork was less than perfect, but he threw crushing strikes. If he caught Rumi with one of his overhand spear thrusts, or sneaking uppercuts, he would be in trouble.

Yomiku struck his opponent with one such sneaking upper-cut; a subtle suddenness that knocked the young man off his feet completely. Rumi winced at the force of the blow and the way his opponent's head jerked back. It was as though someone had tugged a rope attached to his hair. Yomiku grinned directly at Rumi when the opponent hit the ground. He raised his spear and brought it down on the floored opponent with such brutal force that the sound of the blow was louder than the screaming

THE DANCE OF SHADOWS

crowd. Botanicals carried the unconscious boy away with his face painted crimson and feet dragging on the floor.

'Victory by incapacitation,' the umpire announced.

Ahwazi won his first bout. He was an awkward, unpredictable fighter with gangly, guarded footing. He managed to topple his opponent over and force him to surrender with the safespear at his neck. Rumi raised a fist in salute when Ahwazi was declared the winner. He beat his chest and tapped his shoulder in response.

Rumi's name was the next one drawn. When he heard the name Dasuki, his face fell. Of all the Seedlings in the theatre, his was – save for Yomiku – the name no one wanted in an early draw.

Dasuki made his way through the crowd. It parted for him like dust scattered by a gust of wind. He was at least seven inches taller than Rumi, with shoulders like a continent. His face was chiselled stone. Rumi would have liked to have seen him fight at least once before facing him, an opportunity to search for weaknesses or learn where the danger lay. This way Dasuki would have a basket full of surprises for him.

He was of a height with his trainer, Kairobi, and had the same aura of danger. As he stretched, Kairobi whispered instructions just a few paces shy of the fighting pit.

Zarcanis was nowhere to be seen. She was not the sort to whisper instructions from the sidelines.

The umpire called them close. Rumi's heart beat with a booming thump. He searched Dasuki's eyes and found nothing but the self-assuredness of someone who had done this a thousand times. There was no hate, no fear, no anxiety, only duty. A gardener clipping the weeds.

55

A Fighter

ALANGBA

Alangba squinted as Rumi strode into the fighting circle to face an absolute unit of a Seedling. The Seedling was Gu's own design: mountain big, tall, hard as iron. The crowd chanted the name.

'Da-su-ki! Da-su-ki!'

A man tapped his shoulder and he reached instinctively for his security knife, before remembering he was in the Eredo. He straightened as he glanced over his shoulder.

'Easy, ranger.'

It was Griff Voltaine. The darkman himself. Once the King of the Ghedo.

'Is this seat taken?' Griff said, gesturing to the empty seat at his side.

'No,' said Alangba, though he wished the darkman would choose somewhere else. There was still something unsettling about the man, even though it was said he no longer could call the shadow. Alangba had seen him in his prime. A dangerous man.

He let out a breath and his attention returned to the fight. The fighters circled as the umpire gave his instructions. Alangba thought he had seen it before, but now he knew for sure. The way Rumi moved: keeping the power in his trailing foot, light

on his leading foot. He was a fighter. That sort of natural movement took years to learn, not months. Curiously, the boy moved
as though he wanted to use his fists, not a spear.

Alangba glanced back at the darkman. The man was enraptured, fists clenched as he leaned forward, every sinew of his
whipcord strength willing his son to win.

'I'll take one tuber of yam against my two for anyone who
fancies Ajanla,' someone said behind them.

Griff's ear twitched at that.

'Shege, at least make it interesting,' another voice said. 'The
boy can't even call his shadow by name.'

'Fine,' said the one taking bets, 'three tubers.'

'Four and I might risk one tuber,' said the other man.

Griff glanced over his shoulder. 'I'll take your bet. I'll put
down six tubers.'

The gambler grinned. 'I'm not stupid enough to take six
tubers from the darkman. You'll just beat the tubers back out
of me.'

Griff raised an eyebrow. 'Are you saying I'm a cheat?'

The man's smile vanished. 'No, not at all, Griff, I didn't—'

'I promise a clean bet, if you still want it.'

The man thumbed his chin, considering, then held out a kola
nut. 'Make it ten tubers to my thirty.'

Griff nodded, broke the kola nut and turned back to the
fighting circle.

Alangba wanted to laugh, but dared not. Griff had seen what
he had seen. The boy was no festival goat.

The one they called Dasuki held his spear two-handed like
a club, fixing to knock the darkman's boy senseless. His shadow
loomed large behind him, like the falling sails of a great ship. A
terrifying proposition, even at this distance. But Rumi seemed
unperturbed; the boy left just a few inches at the butt of his

spear, starting with a good spear form, *monkey climbs the tree.*
His shadow seemed calmed and patient.

As they closed in, Rumi's form quickly flowed into *snake crosses the valley.* An effortless change of cadence.

Griff was leaning dangerously forward, as though about to jump into the fighting pit himself.

Dasuki swung to test his range and Rumi dodged it. The torque on that swing was incredible. One connection would be decisive.

Dasuki swung again and massively overextended, taking a moment to regain his footing. *Too long.*

'Go now!' Griff shouted.

The boy couldn't hear him over the throng of shouting, but they were of one mind. He charged at Dasuki with *rhinoceros rages.* The end of his safespear smashed the front of Dasuki's foot before clattering his ankle and shin. Dasuki hopped back, but everything was too slow – his footwork, his responsiveness, his strikes, all too slow. A man too used to being the strongest, scariest thing in the room. Before Dasuki could unfurl his long arms, the boy was inside his reach. If they had been fighting with real spears, Dasuki would have been ten times dead. Griff's boy thrust his spear up into Dasuki's throat. It was a violent strike, but fair. The boy had to make sure.

Dasuki staggered back. As he fell, the brute threw a sharp instinctive swing of his safespear. The boy immediately fell into a box split.

Griff winced as Dasuki's swing flashed above the boy's head.

There it was – that was how close Rumi had come to losing all his teeth. An eyelash away from no more solid foods.

The boy recovered expertly and shot forward, fixing to thrust. Dasuki raised his safespear to parry, but Rumi had sold him with a feint that was a work of art. The switchback was so sudden, so beautifully violent that Alangba could cry. He hammered his safespear down on Dasuki's wrist and the safespear spun from the big Seedling's grip.

The big Seedling raised his hand in surrender. 'I yield!'

The theatre was eerily quiet, then it exploded with booming cheer.

'Ajanla Erenteyo! Ajanla Erenteyo!'

Griff raised a meaty fist in the air and turned to the man. 'Thirty yam tubers! You can start with paying me ten.'

56

Softborn

RUMI

Rumi almost did not want it to be over. The whirlpool within had barely come to a full swirl and his heart was thumping with the fighter's high.

He gritted his teeth and helped Dasuki to his feet.

Dasuki could match a gorilla pound-for-merciless-pound, but he was slow. He relied too much on power. Zarcanis would have made him fight on hot coals until he learned to keep his feet moving.

Rumi had not wounded him much, but he could have. He could have killed him in truth. The safespears were blunt, but jab one into someone's throat apple just right and they would choke on blood. He searched for Zarcanis in the crowd, but there was no sign of her.

The crowd was chanting again. 'Ajanla Mbo, Ajanla Mbo, Ajanla Mbo'. *The old dog is coming.*

Rumi caught sight of Yomiku. He made a gesture with his hands like a balancing scale, as though to say 'not bad'.

Rumi's next bout was against a Seedling called Labalaba. She smiled at him before she called her shadow. Rumi smiled back as he striped his other arm. He threw a testing strike of his safespear and she nearly gored his eye. She was no little butterfly to be handled with folly. She was a scorpion preening to pierce.

Their safespears danced for a few turns before he saw the flaw in her cadence. She was fast and precise, but she always struck to wound. She kept the scorpion tail form, but was fixed to it. Overcompensating for the strength disparity. He flooded her with a barrage of disruptive swings, swiping one way and then the other, for no reason other than to throw her off balance.

He gave her a small opportunity to regain her footing and she took it too quickly. He knew exactly where her foot would go and he smashed her shin with such force that he was sure there would be blood, broken skin and splattered bone when her trouser leg was lifted. She gasped. Most others would have howled. Rumi respected that, but he needed confirmation. He raised his safespear.

'Do you yield?' he said.

Her eyes narrowed. She saw his safespear raised to end it. She slammed her head back on the floor. 'I yield.'

Rumi bowed and the crowd flared up.

'Ajanla Mbo! Ajanla Mbo! Ajanla Mbo!'

He examined his arms and the patchwork of wounds new and old. The cost of calling his shadow. How long could he keep licking his own blood to call the shadow? How long before he became like Griff, unable to do it again?

He fought six times and took some brutal hits along the way. His entire body ached. Exhaustion and pain quickly became as much his opponents as anyone left in the tournament. He poured a flask of water over his head, letting it wash the blood away. He was well in the grip of the fighter's high. A Shinala at the races. He was beginning to believe he could make something of the tournament. Yomiku or no.

Ahwazi was still in the tournament too, and miraculously, so was Sameer. Sameer was crafty as smallpox. He moved slick as a lockpick and had mastered what Tinu called running while walking. No one could catch him in the fighting pit, and he worked with the hourglass to win on strikes landed. A winning strategy against fighters who came to compete, but Rumi worried how he would fare against those who came to hurt. All the same, Rumi was brother proud.

Yomiku broke people on his path to the final. No one, perhaps in the entire Eredo, had more pedigree of unnecessary violence than Yomiku. When his opponents made to yield, Yomiku became hard of hearing and continued to punish them until he was dragged off. It was ugly to watch. Rumi's appetite for the fight grew. He had no great need for a grand finale; a dirty scrap in the corridor would be the rub.

When they announced Yomiku would face Sameer, his heart sank.

In between fights he sought Sameer out. 'You've proven yourself, Sameer. When you get in there, yield immediately.'

'I'll do no such thing.'

'Sameer. Yomiku … He has a real bone in his teeth for softborns. He will take it too far.'

'All the more reason for me to stand up to him,' Sameer said, stretching.

'You don't understand, Sameer, he—'

'No, *you* don't understand, Rumi! Would you yield, if it was you?'

'I'm a better fighter.'

'Maybe with a spear, but in here,' he said, touching his chest, 'I'm the better fighter. I won't yield without showing him that. Without showing all of them that.'

Sameer had fire in his eyes, steel-necked resolve. Like an arrow loose from the bow, he wouldn't stop until he hit something. Rumi knew the feeling, the need to show people. To stand your ground. He could not begrudge him that. He closed his eyes and drew in a long breath. 'Dara guide you.'

Sameer lifted his head and turned towards the fighting pit. 'And may His way be yours.'

Rumi shook his head as he watched Sameer trudge towards the fighting pit. Ahwazi appeared at his side. From the look on his face, it was clear he was still thrumming with the hum of fighting. Yet, when he spoke his voice was inhumanly cool.

'Did you ever wonder how a Kuba boy came to live in the fishing villages?'

Rumi raised an eyebrow. 'I did.'

Ahwazi nodded. 'Back in the old days, towns near the ports were a dangerous place. People used to trick strangers and sell them to slave ship merchants. It was quick, fast money. Not done so much now, but in the fishing villages there are still some in the trade.'

Rumi's eyes flickered. 'He was sold.'

'Yes,' Ahwazi said, 'along with his toddler brother.'

'How did he make it here?'

'Sameer was the only native on the ship who could read and write. The captain made him take inventory every day of all the goods on board the ship. Came to trust him. One day, the captain and half his crew fell sick after a night on the bottle. A week later, they were dead and the natives took over the ship. Sailed back to the fishing villages.'

'Sameer ...'

'Sameer,' Ahwazi said, 'the deer that hunts the wolves.'

Rumi glanced down at the fighting pit where Sameer was about to enter. 'Why would they ever give him a name like Ailera?'

Ahwazi let out a sharp laugh. 'He picked that name himself. No one plans for the weakling, he said.'

469

Rumi's mouth drooped. 'A devious man.'

'Pain is the price of wisdom.'

Rumi glanced up at him. 'What's your pain?'

Ahwazi closed his eyes. 'I'm the stupid one in the group, remember.'

Rumi's laugh was so sudden he jerked back but Ahwazi's face had turned serious and his eyes were locked tight on the fighting pit.

The umpire gave them licence to call shadows. Yomiku circled Sameer like a jackal. From his smile and stare, it was plain to see there was no place Yomiku would rather be than in that circle with blood underfoot.

Sameer was patient, taking steps only when he needed to, staying just out of striking range. They circled like two mismatched dogs in the street. There was an instant where Yomiku's foot seemed to catch. It was a moment that felt as though it stretched out into an eternity; there was a stumble in Yomiku's eyes as the slightest opening emerged. Rumi found himself leaning forward, willing Sameer to take it. He did. He snatched across the ground to gouge Yomiku's side. The crowd erupted in cheer.

Yomiku grunted and stepped back. He smiled a predator's smile, rotating his shoulders. A gesture that said, *that was a mistake*. Sameer kept moving, staying out of reach. If he could run away from Yomiku for the rest of the fight, he could...

Better not to have the hope.

Yomiku lunged again, an act of agitation. Clumsy, arrogant. Sameer dodged masterfully and brought his safespear down on Yomiku's side again. Away from the eyes of the umpire, Yomiku held the attacking spear between his hip and elbow, only for a moment. It was an illegal move; spear holding was grounds for instant disqualification.

'Holding!' Rumi said, nearly bounding into the arena but an arm grabbed his shoulder. He turned, teeth locked in a snarl. It was Zarcanis, her eyes as calm as still water and her grip as clean and uncompromising as an executioner.

Yomiku took advantage of the hold and broke Sameer's safespear with a sly brush of his knee. *It was over.* The crowd gasped as the safespear shattered into useless splinters. Sameer looked to the umpire, but he gave him nothing. *Yield!*

Sameer raised his fists.

Yield!

Yomiku smiled and threw his own spear aside, beckoning Sameer forward. Sameer threw a punch, but Yomiku had woken up now. He caught Sameer's arm at the elbow and used his hip to turn him over. Then he locked his forearm around Sameer's neck.

Sameer's eyes bulged. 'I yie—'

Yomiku muffled the sound with his forearm, tightening his grip around Sameer's neck with the other arm. Yomiku turned to Rumi and locked eyes. Rumi made a step to enter the fighting pit, but Zarcanis inched closer, pinning him back.

'They will disqualify you if you interfere,' she said. 'Getting to Suli would be hard with a disqualification on your record. Don't you see there are those who want you to fail?'

Rumi looked around. She was right, there were faces that wore smiles, people who saw the hold and allowed it. *I'm still only a softborn to them.* He saw it in their eyes. What Kuda Kamo had written about. How easy it was to love the brother and hate the other. The words seemed to come to life in his mind: There is nothing special about loving those you see as your own. No great virtue in carrying the pride of the Odu tribe. Even the snake is loyal to its snakelet. Even the scavenging hyena shares the spoils with the pack. There is a higher love. Rumi had seen it. The higher love. Loving the stranger.

Sameer's flailing arms slowed.

'Let them disqualify me,' Rumi whispered. With a sudden jerk of force he broke free of Zarcanis's grip and flung himself into the fighting pit.

He collided with Yomiku and they both ended in a rolling tangle, toppling the umpire over.

Sameer gave a deep, scratchy cough as he tried to draw in breath.

'Are you all right?' Rumi called out, rising from the heap.

Sameer garbled blood. 'I've been better.'

The umpire returned to his feet and lifted Yomiku's hand. 'Victory by incapacitation.'

Yomiku didn't move. His dark eyes were locked tight on Rumi and his shoulders were hunched like a wolf at cornered prey. The umpire was shouting something at Rumi, but between the roaring crowd, the thump of blood pumping and Yomiku's heavy breathing he couldn't make out what the umpire was saying. Yomiku's words were clean and clear.

'We have unfinished business, Ajanla.'

Rumi's heart pummelled his chest. He knew he should have left the fighting pit, knew what Yomiku had fixed in his mind. Instead, he found himself stepping forward, rotating his shoulders. He glanced up at the faces in the crowd. He was a softborn to them. Something less than full Kasinabe. He wanted to contradict their presuppositions. To show them what happened to a person when his life is a series of skirmishes in a long, unending battle. Like Sameer. Like Renike. Like Morire and Yami.

Someone from the crowd threw two safespears into the fighting pit as the botanicals carried Sameer away. Yomiku gestured for Rumi to take one up. He obliged. The umpire shrugged as though the entire affair had nothing to do with him.

A wide grin spread on Yomiku's cheeks.

Before Rumi could set his feet, Yomiku snatched up a safespear and lunged for him. Rumi made to stripe his arm, but before he could get to it, Yomiku was on him. His first thrust missed to Rumi's left, but he caught him flush on the backswing, flipping his safespear into a reverse grip and dragging it back in a quick jagged line. Rumi had seen the move a thousand times in sparring and still missed it. *Focus, Rumi, focus.*

'Call your shadow!' someone shouted.

He tried to lick his blood but Yomiku flew at him again.

Yomiku came like an ocean wave, following his sharp thrust with a firm blow which knocked Rumi off his feet. As Rumi scrambled for his footing, Yomiku shot into *snake shoots venom* and his safespear penetrated flesh, biting a half-inch into Rumi's chest. Before Rumi could scream, Yomiku was on top of him.

The first blow broke Rumi's nose in an explosion of blood. The second was Dara's own honest attempt to kill. The distant jeer of the crowd was drowned beneath the urgent thump of his heart.

'This is no place for a softborn,' Yomiku screamed, 'no place!'

Blood filled Rumi's mouth. Merciful blood on his tongue. *Thank Dara.* He let the drops fall down his throat and his shadow flared up. The crowd screamed. Power filled him to the brim, his fingertips set to burst with the ripple of energy. He shoved Yomiku back.

Yomiku's surprise at the sudden gust of force gave Rumi a moment to think. Half a moment. Yomiku's redoubled attack made Rumi backtrack, fending off the safespear with *shepherd holds the crook.*

473

Rumi watched the sequence and struck instinctively at the lull in movement. The strike glanced off Yomiku's chest, but the bastard pinned Rumi's safespear down with his elbow.

With his free hand, Yomiku crashed a solid fist into Rumi's jaw, snatching his safespear as he sent him spiralling to the floor. Rumi glanced up as Yomiku broke his safespear into two, then into four splintered pieces.

Zarcanis's voice came like a whisper. Mindwalking.

'*I can get you out of there. Give up!*'

'No!' he shouted.

'*Then fight like a Shadowwielder. Don't wait for your emotions to get so fierce that they drive your action. Take the reins for yourself. Do not blame the past. Do not decide first, just do!*'

Her voice faded from his mind as he stumbled to his feet. The crowd was already beginning to cheer Yomiku, but as Rumi got to his feet the cheers dimmed. He had no safespear. Yomiku could do – would do – irreparable damage.

'You fight like a scavenger animal, nothing won well. I will teach you a lesson today,' Rumi said.

In some crazy way he believed it. Warmth draped his shoulders like a cloak of fire. He beckoned Yomiku forward.

Yomiku thrust his safespear forward with enough force to kill. Rumi swerved left. *Dancing feet keep you pretty.* With his safespear gone, Rumi was possessed of all the mobility Tinu had invested in him, but he faced an opponent with murderous intent. He had to find a way to fight on level terms.

Yomiku narrowed his eyes, beat his chest and raised his safespear high. The crowd roared. *There it is.* Yomiku had a wild look in his eyes. He was a man of stories. A man who recited names of warriors long past with the easy reverence of a fanatic. He wanted to show the Eredo how strong he was, prove his old blood. In that folly rested Rumi's only hope.

Rumi stretched his arms wide, offering up an irresistible target. Yomiku obliged like a bull, lurching forward with nothing held in reserve. Rumi pulled in air, waiting. At the moment of impact, Rumi sucked in his stomach. The safespear still penetrated flesh, its blunt edge buried in his belly. If it had been a real spear, he would be dead. Even a safespear would have done for him if he had sucked his stomach in an inch less. As it was, he was wounded, but the pain was not nearly loud enough to penetrate the rushing blood and the roaring shadow that filled him. He gritted his teeth, resisting the urge to cry out, and shot into *puppet snatches the strings.* He brought his forearm down with all available force, shattering Yomiku's safespear.

Yomiku staggered forward as the broken safespear fell from his hands. Rumi drew in more shadow as he let Yomiku stumble to his feet. Then he focused and did as Sameer had taught him, throwing a gag of shadow at Yomiku's throat.

There were gasps in the crowd as both shadows whimpered out. Rumi grinned. It was a Bobiri fight now, his fight. He could not beat Yomiku with the shadow, not even with the spear, but Rumi had been a fighter long before he had any weapons.

He darted forward and dealt Yomiku a rising uppercut that made his teeth chatter. As Yomiku's nose spattered blood, Rumi's fist sang across his cheek, once, twice, a third time. If Yomiku wanted to yield now, he would not have the sense left in him to form the words.

A fourth blow knocked Yomiku clean off his feet. Glaring down at Yomiku, Rumi let the reins of his rage free. He hammered him with blows, opening up cuts and laying down welts. Yomiku's mouth sagged open as Rumi lifted him from the ground the way he had seen Tinu do so many times and brought his limp body down against his knee.

'Do you yield?'

Yomiku coughed blood. Rumi slapped him with an open palm and he splattered blood, staining the closest spectators.

'Do you yield?' he said again. There was silence all around them now, save for Yomiku's uneven breath as he slapped teeth from his mouth. 'I said... Do you yield?'

Yomiku gave a wordless groan.

Rumi turned to the crowd. 'Is this what you're here for?'

The crowd was silent. He turned to the umpire.

'And you? You let this... this jackal get away with anything, for what? Is this what you wanted?'

The umpire failed to meet Rumi's eyes.

Rumi licked a line of blood from his arm and his shadow amplified his voice until it carried around the entire theatre.

'My mother told me that the Kasinabe were the bravest of us. Honourable. Strong. Are these the champions you build now?' he said, pointing at Yomiku. 'What have you become? An army with no veterans! While we play with safespears here, there are Palmaine dominating our land, making servants of native children. You call me softborn, but never have I seen a softer place than this. You never had to wash down the taste of roasted rats with river water. Don't know the smell of a latrine. You live and die well. You are the softborn! Which one of you has the courage of Ailera or the battle vigour of the youngest sentry? Death comes but once, and even if I die slow, the last part of me to die will be my pride. It's time we start being what we say we are. Basmine is waiting for warriors and the Palmaine gunman doesn't care whether you are softborn or old blood. It's time we fight for—'

'That's quite enough,' Mandla said, cutting him off.

But the crowd was already alight. The cheers were deafening. The chants seemed to fill him with new energy, their worship swimming in his veins like blood. Rumi felt infinite, lost to the fighter's high.

'Ajanla Erenteyo! Ajanla Erenteyo!'

The sound crashed against the walls unabated. Rumi looked around the room and saw with new eyes. Mandla watched him the way a dog watches an intruder.

Rumi had not acknowledged him.

'Yes, Lord Mandla,' Rumi said, bowing.

'You are disqualified from the rest of the Ghedo. Humble yourself and we will discuss the rest later.'

Humble myself?

He straightened. 'Will I be made a Suli or not ... Lord Mandla?' Adding the honorific was an afterthought.

Mandla's face was like a covered cookpot: on the surface it was still and plain, but wisps of steam streamed from every crack and crevice. Underneath that expressionless face, he was boiling. He looked at Rumi and his calm baby-faced stare told Rumi there was a part of him that wanted to rip him to shreds.

'We will discuss this *later.*'

The crowd still screamed 'Ajanla Erenteyo'. The power still coursed through him even with his shadow gone. He pried his clenched fist open and beat a simple pattern on his thigh.

'Yes, Lord Mandla. Double hundred apologies,' he said, bowing.

Mandla nodded, but the bubbling anger did not leave his eyes.

After being stitched up and balmed by the botanicals, Rumi was able to watch more of the Ghedo. The Suli competitions were different. They raced Shinala, built siege weapons, and after the shadowdancing, they had a team competition, where groups of twenty fought against one another in a melee to capture flags. It required strategy and teamwork, things that Seedlings did

477

not have to demonstrate. The Suli were great conjurers, too, and could produce shadow seamlessly while shadowdancing – a swing of a safespear could be followed by a flying block of shadow.

Rumi watched the competition intently. The advanced level was clear, the union between wielder and shadow was more complete than anything the Seedlings had shown. The Seedlings were trained to fight, but the Suli were trained to wage war.

The crowd didn't seem to care much. They never stopped chanting 'Ajanla Erenteyo', even when others won. The Sulis didn't like it. When the tournament was over and it was time to feast, Rumi stole out from the room to find Ahwazi and Sameer.

57

The Petition

RUMI

'The Order will be talking about this for years,' Sameer said from his bed in the botanical ward.

'You must be a madman,' Ahwazi added.

Rumi blinked. 'I don't know what came over me.'

'That's twice now, that you have come to my aid without me asking for it.'

Rumi smiled. 'Softborn clan.'

Sameer's eyes widened as he nodded. 'Softborn clan. Still, I owe you a rescue.'

'How are you feeling?'

'Half my face is one, long continuous bruise,' Sameer said, 'but I'm still pretty.'

'Pretty as a—' Rumi sniffed at the air. 'What is that smell?'

The door flew open and Lungelo stepped in, shadow teeming, his face the very spit of fury. The stench was awesome.

'Godsblood,' Ahwazi said, covering his nose.

'Chief—'

Lungelo moved across the room and seized Rumi's wrist. It all happened at blurring speed. Rumi wrestled with his grip, but he had no hope against a man holding the shadow.

Lungelo pressed into his mind. His efforts to resist it were entirely futile. He tried not to think about it, but it was at the

479

forefront of his mind: running from Lungelo's room; waiting for Sameer to drop the bomb. It only took a few moments for Lungelo to read the memory.

'I knew it! *You* are behind this!'

'Behind what?' came another voice.

Rumi looked past Lungelo to the woman who had spoken.

Zarcanis was outfitted in warrior garb; brown earthen robes that covered her from the bottom of her chin to her fingertips and a helmet in the form of a leopard head. She sniffed the air and scowled at the smell as she stepped forward.

'Behind what?' she repeated, without sparing a glance for Ahwazi and Sameer.

Lungelo narrowed his eyes. 'This rat broke into my room and dropped a ... dangerous contraption in it.'

'A dangerous contraption?'

'This is no concern of yours, Zarcanis.' Lungelo waved his arm dismissively.

'With respect, Chief Lungelo, you are holding the shadow and dragging my Seedling by the wrist. It is of some concern to me.'

'I am taking him to Lord Mandla. He is to be stripped of the Bloods tonight. Conduct unbecoming.'

Zarcanis raised an eyebrow. 'To Lord Mandla, then.'

Lungelo dragged Rumi through the corridor, holding his shadow all the while. Rumi was sure his wrist would snap under the force of Lungelo's grip, but his bones proved resilient. They arrived at Mandla's door and Lungelo knocked. Mandla's bodyguard, Telemi, answered the door. 'What on earth is that smell?'

It was the first time Rumi had heard him speak. Before then, they had only communicated in scowls and smiles. The man's voice turned out to be croaky and hollow. The voice a tree would have, if trees could speak.

Lungelo ignored him. 'We are here to see Lord Mandla.'

'Is he expecting you?'

'Expecting—'

'Let them in, Telemi,' came Mandla's voice from inside.

Telemi grunted and stepped aside. Mandla and the five chiefs were all in the room. Another woman, dressed in a ceremonial iro and buba, sat with a white fly-whisk in hand. Only on closer inspection did Rumi realise who it was. *The princess.*

Every face registered the force of the stench, but they all seemed to dismiss it almost immediately.

'What is it, Chief Lungelo?' said Mandla.

'This boy broke into my room,' Lungelo said, throwing Rumi to the ground.

Mandla's face was impossibly blank. 'Is that why you are holding the shadow in my presence?'

Lungelo scowled and reluctantly released the shadow. Rumi let out a breath as the death grip on his wrist slackened.

'He broke into my room,' said Lungelo.

'Tonight?' Mandla asked.

'No, a few nights back.'

'Did he take something?'

'No.'

'Then how do you know it was him?' asked Zarcanis.

Lungelo made a disgusted noise. 'This is Chief's business.'

Zarcanis was not done. 'My Chiefs,' she said, putting both fists together and touching the ground with both her knees. 'I am sure this is a mistake—'

'It's no mistake!' Lungelo interrupted.

Zarcanis nodded, keeping her face expressionless and letting the moment pass. 'It can be resolved without all this ceremony.

How could a Seedling find his way to a chief's room? It is impossible,' she said.

There was an interval of silence.

'How do you know it was him?' Mandla said.

Lungelo's lips formed a tight line. 'I know.'

Rumi rubbed his wrists. Lungelo did not want them to know he had been mindwalking. That was his chance. Twice, he had run to Lungelo's bait like a rabbit in the slaughterman's garden. He had learned from that. Twice, Lungelo had made him look a fool; now it was time to act the fool himself.

He tapped his chin and stared up to the ceiling like a dullard being asked to recite *Belize's Dialogues*. 'The corridor can be so confusing,' he said, making his voice soft as cotton. 'I barely know my way around.' *That is not entirely a lie.*

The hint of a smile tickled Zarcanis's lips. 'My Chiefs, I think we can all see that there is no way he could have found Chief Lungelo's room.'

Lungelo stared daggers at him, his fists clenched tight as rocks. 'This boy is still a god unto himself! A moment ago he was ready to defy our Lord Mandla openly in the Ghedo. I have never seen such vicious pride, *never*. It grieves me to say that the boy has, on more than one occasion, exhibited conduct unbecoming. He tried to call his shadow on me.'

There were audible gasps.

'Is this true?' Lord Mandla said.

Rumi fumbled for an answer.

'It is true!' Lungelo said. 'That is conduct unbecoming, enough to take him off the Bloods. Why should we honour his conceit?'

There was another interval of silence.

Zarcanis fell to her knees. 'My Chiefs, if I may?'

Mandla nodded.

'The boy is … proud. Dare I say, he is not far from a trouble-maker, but he has something in him. Look at his shoulders; look at how he stands. He is a striver, and that is the great strength of our people. We should be dead and here we are, and here he is. He is fresh blood to tired veins, a reminder of why we are here, and though he may be rough, he is good iron. I swear that on my blood.'

'Well said,' said Gaitan.

'I agree,' said Kwesi.

Zarcanis bowed. 'Your words are rain, my Chiefs. I am—'

'My Chiefs,' Lungelo said, cutting her off, 'there is no doubt the boy is resilient, but I have not forgotten the precepts of our law. The enemy will sow weeds among the wheat. It is my right, on which I now stand, that he should walk through the Arakoro, let his seed be shown.'

Zarcanis turned immediately to Mandla, her expressionless eyes giving way to fear.

'Lord Mandla,' Zarcanis pleaded.

Mandla raised a hand. 'He will walk through the Arakoro. If he comes out at the other side, he will be a Suli.'

Rumi opened his mouth to speak, but Zarcanis squeezed his shoulder.

'My Chiefs, he is still young. Still … fragile. He cannot walk the Arakoro,' she said.

'Some things have to be broken before they can be remade,' Karile said.

She looked at Zarcanis. Something unspoken passed between them.

Zarcanis bowed. 'My Chiefs, I am grateful.'

Her knees touched the ground once more. Rumi bowed and then Zarcanis ferried him out of the room.

When they had made half a dozen turns in the corridor, Zarcanis finally spoke.

'That lizard Lungelo,' she said. 'How dare he make an objection to me.'

'Lungelo hates me.'

'Lungelo doesn't hate you, he just doesn't trust you. You are an outsider. He is not the first man on earth to distrust an outsider.'

Rumi hated Zarcanis every bit as much as he loved her, but there was no one in the world he would rather fight alongside. Seeing her vouch for him in front of the Mandla and the chiefs made him feel like a man on the mountain peak. In that moment, he wanted to be a shadowwielder so much it made his stomach churn.

'You impressed me out there. At the Ghedo,' she said.

Rumi's heart jumped. She had never told him he impressed her, not once.

'All the times we sparred and you were never impressed. What was different this time?'

'Oh, godsblood, no, it was not your shadowdancing that impressed me. That was a terrible performance. Still so impulsive and ill-disciplined; you fight yourself before you fight your opponent.'

Rumi raised an eyebrow. 'What impressed you, then?'

'It was the music. By Dara, the *music*. It was the first time I saw that you understood anything about your life. This whole time, I thought you were consumed by rage and that I could only motivate you by making you angry. I was wrong. You're not angry; you're afraid. Afraid of failure, of success, of looking stupid, not being enough. You hold on to your anger doggedly because you know when it is gone, you will be forced to deal with fear, with pain. But there is hope for you yet. I wanted you to find yourself in the fight. But you are not a fighter; you are a musician.'

Rumi was stunned silent. Zarcanis was the last person Rumi imagined would have any appreciation at all for music. Zarcanis, who had once told him that she put duty before desire, that she had killed more natives than sleeping sickness. A lover of music.

'You... you liked the music?'

'Do not look for your glory in it, boy. I know you play the humble one, but you are always hungry for praise. You won't find it from me.'

Rumi frowned, but kept pace with Zarcanis, winding through the corridor with brisk, bounding strides. She glanced at him, her face expressionless, but in her eyes, there was a twinkling.

'Did I enjoy your music? Yes, but only because it came from understanding. Making music is a journey without a destination; the triumph is not in the ending, but in the playing, in the moment. We are the people of music. Give any swaddling baby in Darosa a drum and you will learn that we are born with it. Dancing visits our spirit from the soft kick-kick of the womb and doesn't leave us until our graves are cold. There is something to that. Dara made us so.'

'What are you trying to say?' Rumi said, trying to keep pace with her.

She turned on him. 'I am saying you have to allow yourself to be who you're supposed to be, fear and all. Cut the strings. No compromises, take off every mask. That is what Dara wants for us, freedom. Freedom from fear, from pain. You think surrender is resignation or failure, but sometimes surrender is freedom. Stop trying to find strength in anger, that's not who you are. You don't need to find the vengeance. Be free again.'

Rumi frowned. 'My mother, my brother, so many others...

they died because of me. *Me*. Vengeance is all that I have. I'll never be free of that. Never.'

She looked at him as though she had never met such a fool, then her face stiffened. 'You have no idea what you can be free from. I asked you once before, after you get your revenge, what next?'

Rumi frowned deeply. 'Then my story is over.'

She blinked and squinted, examining him. 'A musician as talented as you, and you believe your mother sent you here to learn violence?'

Rumi let out a short breath, not meeting her eye.

'You miss her, don't you? Your mother, and your brother?'

She reached out to him. As a reflex, he parried her hand away with *shepherd holds the crook*.

Zarcanis made a disgusted noise. 'Well, let's get on with it then. I hate a predictable story. They will come for you in the hour of crossover. Be ready.'

58

The Arakoro

RUMI

There was a solemn silence when Rumi stepped into his dormitory. The story of the Ghedo was still fresh. Ahwazi and Sameer were still recovering in the botanical wards, so Rumi had only his thoughts for company.

When the crossover hour was upon him, they came; men who moved like panthers stalking game. Had he not been expecting them, they would have grabbed him before he knew they were there. As it was, he caught the faintest hint of movement in the shadows and sat up before they surrounded him.

'Come with us,' said one of the men.

Rumi glanced up at him. He stood at least six feet tall. There were four of them, all wearing veils that covered their noses and mouths, and black cloaks that made them one with the dark. They led him into the corridor and down a dimly lit route that opened at a door with a wood carving of a snarling dog at its centre.

'Take your clothes off,' one of the men said.

'Excuse me?'

'You heard the man,' the tallest one said.

Rumi muttered as he stripped his kaftan away, leaving himself bare as his born day save for the priestess's cowrie necklace.

The tallest man nodded, satisfied, and pulled the door open to reveal a long, straight tunnel with the faintest hint of firelight at the other end. *The Arakoro.*

'All you have to do is walk through the tunnel. Try not to get emotional, the dogs can smell emotion.'

'The dogs?'

'Yes, the dogs,' said a veiled man.

The tallest man drew a matchstick and scratched it to flame. For the barest moment, his reddish-brown eyes were visible in the flickering light. Then he threw the matchstick to the floor.

A long sheet of flame carpeted itself from the door to the other end of the tunnel, illuminating the entire corridor. Rumi blinked. A stone walkway provided a path to the end of the corridor but the hot coals and licks of flame on either side meant he would have to take it one careful step at a time. It was a dangerous thing to have to do, but that was not what made his heart want to break free from his ribcage.

Lined along the walls of the tunnel, standing paw-to-paw, were a hundred or so huge dogs. Their tongues hung from their mouths, teeth fixed in a snarl. Their eyes were a vacant white, with no pupils. Rumi gasped.

'They won't see or hear you, but they can smell strong emotion,' one of the veiled men said.

'And they don't like it very much,' said another man.

Rumi could hear the smile in that last man's voice. Probably another man that was itching to see a softborn fail. *Not me.*

The darkness snapped back at him. *A goat on feast day.*

'Shut up,' Rumi said aloud.

The tall man in black stared at him.

'Sorry ... nervousness.'

He tapped a simple pattern on his thigh and exhaled half the breath from his lungs. He turned his head one way and then the other as though to work out the cricks in his neck.

The dogs were big, muscled creatures, tall as a man and broad to boot. Perhaps, if he was lucky and it came to it, he could kill one of those dogs. Perhaps, with Dara's luck, he could manage two, bare-handed as he was. But three would certainly tear him apart. A hundred or so would have more trouble fighting for his bones than killing him. He swallowed again.

'We don't have all day,' one of the men said.

Rumi glared at him. 'Calm down.'

The tall man agreed. 'Give him time.'

He took in a sharp breath and stepped onto the cool platform. The dogs barely stirred. He calmed himself and took a second step. Nothing. He took a third, then there was a blinding flash of light. He raised his forearm to shield his eyes. When he lowered his arm, Nataré stood before him. She was wearing a beautiful blue silk gown that showed the silhouette of her body in the places the light touched. He smiled at her, then quickly gritted his teeth, trying not to let the joy grow strong.

She smiled back and his joy rose like the tide after a wave. One of the dogs let out a low growl. Rumi patted his thigh, taking a step forward.

He had seen that dress on her before. She looked so ...

He froze. There was someone behind her, a man. The man wrapped his hand around her neck and forced her head back to kiss her. It was Tigrayin. Anger flared up inside Rumi. The dogs growled; some barked.

It couldn't be real; it was a trick on his mind. Tigrayin was *dead*. He forced his anger down like a too-large lump of yam in his throat. With effort, he ripped his eyes away from the scene, walking forward. *It's ... not ... real.*

He put a finger into each ear to drown out the sounds and took a step forward, then another, then another. The sounds ebbed away. He glanced back over his shoulder. They were gone.

Rumi took another step forward and was dazzled again by an explosion of light. A child crawled to his feet. When their eyes met, a smile crept across the child's face. A familiar smile. Instinctively he turned away and kept his eyes fixed on the path. He took one step, then another. He heard a voice behind him. He turned, ever so slightly, then he found himself staring.

'I'm sorry,' Griff said, staring down at the crawling child.

He had a large bag in hand and a massive scabbard fastened to his back. He kissed Morire on the head and faded to mist.

Rumi squirmed as Yami appeared. She lifted Morire into her arms and held him close. Then she sobbed, trembling as she pulled Morire to her stomach.

Rumi felt like his heart would fall to pieces. *Morire and Yami.* He heard the dogs start to growl again. He turned away from them, taking quick, deliberate steps to put distance between himself and the sound of Yami crying. He was close to the end now.

There was a third almighty flash of light. He staggered back. His right hand was singed with hot coal as he stretched it out to stop himself from collapsing outright. The first instinct was to cry out in pain, but he controlled himself, absorbing it. He rose to his feet and came face to face with his mother.

'I have no peace, Rumi. I gave my life for you and it was my worst mistake.'

Rumi's heart sank. One of the dogs howled.

'What was I thinking, dying for you?' she said. 'I warned you not to go to the Golden Room. I warned you.'

Her eyes were like arrows perforating flesh.

'You were never brave. Never strong. You let people die

490

because you can't stand up to anything, to anyone. You are terrified by the battles you can't win.'

Morire emerged at her side, as did Kaat and Ndebe.

The dogs were snarling all around him now. He sank to his knees, the edges of his thighs starting to burn at the touch of hot coals.

'Just kill yourself! That is the least you can do!' his mother screamed. 'End this farce.'

Rumi could feel the hot breath of dogs closing in on him. The darkness had come and he had no answer for it. He retreated to the corners of his mind and barely flinched when the first dog vaulted onto the walkway. He was going to die there. He was so tired. Of himself; his false bravery, his failure after failure.

In an instant, three dogs were upon him, sinking teeth into his neck, arm and ankle. He heard ... a drum. Something stirred in his stomach. A talking drum. It was playing a simple beat, *tap tap tap-tap-tap, tap tap tap-tap-tap.* He knew that chorus.

He opened his eyes. Beyond the dogs, he saw her. Zarcanis, the real Zarcanis. She was ... waiting for him.

With a shout he threw a dog from his body. He was emotional, but he needed it now. The dogs howled all at once as though alive to a sudden threat. Rumi was singing like a drunkard in a beer parlour, tears in his eyes.

'Furae Oloola, arise the never-setting sun!'

He sunk his teeth into one dog, sending it whimpering, then threw a fistful of hot coal onto another. Then he flipped around to wrap his arm around a dog by the neck. The dogs hissed and snarled, considering this new threat. *I'm no goat on feast day.*

They lunged at him all at once. Rumi took off at full pelt. It was the only thing left to do.

Ignoring the scalding heat of coals, Rumi ran like he never had before, fending off chasing dogs and sizzling flame. With a final leap he was out of the tunnel and found his feet on beautiful cool ground. He heard the door close behind him on the raving mad dogs and looked up.

Zarcanis was smiling at him. Mandla was there too, with all the chiefs. He was burned and bleeding, but alive. *Alive.*

'That was a close one,' Zarcanis said.

'We need a botanical,' Karile said, wrapping a grey robe around him. 'I can only imagine what you saw in there. The Arakoro turns your mind against you. Poor child.'

Lungelo looked like a hungry man who had climbed ten flights of stairs to find a stranger eating his breakfast.

'She cheated! The Viper cheated!' Lungelo snapped.

'There is no rule against playing the drums in the Arakoro,' Zarcanis said.

'Lord Mandla...' Lungelo looked to Lord Mandla.

'A Suli... He is a Suli,' Lord Mandla said.

Zarcanis's smile was wide as a bridge. She pulled Rumi to his feet and allowed him to rest his weight on her. As they limped away, she pulled Rumi close. 'Do you see it now? Living is your vengeance; thriving is your defiance.'

He nodded shakily. 'I miss them ... so much. I want to cry ... all the time.'

He shut his eyes, unwilling to let her see the tears fall.

She placed a firm hand on his shoulder and squeezed.

'I know,' Zarcanis said softly. 'It hurts to lose someone you love. You never want to feel that pain again, and so you never want to love again. You think it's strong to leave love behind. But the real strength is loving again.' She lifted his chin up. 'For the pain, there is no lasting shelter. But you can love again. You can't help but to love again. I've seen the way you look at

492

THE DANCE OF SHADOWS

your father. You weren't built to hold a grudge. It's time you stop clenching. Live for them. That's the best we can do. Live for them.'

Zarcanis led Rumi deep into the Eredo. They were not going to the dormitory or to the botanical ward. She moved through the corridor without pause. They came at last to a tall black door.

'Where are we?'

She unlocked the door.

Inside there were two low stools, a prayer mat, a closed cook-pot, and a wash basin, where a loosely-closed water tap made a percussion of the steady drip from its mouth. At the back of the room there was a wall-wide mirror, reflecting everything in the room.

'What are we doing here?' Rumi asked, wincing.

'We are going to find your name.'

His eyebrows shot upwards. 'How?'

'Every endeavour has a physical and spiritual component. Failure often involves the neglect of one,' she said, gesturing to the basin. 'Wash your hands.'

He obliged, gingerly scrubbing his scalded hands and face of dirt.

When he was done, she invited Rumi to sit and took the stool opposite him. There was silence, save for the steady drip of the leaky tap.

'Do you hear that?' Zarcanis said.

'What?' Rumi said. 'The tap?'

'Yes.'

Rumi listened. 'I hear it.'

'So listen to it. Listen to everything. Allow yourself to hear all the sounds that are going on around you. Don't try to recognise the sounds you are hearing, don't label them, just... listen.'

So Rumi listened. He heard the steady drip from the leaky tap, the soft *clink* of the keys in the door as they bristled in the breeze.

'I said don't try to recognise the sounds,' Zarcanis urged. 'Just listen.'

Rumi sighed and closed his eyes to listen again. He heard *bzzzzz* and *toing* and *chipilipilipi*.

'Better,' Zarcanis said. 'Now breathe and listen to your breath.'

Rumi obeyed and grew lightheaded. He heard Zarcanis moving and opened his eyes again. There was a drum in front of him.

'The Way teaches us that names are not given; they are discovered. A name exists even when no one has ever called it,' Zarcanis said. 'It is something inherent to all things that have life. When Dara wants to give life, he speaks a name.'

She put her fingers at the mouth of the leaky wash basin. 'Before men called this water, it had a name. To really know yourself, you must know the name Dara spoke. That is why our naming ceremonies are so important; it is not an effort of imagination, but of investigation. That is why, when men and women are stolen from these shores, they take their names and give them new ones. Like trees ripped from their roots, they steal our power. Your name is inside you, and it is the bridge that connects you to your ancestors. Dara has given you the gift to find it. What is your name?'

Rumi blinked. 'I don't know.'

She pushed the drums towards him. 'Must a name have a sound?'

Rumi pondered the question. 'I suppose it does.'

'But are all sounds names?'

'No,' Rumi said.

'Oh yes they are,' she said, thumping the talking drum. 'Who taught you how to play the drum?'

'My brother.'

'Show me what your brother taught you with this drum and I will tell you your name.'

'What?'

'You once told me that I don't know your pain. So show it to me!'

Rumi stared back at her, confused, then he stared at the drums. He started to play a simple rhythm.

'There is a song within you that is playing all the time. The secret of our way is to listen and not to scream. Don't play something you know,' Zarcanis snapped. 'Play something that knows you.'

What the hell is that supposed to mean?

'Just tell me what you want me to do!'

'Play!'

He scratched angrily at his forearm and licked the blood. Shadows teemed from his pores. He beat the drum in four places and scattered it with slaps, Morire's way. Zarcanis nodded, as though the music was telling her something.

The memory of Morire playing stirred something within, shook him from the inside out, made his lips curl back.

The time came when Rumi was playing liberated from notes, fingerbeats of pure impulse. *Play something that knows you.* He understood it; the music fell into all the cracks and crevices in his bones like water, opening corners of his being that he had always known but had never examined. His shadow coated him like billowing smoke, flaring with each beat of the drum, covering his hands with speed unimaginable and power beyond comprehension. He urged the drum to tell him more, pouring everything into his fingers. He heard a sound like the earth clearing its throat in his head and the name flashed in his mind like a thunderclap. The drum dropped and the sound of shattering glass filled the air.

Zarcanis let out a shuddering breath and her mouth widened to a radiant smile as his shadow returned to its normal shape, moving like thick batter poured in a baking mould. He heard his shadow speak; its voice was hoarse, like a man starved of water in a hot place, but unmistakable. Rumi's forehead was beaded with sweat and his mouth was wide open. The mirror in front of him had large spider-web cracks all over it.

'What just happened?' Rumi said.

'You … you spoke your name.'

'That cannot be my name,' he said.

'It is … It must be,' she said, tracing her hands over the cracks in the mirror.

'What … what does it mean?'

'I don't know.'

'Who would believe me if I said my name was Rumi Xango?'

'Don't say it out loud!' Zarcanis snapped.

She quickly revealed a kola nut and broke it.

'Even I should not be tempted with such a name. Tell no one, Rumi.' She offered him half the kola nut and they both hastily ate.

'What does it mean?'

'Think, boy, think. Why do you think your mother went through all that trouble of keeping your name from you, from your father, from herself?'

'What does it mean?'

'Think!' she said again. 'That is a name from a time when gods walked amongst men. Think!'

'Godsblood!' Rumi shouted.

Zarcanis laughed.

'Godsblood indeed.'

'This isn't funny, Zarcanis.'

'In some sweet way, everything is funny.' She rose to her feet and took Rumi by the forearm, adding tattooed lines as she spoke. 'I was wrong about you. Your story isn't predictable after all. And I for one am dying to see the twist.'

59

From Thin Air

FALINA

The Eredo was too warm. Falina rose to her feet, letting the silk sheets fall from her nightdress. There would be guards at her door, of that she was sure, but she needed to walk, to move.

She walked out and sure enough, there were two guards. She was surprised to find Alangba was one of them.

He dropped to one knee and bowed his head. 'Omoba.'

The second guard lay flat on the floor as through trying to sleep.

She pulled Alangba to his feet.

'I want to go outside. For fresh air.'

The second guard frowned at that, but Alangba's expression did not change.

'I will escort you, Omoba,' he said.

Falina nodded and let Alangba lead the way into the corridor. They followed a series of twists and turns in the pathway before they came to a looming stone staircase.

Falina glanced up, then at Alangba.

'You said you wanted to go outside,' Alangba said. 'This is the Eredo's back door. The Thatcher. It's safe up there.'

She grimaced, then made the first step. About halfway up, she needed Alangba to pull her forward with each step. Her nightclothes were damp with sweat by the time they reached the top.

The guard at the top of the stairs gave Alangba a quick look, then studied her. He dropped to a knee.

'Omoba,' he said, opening the door for them to walk past.

Everyone seemed to know who she was. The moon's brightness made her squint as they stepped out into the open plain. A long, flat, expanse of fields dotted with trees, dogs, and men with crossbows.

She looked back at Alangba. The light made him look... handsome, in a way; the way a panther can be handsome in the right light. He never looked at her the way men sometimes did, though; the way Maka did. Not once did he look at her bottom. But he seemed to give her a high appraisal. The times when he did look her way, there was reverence in his eyes. He saw her as a princess, truly, and treated her as such. There was something to admire in that. A man of duty through and through.

They were all men of duty, even Maka. They believed to the very core of their being in a better tomorrow. She had once thought it foolish. Now, somehow, she was beginning to see it as wisdom. They were free from the pull of the past because they were able to look forward.

'The moon is beautiful tonight,' she said, staring at the sky.

'Indeed it is, Omoba. The world is always beautiful when it is still.'

They walked around for a while, touched by the running breeze.

'Have you ever... been in love, Alangba?'

He froze. 'I have ... once.'

'What was it like?'

He stared into her eyes. 'Like suffering and happiness were things that I could share.'

An eloquent man. As rough as a lizard, but as elegant as a Shinala.

'Strange,' Alangba said, stopping abruptly.

Falina glanced around.

'What?'

'There should be more dogs around.'

Almost as a response there was a lion's roar, followed by a woman's gasp, then a barrage of dogs barking in the distance. Alangba's eyes darted like arrows. His face was hard again, like a panther, ready to pounce.

'Stay here, Omoba,' he said, raising his hand.

He darted after the sounds. She gave chase as best as she could. In ten breaths he was wrestling amongst the lion and dogs.

A moment later, a woman materialised from thin air.

'Get off me!' the woman screamed. 'Don't touch me!'

'What are you doing Kayalli?' Alangba snapped. 'Where on earth did you find a ghost stone?'

'It was given to me,' the woman said, glaring at Alangba.

'We need to throw this far away, into the river! Now, quickly, before—'

Alangba froze. A sharp, throaty hissing sound filled the air, and a large mass of black swept across the moon's face.

'Godsblood,' Alangba whispered, looking up.

The woman stared up too, her face a picture of horror.

The lion let out a thunderous roar that made Falina's blood flare from her neck to her fingertips. Alangba threw the woman to the side and pulled his blade free of its scabbard.

'Sentries! To me!'

60

Three Blasts of the Horn

RUMI

Rumi stretched his arms apart as the tailor ran tape across his wingspan.

'Don't start acting better than us because you're a Suli now,' Ahwazi said.

'He already thinks he's better than us,' Sameer said.

Rumi smiled. 'Kneel before you speak to me, Seedlings! I have six lines.'

'This hurts more than Yomiku's punches,' Sameer said, rubbing the long, unseemly scar on his face.

Rumi dropped his arm as the tailor fastened the tape rope around his waist, noting a measurement with a mark on his forearm.

Rumi raised an eyebrow. 'You'll be a Suli soon enough, Sameer. You're smart.'

'What about me?' Ahwazi said.

'Well... there's no rush to be a Suli anyway.'

'Godsblood, I'll be a Seedling forever!' Ahwazi said, his face in his hands. 'I can't imagine watching you *both* make Suli before me.'

'They need Sulis to polish sandals too,' Sameer said.

The tailor coughed back a laugh.

It felt like years ago to Rumi, thinking back to when they had all met outside the smithy.

'Will we still meet at the dining hall?' Rumi said.

'Of course,' Ahwazi said. 'Softborn clan.'

'Softborn clan,' Sameer said.

'Always,' Rumi said.

The tailor completed his work and left.

There was a moment of uncomfortable silence as Rumi turned to Ahwazi and Sameer and fumbled for words to say. He opened his mouth to speak and Ahwazi cut him off.

'Just go. Don't make it all *dramatic*. We'll catch you around, Suli Rumi.'

Rumi closed his mouth, then he smiled.

'I'll catch you around, Seedlings.'

He touched his heart and pointed to the sky. Sameer and Ahwazi returned the gesture. There was a time, not long ago, he'd have been happy to see them gone. But as he turned to leave, his mind impressed upon him his mother's words. *When the music plays . . .*

He darted for Sameer and Ahwazi and pulled them into an embrace. Ahwazi was slow to respond, but Sameer pulled the three of them close at the centre.

'Take care of yourselves,' Rumi whispered.

'You too,' Ahwazi said.

They held the embrace for a moment longer and then broke apart.

'I'll be—'

The crashing sound of the horn broke all silence and speech. One blast. Then another. Then a third. *An attack.*

61

To the Thatcher

RUMI

Rumi, Sameer and Ahwazi barrelled into the corridor. It was utter bedlam. People ran both ways down the corridor with no discernible sense of where the danger might be.

Rumi called his shadow and it obeyed. Power like never before flooded through him. What he had felt of the shadow before was a whisper; this was a roar.

He led them at a run into the corridor. They had barely made two turns when they saw Zarcanis and Yomiku running towards them. She was in a high-necked armoured vest, Yomiku fully armoured with a lion's head helmet snapped shut. Neither of them had called their shadows.

'Suit up and get to the Thatcher. We're under attack,' Zarcanis said, barely slowing her run.

They deviated their run to the armoury. Gaitan rushed past in full armour with a gleaming shadowsteel axe in his hand.

'All shadowdancers to the Thatcher!' he shouted. 'Everyone else to the bottom of the Eredo.'

Rumi ran to his leather armour and dog's head helmet and snapped it shut. The shadow made everything move faster. He fastened his ironwire vest, snatched up his halberd and moved.

Sameer quickly donned his owl-head helmet and Ahwazi grabbed a snarling leopard.

Sameer darted in front, leading them to the stone staircase. The ones called to fight were moving in the same direction, while the others were moving to the lower levels of the Eredo. Rumi's heart was pounding. The Thatcher; Nataré would be there.

He doubled his speed, racing ahead of Ahwazi towards the stairs of stone. The cowrie sizzled at his neck as he scattered the distance with leaps, flinging himself towards the door. Ahwazi called his own shadow, scattered smoky black giving him the power to match Rumi's stride.

The door was open at the top. They came out into a scene from a scare story.

A horde of manacled creatures that looked more beast than man were trying to batter down the Thatcher gates with a thick yellow tree trunk. Rumi winced. *An army of Obair.*

The gate shivered with each thump. It would not hold long.

In the sky, vultures flew at breakneck speed, colliding with eagles and crashing to the ground in bloody heaps. Zarcanis's voice rang out across the plain.

'Shadowdancers! To me!'

Rumi followed her voice and darted to the mass of people set to reinforce the men at the gate. Zarcanis still had not called her shadow. Beside her stood Lord Mandla, holding his wooden staff. Telemi loomed behind him like a tree. All the chiefs were there in full armour shadow, except Chief Karile.

Lord Mandla stepped forward. 'Shadowdancers! How do we make tomorrow come?'

A hundred voices answered as one. 'We build it today!'

'So pick up your bricks and wet your mortar. Tonight we fight for tomorrow. Never before have enemies stormed our gates; our existence and survival is a marvel, a miracle, but every one of us has been preparing for a day such as this. A day when we can fight with the spirit of our martyrs, our ancestors who chose freedom over subordination. Tonight, again, we choose freedom and if anyone means to take it from us, he will have to fight until no man, woman or child with ink on his neck still breathes! I ask again, how do we make tomorrow come?'

'We build it today!'

Zarcanis stepped forward. 'We fight in threes, like this,' she said, drawing a triangle in the air. 'No triangle should have more than one Seedling. We stay compact and disciplined, using our weapons and our wits. Death is a small price to pay for keeping the Eredo alive. But no one dies cheaply today! If we keep our discipline, we will overwhelm them. Remember, they have nothing to fight for, and you have everything! In a moment, they will break our gates down. We will let them advance to the front of the plain and then let the spears sing. Our sentries will attack from the sides and our Chainbreakers will close in at the rear. Lord Mandla, the reserve is yours. When a weakness opens, strike hard. Sulis and Truetrees, you know the formations. Seedlings, today you learn fast.'

A thunderous sound filled the air as the gates took another thump.

'Ajanla! Kubani! With me!'

Zarcanis called her shadow and pulled Silence from its scabbard.

Yomiku joined her on the left. The massive weapon he called *Sword Baba* was slung across his shoulders. Rumi moved to complete the triangle on the right. Zarcanis snapped her helmet shut, and the echo of other metallic helmets doing the same rang out across the Thatcher.

Rumi raised his halberd slightly. He felt the otherworldly surge and swell of his shadow unleashed.

Yomiku leaned in close. 'Ajanla, know this. I know we've had our disagreements, but in battle there is neither old blood nor softborn. I will guard your side with my life and expect the same of you.'

Rumi was pleasantly taken aback. He touched his heart and pointed to the sky. 'On my blood.'

Yomiku nodded. 'It was never personal, by the way, between you and I. When this is done, I will teach you a thing or two about how to improve your conjuring.'

'If we are still standing when this is done,' Rumi said.

'We will be standing, Ajanla. We have the Viper.'

A final crash shattered a hole in the gate. An ink-black horde of Obair burst through, flooding the plain like locusts.

'Shege,' breathed Yomiku.

There were too many of them. Surely they could not win this fight. *Surely.*

Even holding the shadow, Rumi found the halberd shaking in his trembling grip. He remembered the last time he had seen an Obair. He had pissed himself that night. Somewhere, deep beneath the shadow, he was more afraid now than he had been then.

He felt himself take a step backwards. He glanced back over his shoulder to the Eredo. There were a great many places to hide in the Eredo.

Zarcanis stepped forward. Her eyes were cold, focused. She raised Silence high. 'We charge on my count!' she screamed.

Rumi swallowed.

'We fight?' asked Yomiku.

Zarcanis didn't look at him, her eyes fixed on the Obair. 'We always fight.'

Yomiku nodded and turned to Rumi, a fat smile spreading across his lips. 'I bet your heart is pumping now, Ajanla.'

Rumi tightened his grip on the halberd to steady himself.

Yomiku put an arm on his shoulder and locked eyes. 'When you have been looking over your shoulder enough, it is a relief to finally face your enemy. You're afraid. Don't run from it; embrace it. We're all afraid, but we're afraid together. Fight back, like you fought me.'

'One!' Zarcanis yelled.

Rumi's heart threatened to pierce through his chest. His breathing came fast and shallow.

'Two!'

The Obair thundered into the plain in their hundreds. He gripped the halberd like it was life itself. *This is it.*

'Go!'

Zarcanis moved like a wolf to its kill, leading the charge.

Yomiku roared something Rumi could not understand, loud and visceral. Rumi found himself shouting too. They were all shouting, all running like hell into the teeth of an unimaginable enemy.

62

Twenty Obair

ALANGBA

Blood streamed from the wound at Alangba's shoulder. Ijere had already torn three Obair apart. Okafor was low on his haunches, bellowing directions and putting together a strategy. That was why he was First Ranger; he knew how to lead. A better strategist than any, whether in a battle, a siege or a bar fight. Maka was getting stuck into the mud too, his ida sword dancing in the darkness. No Music would be at the centre of it, delighted, no doubt, at a chance to let completely loose. Alangba glanced at the princess.

'Omoba, we must get you to lower ground. Take you back inside.'

'How?'

Alangba studied the Thatcher. The door was near five hundred feet away, and across that distance, there were near five hundred Obair at the least. Even at a run, they would have to see at least twenty. *Twenty Obair . . . can I cut a path through twenty Obair? I will have to.*

'I will cut a path through, Omoba.'

Princess Falina stared at him incredulously.

'Through that?'

'Through that,' he whispered. 'Behind me, Omoba. We move!'

He darted forward with an upraised ida sword. His sword danced with the first Obair to confront him. The Obair had a double-axe that he swung with reckless verve. Huge legs, incredible power. *Twenty of them ... at least.*

His ida sunk into the Obair's stomach.

The princess muffled a scream as the Obair slunk to the floor, lifeless. *Twenty ... at least.*

He moved forward at a run and caught another by surprise, his sword perforating upwards from the lower back until it touched bone. Hot blood splattered his forehead. *Two.*

He crept forward and two Obair tore a sentry apart in front of him in a bloody tug-o-war. The princess gagged. The Obair turned towards them and Alangba raised his sword.

A dancing man cloaked in shadow moved at blurring speed. With his first swipe, the shadowdancer severed an Obair hand at the wrist; with the second he separated a leg from its body. Alangba finished the work with a point-first stab into the stomach of the one-handed Obair. The shadowdancer cut through the other Obair's second leg.

The shadowdancer turned to him. 'Move!'

It was Ladan, painted red with blood, his eyes cold and focused. *Four.*

Ladan danced among the Obair like a swirling wind, leaving blood and bone in his wake. Alangba tidied up and did his bit to protect Princess Falina. Watching Ladan, coupled with the heat of battle, made his blood race inside. The beauty of shadowdancing. They were gods of war, and Ladan was only a few years a Suli. *Give Okafor ten thousand shadowwielders and they will bring back any prize on earth.*

The tenth Obair fell and they were less than halfway to the door. Perhaps twenty wouldn't do it.

Almost as though to put paid to his estimation, six Obair rushed them at once. Gaitan, a bull of a man, moved in a stampede of shadow, lowering the number to four. Alangba's sword clashed with an Obair's crude blade. The power as the Obair imposed his weight was incredible. He ducked under the blade to offset the Obair's balance. *Even the strongest tower has a back door.* With a deft slide between thick legs, he was behind the Obair and sliced him at the heel.

The Obair screamed. It did not sound like a monster; it sounded like a man. Alangba didn't let his mind think of it as he stabbed the thing in the back.

It turned on him. A resilient creature. It swung its blade, searing Alangba on the side of his thigh. He staggered back as the Obair moved again, suddenly twice as fast.

There was a quiver in the bond as Ijere leaped from behind him. With a single bite, Ijere ripped the Obair's throat out.

Alangba breathed out in exasperated relief and climbed to his feet. With Ijere at his side, they ran several paces forward. Ijere brought another Obair down and the door came into view not far ahead. Ladan was finishing a kill when a marauding Obair approached him from the rear – Alangba darted forward, bringing his sword to clash Obair steel. The blow knocked him off his feet and sent his sword flying.

'Run, Omoba!' he said as the Obair raised a blade to end him.

The Obair brought its blade down. Ladan moved to catch the blow at the elbow. Alangba winced as the Obair severed Ladan's arm.

Alangba moved first, driving his security knife deep into the Obair's chest. Letting the corpse slide off, he turned to Ladan.

He was sprawled out on the floor, coughing blood. His right arm ended in a bloody stump.

'I'm taking you inside,' he said, lifting Ladan onto his shoulders.

'If I die tonight,' Ladan croaked, 'I want you to know…You were always worth the risk. Every time. When we were on that ship, hearing you breathe … it kept me alive.'

Alangba's eyelids twitched. 'You won't die here, or anywhere. Not tonight.'

He glanced at the princess, then at Ijere. He raised his sword.

63

Lights Out

RENIKE

A loud boom sounded outside as Toshane screamed. Renike paced around the room. N'Goné had not returned.

'What was that?'

Renike stared at the door. 'I don't know.'

The sound came again. Like the blast of a cannon at close range. Tears welled up in Toshane's eyes.

'Don't worry, she'll be back soon,' Renike said, massaging Toshane's neck.

Abruptly the door flew open. N'Goné stood in the doorway, breathing heavily.

'Everyone is up at the Thatcher fighting.'

Renike locked eyes with N'Goné and nodded. N'Goné reached under the bed and pulled out three stone knives.

Toshane looked at the knife like it could bite. Only a moment passed before she accepted it in trembling hands. Renike gripped her knife firm, the way Baba had taught her.

'Quick, we have to get to lower ground!'

They sprinted into the corridor.

'I suspect someone opened the front door of the Eredo too,' N'Goné said, breathing heavily.

'Why would anyone do that?' Toshane asked.

Weeds among the wheat.

They rounded another corner and heard the low dying whimper of a dog.

They froze.

There was a huge dark figure ahead in the corridor. The lanterns beyond had been put out.

'What is that?' Toshane screamed, backing away.

Renike lifted her knife and narrowed her eyes. 'Who's there?'

There was no response, just the sound of metal dragging on the floor.

N'Goné stepped forward, watching the figure move in the darkness. Renike's heart hammered her chest.

They could run back the way they came, but whatever it was in the dark could pick them off in the corridor. *Better to face it all at once, together.*

She gritted her teeth, trying to wear a brave face. It was unspoken but acknowledged that though N'Goné was the strongest, Renike would be the one to hold their group together. The one to lead.

Renike looked to N'Goné. 'Dara is with us; He is always with us.'

N'Goné nodded.

The figure inched closer in the darkness.

'Whatever that thing is, we will stop it. Then we close the Eredo door.'

N'Goné nodded and crouched low. Her tongue lolled from the side of her mouth as they waited with heavy breaths for the monster to reveal itself.

'Are you with us, Toshane?'

Toshane wiped the tears from her cheek and nodded, firming her grip on the stone knife.

The figure stepped into the flickering light from the lantern on the wall.

It was a bald, tar-black man whose eyes had no pupils, carrying a long, jagged sword.

Toshane gasped, but did not scream or run away. She would not leave N'Goné to die.

Only N'Goné seemed ready, teeth gritted, veins marbling her fist tight around the stone knife.

The man emerged fully into the light. It was not a man at all – it was a monster, with legs thick as trees.

Renike pointed her knife at its chest. 'What are you?' she demanded.

The monster's lips curled into a wide, mirthless smile. Then it blew out the fire in the lantern and the corridor went dark.

64

The Vulture's Banquet

RUMI

Rumi, Yomiku and Zarcanis darted into the fighting. Almost immediately, an Obair with a long, curved sword tried to take Rumi's head off. He smashed the sword back with such force that the Obair's balance was lost. With a second swing, his halberd crashed down atop the Obair's skull with a wet crack. Blood splashed his face as he wrenched his axeblade free.

'Good kill,' he heard Yomiku say as he gored an Obair of his own.

There were hordes of them, but Zarcanis was right; they lacked discipline. Zarcanis herself was something else – at the sharp point of their triangle of death she wasted no swipe of her blade. Silence, she called it. The name was apt; with the blade she brought battle cries and war-shouts to an end. She was a blur of violence. A master artist, calm as you like, painting a masterpiece of death. As indifferent to the bath of blood as the slaughterman earning his pay. She was the beacon, the well from which they all drew the courage to fight.

Rumi thrust his halberd spike up into an Obair's throat, then spun to smash the axeblade deep into another's chest. One used a spear to parry his halberd aside and Rumi's reflex was instant, using the halberd's hook to tear the Obair's calf out. The Obair dropped to a knee and Rumi's downward strike sank down into the flesh between neck and shoulder.

The dying Obair screamed, grabbing at its neck as though to push the blood back in.

Rumi's Shadow reared him on, enjoying the spill of blood. The power surged as he took a step forward and thrust his spike again.

'Do not break the triangle!' Zarcanis cried as she sent Silence halfway to its hilt through an Obair head and shot a gorgeous spear of conjured shadow through another's eye socket. 'We need to cut through their ranks. Whoever brought them here will be at the centre.'

An Obair charged. Rumi smashed his axeblade through its chest, breaking the sternum with an overhand chop.

He shifted backwards and found himself back-to-back with Yomiku, pressed on either side by the enemy.

Yomiku's voice rose like a wave over the battle noise. 'How many have you killed?'

Rumi kicked an Obair back and brought his axe head down on it. That brought his tally to eleven.

'I'm not keeping count,' he lied.

Yomiku laughed as he spun around a battle axe and skewered the wielder like festival meat. 'You are a poor liar, Ajanla.'

'How many do you have?'

Yomiku dodged a blow. 'Ten more than you. Catch up.'

Rumi grinned as he drew on the shadow, filling himself with retaliatory bile.

In just a few moments, corpses lay prostrate at his feet. He made no effort to kick them aside. The sick sound of blade puncturing flesh no longer made him wince. The air was full of the sharp clang of steel and the dull thud of iron thumping flesh.

Their triangle moved deeper into the melee, towards the

centre. The Obair started to come two at a time. Rumi had to shorten his grip for close combat. A charging Obair glanced a crude sword across Rumi's side, leaving his hip wet with blood. It paid dearly for that.

Yomiku was taking hits too. He groaned with each swing of his blade. Twice Yomiku saved Rumi from certain death by closing the triangle and killing an Obair.

'Careful,' Yomiku breathed, as he came up like a ghost to save his life a third time.

They bit into the heart of the Obair mass. Rumi was thrumming to the beat of blood thrill. He couldn't tell if he was crying, but he'd never felt so vital. Strange how being so close to death made him so much more alive. Nothing mattered but the two either side of him.

At the point where the fighting was thickest, he spotted a man and woman approached by half a dozen Obair. He squinted, trying to make them out. Then his heart stopped: it was Nataré.

No Music was at her side. He looked like he had taken a bath in ten pints of blood and they were woefully outnumbered.

'We are close to the centre. Don't break the triangle!' Zarcanis shouted.

The Obair closed in on Nataré and No Music. Rumi's mind flashed back to the Nyme. To Nataré loosing arrows into a horde of vultures, riding towards him.

'Rumi!' Zarcanis screamed. 'Do not break the triangle!'

He was moving, away from the triangle, towards Nataré. With a downward swing, his halberd bit down into an Obair skull. Before the other could whirl on him, he sent it to the Hellmouth with a reverse blow. The third took several steps back as Rumi put a foot in front of Nataré, blocking its path to her. The Obair seemed to nod in salute and fled.

Rumi pulled Nataré to her feet. She had taken bruises and scrapes, but nothing she wouldn't come back from. Their eyes met for the merest moment, then the Obair started to come in masses.

No Music tilted his neck one way and then the other, and started to kill. Rumi swung wildly. He missed more than he hit, but the sheer numbers made his kills unimportant. He drew down on the shadow. Every thrust of his halberd brought death. Nataré was letting the spear sing too. A bloody ballad at that. The Obair kept coming. Wave after wave of them. Rumi found himself pinned on both sides by Obair fighting desperately to keep them at bay. A third strode towards him, weapon raised. It was too much. They could not fight their way out of this. At the corner of his vision he saw a small ball of shadow fly through the air. It struck the ground and there was an almighty flash.

The Obair roared, disoriented by the sudden illumination. A figure appeared a few metres away. Small and thin with an owl-head helmet.

'Move now,' Sameer shouted, leaking shadow.

Rumi grabbed Nataré by the arm. They were running before the Obair could regroup, slashing and stabbing as they did. No Music stayed where the fighting was thickest, taking on all comers.

Rumi cut a path back to Zarcanis and Yomiku.

As he closed in, an Obair slipped inside Yomiku's guard. Before he could shout, the Obair drove a spear through Yomiku's back and out through his chest.

Rumi's heart dropped.

Yomiku fell to his knees and looked back over his shoulder. First at the Obair that had killed him, then directly at Rumi.

With a spear protruding from his chest, Yomiku pulled the Obair into an embrace, skewering him dead.

'I never yield,' he screamed, and with a final outpouring of rage six spikes of conjured shadow exploded from his body, killing Obair as he collapsed.

Rumi froze, eyes fixed on Yomiku's lifeless body. His halberd fell from his hand. All he could hear was the thump of his own heart.

Zarcanis rattled his jaw with an open palmed slap.

'This isn't the time!' she shouted.

Rumi snapped back into killing.

Griff joined the melee with a massive greatsword, cutting Obair in half. Another seasoned merchant in the business of blood.

Rumi glanced back to Yomiku dead on the floor, a spear haft protruding from his chest. *Yomiku.*

'Every decision has a cost! Form new triangles!' Zarcanis screamed.

Rumi reined in his shadow, taking a position between Griff and Nataré. He kept glancing at Yomiku, the spear sticking out from his chest, hoping he would get up.

'Focus!' Zarcanis shouted through heavy breaths. 'Forward!'

She pressed forward like a farmer in the field at harvest, her blade a deathly scythe.

Blood and sweat washed Rumi's body and the horde thinned out. They were at the centre.

The sound of a drum erupted from somewhere amongst the Obair. They formed a circle around Rumi and his companions.

The priestess's cowrie burned.

'What are they doing?' Rumi asked.

Zarcanis's eyes widened and she stared back at the Eredo.

'They weren't trying to get in. They were trying to bring us out.'

There was a ripple in the Obair crowd. The monsters shuffled to form a pathway.

A man clad in all white appeared. He moved at a glide, feet seeming not to touch the ground. Hearing his voice made Rumi's stomach shift.

'The fugitive from death. I knew that ghost stone would lead me to you,' he said, stepping forward. 'Today I will end the iniquity of your bloodline. I will not fail a third time.'

Ghost Stone? He glanced at Nataré as his shadow surged within him.

'Shege,' Griff said. 'Godsblood. Dara's bloody blood, save us.'

They all backed away as he approached, except Zarcanis. She stood her ground.

The Priest of Vultures stopped, arms clasped at the navel. 'You come with friends,' he said, smiling. 'It is not too late for you all. Will you kneel? Will you serve the Son? Or will it be a banquet for the vultures?'

'Damn the Son,' Zarcanis said, stepping forward. Her hand moved to her neck. She ripped her armoured collar down to reveal a brilliant silver necklace with a blue jewel at its centre.

Rumi squinted, looking over the necklace, then his eyes bulged. It was an Odeshi. *The quartercuff.*

He gasped. *How can she stand with it? Godsblood, how can she fight with it? How strong is her shadow?*

'When I remove this, the rest of you run. The battle is over.'

Rumi stepped forward. 'I—'

'Listen to me! Griff, lead everyone back into the Thatcher. Leave no living person behind.'

'I won't leave you—'

She flashed a gauntleted hand through Rumi's cheek, making his head jerk back.

'You will. Now!'

'You don't have to do this, Zaiyana,' Griff said.

She looked back at him, eyes wet with tears.

'I do.'

With that, she ripped the Odeshi from her neck. An explosion of black sent everyone flying.

The circle of Obair scattered. The Priest of Vultures, the only one not thrown back by the explosion, walked forward. 'And the Son shall cast them down, erase their names, their seed in the land.'

He reached for the skies and a shrieking sound filled the air. Rumi stared up. A huge black beast pierced through cloud, dominating the sky. Its shadow darkened the battlefield.

Rumi squinted. A massive, winged lizard. It shrieked and a column of fire bathed the sky in yellow-red. *A kongamato.*

'Run!' Zarcanis screamed, blood streaming from her nose. 'Run!'

Zarcanis's eyes were the red of a live flame. Her hair danced around her shoulders, animated life in each strand. Her shadow was no longer a flowing cape but a raging monster. A three-headed lion, ten feet tall, with eyes of flame scattering all the Obair in its wake.

'Retreat!' Griff shouted. 'Shadowdancers! Sentries! Rangers! Fall back!'

The kongamato swooped down and snatched a fleeing shadowdancer in its beak, belching a cloud of fire down when the man was consumed.

A voice rose over the madness. 'I am the knife edge!'

Rumi glanced back. Nataré, sword in hand, was running towards the Priest of Vultures.

He sprinted after her, catching her by the arm. 'What are you doing?'

She didn't meet his eyes. 'This is my mistake. I will pay for it.'

Her words hit Rumi like arrows in his chest. He looked over the Thatcher. It was carpeted with corpses. Enough dead Obair and shadowdancers to step across the field without treading ground. His feet squelched in blood-wet soil as balls of fire exploded on the ground.

The kongamato illuminated the sky with clouds of fire, snatching life as it swooped down. Brave sentries aimed bows at the creature, undeterred by the screams of their dying comrades.

A circle of space had cleared around Zarcanis and the Priest of Vultures. A fighting pit. She raised a hand and her shadow morphed to form a perfect armour around her. Her sword slowly turned obsidian-black as she stretched. The Priest of Vultures summoned his grey-white sword and beckoned her forward. They were going to dance.

He forced himself to look away.

Rumi pulled Nataré close, leaned in and trapped her eyes with his. 'We've all made mistakes, terrible mistakes. But we have to answer the same question. Will we be defined by our scars … or by our healing?' Tears filled her eyes. 'Today, we have to listen to Zarcanis. We have to run.'

They darted towards the Thatcher door. Hordes of people hustled to get inside. Zarcanis screamed behind them.

He's killing her.

Griff sat astride a Shinala, waving people inside. His face was a picture of solemnity. They were leaving Zarcanis to die.

Rumi caught sight of Strogus among the crowd, his fingers forming a crossroads as he watched the carnage.

Rumi glanced at Nataré, then at Strogus, and nodded towards him.

He drew in a deep breath. 'I won't let her die. Not again; not like Yami. And I won't let you die either.'

Nataré shook her head.

'Strogus, make sure she gets inside.'

Strogus took Nataré by the shoulders. She flailed in his grip and reached for Rumi, but Strogus's grip was final as the grave.

'If I don't return,' said Rumi, 'tell Renike I didn't leave her. Tell her ... Tell her the old dog never dies.'

Tears bubbled in Nataré's eyes. 'Rumi ...'

He swivelled into a run.

A horse, I need a horse. He scanned the battlefield and spotted a stray unbridled Shinala. He ran for it, a thick rope of shadow forming in his hand as he sped. The Shinala bucked and whinnied like a crazed bull as he climbed onto its back, but he subdued it with the rope and kicked it into a gallop.

Rumi gritted his teeth. *No one will pay for my life with their blood again. No one.*

As he rode out, he heard a second set of hoofbeats in pursuit.

'What are you doing?' Griff shouted. 'He will kill everything.'

'I won't run away. I won't abandon Zarcanis to die. He's the one — the one who took Yami.'

Griff rode on without saying a word for a moment. His countenance fell apart for the blinking of an eye and then he drew in a long breath. He raised his chin and was master of himself once more. 'I am with you,' he said, snapping his helmet shut.

It hit Rumi like a fist. He knew his name now. It meant he knew Griff's name. His shadow scoffed, but he pushed it back. There comes a time to set things aside.

'I know our name.'

'What?' Griff shouted, flipping his helmet up.

'I know our name!'

Griff's eyes bulged, his dark face wet with sweat. 'Do you ... want to tell me?'

The screams of death seemed to lull for a small moment.

'Xango,' Rumi said.

Griff's eyes narrowed, then closed. His lips quivered. His knuckles were trembling around the grip on his reins. Then a smile formed on Griff's lips. He nodded to Rumi and snapped his helmet shut once more.

The shadow exploded from him, like a great beast freed from an eternal cage.

Rumi brought his hand up to shield his eyes. When his perspective returned, Griff had his sword raised high, streaming shadow. He roared and the thud of his voice was loud enough to startle the dead.

'We ride!'

They charged forward together. Barrelling towards the heart of the fight.

The Priest of Vultures slashed at Zarcanis's shadow, his grey-white blade cutting it to strips. Rumi kicked faster.

Something whizzed through the air and the Shinala screamed. Blood splattered from its legs as it somersaulted. Rumi was flung from its back through the air.

He landed with a heavy thump. He looked up to see a flood of Obair approach him, led by a tall, lean Odu man with an iron ball in his left eye socket. *Sabachi.*

He reached out for his halberd and tried to stand. His body reproached him, pain slapping every bone as he fell back down. He gritted his teeth. *I won't die on my back.*

He forced himself to his feet and immediately threw out his halberd to stop a slash from a swinging Obair. Then Griff was at his side, going blade to blade with another, showing all the poise that made him a thing of legend. The Obair moved to Griff, ignoring Rumi.

Sabachi locked eyes with Rumi and started to move. Rumi's heart thumped. Every step was an exercise in agony. He swung his halberd and Sabachi parried it easily, nearly knocking him from his feet.

Sabachi smiled like a child told he could play. He stepped forward into a strike and pierced Rumi's armour at the shoulder. Rumi dropped to a knee. Blood trickled down his leg. He bit down on his tongue hard. *I am no festival goat.* He gripped the reins of the last vestiges of strength and surged forward again.

Sabachi was too fast; he smashed Rumi's jaw with a bare fist that sent his helmet flying off. Rumi spat out a tooth and blood and swung his halberd again. Sabachi swiped the axe head aside and floored Rumi with a kick to the chest.

'My Master will have his name,' Sabachi said, raising his sword. 'Madioha is not here to save you now.'

Rumi looked up. Blood in his eye blurred his vision. Pain shot through his body in waves. This was it. The fire-red skies seemed a foretelling of what awaited him in eternity. He had not even reached Zarcanis. He gritted his teeth and moved to stand. *I won't die on my back.*

Sabachi shoved him back down with his heel and loomed over him, sword raised. The priestess's cowrie on his neck burned hot. A growl of thunder sounded in the air. Rumi recounted Sabachi's words. *Madioha ... where have I heard that*—

He snapped his eyes open and was surprised to find the halberd in his fist. He screamed a name, without thought, a name from the far reaches of his mind.

'Madioha Alaye! Madioha, the Son of Ikwere the Brave!'

A flash of blue-white lightning filled the air and thunder roared. Sabachi glanced over his shoulder. A figure stood silhouetted by the fire-filled sky. Rumi blinked as the figure moved with blurring speed. A flash of shadow-strewn cutlass was the last thing Sabachi saw before his head was severed clean off his shoulders. Kamanu had returned.

'Stand up, Rumi. Shoulders back, chin up. The Odu do not die quietly!'

Rumi took Kamanu's hand. The texture of his voice, the intensity, the way every word hit like a punch. It was unmistakeable. He was *real* – his eyes shone like glowing rocks of fire, and he was shrouded in awesome light. Rumi coughed blood as he steadied himself.

'It was you... the Raging Flame.'

Kamanu smiled. 'I was a man once. I told you you knew my name.'

Shuni appeared beside him, a crown of gold on her head and a golden trident in hand. Mandla appeared last of all, riding Yahya, the King of Dogs, like a general in war, towering over the proceedings. His staff shone a blinding blue and his torch was lit with flame that raged as though fetched from the core of the Hellmouth.

'We will give you a moment, Rumi, but that is all we can give you,' Mandla said, staring down. 'Only you can use his name. Enter his mind, break him from within.'

The kongamoto shrieked from above. Shuni tilted her head. 'I'll deal with that.'

She raised her hands to the sky and a loud shriek filled the air. For a moment, the night sky carried all the brilliant red of a full sunrise. A second kongamoto had joined the fray. It darted across the fire-brightened sky, scales shimmering grey with a huge silver horn at the centre of its eyes. Though it lacked the size of the Priest of Vulture's black kongamoto, it moved with blurring speed.

Shuni tilted her chin until her neck clicked. 'I am the song of the living waters. Even the mountain cannot stand against the sea.'

Her kongamoto launched itself at the larger beast with an explosion of fire and ash. The behemoth roared as Shuni's creature drove its talons deep into its chest, showering the ground with a torrent of black blood. The brute struck back with its tail, but the other was too fast. It rounded on the black beast and caught it at the neck with its jaws, biting until its teeth met at the centre. As the gargantuan screamed, Shuni's kongamoto drew its long neck back. Ink-black flesh, gristle and gore dangled from its teeth. The black kongamoto beat its wings, trying to fly free, but the smaller beast had its talons lodged to the knuckle in the beast's back. Like a bull to its kill, Shuni's kongamoto forced its silver horn into the back of its adversary's throat, drew in an almighty breath and blew an inferno through the bloody gash. The sound the creature made was unthinkable. Pure horror.

Rumi watched in disgusted awe.

'It's time,' came Kamanu's voice.

'What?' Rumi said, his eyes still fixed on the monsters in the sky.

Kamanu grabbed his shoulder. 'You are the son of a great woman, Rumi. It's time to prove her right.'

Rumi looked at him, gathering the message from his eyes and turning towards the Priest of Vultures who was still fighting Zarcanis. He stepped forward. Every footfall was a lesson in pain; the sensation in his toes moved through a filter of suffering. *'Embrace the pain till you find the joy in it.'* What a useless thing to say.

Griff appeared at his other side, drenched in blood.

'You can do it,' Griff said, his face hard as stone. 'You are Adunola's son.'

Rumi leaned forward and picked his helmet up, donning it and snapping it shut.

Griff nodded at him with stiff affirmation. Above, Shuni's kongamoto had its jaws clamped around the black beast's wing as it drove it downwards. They hit the ground in a tangle of ripping, slashing and fire. Yahya roared and that seemed to signal the moment. Griff, Shuni, Kamanu and Mandla charged towards the Priest of Vultures.

Sensing their approach, the Priest of Vultures stopped his blade and slowly turned. Mandla held his wooden staff aloft. Kamanu led the charge, and Shuni seemed to glide on air, eyes fixed on the kongamoto. The Priest of Vultures raised his sword, accepting the challenge.

Rumi drew down on the shadow, pulling more of it, filling himself to the brim until he was shaking with cold rage. Until he could taste death in his throat. *He will know my pain.*

'If the Skyfather won't kill you, I will do it!'

The shadow raged within. He struggled for control; it was a roaring wave of fire that he surfed with a tree branch. It overpowered him and seized the reins.

He was alight with power; shadow flooded him till it burst from his eyes. It was enough power to destroy him, to destroy everything. He did not care.

He reached into his mind to find the name he kept in the darkest place. The night of the Governor's Ball. *Tahinta.* Thoughts of that night replenished the shadow; his fear, his rage, his pain. He drank all that and more. He bound his shadow to the name and entered the Priest of Vultures' mind.

The sky was coated in a thick, viscous tar, blocking whatever light the sun or moon had to share. A long, unending road, pillars of white stone at the sides, loomed before Rumi. At the end of the road, at the centre of two large, grey columns, was a bulging white pillar.

The shadowmind. Rumi raised his hands and scalding columns of shadow materialised in the air. *You will know my pain!*

The Priest of Vultures' mind roared to life. White-hot balls of fire fell from the ink-black sky.

A twisted voice filled the air. '*You think you know pain? I will show you pain.*'

Like a sudden crash of lightning, the priest brought all his force against Rumi. He screamed. He realised, as fire seemed to burn him from the inside, that he had never felt pain before. Anything before had been merely a semblance of pain, a fraction of it. This was a discovery, this was true pain.

He saw the Priest of Vultures mind for what it was. A place of unshakeable faith in the correctness of his cause. No doubt. Pure clarity. The power of it was impossible to withstand. Here was one totally devoted to Palman. *No greater tool than religion to make a good man do evil.*

He tried to scream but all breath was gone. Hot tendrils of death pulled him down. They were in battle now, mind against mind, and he was hopelessly overmatched. He scrambled desperately at the shadow, drinking it in, searching for a strong emotion to hold on to. Images of things he had fought to forget flashed through his mind as he drew deeper. He saw through the Priest of Vultures' foremind as he struck down Kamanu with a killing blow, then struck down Mandla. *He is going to kill them all.* The world was on fire, and death had made its demand.

'*Whatever you thought you would become, now you know it is a lie.*'

Rumi made a last desperate reach for the shadow, a last grasp for life. He let out an animal growl through clenched teeth as he drew more shadow in.

Then at the bottom of his stomach, he found something. A weapon, something that was always there: hate.

He bound himself to the burning hatred and found a new source of strength. The hatred he felt for every person who had beaten, cheated or insulted him in his life filled him. He planted a leg to rise. The burning pain seemed to whimper.

He gritted his teeth and found himself standing again. 'Tahinta!'

His voice was not his own. It was deeper, resounding like the first crack of thunder. The energy of the shadow pulsated within him. He was destruction made flesh. With all his strength, with all the hate in his heart, he drew down on the power of the shadow, to the bottom of the well. He took it in entire.

Surging with power unspeakable, he walked forward. He was death. He raised his fists in the air and called out for the Priest of Vultures by his name. *Tahinta! The Accuser of Men! You will know my pain.*

The fire rained down to incinerate him, but he was cocooned in shadow. Waterfalls of fire forked around his dome of shadow as he ran for the shadowmind. This much shadow could burn him from the inside out, but he did not care. *Vengeance is mine.*

A towering gate appeared in front of him, barring his path to the shadowmind, and he raised his fists in the air. The gate opened of its own accord, leaving a clear path to the mind's temple.

He took a step forward and the attacks stopped. The roaring wind in the Accuser's mind calmed to a gentle breeze and all was serene. Any attempt to burn him with pain vanished. It was as though the Accuser's mind had made peace. Had he won? No, the pillar was still there.

Karile's words spun in his mind. '*It will allow you to stay if it thinks you are cut from the same tree . . . To walk in another's mind that long you must see the world as they see it.*'

Another voice flashed in his mind. A voice that had taught him what it meant to be Odu, to be a man. *Yami.*

'Is this who you are?'

He froze. He could feel the heat of a hateful sun raging inside. He was alight with the power, the hate had strengthened him, but he felt *wrong*. Deep down he knew it. He could not hate enough to challenge Tahinta; he could not win that way.

Rumi bunched a hand into a fist. 'No.'

'Then who are you?'

'I am your son.'

Adunola's voice answered. 'My son does not find his strength in hate, or anger, or pride. If you are my son, show them who you are.'

Rumi's eyes snapped open. The blistering heat of his shadow subsided. He felt a peace come upon him. He knew this feeling; he had felt it the night of the Governor's Ball, he had felt it sparring Yomiku. He could see a path to it, to touch the Originate. He drew down to the very bottom of his shadow and there he felt it. The hate of death, the hate of suffering, the pain of a people of generational scorn. The love of his mother, the love of his brother. The power of ancestors untold, hot as white flame.

'Show them who you are!'

A new vein of power flooded him. Unmistakeable. Agbara power.

Tahinta's mind attacked again, but he could not entirely focus on Rumi while tussling with Mandla. This was Rumi's chance. He gritted his teeth as the power reached a crescendo. He felt *complete*.

He focused on the shadowmind, sensing the great torrent of power within it.

He conjured a spear and his mind started its assault. Every part of doubt, of fear, of pain pressed down on him, but he continued to conjure, resolute, clear-sighted. He bound all his hate for the Priest of Vultures with all his love for his mother, his brother, Renike, Nataré, Sameer, Ahwazi, Ladan, Zarcanis, Griff. The marriage of power rushed through him like a flood.

For the first time in his life, he saw the truth of himself. He was not a good man, but he was no festival goat either. He shot out his hand and felt the release of a six-foot spear of pure shadow.

It seemed to touch the pillar with slow, slurring speed. The pillar unravelled. Burning away at the touch of his shadow like the threads of a cheap carpet, one after the other. Tahinta's hopes, loves and fears flashed before his eyes.

He would show Tahinta who he was, and he would hold nothing back. *Even if I die tonight, you will know my pain.*

65

The Last

ZARCANIS

The Priest of Vultures' smile vanished as his sword fell from his hand. His eyes flashed a vacant white and he plucked them out like corn from the cob. Zarcanis stumbled back, tripping over Kamanu's corpse. The Priest of Vultures howled, frothing at the mouth, scratching his face bloody as though to claw his insides out.

She turned to Rumi. He was on his feet, teeth gritted and chest pulsing, cocooned in an orb of thick shadow. She thought, *He is drawing far too much shadow. It will consume him.*

She reached for the Odeshi at her side, and with the last vestiges of her strength, she collared Rumi, locking the cobalt around his neck and wrestling him to the ground. His eyes flickered, then closed.

The Priest of Vultures gasped as ink-blank tendrils of shadow drooled from the corners of his mouth. He tried to force out words as blotches of liquid shadow sprouted on his skin.

It started on his cheeks, spreading to his neck, and in five breaths the Priest of Vultures' skin had gone from translucent white to completely shadow black.

His eyeless gaze looked to the skies. He finally managed to force the words out.

'Palman... My Lord... Why?'

The blackness reached his eyes as he spoke his last words. 'The Son of Despair.'

He went still. More than still; he was solid. The sound of his collapse was like stone hitting the ground.

Zarcanis picked up her sword. His body was frozen in a pose of pure anguish. She tried to stab his head and it shattered. Like a cheap, brittle statue.

'Godsblood,' she whispered, covering her mouth.

She staggered to Rumi, fearing the worst. Mandla lay behind her, nearer death than life. Yahya trembled in a pool of blood. Shuni was a picture of torn flesh and mangled bone. Griff lay spread-eagled in a bloody heap beside her.

She crouched low to touch Rumi's chest in search of signs of life and jumped back when something touched her leg. It was a cat, black with yellow eyes fixed on Rumi. She pushed the cat aside with her leg and settled her hand on Rumi's chest.

A moment passed and she felt the soft thud of an ailing heart. He was alive.

He coughed up blood. 'I am not nothing,' he snarled. 'They will all know pain!'

She slapped his cheek, startling him. His eyes stuttered open and his pupils were like blazing orbs of fire. Her heart jumped. *Those eyes.* A moment passed and his eyes softened, and he was himself again.

'You were almost lost to the shadow,' she said, staring at him.

He touched the Odeshi on his neck and stared up into the sky.

A cough drew their attention. It was Shuni, drooped against the dead carcass of a kongamoto. Her body was more scars than skin, painted red with infinite cuts.

534

'Rumi, Omo-Xango, *Kukoyi*...' She coughed as though ready to die on that breath. 'I am Shuni, the Mother of Sweetness, Song of the River. You have my instruction. Read the *Book of Shuni*.'

Then her face hit the ground and she breathed her last.

Epilogue

RUMI

Rumi glanced down at Renike, asleep in the botanical ward.

'A brave girl,' Chief Karile said. 'If not for her and her friends, much would have been lost. They bolted the front door and stopped an Obair along the way.'

'How did an Obair get through the front door?'

Karile scowled. 'Weeds among the wheat. One of them released Zaminu from our dungeons.'

Rumi thumbed Renike's forehead. 'Will she be all right?'

'She is a fighter,' said a young girl with a scar on her cheek, appearing at Rumi's side.

Rumi studied the girl. She had hardness beyond her years and muscle in her arms.

'She will be fine,' Karile agreed.

'Her hair,' the scar-faced girl said. 'She would want it braided.'

Karile smiled and nodded. The scar-faced girl took a lock of Renike's hair and started to braid it.

Rumi found himself smiling too. *You always find the trouble, don't you, Ren.*

He glanced over his shoulder towards Griff's bed.

'What about the darkman?' he asked.

Karile frowned. 'Dara's will shall prevail.'

Griff's eyes were closed. Under his bandages were wounds most would have died from. The man was in a fight for his life.

Rumi closed his eyes and let out a silent breath. *How many times can I lose a father?*

There were others badly wounded. Ladan had lost an arm; Mandla had come close to death. Yomiku had paid the ultimate price for Rumi's decisions.

'How many died in this attack?' Rumi asked.

'We've counted a hundred, so far.'

His heart sank. *A hundred.* He felt himself drop to one knee as he covered his eyes. He rubbed the cold cobalt Odeshi beneath his leopard-skin scarf.

Zarcanis stepped into the room. 'Death comes but once. Don't die before you're dead.'

He glanced up at her. Her step was aided by a thick walking cane and she scowled a little with every footfall as she moved forward.

'Get up,' she said, pulling him to his feet. 'Always so dramatic.'

Others filed into the room. Alangba with the princess. No Music. Lord Mandla followed, and then Nataré. It was the first time Rumi had seen them since the battle.

Nataré smiled at him. He could count on one hand the times she had smiled at him. He tried to play the cool wind, but found all his teeth exposed.

Mandla looked surprisingly fresh for a man who had grappled with death mere days ago. There was a book in his hand, wrapped in cloth.

Rumi locked eyes with the ranger. It was said that Alangba, a man who could not call the shadow, had cut down over twenty Obair in the battle.

'You are awake,' Lord Mandla said. 'Good.'

The scar-faced girl moved to Nataré and they embraced.

'What will happen to the Eredo now?' Rumi said.

Mandla narrowed his eyes. 'The Eredo is an ancient sanctuary. It was never meant to be a permanent home. It is a place to recover; to re-strategise. Now we see that we will never be truly safe until we face our enemies. We will rebuild our walls, heal up, but now we must make tomorrow come. Plan for attack.'

Zarcanis stepped forward. 'Our numbers are depleted. We are less ready now than we have ever been, Lord Mandla.'

Mandla smiled, locking eyes with Rumi. 'I am not so sure.' He touched Rumi's shoulder.

A sharp tremor ran through Rumi. A sound hit him sub-vocally and he instinctively glanced over his shoulder. Two figures crouched low, mired in shadow. He squinted towards the door trying to make out what they were. A lionhound stepped forward and bared its teeth. *Kaat.* Rumi smiled before another lionhound stepped up beside Kaat and looked straight at Rumi. His heart thumped his ribs. At first glance, he thought it was Ndebe. A second look showed him the truth of it. *Kaat's pup.*

The lionhound couldn't be more than a few months old but already it was bigger than Ndebe ever was when he was alive. Their eyes met and it was as though a shower of cold rain hit. He went completely still and for a moment all Rumi could do was stare. Their emotions mingled – the lionhound was angry, afraid and confused all at once. There was deeper feeling there too – in the hunched shoulders and bared teeth. It was ready. Ready to fight and Rumi's side just as he was at its. Silently, the young lionhound moved to Rumi's side – he said no words, he didn't need to.

Mandla nodded his approval. 'When Jarishma blessed you, I suspected, but it was at the Ghedo I knew for sure. The crowd cheered your name and you seemed to draw strength from it, confidence even.'

Zarcanis's eyebrows shot up. 'Worship,' she said, her voice barely above a whisper.

'Precisely,' Mandla said. 'You are of the old blood, Rumi.'

He unwrapped the book bound in cloth. It was his mother's *Sakosaye*. 'We found this under your bed.'

Rumi took the book.

Mandla smiled. 'There is a chance, a small chance, that one day you will write your own book in the *Sakosaye*.'

'He already has a section to read. Shuni gave him her blessing,' said Zarcanis.

Mandla nodded. 'Go on, then.'

Rumi opened the book and thumbed the index to find the *Book of Shuni*.

No one ever talks about how Xango loved music. Not a gifted singer, but the gift of music and dance he possessed in more measure than any of the Agbara. That was his way, to enchant us with the dance. Even Billisi loved to watch Xango dance. Some say she just loved to watch Xango.

When Jahmine bore Dara twins, Dara called unto Xango, saying, thus shall thou dance in celebration of my children, for they will redeem mankind. And Xango danced and Dara saw that it was good and gave Xango charge of the security of his children.

But Billisi plotted evil, and when she had set the world to burn, she snatched the boy Azuka and tore the girl Shirayo to pieces. And when Xango saw this, he was grieved in his heart, for he had charge of the security of the children and the girl Shirayo had been torn apart. He called upon me, Shuni, Song of the River, to find every piece of the girl Shirayo, such that the girl could be put together again.

I called upon everything that swims and drinks and wades in the deep, and every cloud that holds rain and every green thing that grows, to find every piece of the girl Shirayo.

And it came to pass that each piece, save for her tongue, was found and brought to Xango, at the cloud upon the mount. He blessed me and called forth his wife Oya, my sister, that we might piece the girl back together again. And we did, breathing life anew into her lungs. They came to love the girl, raising her as a daughter. And the girl grew to a woman, powerful in like to her father and brother, with the love of precious Jahmine. And Xango invested in her the gift of music and of dance.

For as we could not recover her tongue, Shirayo could not speak with her words. Instead, she spoke with her hands.

The day came when she left the cloud upon the mount and went out into the earth, and we have seen no sign of her touch, save that she leaves the gift of music in any place that she goes. So we watch, for wherever there is great music, surely Shirayo has been known.

Shirayo lives. Though all the world thinks her dead, she lives.

Rumi closed the book slowly.

Zarcanis hobbled close and spoke before anyone else. 'So, now that you have your revenge, tell me. What more is there to you?'

Glossary

Aferi – the vanishing charm; a magical stone which renders whoever uses it invisible.

Agbada – flowing wide-sleeved robe worn often as a ceremonial garment.

Agbara – literally translated to 'Power'. Refers to any of numerous gods or spirits worshipped by the Darani, i.e., the Odu and Kasinabe people of southern Basmine.

Agbalumo – sweet, tropical fruit.

Agbo – potent and addictive drug derived from dried herbs. Sold in the form of a milk-white stone which is licked or swallowed to experience the intoxicating and hallucinogenic effects.

Alaafin – title of the King of the medieval Mushian Empire (present day Odu and Kasabia).

Aminague – masquerade featuring a woven raffia mask and costume, said to understand and interpret the will of the gods.

Bambanut – tropical fruit with a hard shell and soft, sweet flesh.

Biku – Dara's great axe of bone and bronze.

Blackfae – small winged creatures of human form that possess magical powers.

Bleeding, the – induction ceremony for those admitted into the Shadow Order.

Bloodgeneral – high ranking officer in the Kasinabe army.

Bloodleaf frog – small amphibian with the colours and appearance of a leaf that feeds on the blood of mammals or birds using its two sharp incisor teeth.

Bloodlettering – powerful magical skill employed by gifted shadowwielders that enables them to write things into or out of existence.

Bloodmad – said of a person who fights with wild and uncontrolled ferocity.

Bloodmagic – use of blood to perform magic.

Boylover – *slur.* A contemptuous and insulting term for a gay man.

Brown Sea – one arm of the larger Kesh Ocean extending between Darosa and Paronesia.

Butter-eaters – person with an exaggerated or extreme preference for luxury and social superiority.

Chainbreakers – militant force founded by formerly enslaved men and women whose goal it is to end all unlawful imprisonment and slavery.

Cowrie – small, glossy, porcelain-like shell used as a form of currency in Basmine.

Damudamu – the confounding charm. Said to have an enchanting or fascinating effect on a person to prevent them from acting in opposition to the person who uses the charm.

Dara – supreme deity of the Darani religion. Considered by the Darani to be both the creator and saviour of all mankind.

Darani – ancient religion of the Odu and Kasinabe tribes centred on the teachings and stories of Dara and the Agbara.

Darosa – large and populous continent west of the Brown Sea. Home to Basmine, the centrepoint of our story.

Dashiki – loose-fitting tunic, typically brightly coloured and patterned.

Eredo – underground city occupied by the Kasinabe.

Ethiope – Darosan country just north of Basmine.

Eversmith – honorary name for Gu, warrior god of iron and war.

Firewine – sweet and spicy wine originally from East Basmine.

Florinian flute – brass wind instrument.

Gele – ceremonial headdress worn almost exclusively by women.

Ghedo – set of competitions and tournaments taking place in the Eredo every five years.

Godhunters – (also known as the Godsbane) prophets and priests imbued with magical powers to hunt down and kill the Agbara.

Godsblood – swear word, used to express anger, annoyance, surprise or shock.

Gourdlets – small fruit shell, used as a container for potions.

Governor's Ball – ceremonial event to celebrate and announce the election of a new Governor-General.

Gu – Agbara; the warrior god of iron and war.

Harmattan – dry, cold, dusty season in the last months of the year.

Hashiyeshi – greeting in the Odu language meaning 'Hello, how are you?'

Ida sword – long sword with a narrow to wide blade and sheathe.

Iro – cloth wrapping used as a skirt.

Iroko – large hardwood tree that can live for up to 1,000 years.

Isora – the protective charm. Said to blunt the edge of an enemy sword.

Itara – passionate lovemaking.

Jazzmen – witch doctors who practice bloodmagic.

Juju – ancient magic.

Kamanu – Agbara of thunder and lightning.

Kasinabe – warrior-like tribe from the ancient kingdom of Kasabia (the south-eastern part of Basmine).

Kiwinje – competition where two people face off on a thin bench with the aim of one person knocking the other off with the assistance of a straw club.

Koboko – stick whip made with with cow or goat hide, used as a tool for corporal punishment.

Kola nut – caffeine containing nut, broken as a gesture of agreement or trust between the natives of Basmine.

Kongamoto – large reptilian water-dwelling creature that is able to fly, swim and breathe fire.

Kuba – tribe from the ancient kingdom of Kuba (the northern part of Basmine).

Kubani – Mushiain approximation of the Odu word Kubano, which could mean angry bull or stupid bull, depending on the context.

Kubano – see above.

Kukoyi – Odu term meaning 'He who dodges death'.

Lickhead – person addicted to agbo.

Lionhound – large dog, fiercely loyal, having keen sight and capable of high speed, used since ancient times for hunting small game.

Maicer – enslaved person of particular skill made available for short term hire.

Mgbedike – meaning 'the time of the brave' an ancient war amongst Gods and powerful men.

Mindwalk – magical ability to walk through a person's mind and affect their thoughts and actions.

Mother of Nine – honorary name for Oya, an Agbara and wife of Xango.

Mudskin – derogatory term used against the Odu and Kuba, typically by the Saharene.

Mushiain – both a name for the ancient empire of the Odu and Kasinabe people and the name of the ancient language spoken by the Odu and Kasinabe.

Obair – a godhunter's slave soldiers – creatures formed using mysterious powers to do the bidding of the godhunters.

Odeshi – the quartercuff. A charm used to subdue shadow-wielder's by reducing their power to only a quarter of full strength.

Odu – tribe from the ancient kingdom of Odu (the southern part of Basmine).

Omoba – Mushiain word meaning 'Child of the king', used for either a Prince or Princess.

Ori oil – oil made from the crushed nuts of the Ori tree.

Oya – wife of Xango. Agbara of the Rivers.

Palm wine – alcoholic beverage made from the sap of the palm tree.

Palmaine – both the nation and people of the country known as Palmaine. A colonising nation originating in the northern-most part of the Paronesian continent.

Palman – supreme deity of the Palman religion – practiced predominantly by the people of Palmaine and those living in Palmaine colonies like Basmine. The Palmaine are his chosen people.

Saharene – nomadic tribe, originally from the Sahar desert.

Sakosaye – religious scripture of the Darani known as the living book for it is still unfinished.

Sandskin – derogatory term used against Saharene people.

Sanyan – pale brown and woven beige silk that is obtained from the cocoons of the Anaphe moth.

Seedlings – new recruit to the Shadow Order.

Selistre – harp consisting of nine strings.

Seraiye – turn based strategy game for two players.

Shadow Order – Kasinabe institution for the training of shadowwielders.

Shadowblade – sword formed from Shadowsteel.

Shadowdancer – person who can fight with the shadow.

Shadowmind – deepest part of the mind in the practice of mindwalking.

Shadowsteel – alloy of steel and conjured shadow.

Shadowwielder – (1) person with the power to wield his shadow as a weapon or (2) person who has completed the full training of the Shadow Order and become a full shadow-wielder.

Shinala – large warhorse raised for long journeys and battle.

Shuni – Agbara of sweetness, water, beauty and sensuality.

Softborn – derogatory term used for those born outside the Eredo.

Tesara – erotic use of pain as an inducement to pleasure.

Tiger-eye – semi-precious yellowish-brown variety of quartz with a silky or chatoyant lustre, formed by replacement of crocidolite.

Tilakia stone – near impenetrable stone which is also impervious to magic and juju.

Xango – husband of Oya. Agbara of thunder, lightning, dance and virility.

Zarot – contemptuous and highly offensive word used against the Odu. It means twenty cowries, the old price for an Odu slave.

Acknowledgments

Thank God for this beautiful journey.

To my dearest mother, who taught me to dream, even in a nightmare. To my dear sister Demi and brother Shore who gave what cannot be repaid, but never said 'you owe me'. To my parents, other siblings, cousins and all my family who have supported me all the way. Thank you – I could not have done this without any one of you.

To Jordan, who kept the wheels turning on this long ride. To Marcus, who helped to refine my story and amplify my voice. To Mayowa for the glorious cover art. To everyone at Gollancz and the Blair Partnership who worked to get this book out. Thank you – You all did an incredible job and I am so glad to have the opportunity to work with you.

To my good friend Maro, who saw the vision and ran with me. To Eniola who believed in me before I believed in myself. To Clair who poked at all the brittle bones in my first draft and gave a course-changing critique. To David who was my first beta reader. To Sekemi who always reminded me to write. To my Aunt Yemisi and Aunt Debola. To Omo-B, Olaedo, Erin, Richard and Martin. To everyone who read a rougher version of this book and helped to make it smooth. Thank you all for your feedback and encouragement.

To Sayo, who gave me the most precious gift – the experience of knowing I will always belong. Thank you – words are no true currency to express what you mean to me.

Thank you all for getting me here. And now we go again.

Credits

Rogba Payne and Gollancz would like to thank everyone at Orion who worked on the publication of *The Dance of Shadows*.

Editor
Marcus Gipps
Claire Ormsby-Potter

Copy-editor
Abigail Nathan

Proofreader
Patrick McConnell

Editorial Management
Jane Hughes
Charlie Panayiotou
Tamara Morriss
Claire Boyle

Contracts
Dan Heron
Ellie Bowker

Audio
Paul Stark
Jake Alderson
Georgina Cutler

Design
Nick Shah
Rachael Lancaster
Joanna Ridley
Helen Ewing
Tomás Almeida

Finance
Nick Gibson
Jasdip Nandra
Elizabeth Beaumont
Ibukun Ademefun
Sue Baker
Tom Costello

Inventory
Jo Jacobs
Dan Stevens

Rights
Ayesha Kinley
Marie Henckel

Production
Paul Hussey
Fiona McIntosh

Publicity
Frankie Banks

Sales
Jen Wilson
Victoria Laws
Esther Waters
Frances Doyle
Ben Goddard
Anna Egelstaff

Marketing
Lucy Cameron

Operations
Sharon Willis